Death

and the

MERCHANT

Death

and the

MERCHANT

C.H. WILLIAMS

For Elsie.

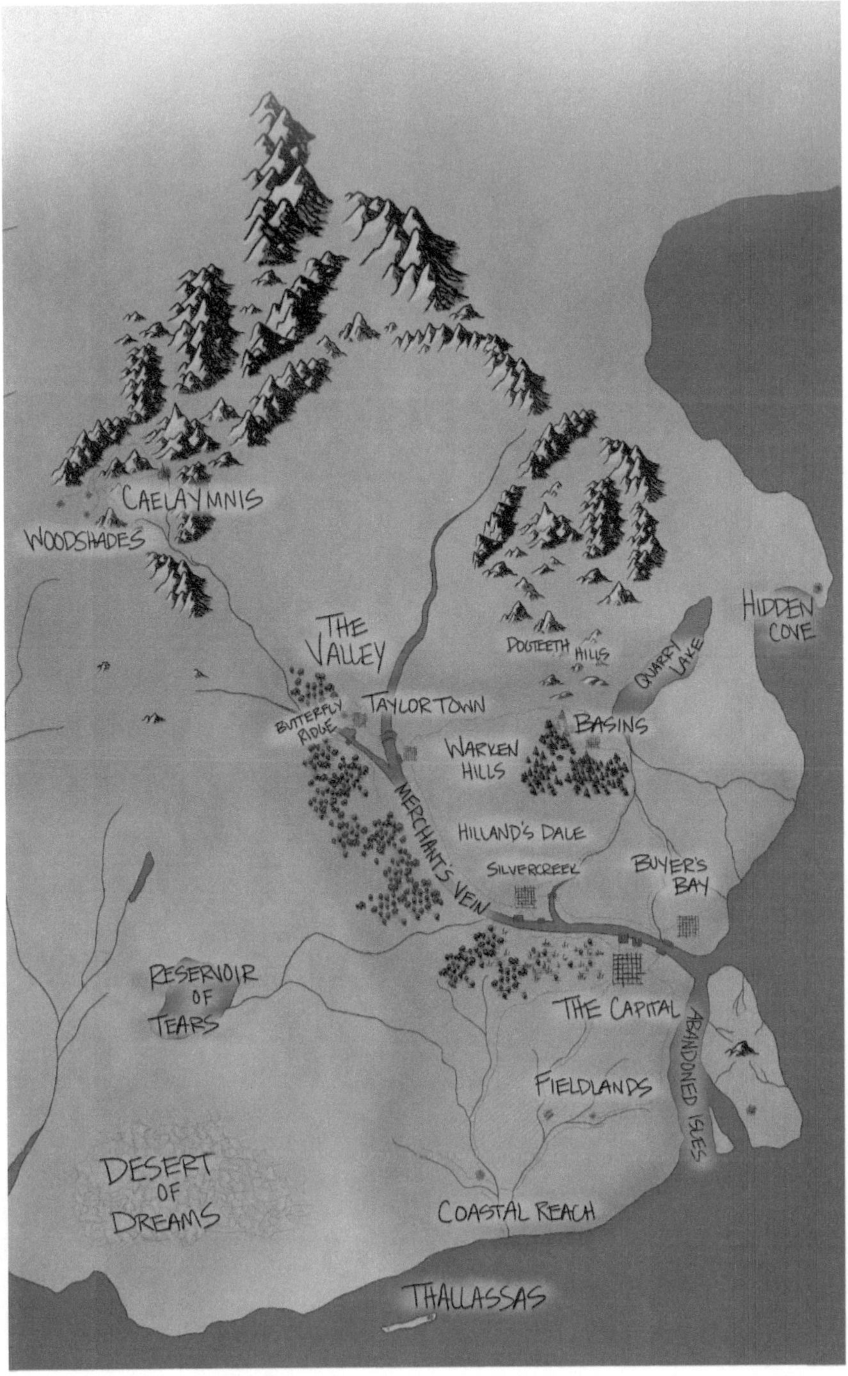

CAELAYMNIS
WOODSHADES
THE VALLEY
DOGTEETH HILLS
QUARRY LAKE
HIDDEN COVE
BUTTERFLY RIDGE
TAYLORTOWN
BASINS
WARKEN HILLS
MERCHANT'S VEIN
HILLAND'S DALE
SILVERCREEK
BUYER'S BAY
RESERVOIR OF TEARS
THE CAPITAL
ABANDONED ISLES
FIELDLANDS
DESERT OF DREAMS
COASTAL REACH
THALLASSAS

PROLOGUE

I was born with one foot in a world of ink and paper. And since that moment, I've spent my life trying to escape into the pages of another world. I'm convinced that's where I'll find Death, and all the other gods, too. Find them, and make them pay.

It was said that the gods wield not weapons but fountain pens.
It was said that only gods write the beginnings.

We're sitting here, trying to think up better beginnings than the ones we got. I didn't want my story to start with defeat.

But I write the endings
I write the endings
I write the endings

THE LETTERS

The Guild is relentless.

They agreed to forsake magic, and now, in their hour of need, they demand ours. Ours, which has been neatly hidden away, protected and protecting. The elves refused, so they turn to us.

And what have I done, but agree to share. I did not even have the decency to broker the deal in secret.

I wonder if this decision will tear us apart. There is already talk of replacing me, either with the blade or with the vote. But the Guild is on a precipice, and good people will suffer without aid.

Already, we prepare the first shipment on the condition of secrecy. Medical supplies. Food. Toys, textiles, anything our city can spare, and the Guild will proffer our wares as their own.

They mock me, here, mock the Guild, too. They call me weak, unwilling to make the difficult decisions, unwilling to let the Guild confront their refusal of magic. But their people did not choose this, and my duty as Chancellor is to humanity.

They call the Guild Commissioners the Merchants of Death, profiting at the hand of one whose legacy is synonymous with loss, and I am not so naive as to rebuke this.

The Guild is practiced at exploiting calamity, and my

City is responsible for much of it.

I am the descendant of the God of Death, heiress to tragedy, and here I am making trades with oligarchs in the name of preserving life.

For fuck's sake, Clark. You better make this work. Don't make me regret this.

~ EXCERPT FROM THE FINAL LETTER OF
MARGARET FAULISE,
LUMINARY CHANCELLOR OF THE HIDDEN CITY AND
THE SOLE LIVING DESCENDANT OF
CORA, GOD OF DEATH,
TO COMMISSIONER CLARK CARSON

FLETCHER

"And she danced in the light to spite the demons, driving them back to the shadows. If only she'd remembered that torchlight is fleeting, and darkness inexorable."

~ 'Enchantress of Frost' and Other Collected Tales

The life of this elf was never quiet.

Dark had long since fallen as Fletcher lingered in the streets of Taylor Town. His ears pricked with the occasional shouts of delight still echoing through the avenues, shrieks of laughter bubbling over from the taverns as the festival-goers continued their revelry beyond the town square. And amid the scuff of boots on the rough cobblestones, the creaking of barroom floors, the rush of a silver piece being slid across the worn wood of a table...

He could hear it.

Da-dum. Da-dum. Da-dum.

The thrumming provoked a wistful smile on his lips.

Somewhere, the hiss of someone taking a drag echoed in the wake of a match strike, and the phantom smell of tobacco reached him, imagined in the rush of noise. The crisp crunching of leaves underfoot wafted through the air, the papery residue of autumn being ground against the street by the soles of worn canvas shoes.

Da-dum. Da-dum. Da-dum.

He was having to strain to hear it, now. Her heartbeat. If the moment had been perfectly still, if not another soul had dared to even breathe, he might've listened a little longer. As it stood, though, the sounds of the night threatened to swallow it up completely, even as he waited, less than a block from the square.

The town square. The normally dreary lot, littered with debris, had been transformed tonight into something utterly transcendent. Lanterns had been strung between the trees, trunks had been draped with gorgeous swaths of colorful fabric...

Then there'd been Elsie.

With an exasperated sigh, he leaned back against the cold brick of the alley, closing his eyes as he tried to hold onto the sound.

Da-dum. Da-dum. Da-dum.

It was faint, now. Or perhaps it'd gone, and all he heard was the reverberation of a memory pounding in his ears.

The humming fiddle had drawn forth a tune, strings whining as the hiss of resistance was sent dancing through the air, set in time to the quaking of reeds, rattling along to the straining membrane of the drum, pulsing, pulsing, pulsing, and that, he knew, had been the music of the spheres—the sounds the gods had hummed when they'd forged the world into being.

Her dress had whispered beneath his hands as they'd danced, murmuring the long-forgotten tune, and he'd almost breathed the words into her ear. Held tight in each other's arms, the faint tang of sweat lacing the air, his heart pounding in tandem to hers, he'd been ready, finally, finally, ready—

But the bell tower had sent a shattering blast through the air, sending the moment crumbling into the oblivion.

Swearing quietly, he opened his eyes. His cheek still burned where she'd kissed him goodnight. The sweet smell about her had soaked into his tunic. She was impossible to leave behind.

Beautifully, mercifully, wonderfully impossible.

The censure was heavy in his jacket pocket.

That Rodion had been sent to deliver the notice was salt in the wound. It was a petty show of dominance on Augustus's part, sending a friend to deliver the reprimand. Just another way to drive home his brother's relentless mantra, pounded into the heads of every trainee.

Loyalty before amity.

It wasn't his fault he loved a human. And it sure as hell wasn't his fault that he was locked by law and loyalty from spilling his secrets. As it stood, though, he was in love with a human—and as far as El knew, she was, too.

He pulled out the notice, the creases silent as he unfolded it for the millionth time.

THE COUNCIL HEREBY ISSUES THE FORMAL CENSURE FOR THE VIOLATION OF THE DIRECT ORDERS FROM A COMMANDING OFFICER, WITH THE KNOWING DISOBEDIENCE

Absurd. It was absolutely absurd.

Staying true to form, his brother had at last pulled rank, summoning the power of the Council to deliver the death-blow to an already crumbling career.

It was a taunt, done in a fit of childish spite. Then again, Augustus hadn't ever mastered the art of a dignified command, in his quick-to-anger voice that barked through them all, his petty scowls of—of irate— of pathetic, infuriating—

Elsie would've had the words for it.

That woman's life moved in metaphors. She'd have said something like, *He doesn't know how to draw bees to flowers.* Not that exactly, of course—the way she'd have put it would've had music to it. Would've somehow been clear, even though the words rung of nonsense. And she'd say it, too, with that faint lilt on her tongue, the flare that betrayed her as a woman Valley-raised, those soft vowels and swallowed consonants making her words flow like water.

Your position, and subsequent investigation, are suspended, pending appearance before Council and Crown

Grinding his teeth, the notice crumpled beneath his fingers, the crackling of crisp parchment filling the air. With a flare, it dissolved to ashes, nothing but glowing embers drifting down from the palm of his hand.

And still, the words burned before him.

Commander Praequintelya is heretofore ordered to cut contact with the Human settlement.

Effective immediately.

ELSIE

"Fortune favors the bold."

~Unknown

In the light of the pale moon, Elsie's fingers found the laces holding the sweat-soaked satin to her hot skin. She gave them a tug, and the gown seemed to melt, pooling auburn on the floor. Cool autumn air brushed her bare skin, sending a pleasant chill down her spine as she drew in a deep breath, ribs reveling in their new-found freedom, and still, his whispered anxiety was pounding in her ears.

I wish that we could never end.

Fletcher had forgotten, in his moment of worry.

Wishes were for fools and cowards not brave enough to curse the gods. For fairy tales and godmothers and crumbling wells, and all manner of creatures make-believe borne of ink and parchment and the disturbed imagination.

They were not for farmers and bastards and broken Valley people.

To wish was to surrender, and Elsie was no coward.

I wish that we could never end.

Elsie frowned. What had even catapulted such a thought into his head, she didn't know. But she didn't like it. The thought of them *ending*.

I wish that we could never end, he had breathed, arms around her.

Anger and affection were warring, her heart the victim. Impulse told her it was a foreboding threat—but sentiment, and perhaps wishes of her own, told her that it was love.

Experience told her the latter was dangerous. To love—to wish to be loved—these were weapons that could be turned against her in a moment's notice.

She flipped a match from the box on her desk, the cheap wood threatening to splinter as it flared to life. It lingered only long enough for her to coax a catch against the lamp wick, guttering resentfully out as warm light blossomed across the drafty walls of the farmhouse bedroom with all the grandiose promises wicks tend to give.

Promises, to her thinking, were rather like wishes.

Her lamp had promised heat.

What she had, though, was a crumpled sweater, countlessly mended, with too-short sleeves, bathed in the cold, yellow light.

It'd been Teddy's. Before that, it belonged to Tom, and before that, it'd been cheap, rough-spun wool, mildewing and sold for a discount.

Still, she could remember burying her face in the scratchy folds of wool as her brother scooped her up on his hip, the leaves turning in the autumns of her childhood, and so she'd been resigned to love it, the scraping gray yarn whispering *safe, safe, safe* into her ears as he carried her home.

But it wasn't warm.

And that had been the promise.

She stuffed the slick gown into her canvas bag, a tight, wrinkled-by-the-time-she-got-to-town, undignified ball of red. It was Sam's problem, now.

Turning to leave, though, she paused.

She'd caught it, out of the corner of her eye, hadn't registered it until her fingers lay ready on the cold brass handle.

A letter, on her desk.

Her gaze flicked back to the twirling script that scrawled her name, curling like ribbons across the thick parchment of the bulging envelope.

Elizabeth.

Two steps, and she'd snatched it up, and frowning, she slit the seal, wax shattering across the worn-wood floor.

This was left, the words seemed to simper, in my possession.

The locket was slender, the golden chain glittering as it caught the light.

So from the mother, so to the daughter.

A Valley quip to blame the bastards.

And thus, yours.

Bastards like her.

Respectfully,

Bastards like Elsie.

Commissioner Clark Carson.

THE MURDERERS

Someone, it seems, has developed a taste for pastries—
and I do not mean the sweet desserts for which our
district has come to be known.

The daughters of the merchants are dying.

Panic has spread, and they are more than content to let
their children be taken by this investigator from the
mountains, for they think it to be a hemorrhagic fever
from the south, and they are afraid of what might be
brought into their doily parlors if vigil for the dead
should be held in their homes.

It is not a fever, as I am given to understand, though he
burns them anyway, as is the mountain custom, which
we can all agree is a more poetic end.

Someone has taken to poisoning the pastries.

~SAM ALDERTON,
EXCERPT FROM A LETTER DATED AUGUST 25TH

AUGUSTUS

"Knowing, they say, is half the battle. Even so, it's no guarantee you'll win the war."

~Risa Barrett

"General?"

The hesitant tap of knuckles on the barrack door roused Augustus from uneasy sleep.

Rolling off the cot, he made for the washbasin by the closet. Dress uniform, three standard-issue sets of fatigues, three sets of training garb, all were hanging inside a glorified cupboard. No more than he was permitted. No less.

A departure from the royal accoutrements of his adolescence, thank the gods. He never asked to be a prince.

The water was brisk against his skin, drops skittering down the surface of the basin as he shook his hands off, reaching for a rough towel, and at last he glanced to the door. "Enter."

"Sir." An aide pushed the door in, a rush of chilled mountain air curling through the veritable closet of a room, already the wood beginning to creak and groan with the reluctance of the cold.

"Close the gods-damned door, Epherias, let's leave a little mystery for the rest of the barracks today, shall we?" Snapping up a pair of undershorts, Augustus didn't break the aide's gaze. Epherias's cheeks turned bright pink, those pale eyes looking nervously away, searching, trying to light on anything, any place, except Augustus. "Report."

The boy oozed privilege.

Three months an aide, and still, Epherias couldn't see any of them as the soldiers they were. Every morning, pounding on Augustus's door with the nightly report—half the time apologizing for the interruption, like he was a serving boy bringing breakfast—and Epherias was a trembling mess. He'd trail after Augustus, making for the mess hall, and more often than not, end up frozen in place as Cook dished the steaming porridge into his bowl, lost in his own anxieties. And, of course, he'd sink down with the rest of the cadets, gulping down a few bites of food before the end, but not daring a word to any of them.

Any of them, save Lya.

Lya, his betrothed, and they'd joined together—or, she'd joined, and he'd followed, which made Augustus want to hurl.

But Epherias would pad after her to the training hall, all the same, where he'd lurk by the sidelines, wringing his hands until Augustus pushed him into the ring, and whimpering, Epherias would throw a few feeble punches at the woman he so deeply loved, Lya, all the while, pinning her fellow cadet in a few quick moves. And with tears in his eyes, he'd brush himself off and slump against the wall, waiting for the next round of pummeling.

Just like Fletcher.

Only, Fletcher hadn't followed a betrothed to the compounds.

He'd followed an older brother.

"Report," Augustus echoed again, louder, snapping his fingers in annoyance. "I don't have all day, Cadet."

"I—I, um—it's the human settlements," Epherias stumbled, "they— they're marching towards the western g-g-gate, it isn't, um, many—t-

14

twenty or thirty strong, b-b-but they're angry, and—and armed..."

He froze, fingers half-way through buttoning his gray trousers. "Armed with *what*, Cadet."

"Stolen magic, sir. O-O-Our magic."

Jaw clenching, he could still feel his scarred forearms burning, welted with still-fading slits running elbow to wrist where they'd tried to drain him not a year ago. It was a crude attempt at noble magic, for they used no beasts nor draughts to achieve their end. No, they would have simply drained him like a slaughtered lamb and used their wretched spices and their massive vats to draw forth the magic.

There was an uncomfortable slickness to the scars, his calluses not catching quite right against the strained, too-tight skin. The medics had given him ointments, of course. But they might as well have given him cucumber water, for all the good it did.

He didn't dare seek the touch of a Healer. Not that he'd have permitted a human to touch him, not after what they'd done to him. The elves could do nothing more than mend with salves and tonics, for Asa, God of Healing, had only allotted their magic to a handful of humans.

Damnable fool of a god.

Augustus yanked the gray coat from the closet, metal clattering as the hanger tumbled percussively to the floor.

Blood magic was as old as time itself. Perhaps it had once been used justly, as the stories claimed, but Augustus did not care for heroic would-be's of the past.

His attention was firmly focused on the now, and now, those dwelling in the Woodshades were stealing Caelaymnic magic. The scantly forested river settlement on the western plains beyond Caelaymnis, the Woodshades were littered with humans disinterested in Aerdela's Guild and discarded from the Hidden City, with elves who eschewed the Caelaymnic monarchy, and with anyone else rife with anarchical inclinations.

As a child, Augustus had found this notion rather grand. In his early memory, he knew they'd gotten along well with the Woodshades, having brokered a tentative peace.

But something had fractured, these last years.

Wartime had taught Caelaymnis to keep watch for dastardly magics, and so when bloodless bodies began to surface in the Weir, washed downstream from the Woodshades, the message could not have been more clear.

We have your magic.

And we are coming for you.

~ • ~

There was bloodlust on the air.

Valoxus pawed the ground, nickering as Augustus pulled the reigns taut. A monstrous warhorse, black as sin and silky as night, the muscular back rippled beneath his legs, nothing more than the barest tack lain upon the glorious creature. Horse and rider were one—leather and steel and pads and buckles, it was superfluous to the bond they shared.

And atop the magnificent beast, he knew he was the picture of power. That gray uniform, those glossy black boots, the dark bars emblazoned on his breast to boast his historic rank—twenty-one and a general—it was nothing compared to the strong jaw, the cropped-short blonde hair, the pale gray-green eyes, just like his father's, and gods, his physique, honed through years, towering above them all as he'd pushed past six feet with ease. That, and the gleaming silver blades flashing in the morning light, the spark of power rippling through his very being, a taste of the clash to come...

They feared him.

He could see it in their eyes, riding before the line.

Fifty pairs of eyes followed him. Fifty pairs of eyes, terrified of what he would do if they looked away. Fifty pairs of eyes that lived for the taste of their general's curt nod of approval like it was the bread of life.

Through the pass to the sprawling plateau, Augustus inhaled the sweet air bled from the snow-capped peaks.

He could hear them, in the distance. They all could.

The heavy breathing, clodding feet pounding carelessly against the painstakingly flattened pastures of the highlands, the hissing and spitting of angry words through yellowed, rotting teeth, the worn leather sword-belts clanking with dull iron blades, blades he knew well, blades he could still feel, needling deep into his skin, draining him of the blood to craft the dark magic they craved so badly.

Human.

They were so painfully, tragically human.

These were not the docile, submissive creatures that had allowed themselves to be corralled within the sequestered lands of Aerdela. These were not the humans that had been all too happy to forget their world was teeming with magic, to forget that there were others in this life beyond themselves.

These were the outliers.

The ones forgotten by their brethren, the ones that still recalled the taste of magic.

And their blades, the ones he knew so well, the ones he could still feel, those blades would lay discarded on blood-soaked earth before the morning was done.

ELSIE

The tang of stagnant water filled the air as waves lapped against the stone walls of the harbor.

A spray of white frothed into the air, the hewn obsidian surface gutted by the keel of a barge, and Elsie wiped the cold from her cheeks with the back of her hand, grimacing.

The chain of the locket was grinding into the back of her neck, yanking on the wisps of hair ill-contained and trapped beneath her scarf.

Stupid.

Stupid, stupid, stupid, and what had she done but slide the locket tentatively over her head, only to bury it with shaking fingers a moment later beneath her tunic, face heating in deep, childish shame.

My mother is gone, she is dead, she isn't worth the air you breathe, because who would just brazenly abandon their baby with back-district trash and still, the locket sat, the metal warm against her skin.

"This place smells like death," Elsie muttered, nose wrinkling in disgust.

Death.

The word itself was a wash of darkness across her.

Fletcher gave her a side-long glance before returning to his study of the docks.

Where words usually ran freely between them, he was quiet, hazel eyes cradled in hammocks of purple.

She'd found dawn on the streets, and Fletcher, too, striding purposefully for the harbor, smelling of ash and pine.

Stray strands of hair were sent whipping across her face, phantom spiderwebs yanked forth by the cold burst of wind off the water. Hands stuffed in rough coat pockets, her fingers toying with the familiar holes in the slick lining, she traced the stains bleeding into the cobblestones, the toe of her boot dragging across the crevasses and cracks where the body had been.

The only evidence the girl had ever lived.

Had ever bled.

Had ever died.

Fletcher brought whispers that this plague of poison was sweeping through the Guild. Tarts in the Capital, men rumored fallen. Confections in the Coastal Reaches, people toppled just when they'd been poised to power. And now, pastries in the Valley, the daughters of the merchants picked off one by one.

The marks were sequestered beneath the empty branches of an oak peering over the dock wall. The girl been dumped, cold and alone, on the shores of a stinking harbor to die amid the sounds of clanking bells and swearing harbormen.

A few of their delectable daughters in their pastried gowns, driven to the edge of madness, dying in delirium in the streets of their little town, and the scandal was quietly swept aside.

The merchants were predator, not prey, and anyways, the gulls didn't care if a few pastries bit the dust.

This one had been a pastry, too. The one who died last night.

The one who died while Elsie had let herself forget the world for the sake of a fairy tale beneath the glittering festival lights. That's what it had to be, right, to feel so loved?

"Did she burn," Elsie asked quietly, guilt overtaking her. Even pastries shouldn't have to die lonely.

Fletcher nodded, not taking his eyes from the marred cobblestones. They all burned, in the end.

She'd never bothered to ask why the boy from the mountains set them alight atop the pyres, because it seemed better, anyway, than rotting in the ground, forgotten in decay.

So they burned.

Eights souls, all burning, for the price of a love that didn't hurt, that'd been the ferryman's toll. Eight souls, and she kept him a while longer, because if they stopped dying, stopped burning, there'd be nothing to keep him here.

Eight souls, anointed with poison, sanctified with blood—and consecrated with a cunning scheme to send the Guild crashing to the ground, it seemed, for why else would the merchant's daughters be falling with alarming speed.

Eight souls, and time was running out.

"How much longer are you going to stare at the blood stains," Elsie muttered, breaking the silence to answer her own thoughts.

He said nothing, lost in thought as he crouched down, hands hovering above the stain as if before a fire. His tic when there was a puzzle he couldn't solve. As if he might reach out and snatch the answer from thin air.

Elsie kicked her boots together, bringing some life back into her toes. They'd been standing here for over an hour, and the cobblestones were blocks of ice beneath the thin leather.

It'd been polished.

The locket.

Lovingly cared for, painstakingly preserved.

Almost like new.

Almost, save for the worn filigree heart etched, fading, on the front.

Sam.

That was probably it, it had to have something to do with Sam.

So from the mother, so to the daughter, or maybe, so to the son, because Sam was a bastard, too, and it was the ill-breeding of their mothers that'd marked them so from birth, so that was probably what it had to do with, the Commissioner, trying to get under Sam's skin. He'd been difficult of late, Sam had said.

Even still.

She didn't know if she was ready to share this, just yet.

A little tiny piece of who she could be. And if it was just to get under Sam's skin...

Well, no use making waves.

Rising, Fletcher's gaze darted around the harbor, eyes unseeing all the while, brow furrowed in contemplation.

He hadn't even bothered to change after the festival. Hadn't even bothered, if she knew him, to go back to the damn lodge to even get a bite to eat.

"You okay?"

"I'm just...not ready to go," he said quietly, eyes flicking to hers.

She scowled. "I am." Lingering here was making her bitter, reminding her that the only reason Fletcher was even here at all was death.

And when they stopped dying, he would leave.

21

I wish that we could never end too, Fletcher. Guess that makes me a gods-damned coward, doesn't it.

~•~

The sounds of the town awakening overtook them as they at last left the harbor behind, the clatter of commerce once more filling the streets of Taylor Town.

Shouts filled the air as street vendors cried for coppers, and the vague smell of hot-inked papers and burning bread curled in her nose as she side-stepped a dark-suited merchant, rattling off a list of complaints to an already over-burdened secretary as he snapped up one of the papers. "Steel securities are up, good, good—schedule an appointment with the Commissioner, we're buying on the margin, need to get a meet-and-greet—we'll see who's 'Commissioner' after this..."

Elsie gave a snort of derision, rolling her eyes. The epitome of a tart, with his perfect little necktie and crisp lapels, bouncing along like he owned the damn place, an up-and-coming young confection fumbling with their notes as they trailed after the tart.

Pride before the fall, and greed precedes the grave, that was how the saying went.

Only one man owned these streets. And he did not share.

Her hand was half-way to the locket before she caught herself, tucking a strand of hair unconvincingly behind her ear instead.

Commissioner Clark Carson dominated the Valley. It was a small district, to be sure, barely eking out survival, and yet, he'd managed to wring a pile of gold from it bigger than that gods-forsaken mansion he laughably called a home. And when he'd started climbing that pile, he hadn't stopped until he was running the Merchant's Guild.

So what is he doing, handing out trinkets to a broken little bastard.

Her gaze drifted down the street.

She spotted Sam first, of course. His spun-gold hair was hard to miss, and anyway, his voice carried through a crowd. But a few more steps, and she saw her brother's dark navy coat—she'd gotten particularly good as a child at spotting it amid the chaos that was Taylor Town, a talent that had not diminished as she'd gotten older.

"Come on," she sighed, nodding to the boys down the busy sidewalk. "I see breakfast."

ELSIE

"In the cold of winter, it was the breaking of bread that kept them from breaking themselves."

~from 'The Advice of The Long-Dead' and Other Essays

Leaning on the counter of the general store, Elsie pulled off a chunk of her sweetroll bleeding with sugar and cinnamon, watching idly as Teddy pulled his apron on, fingers deftly tying the strings behind his back. Her brother's blue eyes flicked up to hers, and he gave her a small smile.

The paper crinkled pleasantly as she blotted up a pool of glaze with a hunk of bread.

These were their moments.

The four of them. Elsie and Fletcher and Teddy and Sam. Moments when the rest of the world lay frozen, quiet, and they were permitted temporary reprieve from what lay beyond.

Not that there was much solace to be sought on a morning like this.

On a morning so heavy with death.

Sam shrugged off his suit coat, tossing it down the counter out of the way of the sticky glaze oozing across the brown paper bag. Joining Elsie at the counter, he eyed the sweetrolls, relenting after a moment to the precariously delicate one nearest him. "I'm surprised to see you here, so early," he put forth, eyes sparkling with mischief as he glanced over to her.

Elsie swallowed the massive bite of sugary dough. "What? Why!"

"You two were still dancing when we left," Teddy said quietly, amused as he, too, joined them in the sweetrolls.

"It was too lovely a moment to end." Fletcher was gently folding his gray winter coat up, setting it down beside Sam's bag. His eyes met Elsie's, worried. "Were we out too late?"

She shook her head, a grin edging at the corners of her mouth. "No. Not at all." Forget the fact that she hadn't slept, that she'd changed from her festival wares, grabbed that damnable locket, and hiked back to town, worrying all the while.

Sam looked askance at Fletcher. "Forget El, what about you?" His voice was soft with concern, the familiar kind of care that Elsie had long come to expect from Sam. He was a gentle soul. "Fletcher, you are still in your festival clothes—you're quite dashing, but if you need to change, and rest, please do. We enjoy your company, but you are under no obligation to meet us for breakfast—"

"There was another murder last night." Fletcher looked away. "I...was notified by one of my informants that they'd found a body at the harbor, and...well." His gaze flicked to the sweetrolls. "Another pastry."

"You're sure," Teddy asked, eyes wide, voice hushed.

Fletcher nodded.

There was no question, the murder of the girl by the harbor still belonged to this string of gruesome deaths. The symptoms of the poison were unmistakable.

Wan skin, bloodshot eyes, and everything bled, when they died. Like they were dissolving from the inside out, and even still, the merchants seemed convinced of their own infallibility.

"Which one," Sam asked darkly.

"Thompson. Deb Thompson." Fletcher closed his eyes, hand on the counter.

"She's not even from this district," Sam said with disbelief. "She's from Buyer's Bay, how…"

Fletcher shrugged. "I do not know. My best guess is that it's to send a message to Commissioner Carson."

Sam paused, a piece of bread drenched in cinnamon poised elegantly between his forefinger and thumb. "Perhaps."

"A merchant is going after their own, and not just the ones in the Valley." Elsie glanced between them all. "The merchants truly do not realize they're under attack?"

Teddy paused his whispered count, stacks of coins balanced precariously on the strip of wood before the till. "Are you sure it's a merchant that's behind this?"

"Crossing district lines, luring some of the most well-guarded people off without so much as a whisper of a suspicious disappearance, dumping bodies in the street without a single witness…who else could it be," Sam said quietly.

"Sam's right," Fletcher nodded. "A gull could never afford to be so brazenly messy." His gaze flicked to Sam. "What do you know about the Thompson girl?"

Sam shrugged, eyes distant. "Not much. Her mothers have an estate across the river from the Capital. Neither were merchants by birth, it made a lot of waves when they climbed ranks. A lot of people thought they were gunning for the Capital commissionership."

Elsie listened, fighting the urge to reach up and touch the locket. It set her ill at ease, that in the midst of a crisis amongst the merchants, Clark Carson himself had dared to draw her in.

"Baynard—she was a ward like me, poised to climb quite high, too. Diegel was also not a merchant by birth, her family worked their way up, and Foster I remember making waves by vocally opposing the

Guild... Johansenn, Reginald, both of whom were accused of being illegitimate, Forescue was confirmed a bastard, her father never saw any shame in that, Tibbets—another ward, but her family is quite well liked, and Gough—bankers, I heard they misplaced a vault, and they haven't been able to shake accusations of being thieves, Cele herself told me that their rise was unusual, too, nobody had seen them in quite some time— Mattie thinks the real Goughs were killed by bandits, who subsequently replaced them," Sam muttered, ticking off the names with quiet counter-taps, "and now, Thompson. They've made waves with anyone and everyone—but so has every merchant holding their position."

"They all share a question of legitimacy," Fletcher mulled.

"Merchants are gods-damned rumor-mongers," Elsie put forth, bitter. "Gods only know what to believe."

Quiet washed over the store, a tiny respite from the storm beyond. It wouldn't open for another fifteen minutes. And for those fifteen minutes, it was their refuge.

A merchant, on a quest for vengeance against his fellow plutocrats.

Given this, it made sense that Fletcher had come to the Valley.

The territories outside Aerdela were growing restless, the whispers said, their petitions for districthood falling on increasingly uninterested ears. A few scant towns, lining the edge of Aerdela, that was all they were.

All they were supposed to be, anyway.

The territories were further flung than Elsie had realized, it seemed, if they stretched so far west as to hit the mountains.

That a territory boy had come, crawling from the mountains, sniffing out scandal—and if it was a merchant behind this, if there was tangible, blood-soaked corruption, if this was the weakening of the Guild...

Perhaps there was something growing beyond the borders of Aerdela.

Something bigger than they realized.

A merchant gone rogue.

Elsie watched the sunlight crawling across the floor, leaving a layer of dust dancing in its wake.

It was funny, how people talked about the sun like a faithful friend. The sun was a liar. A liar and a coward. Too deluded by the half-truths of shifting light. Too scared to stay and face the dark.

Morning had fully dawned when she met the street once more, and still, the sun was all wrong, with its false hope.

Cold rays lingered between her shoulders, and she had been betrayed by the blue sky above, cold and unfeeling in its broken promises. A day like today should've been warm, but without the blanket of clouds, coupled with the biting wind rolling off the foothills, the empty sky brought nothing but bitter autumn cold.

His hand brushed her shoulder, giving it a gentle squeeze, and there he was.

Her Fletcher.

Undoing the broken promises of the lying sun.

TEDDY

"Doubt percolates in the troubled mind."

~Dradan Proverb

"You saw it, right?" Teddy asked, frowning. The tang of copper lingered in the air as he closed the till, and he glanced over to Sam, dubious. The gold seemed to melt against his sister's olive skin, chain flashing against the back of her neck as she'd tilted her head low over the sweetroll.

Sam's cinnamon eyes gazed back at him, now molten in the morning sun. Even with hardly any sleep, he was beautiful, golden hair catching the light, his sun-kissed skin warm with sandalwood and cloves. "What, that pretty little thing she thought she was hiding beneath her shirt?"

"She didn't—"

"Ugh! Shame on you, Theodore Mirabeau," Sam scoffed, straightening up. "She steals *one roll—once—*when she was *eleven—*"

"It goes well beyond that, and you damn well know it—"

"It is the morning after a night of dancing and romancing beneath the stars, and given that they were hopelessly tangled up when we left— which was late, mind—I find it disturbing that your first conclusion is blatant thievery. It's probably a gift. You saw Fletcher—he was a nervous wreck. He knows El, he was probably apprehensive she'd—I don't know, berate him for the sheer non-utilitarian-ness of it—"

"Gods, fine!" Teddy snickered, relenting to the smile tugging at his lips. "Fine, point taken. I just worry."

"As is your brotherly duty, I should think."

"Don't let El hear you say that."

Sam grinned, giving a reflexive double-tap on the counter. "Fine. *Point taken.* I'll see you later?"

"See you later."

The bell over the door sent out a tinny call, and Teddy braced his arms on the counter, clinging to the scent of spiced tea that lingered in Sam's wake. A moment later, though, it'd vanished, overwhelmed by the streaks of vinegar on his dark apron, evidence of inattentive fingers and a shattered jar.

It was probably just as well.

Those crates weren't going to unpack themselves.

The storeroom was stale, the air heavy and thick, no matter how many times Teddy had run a broom and rag over the camphor-soaked wood—an atmosphere, he thought bitterly, which wasn't like to help his exhaustion.

It would've been nice for Sam to stay a little longer. A couturier of prodigious skill, though, he had his own work waiting for him back at Mulligan's. That man was unquestionably an artist with the needle and thread—this, even Teddy could recognize, despite having what Sam lovingly called an uninterested eye for fashion.

It wasn't that he wasn't interested.

A farmer's son didn't have the luxury of silk neckties and olive bath soaps, that was all. A merchant's ward, though...

The crack of fresh pine and the faint hint of mildewed straw met Teddy as he took the cat's paw to the crate. Salary was due today. A silver stack to Dad—it was more than Teddy pulled from the general store, but his father accepted no excuses, and besides, he'd seen Sam slip something in his satchel, anyway, gods bless that beautiful man—and he'd split the rest between himself and El—

Teddy's arm caught the corner of a crate as he turned to move, and before he could fully register the impact amid his daydream, a sting of wood in flesh tore jagged against his arm. Swearing, he dropped the cat's paw with a loud clank.

Careless. Careless, careless, careless—

A nauseating, caustic smell lingered in the musty air as blood welled down his arm.

He'd been wrung breathless, was suffocating as his eyes stung, fire prickling deep from within the cut, his lungs burning of something sterile, clean, the incense of his own skin in concentration, and he could feel it, deep within his chest.

The Thread.

Water hit the steel basin like thunder, the shock of cold like ice in his veins.

His heart was humming, and eyes pressed closed, his lungs filled once more with the stale stockroom air as he pictured the whirring little machine spitting stitches into bolts in the back of Sam's workroom.

The Thread.

That'd been Sam's name. The Thread. His grandmother had called it The Touch, but she was from the Basins, and anymore, nobody would've dared invoke such a dated superstition.

He had a knack, that's what his mother'd said.

A knack for helping.

Now go feed the chickens.

A knack for helping, *now go fetch your brother.*

A knack for helping, *now go wash the dishes.*

Her own personal form of denial. *You're a loon,* she'd snip, when Granma Geanie would croon over him, feeling his palms, murmuring prayers to her ancient gods. *Gods, Ma, let the boy be!* And she'd turn, muttering under her breath, *gods know, there's nothing divine here,* because she hadn't really wanted any of them but was too afraid to confess she hadn't been built to mother.

Billy Townsend had a knack, too, except his was for setting a string of barns alight the summer he'd turned sixteen.

'Course, nobody really got into it.

But Sam wasn't nobody.

Teddy! That's—you're—why didn't you tell me? Sam's eyes had been wide, his grin one of unmistakable youth, and it'd been a hot afternoon so many years ago on the shaded riverbanks filled with the sound of Elsie tossing rocks into the water with the responding *plunk-splash, plunk-splash* that awoke in her something destructive and chaotic, and there'd been a little bit of mutiny born in her eyes that day that had yet to fade.

It's nothing, Teddy mumbled, and he could still feel his face burning on the banks with his best friend. Sam's wet hair had been sending cool little beads down the back of his neck, rolling lazily down his tanned chest, an earthy smell, crisp and damp, clinging to them both as they'd sat in undershorts on the baking boulders, soaking in the sun. *I've just...got a knack for that sort of thing, that's all.*

That memory had stayed sweet, through the years.

The youthful memory of the hot summer day by the river.

Teddy opened his eyes, the tap squealing shut, water sputtering to a halt as he ran a hand across the smooth flesh of his forearm, no sign of injury marking him.

Just a knack for it.

ELSIE

"I will fight for you. Fight to the death for your
unequivocal right to not be afraid anymore.

This, I swear to you."

~Sam Alderton

Hissing grass, prickly and brittle, bristled against Elsie's thighs, her eyes darting down every so often to follow the game trail that circled back, surpassing the sprawl of the Valley as it opened up to the western farmlands.

Fletcher's fingers were tangled up with hers as they wound their way through the fields, Butterfly Ridge reluctantly poking up in the distance.

One, two, three chimneys to the left. Even from this distance, it looked dreary.

But fortunately, that distance—for the moment—was quite far.

Shortcut, indeed.

With coy smile, Elsie twirled around, catching Fletcher in her arms as he nearly walked into her, pressing a quick kiss against his soft lips. He went up almost imperceptibly onto his toes, just a fraction taller than she was for that one moment, catching his balance and another kiss before sinking back down to meet her eye line.

"Love you, Elsie," he breathed, lips tugging up, eyes alight.

He mended the broken promises of the treacherous sun.

They were loving as-is, in present condition, no questions asked, no heartache sold here, and she was alive, so gods-damned *alive*.

Tangled together, she followed the steady rise and fall of his breath with hers, tracing the gentle lilting of his ribcage with her hands—her hands that had already undone his buttoned coat, her hands that slid atop the over-starched tunic, making him laugh quietly, even as he winced against her icy fingers. "Love you, too," she murmured, squeezing him tightly, never letting go as she nuzzled into his neck.

The bitter wind was roaring around them, and there was a quiet voice inside her, pulsing next to the beating of her heart.

Safe.

Safe.

Safe.

Safe.

Safe.

Safe.

Safe.

~•~

She left him in the field, the taste of his lips still lingering sweet on her own.

It didn't do to cross lines like this, to bring him to this place where she was someone else. Not just yet. Not while they were still shiny and new and beautiful and clean and everything that she needed them to be right now.

The ragged pastures bathed in ghostly light were shifting, warm windows of creaking cottages speckling the countryside. Butterfly Ridge was a pathetic outcropping at the edge of the Valley, a hub for the farmers to drink and trade amongst themselves whilst the world moved beyond them.

"Hey!"

A familiar voice staggered through the air, and she didn't turn. That fucker wasn't worth the mud on her boots. Not anymore. Speaking of crossing one too many lines—

"Hey, Elsie!"

"The fuck you want, Percy," she snarled, whirling.

His greasy hair and stubbled cheeks were set into relief by the light from the bar, alcohol oozing from his flushed face, making her nose crinkle. "Hadn't seen you around too much. Can't I just tell m'girl hello?"

"You can try," she hissed, snapping a switchblade from her coat pocket, taking a step forward, "but I don't think it's a conversation you're going to like."

"Easy, now. Don't want no trouble—"

"Then walk away."

His jaw clenched at the command, a sneer she knew so well tugging at his face. "I heard," he began softly, frozen ground crunching under foot as he started a slow retreat, "that you found yourself a little tart to play with. An' that was you, wassinit, last night? All dolled up, a sweet little pastry?"

She moved on him, carving a warning into the cold night air. "Leave. Now."

"You think you're really so much better, now," he snickered, shaking his head. "You got all up on your high horse, just 'cause you got a tarty, now. He know that Princess Pastry's got sticky fingers? And it ain't from no sugar—"

"Run home, Percy Wilson." Her voice was low, and he was cornered, her blade poking dangerously into his gut. "Run along home to whatever you scraped up off the tavern floor and *leave me alone*."

"Or what," he whispered, a malicious smile on his lips.

Her heart was racing, and the night was sharpening with a renewed rush of adrenaline.

Percy just clicked his tongue, rolling his shoulders as he took a step back. "Feisty. Missed that about you, Elsie-bells." And with a derisive laugh, he left, muttering to himself. "Jus' like I said. Same as ever."

The blade clicked shut, fury roaring inside her.

Princess Pastry.

It was hard not to go back, to grab his shoulders, to shake him violently, to scream until he had no choice but to hear her words.

But boys like that never listened.

Fletcher did, though.

A tart, she thought bitterly, resentful. Fletcher was anything but.

Warm blueberry pie with a dollop of vanilla cream. That's what he was.

Sweet stains of purple and bitter blues buried inside an egg-washed crust, because really, wasn't that all any of them were, a mashed-up filling of what was right and wrong and good and bad and secrets and lies and truth and justice, all stuffed inside a crumbling shell, a dessert delivered in the cool nights of autumn when the sun had faded and still, they hoped.

And such an intoxicating hope it was.

That things could be different.

That they could be more.

There was a fire in her chest, and her fast breaths were curling on the night air, eyes never leaving the lights that flickered out before her, and she wondered if this was what it really felt like, being in love.

They would be more.

Marlene was waiting, plopped on the thread-bare sofa darning socks. In her ill-fitting cotton shift and stained, pink apron, she seemed to be trying—and failing—to evoke the cheery affect of the farmer's wife. She might've been the classically jolly matron, had it not been for the bitter expression carved on her face, her lips twisted into a permanent frown.

There was something sadistically dignified in those gray eyes, a look of righteous vindication in the puckered corners of her wrinkled lips.

And the locket suddenly didn't sit so heavy on Elsie's chest.

Did he know.

Did he know, when he'd sent his crony crawling through her window, that he'd sent not a locket but freedom.

I don't belong to you.

It didn't really matter if it was real or not, because she'd been left, and lockets didn't change that, but all the same, it was a strange sort of defiant reminder that she didn't belong to them.

She didn't belong to anyone. And she didn't belong here. Not really.

Kicking off her boots, Elsie turned for the hallway, Marlene's voice lemon in milk behind her, curdling any warmth put off by the crumbling fireplace, an insistent pudgy sausage of a finger thrust towards the back door.

Then again, Elsie supposed it didn't matter.

None of it mattered.

Because defiant rebellion or no, tonight's ending didn't belong to Elsie.

It belonged to the page-rippers.

SAM

"They peddled war, proclaiming it was peace. They sold famine, saying it was gluttony. They dealt in darkness, gambled with greed, and in their wake, whispers filled the street.

Beware the Merchants of Death."

~from 'Merchants of Death'

Pale satin dresses turned brilliant shades of burnt orange and lilac in the shadow of the sinking sun, and Mulligan's Finery looked a sunset for the taking.

Sam paused, on his way out the door, sewing kit tucked neatly in his leather satchel, shoulders aching from an afternoon hunched over hemming gowns, paused to look himself over in the tri-paneled mirror, gilded and shining at the center of the shop.

The brown suit was a bit summery—perhaps his own reluctance to bid farewell to the warm weather that had long-since departed.

But it was *perfection* with the ivory tunic, the accompanying vest, the caramel-colored cravat, dotted expertly with a golden tie pin.

A favorite combination.

And it screamed *tart*.

It was supposed to be a slur.

He'd never been called a tart, at least not directly, not until he'd met them. Elsie and Teddy.

'Course, Elsie been shorter, then. He'd still been able to look down on the top of her head when she'd been ten and viciously precocious. He'd been fifteen, and she'd walked straight up to him, tome in hand— a tome hopelessly expensive, that she'd never afford, but the shopkeep let her read, anyway, when she'd come into the bookstore after school— she'd walked straight up to him and *demanded* to know the meaning of the word 'ameliorate.'

Like her right to knowledge had been unequivocal and inalienable.

He told her, and she went right back to the armchair in the corner, reading away, and he went back to perusing back-shelf novels while his sisters waited in line, and really, he hadn't thought much more of it, until he'd gone to leave, parcels in hand, and she'd been waiting at the front window, book bag clutched to her chest, staring with worried eyes out into the dark. Waiting.

Oh, lovely. A tart, Teddy had muttered, lifting Elsie up onto the counter of the general store while Sam had lingered at the door. He'd realized what he'd said immediately, of course, face turning bright red, eyes going wide, and there'd been apologies, and a *thank you for walking her over* and more apologies, but it didn't matter, because even if only for a moment, he'd spoken his truth.

Sam's thoughts drifted down the street, to the now-dark general store.

Teddy's eyes, usually bright blue like the deep Southern oceans, had been muted and dull this morning. They'd been out late last night, and Teddy didn't relish the crowds or the noise or the beautiful chaos beckoned in on the velvet night. But tangled up on the sofa in Sam's apartment, lost in idle talk and mulled wine with nothing but the sound of the roaring fire to serenade them...

Those blue eyes had filled up page after page of his sketchbook for years beyond count.

The first time he'd drawn them, his hand had been shaking so badly it'd been nothing more than a wash of deep blues and blacks set across the paper. Love unreciprocated was terrifying.

But each time he drew them, there was a little more clarity. He'd find the starbursts of gray buried so far beneath the waves of azure. Would realize how the light left little bright pinpricks across the glassy surface. And finally, finally, he'd at last seen himself reflected back in them. Had at last been able to find some clarity.

Had been able to see who he was, more or less.

There was an indelible smile dancing on his lips as Sam settled the leather satchel draped across his body, stuffing his hands in his pockets.

Of late, he could see their future, too, in those eyes.

Hell.

Those eyes *were* his future.

Soon. He'd propose soon, when the moment was right.

The world was starting to take on a sort of brownish hue as the sun began to disappear. Shining mares with angry breath curling on the evening air had been plunged into shadow, their darkened carriage widows reflecting the ostentatiously gilded shop windows alight with commerce. Women bathed in silks and satins of the most brilliant plumage began to litter the street, men in deliciously regal tails and ties sporting looks of lust at their little birds.

"...dues unpaid," a voice carried through the street, and Sam felt his blood run cold.

If they were pretty little birds, dancing in the street, *he* was caracara, picking them to pieces.

"Given the acclaim of your establishment, it's simply unacceptable."

"Please, you don't understand," a shopkeeper was pleading, "I paid them, I swear—"

Clark Carson stood, arms crossed, a look of derisive pleasure behind his cold eyes, his black hair slicked back for the kill. "Your pathetic whimpering might have swayed my actuary, but I care not for this charade." He gestured to one of his lackeys, who yanked the shopkeeper's arm and began dragging him towards the forebodingly unremarkable carriage in the street.

Sam side-stepped the display with an air of casual inconvenience.

Like it wasn't odd, running into the Commissioner himself exacting penance for the unforgivable sin of unpaid dues.

The shopkeeper struggled against the lackey's strength as he was forced into the windowless carriage, futilely arguing all the while. "My family—"

"—is not my concern," Clark shrugged, brushing an invisible speck of dust from the plumage. "Acquisition, Distinction, Protection—is this not the motto we live by, in the Guild? Pray tell, how might I execute the latter if the former two are neglected?"

"My children, they did nothing—"

Clark's eyes flickered up to the shopkeeper. "Children are such fickle things, aren't they?" There was a sickeningly sweet tone to his quiet voice. "One moment, they adore you, the next, they ignore you as they pass by on the street."

Sam rolled his eyes, scoffing as he shifted the satchel strap on his shoulder.

"Mr. Alderton?" Clark's voice cut through the night air. "That's what you go by now, isn't it, Sam?"

Turning smoothly on his heel, Sam met the scene with a sardonic

41

stare. "It is. And after six years, Clark, I'm glad word finally reached the manor. I was starting to worry."

Clark gave a dramatic gesture to the shopkeep, the sidewalk a theater as the caracara declaimed. "You see what I mean. We raise them, love them, nurture them, give them the world on a silver platter, and they toss it in the gutter like refuse."

"Oh, gods below—"

"That's it." A sharp clap through the air sent the carriage rattling away, one of Clark's lackeys waiting nearby, eyes darting between the two of them standing there in exasperated silence.

"Well, go on," Clark snipped, waving the lackey away. "Shoo.

"Commissioner, I don't think—"

"You are superfluous, you intolerable clod. It's just Sam. He's my son, not a flagrant shop-keep with a temper," Clark muttered. "Go."

"I'm not your son," Sam remarked, trying to mask the air of irritation with a look of vague boredom. As if familial disownment were casual conversation. Of course, it'd only been said a thousand times, for all the difference that made—

Clark only sighed, eyes meeting Sam's as he gestured to the street ahead. "Let's take a walk, shall we?"

"Teddy's waiting for me."

"Well, let's grab this fellow and make a date of it, I admit, I'm rather peckish—"

"No."

"You do spoil all the fun—"

"—yes, yes, I know, I'm an ungrateful thing, you've said so to anyone who'll listen, Clark, now what do you want?"

Clark frowned, any amusement derived from his playfully horrendous banter dissolving. "Fine. I'll be brief. The absence of your correspondence has been noted."

42

"I've been busy, with the season about to begin."

As if they both didn't know the oversight was deliberate.

"We had an arrangement, Sam. Is her life really worth clerical neglect?"

He never said her name.

He didn't have to.

That was how deftly he pulled the strings, to evoke her with just a breath.

"I'll be watching for your notes, love."

Sam put a hand reflexively to his heart, fingers brushing the bulge of the letters tucked inside his coat.

The very notes that Clark demanded.

It was cowardly, to carry them around. Like Sam couldn't make up his mind about whether to hand them over or guard them close.

So casual, Clark was, now turning away, hands in his pockets, as if he hadn't delivered a death threat.

As if Sam wasn't carrying her beating heart in the breast pocket of his coat.

As if it wasn't an armament to his own guilt, some sick kind of assuagement to his own culpability.

As if he loved a single soul in all the world that he hadn't eventually betrayed.

As if this was all for something more than themselves.

As if they were fighting the good fight.

As if they were good men.

As if.

THE BEAST

"Truth is in the eye of the beholder, and lies on the tongues of the well-meaning."

-from 'The Advice of The Long-Dead' and Other Essays

The Beast had been borrowed, and now stood with the Master, waiting together beyond the grand house in the Valley.

"Clever," the Master mused, delighted. "I'm sure this one's the one, she must be...He has done well, has he not?"

Magic curled in the Beast's nostrils, whetting its taste for fear. It cared naught for the Master's words. It only longed for the hunt.

"Ask, and you shall receive, and so the gods shall not leave their children wanting," the Master purred. "You shall not be wanting for much longer, love, you understand."

But the Beast didn't understand.

The Beast only knew hunger. The hunt. And pain—lots and lots of pain.

ELSIE

.

"Certainly, sleep is not a requisite of nightmares. You understand, now, our fascination with fairy tales—all we wanted was to imagine a better world. We all pretend, in our own way."

~Elizabeth Clement Faulise

"What would you say if I asked you to marry me?"

"If you did something so ridiculously stupid," Elsie mused, not looking up from the stack of papers littering the floor of Fletcher's room at the lodge, "I would tell you no, because the whole notion is absurd."

They'd spent the morning buried in records, chasing the so-far unanswered question of who the girl at the harbor had been, armed with a pot of acidic, dark tea and quiet conversation. Settled on the hearth-rug, she let the heat from the crackling fire soak deep into her aching back, reveling in the now-hot knit sweater against her skin.

"And would you say it's absurd, because the essence of a thing isn't so much in the name as in the details, and adding a wedding band doesn't change the details of us?"

She felt her lips tugging upwards as she glanced up. "I do love you, you know that?"

He nodded, a sweet smile on his lips. Legs crossed, leaning against the sofa, he looked at ease, a notebook balanced precariously on one knee, a stack of parchment on the other. There was something mischievous in his eyes as he watched her.

"And what would you do," Elsie relented, taking the bait, "if I said no?"

"That's predicated on the assumption I'd be so stupid as to ask," he countered. "I'd be more inclined say we should get a cat."

"Mm, smart companion," she snickered, returning to the ink-laden sheet before her. He knew her well. She admired the fierce tenacity of their barn cats, and had long nursed a soft spot for them, going so far as to leave a bit of milk in a dish on particularly cold winter mornings. Scrappy, feral, dangerous—not a bad thing to be.

"I was thinking," Fletcher went on, sounding a little cautious, "that maybe after the investigation is done...maybe we could do that. Get a cat."

His words settled over the quiet room, and her breath caught in her throat again and again and again, refusing to leave.

"Elsie?"

She didn't move her eyes from the now-illegible scrawls flooding across the paper, and she could feel the thin parchment starting to give as she gripped the edges with white knuckles.

Raw.

That's how she'd been left. Stripped raw, left oozing when she'd barely had a moment to scab, and anymore all she wanted were the scars, the welted, pulled-too-tight scars to cocoon the wreckage that was left, but here he was, and maybe she didn't have to fight for scars anymore. She'd been left inevitably betrayed by her affection, for the world would turn each love against her eventually—until now, when he'd borrowed from the things she loved and turned them into an emollient.

Once upon a time, there was a girl.

Teddy had first told her the story when she was very little. The beginning was always the same. It was the endings that her brother liked to change. He couldn't very well change their beginnings, he'd told her—only the gods above and below had the power to spin the beginnings of a story.

But in spite of the best efforts of a cruel world, Teddy had instilled within his little sister the very dangerous notion that she might change the ending to her own story, if she wished.

Some men, Elsie had come to realize—Gregory Mirabeau, Percy Wilson, hell, Clark Carson, probably—they were the kind of men that commandeered another's story. They opened the cover, ripped out the pages they didn't like, scratched out the lines he wanted to change, and when it was done, they'd discard the book like the piece of trash they knew it to be from the start.

She knew that Fletcher's hand had brushed against hers, that he'd slid beside her, his knee against hers, but everything was numb.

Deadened, for it felt like her body had fallen into such disuse it could hardly remember.

Nobody is coming to save you.

If what came before had been such lonely pages, that was how they'd have begun, for it was hard to imagine that if she had been one of the fallen pastries, Fletcher should've come for her.

No matter what Clark's letter implied, she did not think so highly of herself to be paid such care.

Yet, here Fletcher was, caring, talking about cats and not-proposing, and...and their life together, after the investigation.

And suddenly, his love wasn't contingent on death. Suddenly, Elsie wasn't responsible for how dead those girls were, because even though she played no part in their demise, she had not wanted Fletcher to leave, which surely meant she wanted the pastries to continue to fall—

"Did I say something wrong?"

What is this what is happening why do you feel hope you know that's foolish

"No." She dared a glance his way, but he was just a watery mess of worry and love. "Where, um…where would we keep this cat?"

Why the fuck are you crying stop stop stop

"Anywhere you like," he said softly.

Why are you still crying, get a grip—

"Like somewhere with you and me and nobody else."

Weak weak weak strong girls don't do this chase boys like this run after them and you do it because you're desperate, desperate and pathetic—

There was a faint smile on his lips as he gave her a small nod. "Somewhere like that."

It's not real none of this is real he doesn't love you—

Her eyes found his, burning and flashing in the firelight—flashing so impossibly with joy, a soft pine forest streaked with amber, and the world went quiet.

Quiet for just a moment.

"Sorry," she breathed, breaking his gaze at last as she brushed the tears from her cheeks.

"Why?"

"Because….this." She gestured vaguely to herself, shaking her head.

"Because you're crying?"

The question sent her eyes stinging raw again.

But when he spoke next, his words were unfamiliar, his timbre dropping almost imperceptibly, the sounds curling through the warm air.

They stirred something deep within her chest, a spark hidden in the raw and oozing recesses of her heart. "I don't know what that means," she said quietly as her fingers worried the unraveling hem of her leggings, eyes intent on the tight weave of the soft, dark cotton.

"It's a saying. From the mountains." There was a soft smile on his lips, his shoulders swaying in easy time to a song she could not hear. "It means that a few drops of rain muddy the path, but a torrent washes it clean. Elsie, I've never seen you do anything half-heartedly. You're— you're not a muddy path kind of person. You're a downpour. A barrage. A cloud-burst with thunder so loud it makes the window panes shatter. And you don't need to except your tears from that way of life. It's okay to be torrential."

She chuckled wetly, shaking her head. "I thought you didn't do metaphors."

"I don't do your metaphors," he corrected, grinning.

Being torrential. She rather liked the sound of that.

"My metaphors," she snickered, drying her tears. "Who are you, Fletcher Praequintelya?"

And he paused.

He paused, and there was something on the tip of his tongue.

But he merely shook his head, his voice a half-whisper.

"I wish I knew."

FLETCHER

"We love, and we trust—and we hope that it's enough."

~Theodore Alderton

Leaves clanked together like pots and pans, their skittered reverberations filling the air as Fletcher trailed the traces of magic burning like lines of fire through the countryside.

A cat. The thought made him smile. Soft little paws on a hard-wood floor, pitter-pattering to the low-hum purr, and Elsie's laugh would fill the air, crisp and sweet, because she would be happy.

He would be happy.

He could do this, keep this up. She didn't need to know about magic. They could simply exist. His powers would grow weak in disuse, would ossify into a bittersweet memory, and perhaps he'd no longer be a river on the constant verge of overflowance, always fighting to stay afloat while his lungs still filled with water. And they'd have their quiet future.

A future that regretfully felt worlds away tonight.

The grass beneath his leather boots cracked and snapped, soft earth sighing gently under his weight. The kobalde's trail was growing stronger.

His pace was quick, magic flaring instinctively in his palms with a sparked sizzle so high it seemed to float above the heavens. The kobalde were mischievous creatures, cunning, dangerous masters of deception, and their whining—gods below, their whining was incessant, already, the trails rang nasal as he closed in.

That one had appeared in the Valley was not, in and of itself, concerning. Attracted to the chaos of a trading district, they thrived on the mayhem wrought in the shops and homes of workers and merchants alike. Their love of crowds and confinement and chaos and cacophony was—how did Elsie put it—butterflies to candles?

That couldn't be right.

No matter. Whatever force drew the kobalde to the trading hub had slackened, it seemed, because the little threads of magic scampering through the fields were headed straight to the district's outer edge. The drone of cattle lowing was on the air, piped as shadows began to linger long over the plained horizon.

And in the pastoral haze, something snapped.

Something intangible and distant, close and screaming, and his magic sent a little sting through his heart, burning and writhing.

Fletcher froze.

A tripwire.

He'd set them snaking across the Valley, little strands of magic listening for the call of the like craft, waiting to be disturbed by creatures and conjurers that ought not to be crossing the district bounds—though the waiting, it seemed, was over.

No magic was permitted to contaminate the bounds within Aerdela.

This remained the highest law, the most unbreakable.

That he'd willfully disobeyed, in the name of this investigation—it was no matter, the way he saw it.

The secret stayed safe.

Nobody knew about the bloodied magic seeping into the sequestered lands. Nobody knew a dishonored—soon to be discharged—warrior prowled those same sequestered lands, seeking to oust the illicit practitioners.

But something had disturbed the tripwire.

The tripwire laid carefully, no less, winding beyond the house he'd expressly been forbidden to see.

Behind the house of the one he loved.

Swearing angrily, a renewed wave of adrenaline flooding his body, he disappeared into a shimmering whirl of mist, bracing himself.

ELSIE

"It is only when the torches die and the darkness encroaches that we can truly see the fabric of reality."

~from 'The Advice of The Long-Dead' and Other Essays

"Bells!" Elsie called out, exasperated as she strode through the darkening pasture. That fucking cow. And what a ridiculous name.

Great fat thunderheads were burgeoning, bruises of black and purple beneath whipped cream heads, and another clap of thunder was sent echoing through the fields. She pulled her coat closer, grimacing as big, fat drops began to plunk down, splattering wildly against the cracked earth. The wool scraped the back of her neck, the collar steadily untying the loose braid as she turned her head from side to side, searching.

"Bells! Bells, you insolent sack of milk, where..." Her voice trailed off as a movement near the road caught her eye.

The air was electric and dark, and the little girl strode through the grass in her little blue pinafore apron and gathered black dress and sweet red hood, not seeming to care that the sky was rebelling.

Careless, letting a child wander. And it made her heart ache.

Does your family know you're not at home?

"You shouldn't be out here," Elsie called out, pace quickening through the tall grass. "Storm's coming in, it isn't safe."

"I'm in the middle of my game—"

"Go on. Get out of here. You can finish your game another time." Her voice was brisk, colder than she wanted it to be.

"No." The little girl's face had wrinkled into a pout.

"It's dangerous."

And the girl paused.

Her frown flickered out, a malicious smile curling on her lips. "Yes," she grinned. "Yes, it is dangerous, isn't it?"

Even before her tiny shoe smacked the ground, even before that little girl had raised her foot to stamp the earth, Elsie had known. Had felt a hum through her bones.

Elsie was falling, a loud crack filling the air, and a dark burst raced forward, pinning her to the ground with suffocating force as she gasped for air, her bones stinging—

Something moved through the grass, something making it whisper and hiss, a snake of cold, biting air—

"No, no, no, no, no!" The little girl was screaming, furious. "Not fair! That's cheating, it's not part of the game, that's—"

What it was, precisely, Elsie would never know.

Because someone's hand was on her shoulder, and the world had dissolved into bright whirls of color, spinning, spinning, spinning...

~ • ~

Whether the world had pieced itself back together or not, Elsie wasn't sure. Hers was still moving far too fast, her blurred vision dotted with black spots. She was shaking as she pushed herself up, dead leaves and pebbles sticking to the palms of her sweaty hands. The bile biting at the back of her throat, the nausea rising in her gut, the pounding in her head—it all proved too much to fight back.

She retched, losing what had barely passed for dinner anyway on the forest floor. Someone was pulling her hair from her face, a familiar hand braced gently on her lower back as she coughed, spitting out the vile taste of vomit that lingered on her tongue.

"Are you okay?" Fletcher's warm voice met her ears.

Sitting back, eyes watering, she glanced over—and started, ripping herself away from his touch.

Her fingers dug into the pungent dirt, packing the grainy bits painfully beneath her nails, and she could not look away, because her mysterious mountain boy...

Delicately pointed ears cut through his dark blonde hair, acuminous nails at the tips of now-slender fingers. She found his eyes, but he shifted, and they caught the light all wrong, flashing like a wolf in the dark.

"What are you."

"Drada," he said quietly. "Elsie, I am so sorry. I..."

His words faded into nothing but a roaring in her ears, the beating of her own heart like some sadistic drummer hoping to rupture the head.

She should be scared. Little girls couldn't bring down a person with the stomp of a foot, worlds didn't just disappear in the blink of an eye, Drada—whatever that was—didn't exist, and she sure as hell knew that if they did, her companion wasn't...

Drada.

Maybe she'd said the word, because the taste of crisp ozone air was on her tongue, an echo of a sound on her lips, and he was giving her a quiet nod.

She pulled the switchblade from her pocket. It flicked open with a satisfying click, and she could feel her heart starting to slow. "A Drada is...what, exactly," she challenged, voice low.

His voice was measured, brows knitting as he eyed the knife in her hand. It didn't make a difference, though, what his voice sounded like, because she couldn't hear him above the din in her own mind.

Her knuckles were white, the crevasse of the handle digging sweetly into her skin, and she could not take her eyes from him. Searching, she was searching violently for the man she knew, she loved, beneath the leather bracers, beneath the knife-belt, beneath the dark clothes woven from midnight itself.

"I'm not going to hurt you," he was saying softly, hands lingering in surrender, and gently, he rocked, back and forth, a lilt she'd memorized, a tic she'd seen a thousand times and loved a million more.

"No. No, you're not." She shifted, her legs beginning to prickle with pins and needles.

Then, exhaling deeply, she flicked the blade shut, gripping it in a tight fist. "That thing, the girl..."

"A kobalde. A demon." He was searching, too, his flashing eyes refusing to flit away. "Are you alright? You're not injured?"

"No." Her fingers grazed the back of her head nevertheless, meeting the unbrushed mess of a braid peppered with pokey little seeds burrowing into her dark hair. A bit tender. But she'd had worse.

The barren trees overhead reached up towards the dark, rumbling sky, the dead leaves shivering with raindrops. "Where are we?"

"Out of the way. For the moment, at least."

And there it was again.

Beside her heartbeat, tucked safely in between the spaces of her ribs.

Safe.

Safe.

Safe.

And not numb.

Gods, was she so not numb.

There was thunder in her palms and lightning in her eyes and this, this was what it was, to revel in being.

She was on her feet, brushing dirt from her leggings. "So. A Drada." Her eyes flicked over to him. *Mysterious mountain boy, indeed.*

Fletcher was rising, black cloak giving a faint flutter in the breeze. The shadows didn't become him. If they'd meant to conceal him, they'd utterly failed—he would've blended better to sun and sand. The ears, though...

"It suits you. Being...Drada." Whatever that was.

"Thanks," he said quietly, disbelief in his eyes.

"So, you're obviously hunting," she sighed, gesturing vaguely at him. "I'm going to take a wild guess and say it was the—what was it, kobalde?—that you were after."

"Something like that."

"And she attacked me because?"

"No idea. One moment, she was circling the border, the next..." He trailed off with a quiet sigh, and his eyes found hers.

I wish that we could never end.

Seven words, and they'd betrayed his fears. Seven words, and they'd been an apology for sins of circumstance that had slipped through his fingers while he'd held her close.

Seven words, and she could see it in his eyes, now.

This will not be how we end.

Seven words, and he remembered that she wrote the endings.

She blew out a breath, eyes trailing him up and down once more. She'd been praying for this fairy tale for a long time, now. It seemed foolish to abandon it before it'd even really begun. "Alright," Elsie said softly, eyes flicking past him to the forest beyond. "Let's go get her."

Fletcher gave Elsie a curt nod, and she could've sworn she saw a faint smile tugging at his lips in the low light. "First thing's first." With a small gesture of his wrist, a glowing orb appeared in the palm of his hand, pulsing softly in the darkness. "This is a lucent. Throw it, as hard as you can, at anything that comes towards you."

Her fingers brushed against his as she took it, his skin sparking warmly against hers, familiar and soft. And the lucent—

"Amazing," she breathed. A smooth, velvety membrane of warmth seemed to be all that kept the light inside from spilling into the dark. Grinning, she pocketed the lucent, gesturing for another.

"Second," Fletcher nodded, obliging, watching as she stuffed her pockets with lucents, "kobalde are tricksters. They thrive on discomposure, and they're wicked clever. My brother was fond of saying that truth is irrelevant on a demon's trail—and gods, I can't believe I'm saying this—he was sort of right. Confused prey is easy prey, so just be on your guard when it's cornered. They've got tongues like knives."

"Noted."

"Ready?"

"Ready."

He held out his hand.

She took it, savoring him, sweet and warm in the cold air, and the world dissolved around them.

ELSIE

"Dark of heart, dark of mind,
And in the dark, should demon find,
To run, to scream, to fight, to flee,
Lest the darkest heart consumeth thee."

~Emilyon Dresada, 'Chant of the Night' from 'Collected
Dradan Poetry'

Elsie felt a renewed wave of nausea in her stomach as she gripped his hand, waiting for the world to still. They were on the western border of Butterfly Ridge, where the farmland slowly began melting into the forest beyond.

Even as she blinked back the specks of white light still burned into the back of her eyelids, Fletcher had his head cocked, his movements unnaturally still. Then, ear twitching slightly, he nodded south, to where the tree line grew dense as it neared the river. "That way," he breathed, giving her hand a squeeze before letting go.

The swollen purple clouds above them had dimmed what little evening light they might've had, pelting raindrops smacking haphazardly against her cheeks with cold determination.

The weather willed her home.

The weather, she mused, would've done well to remember.

I write the endings.

Her fingers were around a lucent, turning it idly over in her hands, eyes darting up and down the banks of the roaring river as they walked, every nerve alive with anticipation. Air, crisp and sweet, filled her lungs, lighting crackling through the clouds.

One, two—

Thunder barreled through the earth.

On the heels of the shaking ground, a grinning little girl with inked eyes and a cloak of blood.

Elsie sent her lucent flying with lethal precision—

But the little girl gave a flippant wave of her hand, and it melted away, ice against a hot stove.

"Oh, isn't this a precious little game," the kobalde snickered, brushing off her hands. "Princess Pastry and Good Sir Tart, come to play. Grishka!" Her voice clapped through the air. "Grishka! Come out and introduce yourself! I'm Chim, by the way," she beamed, sparing a mocking curtsy and a flashing, fanged smile. "And it is so lovely you've come to play."

Behind her, branches were cracking beneath shadowed swipes, shuddering trees sending sprays of water droplets peeling to the ground as great booming steps pounded through the foliage, Chim squealing with excitement.

Fletcher's own fiery lucent bore into the dark wood without warning, not waiting for the creature to emerge. An ear-splitting roar filled the air, and Elsie's skin was crawling, her jaw clenching—

It was terrible, the thing dragged from the shadows. Slits for nostrils sucked in the night, steam curling with hot, heavy breaths, and loose, mangy skin hung from bones, greasy and slick with rain, a sickly gray scabbed with blue. Towering at no less than twelve feet tall, great black plumes gathered at its fingertips, coalescing amid the cackling laughter.

60

Impossible.

It was impossible, the billiard-ball lucent clutched in her fingertips, against the beast with blazing eyes.

A pernicious little giggle bubbled through the air, and the kobalde's eyes were on her, maliciously amused. "So sweet," she simpered, throwing a hand up to dissolve another lucent, "letting your little princeling do the work. Is that what mommy taught you, before she dumped you here?"

"No! Elsie, don't—"

But Chim was running, laughing wildly as she danced through the trees.

A blur of red twirled through mangled brush and the air was burning in Elsie's lungs, the bellow of the river drowning out the pounding in her ears. The spindly fingers of branches and bramble clawed through her coat, yanking her hair, but it didn't matter because there was fire, fire burning hot inside her chest, she would pay for those words, pay dearly—

Taking a chance, Elsie hurled a lucent towards the giggling blur of red—and watched as the girl was sent crashing down, rocks squealing at the impact.

"Mean," the kobalde was whimpering, pushing herself to standing, dusting off her smock with a crinkled nose. "You're a mean girl. That wasn't fair, I wasn't ready!" Crocodile tears pooled in her eyes, spilling onto her dirty cheeks.

"Too bad," Elsie smirked, tossing the lucent in the air, catching it in the palm of her hand. "Why'd you attack me?"

"Because those are the rules of the game," Chim sniffled, pulling a hand across her face.

"It's not a very good game, then, is it." Turning quickly, she sent the lucent in a piercing line to the kobalde.

"Mean and stupid," Chim snipped, swiping the lucent aside with ease. "You just don't know how to play."

"Then tell me why you attacked me in the pasture."

"No. Why don't you run back to your little princeling before I decide to give you a penalty for breaking the rules."

Elsie clicked her tongue, pacing as she tugged yet another lucent from her coat pocket. "Not good enough. You attack me. You insult me. I want to know why."

Always, needing to know the *why*. As if Marlene Mirabeau hadn't given her the *why* a thousand times.

Still, she asked.

Still, she hoped one day to find the answer.

The little girl inclined her head, dark eyes wide, unblinking. Her gaze was disconcerting. Where the whites of her eyes should be, where the concentric colored circles ought to be running towards a dark pupil, lay only a black void.

"The Master's been giving me ideas," she said salaciously. "You know the one? The one with a taste for pastries?" Then, with a devious smile on her lips, she straightened her hood. "Must be getting home for supper. Those are the rules." And in a whirl of inky black, she disappeared.

Elsie sent the lucent flying towards the dark cloud—her efforts were in vain, though, the lucent crashing into the tree behind where the kobalde had stood.

The Master?

Gravel crunched behind her, and she started, whirling.

"Just me," Fletcher murmured, hands in surrender.

"She—she disappeared," Elsie breathed in outrage, "I tried—"

"You couldn't have stopped her." Fletcher's hands were outstretched, as if he were warming them by an unseen fire as he surveyed the disturbed earth where the kobalde had fallen. "Lucents can slow a kobalde. But they aren't shackles."

"What about that—that other thing," she asked quietly, glancing over her shoulder, as if expecting it to come tumbling through the trees at any moment.

"A beluae. Dead." He said the word like it killed a little part of him, too.

Elsie could still feel the phantom lucent against her fingertips, now stinging with regret.

"She's certainly gone," Fletcher murmured. "Where, I do not know. Beyond our reaches, no question."

"Can't you find it again? Do the thing—with the, um..." Her hand danced in the air, searching for a word she realized she didn't know. "The disappearing, or whatever?" Her heart was pounding, body flooded with adrenaline from the chase.

"Evanescing. That's what it's called." He shook his head, rising from where he'd knelt to examine the ground. "The kobalde are deceivers. They have a gift for disappearing when they do not wish to be found."

Rainwater was already pooling in the little indentations made by the kobalde as she'd skidded to a stop, tumbling over herself. Elsie was soaked to the bone, the water clouding her vision. Not water, she realized—tears. Tears of failure, and bitter anger.

"Elsie." Fletcher gently brushed the moisture from her cheeks with a soft finger. His skin was stained with blood as he pulled it away, her own stinging with salt and water.

"We should find—"

"You're hurt—"

"I am *fine!*"

"Elsie, you—I—" He sighed, exasperated. "Even if I wanted to, I can't track a kobalde over those kinds of distances. Nobody can."

Grimacing, she scoffed her frustration. "No. Of course, not. Because why—why would anybody..." But the words caught in her throat, stuck between her constricting chest and heavy disbelief.

She grabbed his hand, slick with rain and chilled to the bone, gripped it hard, as if the mere act of his skin against hers was enough to dissolve this miserable scene. "Fine. Let's get the fuck out of here."

ELSIE

"Never let propriety get in the way of finding what you need."

~Risa Barrett

Ringing out her hair, Elsie frowned, watching the veritable waterfall splattering onto the soft hearth rug below. Soaked to the bone didn't really do their condition justice.

With a grimace, she sent the droplets lingering on her fingertips towards the flame-licked logs, the fire hissing and spitting in protest. The steady *drip drip* of water on brick evidenced the still-waterlogged state of her clothes tossed hopelessly on the grate, vainly soaking up the heat. She pulled her borrowed dressing robe closer—gods, it smelled like him, like tealeaves and bread, beyond familiar, verging on intoxicating—and she sighed.

A Drada.

Her eyes skirted the lodge room, looking for...well, looking for whatever it was elves left lying around that would've been particularly elfish. A cobbler's bench, maybe.

But there was nothing scattered about that would've betrayed magic, save for the elf wringing out a sodden tunic in the bathing room sink.

Retrieving her steaming cup of tea from the mantle with a quiet clatter of porcelain-on-stone, she padded over to join him, letting the doorframe bear the weight of her exhausted self. "So," she said dully, watching as he tossed the tunic over the edge of the tub. "Princeling. You think she knew it was by birth, or did the kobalde assume it was by your esteemed relation to Princess Pastry?" The taunt still screamed in her mind, the kobalde's childish voice mocking and cruel. But his *was* a title given at birth, that much, he'd confessed long ago, in July, by the fountain. Only then, it'd been the kind of meaningless title everyone wore, like calling someone *Lord* or *Mister*, and since she'd believed him to be from the *human* towns seeking districtship beyond Aerdela, she hadn't questioned that they'd adopted the titles in defiance.

"The former, I'm sure," he muttered, not daring to meet her gaze.

"Well, I confess, I'm a bit disappointed the settlements hadn't taken to crowning their own royalty. Could've given the Commissioners a run for their money—I mean, a self-made King? That's an easy sell, especially with the summer we had. Though it's a bit tropey," she added in an undertone. "An elven prince..."

Her eyes lingered on him. On his loose, too-long trousers sitting low on his hips. On his bare chest, smooth save for a fine dusting of hair on his soft stomach, the kind perfect for hugging.

"So, how bad is it?"

He turned, eyes wide at the almost-accusation, the dripping socks forgotten in his fingertips. "How bad is what?"

"These murders. You're a good man, Fletcher, and you have a good heart, but this is not the only streak of violence within Aerdela. People die all the time, and I don't imagine elves come running every time someone gets gutted in a back-district alley. And someone calling himself the Master is ordering demons through the brambles, bragging about—about having a taste for pastries, Fletcher, that's not *ordinary*. At least, not here. So, tell me. Tell me what crime was so heinous that a *Dradan prince* was sent to find the answer."

Fletcher's brow was knitted. "Blood magic," he said quietly. "But nobody sent me. I'm not supposed to be here."

FLETCHER

"Blood-soaked are the hands of the living. We are all sinners, to have survived so long."

~Adrian Lynch

The rain had stopped falling by the time Fletcher returned to the riverbank, leaving nothing more than squelching mud beneath his boots as branches above groaned beneath the fat, lolling beads of water.

The body of the beluae lay where it'd fallen, the ground stained with its dark blood.

"Odd," a delicate voice said from behind.

Fletcher knew she'd been there. He'd heard her words long before she spoke.

"What, pray tell," his sister went on, making for the creature, "is a beluae doing so far north?" She brushed back the hood of her cloak, a great cascade of curled, dark blonde hair tumbling down her back and shoulders. The skirts of her gown chattered eagerly as she circled the body of the monster, pale hazel eyes curious.

"Your guess is as good as mine."

She nodded thoughtfully. "And a kobalde, too." Not a question. "Do you care to do the honors, or shall I?"

"Be my guest," he muttered, stepping back.

A moment later, great white flames engulfed the body of the beluae, the sound of crackling flesh filling the air despite the damp.

Consigned to the flames.

It was silent as they prayed.

May the fire release your soul from the confines of your mortal body.

May the light of the gods lead you safely to the afterlife.

The first two lines of the Rite. He wouldn't offer more. What the beluae believed—if they believed anything—he did not know. Whether he ought to offer the Dradan words, said to help guide the soul to take its place as a pinprick star in the night sky—whether the beluae soul might even be inclined to take the journey—he wasn't sure.

But the first two lines were surely enough to usher the creature to whatever afterlife existed for it. If one existed at all.

"Oh, come on, Fletcher. Have a little faith."

He glanced over to his sister. "It's rude, you know, to Listen while someone's trying to pray." Trying, he mulled, being the operative word.

"You seemed a little stuck," Alva offered matter-of-factly. It was a rare gift, Listening. She remained the only child to have inherited their mother's talent for traversing the thoughts of others.

It was difficult to be truly bothered, though, that she'd once again lost her focus, had drifted beyond the borders of his mind unbidden. Such powers took time to hone, and at sixteen, she was still coming into her abilities, and somehow it was easier, that she simply knew. The night drew on, and the words were slipping through his tired hands, each one more arduous than the last.

"I confess, I was hoping Elsie would have joined us," she went on, the white flames of the burning beast reflected in her eyes.

Elsie probably would've come, if he'd told her what he was going to do.

That woman redefined strength itself.

He could still feel the graze of her soft fingers against his cheek, taste her sweet lips on his tongue. *I'll see you tomorrow*, she'd whispered, emerald eyes sparking in the firelight. Like it'd been nothing. Like today had just been another day.

Explanations had drifted into silence, and she'd been nestled in beside him, her head on his chest, nothing but *da-dum, da-dum, da-dum* filling the room, her breathing slowing with each passing moment, her fingers relaxing from where they'd been tightly curled around his own, and he had prayed she had drifted off.

But there'd be other nights. Other fires to savor, other storms to weather.

And he had his duties to attend to.

Even if his rank as Commander was nothing more than a technicality, after the censure he'd received.

The white flames hissed as they devoured the creature, venomous plumes of steam and smoke rising in the dark.

He hadn't meant for the beluae to die.

But it'd seized on his momentary distraction when Elsie ran, had sent a painful blow into his ribs, knocking the wind from his lungs. It'd gained the upper-hand, had been drawing up another wave of power, the concussive force palpable even before it'd been released. Throwing a shield up, its attack had rebounded at precisely the right angle, leaving the beluae on the forest floor, body convulsing sickeningly. A freak accident.

It hadn't been fair. That blow might've knocked Fletcher over, cracked a few ribs at worst, but the beluae were vulnerable creatures. Its soft skull had caved at the pressure.

He'd taken lives of demons before. He told himself it was never wanton. That, when he did it, it was because he'd had no other choice.

That truth was irrelevant on the demon's trail.

70

It was all bullshit.

Fletcher dropped quietly to his knees, icy mud soaking through. He hadn't said the Enumeration in years. Wasn't sure if the gods could hear him now, or if they did, whether they'd even care.

Still, he didn't know what else to do.

I have transgressed.

Straying from the guiding path, I have wallowed in the mire.

Let my misdeeds be judged by the gods above and below, let my faults be swept into the beyond so that my path may be renewed.

I have transgressed.

ELSIE

*"What the hopeless might dare to do was so terrifying,
the gods themselves trembled with fear."*

~from 'The Advice of The Long-Dead' and Other Essays

Collapsed into the carved wooden chair in Sam's dining room, Elsie cradled the warm cup of tea in her hands, idly tracing the etched design around the rim with her fingers, the occasional drop of tea catching beneath, dragging pleasantly between skin and porcelain. The too-short sleeves of Fletcher's borrowed tunic had been pushed up to her elbows, the cotton holding tight to her arms.

"I don't understand," Teddy said softly. His brilliant blue eyes were incredulous beneath his crinkled brow, chestnut hair more ruffled than usual. "Magic?"

She blew out a breath. That was the word they never said. The thing they pretended wasn't real, and it was bullshit that Teddy, of all people, said he didn't understand.

"Magic. Drada..." Elsie's words were a whisper.

Teddy was leaning forward on the table, waiting.

She had arrived on their doorstep at two in the morning, muttering about gods-damned elves and fucking kobalde, and she wasn't like to get away with such a vague explanation.

"Er, Drada...Fletcher isn't human," Elsie hedged, wincing. Even with his blessing, it felt weird, relaying this without him here. "Drada means...it means *ally*. There's an alliance—not with us. Obviously. With the other...elves, there's three realms..."

Sam lingered at the threshold of the dining room, arms full of linens. He'd invariably make up the sofa for El when there was a lull, but for now, his expression was rapt with attention. "The *other* elves," he said quietly, eyes alight, a smile at the corners of his mouth.

Elsie nodded.

"And why is he here," Teddy asked, quietly cautious. Leave it to her brother to find the problem in everything.

"It's like he said," Elsie put forth, a bit defensive. "The pastries are dying." Fletcher hadn't been lying, technically. *Right?*

Sam looked quizzical. "Why does a fantastical man such as himself care if the pastries are dying? Not that he wouldn't otherwise, but...well. He's here, that's substantial, on account of our alleged naivete of magic." His cinnamon eyes flicked to Teddy.

"It's not just that they're dying." Elsie looked down into her teacup, watching the sediment twirl around the bottom as she fidgeted. "It's *how* they're dying. And why."

Silence fell over the dining room, the boys watching her with matching looks of apprehension.

"There was a war," Elsie breathed. "A long time ago. And everyone agreed that they should go their separate ways, and Aerdela..." She made a sad sound of disdain. "Aerdela just got left in the dust." And she began to relay what Fletcher had explained.

With exacting detail, he'd told her the practice had started with magical beings as old as time and their foul pets, the barghests.

The reputation of these Insidiae for bending the natural magics

73

reached back to the beginning of time itself, and the barghests were no exception. Mortals tormented until they assumed a beastly form, the barghests in turn became harbingers of fear, feeding not on flesh but on the terror of its victims. Give them a dose of dhacrym, the draught of fear, and it was the perfect storm. Doubly afraid and given to the barghests, they would bleed away their magic, a puppet string of tenancy was waiting for the deft fingers of the Insidiae.

The Insidiae used this tenancy as a check against renegade politicians and power-hungry dictators. One tied by bloodlines to a leader would be designated as the balance, a kinsman who would give their blood so that the Insidiae could rein in the relative who reneged on promises. It was a reminder of the responsibility of leaders, and a promise that their family—with the help of Insidiae—would hold them accountable.

Family.

At least Elsie had not been cursed with ties of blood to those she called family. That was a bittersweet truth, though, and she knew it.

Sam must've seen the look on her face, now, because he sighed heavily, and shifting the bundle of linens to one arm, padded over to give her a half-hug with his free arm. The soft satin of his dressing robe was cool against her hand, catching as she wrapped an arm around him to hug him back.

"They're playing gods," she breathed, pulling away. "That's what they're doing. It's magic meant to check renegades, and now…" The dregs of her tea were bitter against the back of her tongue, a grainy wash of debris making her throat itch.

"I still think that's the least surprising part of it all," Sam muttered darkly, making for the living room, snapping out a sheet before letting it drift lazily over the sofa cushions.

Teddy frowned. "How's that?"

"Don't get me wrong. It's sick. Absolutely sick. You're telling me, though, that some arrogant sonofabitch got greedy and took something they'd no right to in the first place, all for the sake of gaining control over someone else—I'm relatively sure that's the unofficial motto of the Merchant's Guild. It's how Aerdela was built."

"Well, you're not wrong," Teddy mumbled.

Sam's brow was furrowed in thought as he tucked the sheet into the sofa cushions. "Someone is doing this blood magic business with the pastries...someone's trying to infiltrate the Guild, is that what the concern is? It sounds as though no one has to die—it's fallen into the wrong hands, someone who doesn't understand...and to send an—an emissary—"

"A prince," Elsie breathed. That part had been true, too.

"Ah." Sam paused. "That...isn't better, El. That doesn't bode well..." He trailed off, turning back to the couch, lost in thought.

Teddy's eyes flicked to Elsie. His gaze lingered on her cheek as he rose, chair squealing with resistance against the polished wood floor. Two steps, and he was in the kitchen, pulling a soft cloth from a drawer, dousing it in a stream of still-steaming water from the kettle.

"Teddy, I told you, I'm fine—"

"I know."

His fingers were still damp as he gently tilted her head back, dabbing the warm cloth against her cheek, and she closed her eyes, letting him work. She'd made a hasty mess of cleaning it up.

A chilled draft swarmed over her skin as he pulled the cloth away. He was warm, though, his hand returning to linger, cupping her cheek with the lightest touch.

It was such a curious sensation.

Hot prickling tickled pleasantly beneath her skin, a faintly sterile tang in the air washing her back to the skinned knees and scraped palms of her childhood.

"You should tell Fletcher," she said quietly, opening her eyes. She found his gaze, and his eyes were a deeper blue than they had any right to be as he pulled his hand away.

He sighed, scooping up the cloth from the table. "There's nothing to tell."

Her cheek was soft and smooth, no trace of the rough scabbed slice remaining against the warm skin.

Nothing, indeed.

THE BEAST

"Incompetence is an unforgivable sin."

~Anscip Xavishia, Insidiae in the Coalition

"You mean to tell me," the Master growled, slamming his fist down, "that after endless searching, after running through lists of babes and bastards and all assortments of discarded children, after we at last found the one, she got away?"

The Beast could taste the fear in the air—sweet, delicious fear, curling from the creatures before the Master. It was juicy and fresh, the kind borne of true foreboding.

"I gave you strict instructions—bring the girl to me," the Master hissed. "Bring her alive, and unscathed, and yet, here you stand, empty-handed."

"That was not part of the game," the Little Girl snapped, eyes venomous. The Beast didn't like the Little Girl. Her fear was putrid and stale. Not at all like a little girl's fear should be, raw and ripe for the picking.

With a wave of her hand, she conjured a cloud of smoke, and a mirror of the Master and the Little Girl and the Beast appeared in miniature before them.

"You are the key, my dear," the Master crooned. "You will bring erudition."

"Such is the game," the Little Girl conceded with a bow.

"I need her, you understand? Alive," the Master purred.

The Little Girl nodded. "I understand."

"See?" the Master growled.

The Little Girl's eyes grew black, the depths darker than sin. "All I saw," she condescended, "was a promise for information. And that is what I have delivered."

"You said my meaning was understood."

She cocked her head to the side. "It was. That is not the game, though. Understanding and agreement are not one in the same." Such was the Deceiver.

Working the loopholes insidiously.

Reveling, in Chaos.

AUGUSTUS

"We cling to what we can. Sorrow, resentment, hatred—
sometimes that's all we have."

~Alva Praequintelya

The sound of death filled the mountain city.

Bodies had been lined up, row after row of silvery mounds decorating the compound borders, Dradan outlines prone on the earth and draped in shrouds, awaiting the pyres. Augustus watched with unseeing eyes as the medics led civilians through the maze of corpses. But the sound of tears was inescapable.

Some of them were quiet. Saltwater rolling down cheeks flushed with grief, clinging to the divots and the curves of a face very much alive, until they gave way to sleeves or fingertips or kisses of loved ones they'd never feel again.

But most of them were raging rivers, screaming in grief.

This was not their time to go.

Already, bonfires lit up the fading sky as the souls of the dead were released through the flame.

Fifty had left Caelaymnis that morning.

Seventeen had returned.

He'd anticipated casualties, to be sure. A good commanding officer didn't lose themselves in false hope. But this...

This, he would not forget.

This, he would relive, until he could live no more.

The guttural battle cry of the addled settlers still seemed to carry on the night wind, howling and screeching through the streets, and he could see them still, their engorged pupils bloated with magic that did not belong to them as they tore through the ramparts. He'd felt their fingers, clawing at the unseen shield conjured from sparking palms, clawing through the very blood in his veins, and one...one of them almost crawling inside, deep in the recesses of his mind.

Iron pierced flesh, and the singed stink of burning bone and blood had curled from the field of carnage, the screams of the hurt and dying curdling the sky.

And he had led them onto a field of battle where a man in rags had lifted his hands to the heavens and become lightning in the flesh, the earth crackling as he had sent entrails flying before he himself had erupted, eyes bursting, skin crackling, the very sinews of his being hissing and steaming—

Augustus ground his teeth, forcing his eyes on the temporary morgue from his perch inside the medic's tent. The sound of whispers from beyond the canvas partitions followed by the sound of blood hitting stone and boots running for bandages made his skin crawl.

Seventeen.

No more.

No less.

"Captain Mirestva, report," he growled, watching the medic brush past the canvas.

The captain raised an eyebrow, pausing to unroll the end of a linen spool. "They'll be fine, nothing the senior medic, some cotton pads, and a little time can't mend." The smears of blood on the sleeves of the gray jacket and the suspiciously empty black triage vest boasted otherwise, though.

"Tend to the rest—"

The captain's gentle fingers pushed up the left sleeve of Augustus's coat. "They're alright."

"That's an order—"

"You," the captain said slowly, as if explaining something to a very small child, "General, are not my commanding officer. When I am a soldier, I report to Commander Kastarae, who reports to General Adritas. When I am called into active duty as a medic, I report to the Chief." A pair of black eyes drifted down to the arm now cradled carefully in Mirestva's hands. "And refusing treatment would be...ill advised."

Great fracturing lines of deep purple splintered in jagged bolts across the paled flesh of his arm, radiating from his now-bluish fingertips. A hastily thrown up shield—one that should've stopped the onslaught, though, nevertheless. But she'd had a fevered look in her eyes, the woman who'd thrown her body into the shimmering wall. The aftershock had sent his bones stinging as he'd dropped to the ground, that wretchedly familiar fire licking his veins, and in a clash of sparks and magic, he had been branded.

Stained, with a sin that didn't belong to him.

His hand was throbbing with the sharpest pins and needles as the captain extracted a tin from a deep vest pocket and set to work, massaging a putrid purple cream into the strikes with hands he knew had to be warm, fingers he knew had to be gentle, because he'd felt them a thousand times before, running along his cheek, his chest, but there was nothing, nothing but cold, jabbing skewers.

"Prognosis, Medic," Augustus growled, more as ritual than anything

81

else, a reminder that here, they were general and captain, two loyal servants of His Royal Highness King Bowyer Praequintelya, Guardian of the City of Lights. Nothing more. Nothing less.

The captain was nodding, now, reaching for the linen. "Good. Ointment, three times a day, and I'm bandaging it for the sprain, but the shocks should mostly subside in the next forty-eight hours, and you should regain feeling completely within the next two weeks."

"And the—"

"The bruising will fade along with everything else—though the pattern is undoubtedly one for the record books." Deft fingers pulled the linen in even loops around the swollen purple flesh, and silence overtook the tent.

The sieges were growing more violent, the losses more catastrophic. Raids had turned up desperately little, beyond the corpses of the Drada, drained for the magic in their veins. And no longer were they simply those who'd strayed beyond the wards.

Caelaymnis was no longer the sanctuary it promised to be.

How the humans acquired such a potent supply of blood magic, he wished he did not know. Or where they'd gotten so much—

"General." Epherias was standing at attention, having mustered what Augustus presumed was supposed to be an air of stoicism.

Mostly, he just looked afraid.

Mostly, he just looked dead.

Because it wasn't Epherias.

Because Epherias was burning on a pyre at the edge of the city as his mother wailed and his father cursed the gods.

Because he'd taken that fatal blow that ripped through his chest, some hellish monstrosity of a lucent hurled with such frenzy that bone and flesh and sinew and blood had been spilled across the grass, mangled before the eyes of all.

"Report," Augustus prompted darkly. "Cadet..."

"Volentia. Sir, they've taken the captive to your sister's for an...an interrogation."

~ • ~

Augustus flexed his bandaged wrist, a spray of numbness and the prickling of nerves awakening shooting up his arm.

The cell was dark. But Dradan eyes, those ancestral flashing eyes...they pierced the dark with ease.

He paced lazy circles around the man lashed to the rickety chair, taking care to drag his boots deliciously across the damp stone floor, to inhale with salacious predation. A wolf, circling his prey.

The humans wished to spin their stories? Fine.

Fear was a powerful drug, and the imagination, a thirsty addict.

ta-dat ta-dat ta-dat ta-dat ta-dat

The man's heart was racing, the sweat of withdrawal clinging to his brow, sick dribbled down his blood-stained tunic.

"You have committed a fatal mistake," Augustus mused, stopping before the man. The Vernacular words were heavy, bulky on his tongue, and he could hear the lilt of a Caelaymnic accent as his lips formed the cacophonic sounds. "Most that we take think they ought to have evaded capture, that this was their error." Then, lacing his hands behind his back, he resumed his pacing. "It is not. You see, you have taken something. Something that does not belong to you. You have taken the blood of my people."

"It is ours by *rite*—"

"It is not. And for the sweet taste, you are paying the price. You were greedy. You took, and took, and took, and now your own flesh has begun to turn against you. You drank from the tainted well far too deeply, and now, you will die. Not by my hand—though, I promise, you will beg for my blade before the end. They all do. And you will, too, unless you tell me what I need to know."

Cold silence filled the cell.

"So that is it, then. My death is sealed. Gods-damned *vora*—"

The crack of skin-on-skin and the clattering of the chair filled the cell, the back of Augustus's hand stinging with the impact as the man lay, half-coughing, the tang of blood lacing the air as he spat out a tooth onto the stone floor. "You dare to hurl such vile words," Augustus growled, giving the chair a resounding kick for good measure, "when I might offer you reprieve?"

The breathless half-words choked in a blood-filled mouth were the only answer.

Scoffing, Augustus turned, folding his arms across his chest. *Vora*.

An old curse, from days long gone. From a time when the Drada had been hunted like beasts and slaughtered for magic they couldn't control.

The word was ancient and so pathetically human. It'd faded, elsewhere, drifted away out of memory everywhere save the Woodshade settlements.

And it brought everything back.

The crisped pine bark grinding into his bare back as they'd bound him to the tree, his shoulders aching, his skin prickled with goosebumps as big, fat spring-snow flakes came tumbling down from the midnight sky. *Vora*, they'd hissed, dipping the iced iron deep into his flesh. *Vora. VORA*.

"R-reprieve," the man panted, his voice betraying his pain.

Already, it was beginning. The unraveling.

"Our medics cannot help you." He didn't bother to keep the vindictive satisfaction from his voice. "But if you talk, we will keep you in good supply until the end."

The man craned his head from the stone floor, desperation in his eyes, searching the darkness. "Good supply?"

Augustus crouched down beside the man, so close even those damnable human eyes had to see something. "I will *personally* see to it that you are given a generous helping of that swill you covet until you meet the gods. Do I make myself apparent?"

He was nodding, now, viciously, violently, already his thirst overwhelming reason.

His words spilled freely to the dark, too, his tongue a slave to his appetite.

And when he had given everything, when he had betrayed the people he professed to love, when he had signed the death warrants of his fellows-in-arms, when he had relinquished what he'd claimed to hold sacred, Augustus rose, calling for the guard.

A slender vial as black as the night and filled with a draught of fear was tipped into the man's mouth. This was no crude attempted theft. This was ancient and noble magic.

Augustus turned for the cell door. Already, the growling of the beast could be heard, claws screeching against metal, chains clattering against stone down the corridor, and he didn't look back as his command echoed through the terrorized shrieks and feral barks. "Commander," he snapped, and he could feel a guard springing to attention. "Bring in the barghest."

THE LIARS

We deceive, all of us.

Ourselves, others, the gods...it makes no difference.

~SAM ALDERTON,

EXCERPT FROM A LETTER DATED OCTOBER 23RD

THE BEAST

"And the gods played their games, convinced the mortals
would not win."

-from 'The Advice of The Long-Dead' and Other Essays,
'Songs of the Underworld'

"Beautiful," the Master whispered, running a finger along the mirrored ledge.

Upon it, three vials.

Each, the darkest red, and each, dripping with fear.

Ruby Tears.

The sweetest of all such blood magics. Pure. Scintillating.

And powerful. So powerful, even the Beast could feel it, arching its back across the hearth rug. A faint shimmering, sending the earth trembling beneath its massive paws.

Such chaos. Such order.

Such *fire.*

The glass cabinet clicked shut, and the Master turned, snapping at the servant. "Send him in."

The Warrior smelled of magic, stolen twice over.

"I believe," the Master crooned, sinking into the armchair behind the desk, "I have found the answer to your problems."

The Warrior was stone-faced before him.

Arrogant.

But that's what the Master wanted. He needed the alliance with Caelaymnis. He needed this conflict.

"An answer," the Warrior remarked gruffly. No respect, no reverence, no *fear*—

"Do you not still struggle to push back the Woodshade effort?"

The Beast barked, and it would've been a laugh, for the Master knew well that the Warrior faced a difficult battle. The Master himself had orchestrated such things, for he worked the will of the gods with deft and dastardly plans.

"We...fight."

"How many died today, General?"

"Too many."

"There is a girl," the Master went on softly, steepling his fingers, "a girl that could remedy both your problem and mine. There is life, in the blood—this is our tenant. In some, there is more. But importantly, in some...there is less."

He spun the Warrior such a beautiful story.

Once upon a time, the story went, there was a girl.

And she was Death.

Where she trod, Life did not, and so it was.

But she was dangerous. Life was so fleeting and Death, so permanent, and so, they hid her away. Tucked her into the reaches of the unknown, buried her beneath the rags, and prayed that she would forget herself, in the end.

Forget herself, she did.

But when she came of age, she began to remember.

The Beast had wondered how she remembered, but the Master did not say.

She was Death. This was all they needed to know.

And only a Warrior who knew death so well could recruit her to the side of justice.

The tears of the others were but raindrops on the path, the Master said. Good for nothing but muddy ground. This girl, though...

She was a deluge.

RISA

"There's never a good time. Merely the time that we're given."

~*Risa Barrett*

An alarm clock clattered across the nightstand, jangling with giddy anticipation straight off the edge, landing with a gleeful crash on the bedroom floor. Swearing under her breath, Risa rolled over, dangling her arm over the bed as she searched for the run-away, fingers finally meeting the lever with a satisfying *clunk*.

Another fucking glorious day.

Four years, and she'd nailed the routine. From laying in bed to out the door in fifteen minutes—ten, if she skipped coffee and breakfast.

Today, she did it in eight.

Eight minutes, and she'd tossed her chestnut hair into a bun, running a hot washcloth across her face. Eight minutes, and she'd pulled on the pressed gray trousers, the silken navy blouse, and a pair of slick black heels that clicked marvelously across the marble foyer of the Chancery. Eight minutes, and she'd stuffed her notes back into the leather satchel, pulled her coat on.

It would've been seven, of course, but she lingered in the doorway of her tiny bedroom.

Risa had left Lea in bed, wrapped in the pale pink quilt Nerene had bought.

She was so gods-damned beautiful, sitting there in the morning light.

And she didn't belong here.

Not in this closet of a bedroom, stuffed into a shoe-box apartment overlooking 47th Street. Not on this block of the City, running on coffee and patent-leather briefcases and tomorrow's stolen time.

She should've been on the beach.

Not the rocky strips of sand that lined the eastern borders of the City, either, beaten by the angry sea of a Northeastern winter.

Lea should've been lain bare against the hot sand of Thallassas with nothing but a turquoise sea, a cold carafe of wine, and a platter of sticky figs, sweet and chewy. It was a fucking shame, too, because that woman—she was summer. Unadulterated, undiluted, unrepentant summer.

"You're really sure, then." Doe-eyed and regretful, Lea pulled the quilt closer, her lips already starting to pout.

"I am," Risa said softly.

Lea nodded, swallowing. "Yeah. Okay, then. I, um…good luck, I guess?"

"You too."

Risa turned, eyes locking on the front door.

And when you've closed a case, she could hear Adrian saying, *you don't look back. You don't apologize for the verdict bought with your blood, sweat, and tears.*

No apologies. No prisoners.

She was Theresa Barrett.

She was a gods-damned Advocate.

And she owned today.

95

RISA

*"Absolution isn't real. Justice is subjective. Your job,
though, is to act as though forgiveness and truth are
indisputable facts without believing the lie you're
actually telling. If you can't do that—if you're not
prepared to live the dichotomy—you know where the
door is."*

~Adrian Lynch

Risa found the City shrouded in white as she pushed out of the stairwell into the street below.

She'd heard Lea's crying in the hallway—not that those cardboard walls would've stopped it, mind.

It should've been a clean break.

It remained, though, shoddy work, fracturing the two of them the way she had, with wine and regret.

Bicycle bells clanged up and down the already-clear sidewalks, bicyclists appearing moments later from great clouds of steam billowing from the street grating, swerving in-between passersby at break-neck speeds, eliciting screams of indignation from pedestrians and streetcarts alike, and the City was alive. She paused, a reluctant smile on her lips.

This place was in her blood.

She dared a glance up, tracing the buildings that held up the glacial sky domed above, lofty high-rises forced up from within the walled perimeter. Even by City standards, they were impressive feats. As a child, she'd been afraid of them—they might topple in the wind, she'd anxiously whispered to Nerene, gaping at the skyline.

But there was a rush, looking out those windows and knowing deep in her gut she would not fall, a rush Risa had never quite been able to find again.

Ice remnants crunched under foot, the smell of yeast and coffee beans drawing her to the stand on the corner of her block, one of many that littered the smooth-paved streets, an obnoxiously bright yellow-and-green home-away-from-home.

"Sonofa—I know your mother, you little—"

"Morning to you, too, Sal," Risa snickered, watching a knit-capped boy shooting off down the street, waving a bagel victoriously in the air, the veritable flag of success.

"Third time this week, Barrett. *Third time.* Kid's out of control," the man behind the cart grimaced. "I swear, it makes me want to just—" The blue flames licking the aged vat of coffee began to climb viciously up the side, the lid beginning to dance ominously as rolls of acrid brown coffee rolled down the sides.

Risa tossed a fiver on the counter. "He's just trying to get a rise out of you. And if it's not too much trouble, Sal, try not to burn the coffee? Assuming there's any left—"

"He's a thief! You're an advocate. Arrest him!"

"Not 'til I've had breakfast," she retorted, tapping the note. "Muffin and coffee, double sweet."

Sal glowered, turning. "Told me that last time, you did..."

Snickering, Risa stuffed her hands beneath her arms, watching as a gurgle of suspiciously sluggish coffee steamed into the paper cup. "Asking a Treatist to bust your own kid, Sal. That's desperate, even for you." Her eyes flicked down the street, the boy's chaos long-since swallowed up by the burgeoning crowd taking to the City in the morning light.

"Sal, make that two of whatever she's having," a cool voice cut in behind her, and Risa turned, raising an eyebrow. "And thank your lucky stars she's not charging you out the nose. An up-and-coming authority on our beloved Treaty, she's liable to take your first-born...though I suppose that would suit you just fine."

There was pride in Adrian's voice, bragging about his protégé to the man in the coffee stand.

Then again, the Treaty was the pride and joy of the Hidden City.

In the wake of a vicious war, at which the possession of magic had been central, the Treaty had been crafted to protect the humans—especially the ones with magic of their own.

As with so many things, it'd been the path of least loss, and to call it a victory felt wrong.

The City might remain protected, hidden in the bay and brimming with magic.

The same could not be said for Aerdela.

Aerdela, which was alone. Isolated. Aerdela, where magic was forgotten not by ignorance but by mandate and mutual agreement.

But it was easier, on mornings like this, not to think about the people left behind.

Risa rolled her eyes at Adrian. "Since when do you take your coffee double-sweet?"

"First lesson, Risa," Adrian sighed, hands stuffed in the pockets of his dark woolen coat. His piercing eyes found hers, reveling in the morning chill. "Don't ask questions you don't want the answer to." The snow-coated City seemed to set his rich, tawny skin into relief, and even at the coffee cart, he felt larger than life.

Advocate Adrian Lynch.

Three words guaranteed to get shit done.

The coffee was scalding against the walls of the thin paper cup—and her tongue, Risa thought resentfully, courtesy of Sal's flaring temper. That, right there, that was how Elementals got a bad rap. No training and no restraint, and they'd raze a city to the ground.

"So, how'd Lea take it?"

Risa let the question settle, her heels scuffing against the sidewalk. "It could've been worse."

"And you?"

"Hurts like a sonofabitch. I liked her, Adrian," she sighed. "She was a sweet girl. But she didn't like the long hours." Or the late nights in the library. Or the traveling. Or any gods-damned moment when Risa's attention might've been on anything else. "We tried. It was an unmitigated disaster."

He took a sip of steaming coffee, grimacing. "On the note of unmitigated disasters, Regent Chancellor Vaupellum is reviewing trading charters with the Senior Advocates and the Advisory Council until noon, and I don't need to express to you the urgency in the referendum drafts. I need them on my desk by eight tonight—which reminds me," he added, giving her a side-long glance, "clear your plans, because *our friend* has filed a formal petition with the City that needs swept under the rug."

Swearing under her breath, Risa crammed a worn oneie into a paperboy's hand, unfurling the roll he'd stuffed into hers.

'Stricter Protocols' After Breach, Demands Vaupellum.

"Don't know what he expects, petitioning the Chancery," Risa muttered, eyes skirting the headlines. *Blizzard Buries City*—like that was news to anyone not living knee-deep in their navel. *Caelaymnic Council to Petition for Modified* blah blah blah, it had to be the altitude, because the mountain Drada were always begging for something else from the City. *Six Dead in Tunnel Raid—*

She was a mask of ice, eyes flying across the page.

In a late-night raid near a sewer grate in the south-west end, authorities moved to seize a band attempting to gain access to the City. Aided by the so-called Rescindants, a terrorist organization responsible for the lethal Cornerstone Protests, five individuals were smuggled beneath the City's wards before authorities attempted apprehension. After utilizing what was thought to be a classified concussive device to evade capture, the Rescindants collapsed a portion of the main sewer, killing all five illicits and one member of the City Guard—

She looked at Adrian askance. "You saw this?" It was infuriating.

"Asher stopped by early with the news," he muttered.

Risa stuffed the paper under her arm, fuming as she cradled the hot coffee with both freezing hands. "Our *friend's* petition. And it's too much to hope it came with a unanimous vote from the Guild?"

They'd been seeking the vote for years. All nine commissioners, in agreement on one matter, and one matter alone.

To join the City.

To seek protection, unlimited trade, and above all else, magic, the likes of which they couldn't even begin to imagine.

Perhaps Aerdela was inclined to forget. But it was impractical for its leaders to wholly dismiss the notion of an enclave of their brethren living in the City, not when Aerdela nursed a long and quiet history of dependence on the City.

Words like *hidden* and *forgotten* and *forbidden*...they were relative, truth be told.

To grant this—to dissolve the Treaty that had kept them sequestered in the wake of the Clash—well, Risa had made a career out of breaking down walls, and she saw no reason this would be any different. Beyond the back-door deals with commissioners that the Chancery was happy to overlook, this would mean letting magic flood fully amongst the districts. No more vaguely illicit hand-shake agreements delivering ointments and tonics onto the medicine shelves of merchants.

Magic would flow free again.

"If he had the unanimous vote, he wouldn't be flooding my desk with this bullshit," Adrian snipped.

She blew out a steaming breath, headache already throbbing behind her temples.

Fucking Factionist bastards, killing good, innocent people.

Fucking Guild, fucking merchants, fucking Lea—

"I have a query for you, Ms. Barrett," Adrian mused, his voice lethal as they paused before the steps.

The Chancery stood tall, a granite monstrosity beyond the hewn steps, its great squared pillars shining polished in the morning sun, the whole building was a mass of perfect corners, like justice could be shoved in a neat little box and delivered, a parcel to be purchased.

"What do we do, when they tell us there's no hope?"

"We prove them wrong," she said through gritted teeth, a familiar refrain pounded into their heads from their first step through the Chancery doors.

"And what do we do, when they tell you there's no point to this endless fight?"

The sun was cresting over the skyline, now, great shafts of sunlight hitting the frozen pavement beneath their feet.

"We prove them wrong."

"And what do we do, when they tell you you're on the losing side?"

She met his gaze with ice-shard eyes. "We prove them wrong."

SAM

*"A picture says a thousand words? Then I can't imagine
the story one might stuff into an entire ball gown."*

~Sam Alderton

"It just doesn't pop." Frowning atop the stool, the woman was swaying
back and forth, watching the skirt dance in the tri-fold mirror at the
center of Mulligan's.

Sam let himself fall back onto his heels from where he'd been trying
to pin the pink satin hem amid her fussed and frequent movements, and
glancing up, he gave a small sigh. "Des, hon, if it pops anymore, you're
liable to hurt someone."

"There's a month," she murmured, smoothing the skirts, preening.
"You've got time."

"No, *you've* got time. I'm booked from now until February, love."

"Just...hmph. A bit of lace, maybe? At the hem?"

"Desi..."

"Please, Sam? You're only introduced once, and everyone talked
about *your* introduction for *years*," she pouted, not taking her eyes off
the mirror.

Lips pursed, he pushed himself up, giving her a once over.

He hadn't been joking about the pop. He'd emblazoned the bodice himself, a brilliantly deep champagne diamond set right at the apex of the sweetheart neck, the rest cascading down to catch in the folds of her skirt. It'd been so heavy, the dress form had nearly toppled over—and he'd had to cinch it to poor Desi, which she'd taken in good spirits. Of course, she'd be dead on her feet by the end of the ball, touring the floor in that damnable thing. And now, the lace...

Everyone talked about your introduction for years.

She wasn't wrong.

But they hadn't been talking about what he'd been wearing, that was for damn sure.

When he'd stepped down that grand staircase at seventeen, he'd become the single most desirable bachelor across all nine districts, and next to Cele Carson's introduction the next year, it had remained one of the most highly anticipated events of the decade.

Clark Carson's ward was available and looking.

Sam had taken the first dance with Cele—a power play, the whispers said, to throw speculation about the favored suitors.

The whispers weren't wrong.

The problem was, though, the more that he thought about it, it seemed like his favored suitor might be sitting miles away, curled up in a worn armchair, reading with his little sister.

This had been after his first kiss, the one with the wrong boy that was actually the right boy.

All the same, Sam danced with Edmund, the strapping young son of a Buyer's Bay merchant and heir to a shipping empire that reached up and down the eastern coast. He danced with Vivien, the sweet daughter of the Commissioner from the Coastal Reach—not really his type, but Edmund, it turned out, wasn't terribly light on his feet, and Sam really did love to dance, and Vivien was a goddess on the dance floor. He'd

103

danced with countless others, too, all their faces and names blurring into one nondescript suitor with their arms around his waist.

But it'd been Mattie that Sam had been eying.

Matthew Fieldson would've been a good match, arguably the best match, and Sam's turn about the floor with his sister hadn't swayed the whispers from saying as much. A son of the Capital—and more than that, the son of the Capital's commissioner himself—Matt was more than the bastard of a prostitute could've hoped. And they got on well, too, Mattie and Sam.

He remembered thinking that maybe they could be happy together.

It was Mattie's fault, that Sam kissed the wrong boy. Mattie, and his gods-damned eyes, so dark and wide, his little *oh* of a mouth when he was trying not to act surprised, and Cele, she'd been after Mattie, too, but she still had a year, which meant everything was riding on Sam's introduction.

Mattie had walked up to him, as the evening had started to wane. Had asked for a turn around the floor, had held Sam close, his breath on Sam's cheek as they whispered about the whisperers, and still, it'd been the echo of Teddy's lips against his own that had consumed his thoughts.

Teddy, the wrong boy who'd been the right one in the end.

Mattie had led him to the garden, where the roses were just starting to bloom, and the pin-prick stars above them were glittering like candles.

This was it.

There's a lot of speculation, Mattie mused, fingers trailing against Sam's cheek in the moonlight, *about your suitors. Word is, you're not even going to leave your own introduction a bachelor.*

That depends, Sam had murmured, breathing in the bergamot of his city boy.

On what, Mattie pressed.

On you. And leaning in, he took his second kiss, from the right boy that was the wrong boy, in the end.

Mattie, as it turned out, had always been Cele's.

Clark made sure of that.

And Sam...he belonged to Clark.

They didn't remember Sam's introduction as the night Aerdela's most eligible bachelor met society.

They remembered it as the night Clark's ward left.

Desi was right, in that they did talk about it for years.

How he'd taken a small apartment off of Main, how he was working, with his hands, to actually earn a living, how he found a lover in a back-district farmhouse.

How he'd lost every single person he'd believed to be his friend.

Every person, that was, except two.

Except Elsie and Teddy.

Desi's would be a different fate, though. She was sweet and bubbly and, gods, so smart—she'd find someone.

And he'd be damned if he stood in the way of giving her the night she was dreaming of.

"Fine," he relented, a reluctant smile on his lips, dusting off his hands. "But this is the last thing, Des, I can't fit in anymore, I'm already overbooked as it is. I can have it for you Tuesday—"

"Actually, my dear, I'm afraid Tuesday's a bit soon." Mrs. Mulligan was sweeping across the show room floor, her crushed velvet wrap half-trailing absentmindedly behind her as she hustled towards the pair, looking rather grim.

Oh, gods, she's taken another commission—

"Desdimona, sweet, be a good girl, and go get changed," Mrs. Mulligan was fussing, helping her off the stool and shooing her towards the back hall. "Edith's back there, she'll help you out, there's a pretty dove. Now off with you—you'll get your lace, you never mind that," she added, shaking her head. Then, heaving a sigh, she glanced back to Sam, voice soft. "It is a lovely gown, Mr. Alderton. You've...well, you've come a long way since you were stitching muslins in the back room, I'll dare say."

"But," he pushed warily.

"But I've had a visit from your father." Sucking her teeth, she drew her wrap back 'round her shoulders, eyes darting about the room. "I think, sweet, we both knew it was a risk, bringing you on. And I didn't mind, not with...well, not with gowns like that piling up," she nodded, gesturing to the hall down which Desi had disappeared. "He's fining me dry, though, Sam, and he's even threatened to pull my license and lease if—if I don't let you go."

His fingers found the cloth measuring tape hanging about his neck, fiddling with the ends, eyes skirting the shop.

Let go.

Words failed him.

Let go.

A nightmare.

Panic was setting into his chest, deep, unmovable. This wasn't happening, it wasn't real—

Let go.

This was the price he paid, for her.

For the letters, still tucked in the breast pocket of his brown suit, hanging neatly four blocks down in the cedar wardrobe.

Let go.

ELSIE

"We dream of normalcy, but it isn't real. We all simply
do the best we can with what we're given."

~Sam Alderton

Lingering in the back of the drafty inkshop, Elsie's eyes wandered to the shelves—and to Fletcher, intently focused on the contents therein, weighing pens in hand with chilling determination.

Nearly a week, and she had come to dislike the facade.

That was what he called it, waltzing around like some run-of-the-mill human, his round-eared lie. A *facade.*

And the more she watched him drifting between worlds, faces, lives, the more she realized: he disliked it, too.

It strained him. He adored this life, the inkshop-on-a-Tuesday sort of life, with sweetrolls and engagements and *I-broke-the-nib-to-my-favorite-pen* kind of worries. But it was taking its toll, guarding his words, his movements, the very magic that flared in his fingertips, a beating-heart reflex. And he'd been ready, she'd begun to realize, ready to endure that. A lifetime of exhaustion. Of being worn to a nub, of abandoning his people.

Love was all kinds of misguided, sometimes. And she hated herself, for thinking it was sort of sweet.

Love wasn't supposed to make people hurt.

"Any luck?" she prodded, turning over a stack of parchment in her hand. Bound in twine and butcher's paper, a single sheet had remained atop the wrappings for identification. It was thick, with deep, angry, crevasses, the kind that ripped charcoal from pencils and drank up watercolor with greedy ambition.

Fletcher's only answer was a knitted brow, lips pursed as he ran his fingers along the carved wood. Then, with an exasperated sigh, he plunked it back down in the jar, looking irritated. "Wrong."

She glanced around—the inkshop was a closet of a store, and he'd spent the better part of an hour fiddling with the rows of pens that lined the shelves in their gleaming crystalline jars. Diving into the last row, he began again, scooping up a rather simple pen, stained a deep red, a brass band around the tip. A neat *2Ss,4c* had been scrawled on a card before the cup, boasting the exorbitant asking price. "Two Stacks silver," she muttered, fingertips brushing the golden-tipped pens. "Absurd."

The remark earned her a glare from the shopkeep.

In another life, she'd have slipped one up her sleeve to spite him.

And in another life, she thought sardonically, it'd cost Sam more than a few stacks to bribe the mercenaries who'd have shaken her down, if she'd been stupid enough to get caught.

She wasn't stupid, though. Not usually.

The first time had been the failure of a novice.

It'd been a stale roll, with smoked ham and hard, yellow cheese slammed onto crusty bread. Pathetic street food, and not worth six coppers, but day in, day out, it lured her in. She'd been eleven and hungry *and before that ten and hungry and nine and hungry and eight and hungry...*

Her reflexes had been dulled by winter, and she'd overestimated her stealth on a street devoid of chaos. She'd tried to run, of course, but the

108

mercenary's vice-grip around her arm had foiled any hope of escape, and there'd been tears stinging her eyes as she'd watched him kick the roll into the street, grinding the whitebread into the cobblestones with the heel of his boot.

The debtor's prison had been filthy, crowded, reeking of sweat and soil and the brackish water of the docks.

Crammed against the bars, arms clenched about her stomach, she'd been dully imagining her fate. She'd work off the debt, no question—and with interest, no less. Maybe a few months a servant, if she was lucky.

Rats squealing, hands groping, women crying, and it was dark when she'd been yanked out of her corner by a bearded mercenary smelling of roast hazelnuts and money.

But it hadn't been a procurer waiting in the dingy office.

It'd been Sam.

She never asked how he found her there.

She'd known Sam for less than a year.

It'd been a singularly poignant sensation of relief, seeing him, and in that moment, she'd felt every bit the child she was. She forgot to be embarrassed, forgot to be quiet, forgot to hold herself with decorum, had, in truth, forgotten everything that didn't really matter in the end.

The mercenary had released her, and she'd run towards Sam. He'd caught her with a tight hug, smelling of sandalwood and cloves and the cigarettes he used to roll with idly elegant hands, had only murmured quiet comforts while she dried her silent tears on his waistcoat.

She'd been supposed to meet him at the bookstore, like she had every day this last year.

After school, she walked to the bookstore, and they would read together, until the dark finally fell, and he'd walk with her to meet Teddy at the general store.

That was how she'd met Sam.

At the bookstore.

A guard or someone had pressed a note into Sam's hands, *Receipt of Debtor*, she remembered it saying, worth *20Sg*, twenty Stacks gold.

That number had branded her for the better part of the year. Twenty Stacks, twelve coins each.

Two-hundred and forty gold pieces.

A tangible badge of her worth, one she'd worn proudly, albeit secretly.

Teddy had been beside himself, pacing up and down the general store counter, the sign boasting *Closed* but the lamps still lit all the same as he worried his cuticles to bleeding.

I'm so sorry, Sam had pressed, voice remorseful, *we stopped for a small bite, and I completely lost track of time.*

Not a lie. They *had* stopped for food. She still had half a bun from the bakery in her pocket to prove it. *Tomorrow's breakfast.*

No, no, you—you can't just lose track of time! I thought something had happened! You weren't at the bookstore, I—I trusted you with her, a-a-and you—

His tears, though, she remembered better than the blur of words. Blue eyes brimming with panic, he'd held her tight and kissed her forehead. He had, hands under her arms, boosted her up to sitting on the counter, and looking her over, tucked a strand of hair behind her ear.

He didn't speak to Sam for two weeks after that. But that had been the last time Elsie could recall being really, truly, hungry.

It was not, however, the last time she'd met his embrace in that office.

She ran her fingers up and down the slender pen, sucking her teeth.

Easy.

Two Stacks silver—tax to the Guild and Commissioner had to be, what, maybe half that? A few coppers to the poor soul who'd turned the damn thing, and the shopkeep would be sitting pretty in a rain of silvers. And what would he do, but thank the gods to be the shoe, not the bug.

The sound of beetles crunching underfoot must be rather pleasant, from so far above.

Elsie bit her lip, thinking.

Does he know that Princess Pastry has sticky fingers?

The pen clattered into the cup, her fingers moving to worry the locket instead.

Debtor's jail to gilded gifts.

It was a long way to come for a bastard.

~ • ~

They found the lodge in awkward silence, a fire dwindling in the hearth. Their half-eaten breakfast had been cleared from the coffee table, the rumpled bed freshly made, and even when the door had fallen shut behind them, Fletcher didn't shift.

He left the parcels from the inkshop on the messy writing desk in the corner, and still, he didn't shift. He tugged his coat off. Ruffled his hair, looking around. Saw a stack of letters, bound in twine, waiting on the nightstand.

And still, he remained uncomfortably human.

"You're not...are you going to stay like that?" she asked softly, hanging her coat on the hook by the door, watching him skim the letters left waiting. She'd borne witness to the courier who brought those letters, once, a few days ago, as she lay nestled into his bed, bathing in the late-morning light. It'd been just past eleven, she recalled, and a cadet, all in gray and belted with black, had appeared on the hearth rug, standing at attention as Fletcher sat up, pulling the blankets up a little closer.

111

Sorry, sir, I—I didn't—

Fletcher had given Elsie a sidelong glance, apprehensive. And she'd grinned, pulling herself up to lean against the headboard, sheets tucked tight around her. Any glimpse into his world was exhilarating, and the chance to meet another Drada...she wasn't going to pass that up.

It's fine, Fletcher had sighed, giving her a reluctant smile before gesturing the cadet forward.

Notice from the general, sir, he's still furious you haven't answered the censures—

Censures, Elsie had cut in, frowning at Fletcher, *as in, censures, plural?*

—and the situation on the western border is escalating, sir, the aide continued hesitantly, giving Elsie a scrutinizing look. *Beg your pardon, Commander, but...permission to remark?*

What, Fletcher asked, raising an eyebrow.

The cadet had paused. And then, the brightest smile Elsie had seen split across the boy's face. *It's so lovely to meet you, my lady,* he gushed. *Fletcher—well, the Commander—he speaks of you often, and—well, it's lovely, finally making your acquaintance.*

Leaving Fletcher with a stack of parchment and Elsie, flushed bright red, the cadet vanished a moment later.

That'd been a lovely morning.

Not having to pretend like things were normal.

"Fletcher," she echoed dully, and his head snapped up.

"Sorry, yes, I will, but—Siddeus," he stumbled.

"Excuse me?"

A few steps, and his arm was outstretched, passing her a letter full of scrawled script she couldn't read. "One of my captains. Mia Siddeus. She thinks she may have found a den, and it isn't far from here." He caught her gaze, a smile dancing on his lips. "El, we may have found our kobalde."

TEDDY

"Ah, reality. Our fickle and ever-shifting friend."

~Alva Praequintelya

Bell clattering angrily, Sam was glaring as he slammed open the door. "That gods-damned piece of work had me fired!"

Teddy stopped mid-way in reaching for the ledger beneath the counter, frozen in incredulity. "Wait, what?"

"They let me go! A whole thing about how Mrs. Mulligan didn't want to part with me, but she couldn't justify the fines from the Commissioner, and the law is the law and it is such a load of *bullshit!*" The word rang through the store as Sam tossed his satchel down on the counter, furious.

The air was laced with rage, a tangible tang lingering in the back of Teddy's throat as Sam paced the length of the counter, burning off the fresh fury curling in his veins.

And inside, it stirred.

The Thread.

"I earned my place there! And she turns around and acts like she did Clark a favor, letting me stay on? Like this whole thing is some big play-act?"

"They can't do that," Teddy put in darkly as he came around the counter. The countless hours Sam had poured into the needle and thread, the tears, the pin-pricked fingers, the tangled bobbins, the complete brilliance with which he'd shone, seeing that first gown on the mannequin—

"But they did! They did, and there isn't a damn thing..." Sam's voice cracked, brown eyes glistening as he slammed a hand on the counter, grimacing.

With a gentle brush of his hand against Sam's shoulder, the soft reassuring squeeze melted into a deep hug, arms tight around each other because those damn ribs had failed again, failed to guard that quivering mound of muscle so laughably called a beating heart.

"It will be alright, in the end," he whispered, and it was the meadow all over again.

Quiet peace when Sam was falling apart at the seams.

"You can do this," Teddy breathed, and Sam's hands gripped the back of his tunic, because he was, he *was* fighting, tooth and nail, to keep standing, right here, right now, and *You will fight, and you will keep fighting, because I am here with you, Sam. You will fight because you don't have to fight alone,* words conjured with a breath, words to safeguard what the ribs had betrayed.

Sam's jagged breaths were forced, hot against Teddy's neck, willing composure.

"Hey." A gruff voice shattered the meadow, and Teddy's eyes flicked threateningly to the harborman loitering with disdain, a one-man queue.

Pulling away, Sam's jaw was clenched, face red as he yanked his satchel off the counter, turning for the back room.

With a huff of derisive amusement, the man tossed a box of nails and a package of what would prove to be stale, hard cookies wrapped in butcher's paper before the till.

"Something funny to you?" Teddy asked, voice low, returning behind the counter with the taste of rust and sugar bitter on his tongue.

"Just wondering," he snickered, rustling in his pockets. "And maybe you can answer this, seeing as ya'll're so close—why is it, these tarts walk around, actin' like a bunch of fuckin' flowers—"

"That's enough." There was an edge of ice to his voice, his knuckles white against the counter.

A sneer rolled across the man's face as he flicked a worn slip of paper out.

"And no cheaters," Teddy added, eyeing the paper.

"Why the fuck not? That's good money."

"Not here, it isn't. Hard coin, or no deal."

Only a scant few shops in town would take the risk of accepting a promissory note from the Guild. And it'd never been a problem, not here, anyway. Frequenters of Williams' General Store, as a rule, mistrusted the promises of merchants, and had a taste for copper between their teeth.

And kinder words on their lips, Teddy thought angrily, not breaking the harborman's gaze.

They were shrewd people, the Valley people. Quick, too, to have survived here for so long. They could not afford to gnash their teeth at one of their own, not when a weak link in the chain could be the ruin of them all, not when solidarity was in their blood. And Sam was one of theirs, they'd decided.

Nine years loitering around the store, and they'd taken him in—bitterly, warily, resentfully, it was true. But they'd taken him in, all the same.

Swearing under his breath, the harborman slammed a fistful of coppers on the counter, snatched up his goods, and left without another word.

In his wake, a little girl.

Hidden behind his massive form, she took one silent step towards the counter. Then another.

"Rude," she remarked, matter-of-factly, standing on her toes to put an overstuffed bag of candies on the counter. She couldn't be more than five or six, with eyes as dark as coal, her blood-red hood pulled neatly back, a painfully white pinafore smock riddled in ruffles over a navy dress.

His eyes flicked around the store. Empty, or so he'd thought.

"It is 'please' and 'thank you' and be wary of strangers, and he mustn't know the rules." She paused, glancing at the door. "What an ass."

Heart still pounding, adrenaline flooding his jellied muscles, he felt an echo of a smile on his lips. "That's not a very nice thing to say," he offered, leaning on the counter. *Even if it's true.*

"He wasn't a very nice man."

There was the quiet shuffling of shoes on wood, and Teddy glanced over towards the back room. Sam was leaning on the door frame, arms crossed, lips pursed into a reluctant smile, eyes still damp.

"No," Teddy sighed, "no, he wasn't." He turned back to the little girl. "I like your hood. Red, just like from the stories."

"Yes. From the stories." A rather mischievous grin split across her face, a row of small, pearly teeth flashing.

"Just the candy?"

"Yes, sir."

"Well, it's on me today."

She beamed, taking the bag. "Thank you, sir." The girl took a moment to neatly tuck the little bag into the pocket of her smock before looking back up to him. "What's your name?"

"I'm Teddy," he offered.

"It's nice to meet you, Teddy," she smiled, "I'm Chim."

ELSIE

"Fear is the mask, and Doubt becomes her."

~Dryadic Proverb, from the Book of Adagic Texts

"Gods below," Elsie panted, wet, trembling fingers still clinging to the cavern wall. They'd been bathed in an eerie light, and even in the cold, steam was still curling off both of them in time to the pit pit pit of water droplets against stone. Slowly, she let herself sink down, her shaking legs unable to keep her upright anymore. "Gods..."

Fletcher's chest was heaving, his eyes wide and unseeing as he surveyed the tunnel. "Shit—El, I...I'm sorry—"

"It..." She shook her head, swallowing down the moist air, the smell of sulfur swimming. A smile was tugging on her lips, watching him pace.

His eyes flashed in the aquamarine light bleeding through the icy windows swirled into the stone. It'd be flooded, where she sat, come spring, the waterfall crashing down.

Laughter was pressing at her, making her ribs ache all that much more as the sheer absurdity of it all starved her lungs, and he was laughing too, pushing the soaking hair back off his forehead. One glance at her, and he sank down next to her, leaving wet footprints on the cavern floor and a great dark splotch in his wake as he slid down the wall to sitting. The stench of minerals from the hot springs below clung to them, both of them soaked from the dive into the turquoise pond.

Wordlessly, she took his hand, grinning as she tried to catch her breath.

"I, um..." Fletcher's voice was breathless, and he closed his eyes, a smile on his lips. "I can hear your—your heart. Racing."

She glanced over. "Yeah?"

He nodded. "I—I can hear it, from, like, three blocks away, too. Which is pretty good, for us. With the—the background noise, and everything." He was watching her intently, something playful sparking in his hazel eyes.

He never talked about what he could do. Not really. Not like this. It was all lucents and evanescing.

This, though...this was them. Together. Elsie and Fletcher.

"So," she snickered, brushing a kiss on his cheek before rising. "Wrong kobalde."

Laughing, he dropped his head in disdain. "Wrong kobalde."

~ • ~

The evening was crisp as the dirt beneath Elsie's feet gave way to cobblestones just inside the town limits. Their clothes had dried quickly, by the roaring fire sparked in the secluded corner of the foothills, and she'd been savoring the moments, being free. Watching him being free, too. Being free together.

The problem, though, was when he'd gone back.

When he'd shifted. When his eyes dimmed, his ears rounded, when his frame seemed unsettled and graceless, when there was a look of deep discomfort on his brow, unerasable.

Because when he went back, anything between them seemed to fizzle out. The conversation would die, the soft touches would cease, and nothing would remain but stilted words and unsure movements, neither really knowing what to do.

"So," she mused, trying to break the quiet. "What do the Drada dream of?"

"I beg your pardon?" Fletcher's brow knit as he gave her a side-long glance.

The locket was sitting, warm against her chest, and she fought the urge to reach for it. "Human children dream of magic and elves and all the things we think are impossible. But if you live the fantastical, what do you dream of, when you want to escape?"

"Depends. Cam fancied herself an explorer, I think—she used to talk about traveling the world. Augustus only ever wanted war. He was born a soldier, my father used to say. But I think Alva and I always just wanted some quiet," Fletcher shrugged, giving a stray pebble an idle kick. "Listening, I think, takes a toll on her. And my world is just...it's too loud."

Words had trickled intermittently between them as they walked, no destination set.

Fletcher—and Teddy and Sam—they didn't know about the locket. She'd meant to tell Sam, but somewhere along the way, she'd gotten drunk on this idea that maybe there was a tiny piece of her life that belonged to her, and her alone.

And it wasn't like she owed Fletcher any sort of secrets, to be sure.

"Were you ever going to tell me?" She'd toyed with the question, on and off, not really knowing if she wanted the answer, other times telling herself she knew he would've, only the timing had been wrong, and it was difficult, and she wouldn't have believed him, anyway, and—

He heaved a sigh, shoulders shifting uncomfortably as he pushed his hands deeper into his coat pockets.

He was so utterly human.

So human, it was sickening. In the blink of an eye, he'd dissolved, and it was like nothing had happened. As if he hadn't come bearing secrets that would have undone all of Aerdela. Undone their world.

"I knew, very quickly after meeting you, that you were not someone I could walk away from," he said at last, hesitant. His voice tiptoed across the thin ice, each word liable to plunge them into the freezing depths below. "And clearly, there would be...considerations, in a relationship, that would—but you and I—"

"Yes or no, Fletcher," she snapped, stopping in the road. "It's a simple question."

"I—"

"Yes or no."

"No."

The word cut her to the quick.

"No," she echoed, and it was almost funny, in a sick and twisted sort of sense, because of course, this was a secret he'd have died with. He was so damned charmed with her simple life, so, of course, he'd have been chasing his quiet dream, of course she'd be the fodder to the romantically quaint life of humans, a means to a fucking end. "So, what? You were going to spend our lives lying?"

"I never lied—"

"Bullshit!"

And she could feel it, deep in her bones.

The change. The overcoming of love with anger. A script she'd played out again and again, a part she never wanted to play, but always did, when it came down to it.

"You understand, Fletcher, I had no idea who you really were?" she snapped, and she was coming undone.

"Semantics! Aside from the fact that I doubt you've shared every detail of your personal life with me—"

Liars, both of them, liars, because she could not be different, she

120

could only be trouble, *always so much trouble—*

"My personal—this isn't about me," Elsie snarled, taking a step forward. "Don't you dare try and rationalize this, because you know if I'd been in your shoes, I'd have said something!"

"I could've easily invented some story, that's what you're not understanding—"

"Easily? *You,*" she scoffed, "you could have easily invented a story?"

"—but the pieces I did tell you, they were the truth!"

"The truth?"

"I said there were repercussions from disclosing—"

"You made me think that people would keep dying if you said something! That me knowing anything about why you were interested in this investigation would compromise your ability to stop what's happening!"

"And it would have!" His voice was loud across the howling wind as he glared at her with flashing eyes. "Elsie, you're not supposed to know about this, any of it! I violated a treaty, the laws of our realm, direct orders from my commanding officer, my father's explicit directions— you could be arrested for treason, knowing what you know! And we haven't even gotten to the actual reasons that I'm here—"

"I trusted you, Fletcher! I trusted that you would've told me, after this was over, and you were—were taking advantage of that! Of the fact I trusted you!"

Her tears were cold against her cheeks, and the ice had fractured, they'd fallen down, down, down, and she was drowning.

This was heartache. Heartbreak.

And she was Elsie Mirabeau, the scrappy girl that picked fights with anyone that pissed her off, that took no prisoners, that, with venomous vitriol, would push, and push, and push, until there was nobody left close enough to hurt her.

FLETCHER

"Together, we are stronger."

~Lucenia Maladictus, Desai of the Coalition

Storming down the snow-packed road, there was a discomposed glare etched on Fletcher's brow, because he couldn't quite recall ever hating a human settlement.

But right now, he hated that place.

The pasty, over-seasoned and yet somehow tasteless food, the mud so laughably called ale, the unfamiliar streets, gridded and numbered like it made any sort of difference in this chaotic world—he'd been a fool, thinking this was paradise incarnate.

And even still, he'd taken two steps on the icy boulevard here in Caelaymnis, had breathed in the delicately spiced meats and the sweet pies, the cider so sharp it could slice through cold butter, had been ready to walk those swirling city streets that looped in steady wheels, spiraling to the temple spires at the center of it all, and...and it was wrong.

It wasn't home, because she wasn't here.

His hands were still shaking, adrenaline overflowing as he tapped the compulsive rhythm against his leg, *pit bi-di-dit, pit bi-di-dit,* percussive like the language that flowed so easily off his tongue, that now had begun to permeate even his thoughts, his dreams, and he was himself disbelonging, the act of being a sum of parts disparate from any whole.

Snow was falling with quiet *fft, fft, ffts* on the metal barrack roof, windows glowing warmly, the sound of laughter and the smell of cinnamon liquor boasting the end of a long day.

He didn't really know why he'd come to this place.

Even when he'd been in better standing—never good standing, mind, simply better—he'd barely tolerated the cold flat, and besides, Sentinels boasting the rank of captain and above were never tied to the compound. It'd just been instinct, coming back.

Report, he could hear his brother saying.

The only person I've ever loved told me that I made her sick. She told me that I hurt her. And she screamed and cried and yelled and I am lost. I don't understand what happened. I don't understand how I fucked this up. But I did.

I did.

Some report.

Gritting his teeth, he turned on his heel, leaving the barracks to his back.

The house wasn't far. It was a quiet street, too, with a scant few shops wedged in between the domiciles. Nothing glamorous—certainly not like the monstrosity his sister had erected across the city, a miniature shrine to the palace itself. No, this was simple, a two-storied thing, unassuming with its pale yellow walls and deep brown trim and white curtains shading the inside from the street beyond.

It was as he'd left it.

Darkened and cold, he sent a couple warm lucents bobbing overhead in the entry way, illuminating the carpeted stairs that opened up from the foyer to a regretfully empty second floor, save for the bedroom at the end of the hall. To the right, a barren living room, furnished with a piano in the corner and a messy desk, heaped with reports he'd sifted through, letters he simply hadn't bothered to throw out, notes scribbled in his own illegible handwriting that only his eyes might decipher. To the left, a kitchen with nothing more than a dusty bottle of wine and a few glasses, dried little coins of red left in the bottom where they sat in the sink from when he'd last shared a drink with Rodion nearly six months ago.

And this was the place, he thought bitterly. The place she'd been dying to see.

This jumble of mismatched furniture in which he'd built a chaotic little nest.

His fingers trailed the polished banister, little bits of snow still clinging resentfully to the carpet as he summited the stairs.

The worst part was that he knew she'd have loved it. That she'd have grinned, stepping through the door, just happy to be here.

He sank down on the edge of the bed, running his hands with a whispered *shhhhh* across the comforter, breathing in the dust.

This place did not know her.

And it seemed a little dead for it.

She brought life, wherever she went. Vivacious, unrepentant life, lived so fiercely there was no choice but to keep on living.

Fletcher let himself fall back onto the bed, the down heaving out a sigh as he found himself staring up at the ceiling.

The memories rained.

A barrage, like Elsie. Sweeping clean the muddy path.

And in them, he was happy to drown.

~ • ~

She was crawling into his bed at the lodge, her black hair in loose waves, her chilled body covered in goosebumps.

The first night.

"You don't mind if I stay?"

His smile was irrepressible as he shook his head. "Of course, I don't mind."

She grinned, pulling the covers closer above her crossed legs, and set to work on braiding her hair into that thick, mussed braid that eventually he learned meant she was getting tired, and he'd listened to her fingers brushing the groaning tangles out as he'd torn through his wardrobe, praying for pajamas he knew he hadn't even bothered to bring.

Panic was starting to rise, and he'd glanced over at her, humming quietly to herself. She'd met his gaze, cocking her head to the side. "Everything okay?"

"Yeah, I...I'll be right back," he muttered, snatching a crumpled dressing robe from the wardrobe floor, pulling the bundle to his chest as he turned for the bathing room.

No sooner had the lock clicked shut than he'd dropped the robe to the floor, the bathing room of the lodge vanishing in a whirl.

Caelaymnis had been chilly that night, he remembered, and there'd been snow starting to drift down in great, white clumps. It'd taken two minutes, running upstairs, to find the soft mossy pants he neglected in his solitude.

Of course, he'd come back with snow in his hair.

He'd brushed it off over the sink, but she'd still noticed when he climbed in beside her.

"Your hair's wet," she snickered, running her fingers through it, curled close beside him, their legs already tangled together.

"Your hair's wet," was the only retort he'd been able to think of, and she'd lost it, face crinkled with laughter.

It was a beautiful sound, her laughter.

Not like bells or chimes or any of the other pretty things people said laughter was like.

It was sort of breathy, through her nose, unless something was particularly amusing, then she'd fall completely silent, ribs shaking, eyes streaming with tears. There was this cascade of vocalizations, too, harmonics hit with diaphragmatic jolts, almost half-cut hiccups beyond what she could herself hear, and those—he lived for those.

Her kisses had been damp, after that, soaked with joy and salted to perfection.

He'd become adept, in those moments, at writing off his own hesitation as belonging to her, and her alone. She didn't want to know who he really was, right? She couldn't. It wasn't that he was not ready to be known to her, because what right did he have to hesitate like that?

There were moments, though, breathless moments, quiet moments, moments where he wavered, hope edging in. They left him stranded, fumbling. What he wanted...what he wanted was to lose himself with her. He wanted to hold her, to press his eyes closed and listen as her heart raced, to surrender, he realized now. He wanted to surrender. To hold his hands in the air and give up on it all. To confess every last piece of himself so that she could be the one to help guard his secrets.

But he'd spun himself a most romantic tale. He'd spun a tale where the end of the investigation meant an end to the doubt, the end of his life before, the making of a vow, that he would live and breathe and love and die as nothing more than a human.

That night, the first night they'd shared his bed at the lodge in the Merchant's Quarter, he had broken his facade.

He awoke to a darkened room and a cold hearth, heart pounding, unsure at first what had roused him. Elsie seemed dead to the world, her arm around his waist, her head nestled into his shoulder, one leg thrown haphazardly across his hips. But it was not a human she'd snuggled up against.

How to bring back the facade without waking her.

He couldn't.

He'd felt his skin tingling with familiar warmth, his magic tired and sluggish, his body reluctant to be contained, and gods, did it feel good, *so good*, stretched out there, unfurled beneath the blankets, beneath his friend, his lover—

Something made her stir, though, and exhausted eyes met his, wide and full of terror.

And in a blink, he was human again, panicked and awake.

Her fingers dug deep into his skin, her breathing fast, the taste of fear and sweat lacing the air as her heart thrummed, *dadum-dadum-dadum-dadum-dadum*, and she'd pushed herself half to sitting, swallowing hard, looking around the room.

"Elsie," he hardly dared to whisper, "please—"

At his voice, her head snapped back to his, a look of recognition dawning across her face, and already, her eyelids were heavy. "Just…a nightmare," she murmured, letting herself drift back onto the pillow, rolling onto her side.

A nightmare.

That's what he was to her.

And she deserved so much more than a nightmare.

It didn't take keen investigative skills to see that she had more than enough of those, already.

Human. For her, a human.

The next morning brought her no recollection of her waking dream.

She remembered now, though.

Fletcher let the silence of the deadened house wash across him.

Now, she remembered.

ELSIE

"People believe that freedom tastes like morality, justice,
goodness.
It does not."

~Mariann Bell

There was an unnatural stillness to the night.

Like even the wind didn't dare to breathe.

Run, it would've whispered.

Run.

The locket was warm against her fingers as she worried it, a reflexive tic to pull her through the minutes of solitude.

Was it really yours.

No.

Probably wasn't.

And still, she'd memorized the filigree heart, curling in the soft metal. The smooth joints of the hinges, hiccupped with hairline fractures, the sweet dig beneath her fingernail as she clasped it open, the ridges of the empty frame curled atop the diamond-patterned texture.

"You know, I quite thought I saw someone lingering beyond the window."

He was meandering down the carriage-house path, hands stuffed with casual nonchalance in his trouser pockets, like he greeted all trespassers with such friendly warmth.

"Did you know her." Elsie's voice was hoarse, cracking in the cold.

No pretenses.

No games.

His smile faltered, an expression of gravitas washing the light from his eyes. "This is not a conversation for garden walk-ways, Ms. Mirabeau," he said quietly, gesturing to the carriage house. "Please. After you."

~ • ~

Perched on the edge of a puckered leather chair, pulled before the great carved desk, Elsie's knee was bouncing with quiet apprehension.

"There's no need to fret," Clark muttered, glancing up from the drawer he was thumbing through.

She swallowed, saying nothing.

An idea, in the back of her mind, simmering, and in a moment of heartache, she'd succumbed to her own burning curiosity. Alone, watching Fletcher walk away, and she was tired of not having the answers to her own life.

You should've found Sam.

Sam, who'd have had the good sense to talk her out of storming to the manor on the hill, into the den of the monster on some half-cocked plot to demand answers.

Clark gave a soft chuckle, like he'd heard the thought. Pulling out a thick portfolio, deep butcher's brown and bound in twine, he tossed it onto the desk, falling gracefully into the accompanying armchair. "You know, it isn't all true, what he says about me."

129

"What?"

"Sam," he carried on with an exasperated sigh, a smile still playing at the corners of his mouth. "He's a sweet boy, but prone to hyperbole. I am not the big bad wolf he would have you believe."

You are you are you are

"I'm not here to talk about Sam."

"Oh, you are, love. You most certainly are." And with a single finger, he pushed the folder across the desk.

The twine was shedding beneath her fingers, freshly wound, and she let it fall in hopeless curls on the soft carpet as she glanced inside.

No no no no no no

"Go on, love. Take a look."

Her hands were shaking as she pulled the stack from the envelope, because she knew the hand that'd penned those twirling words, knew it, loved it—

"A bright young girl," she murmured under her breath, eyes flying across the page, "she is taken with her books and the idea that there is simply more...what the hell—"

Her. This was a—a documenting of her life, laid out in Sam's own hand.

She adores her brother—

A moment-by-moment account of her loves and hopes and heartbreaks, recorded meticulously by the man who was supposed to be her friend.

...a most vivacious response for a fourteen-year-old, though doubtlessly appreciated...

She flipped through the pages, watching the years of cataloging fly by.

Years.

He'd been doing this for years.

Utterly unrepentant, roguish, even, and her remarks are beginning to fall, as she neglects her schoolwork in favor of P.W.

Elsie's eyes snapped across the desk. "Bullshit. He wouldn't—"

Wetting his fingertip, Clark slid a single sheet of parchment off the desk. "She is mistrustful, to the highest degree," he read, "and though I am reluctant to betray such trust, I find it the necessary evil, when given...the choice." Clark tossed the paper aside, letting it flutter down between them. "He would. And more than that, love, he did."

"I don't understand—"

"I knew your mother." His eyes were polished coal, hands folded neatly before him on the desk. "She was a shrewd woman. Powerful. Great, even, and that...that is a word I do not offer lightly. You can be, too. But you are soft. You've known my son for how long? And not once did you question why the charge of the Commissioner—the heir to the district, heir to the Guild, even—would befriend a poor little farm girl. You never stopped to wonder, and now, in your hands, you hold the answer to a question you were too naive to even ask."

She was on her feet, tears stinging in her eyes, piercing, biting, gnawing—

"No." A resounding clap of thunder through the quiet carriage house echoed *no, no, no* with phantom whispers against the polished wood, and they were lying, lying little echoes—

"Yes," he said in a low voice, rising. "He may like you, he may care for you, he may even love you. And yet, he still betrayed you, Elizabeth. You cannot fill your mother's shoes, believing that he was anything other than a means to an end for someone else. And you're lucky, this time. Lucky that someone was me. Lucky that I had your best interests at heart. Because next time, it will be someone else. Someone who would rather see you dead than reaching for her torch."

She blinked back the hot tears, eyes darting about the carriage house. Sam.

Her Sam.

The one who'd paid her way out of the debtor's cells, who'd shelled out the gold to pay off the mercenaries, the one who'd helped feed her, clothe her, who'd loved her—supposedly—and for what.

So that he could chronical her life for the Commissioner.

"I understand this is a great deal to take in," he went on softly. "And I do not relish shattering what little comfort this life has offered you. But they have hunted her, Elsie. They hunted her, and they found her, and they killed her, and they will do the same to you, too, if they're given the chance. You have a good heart, love. It truly is gold. And they will use it against you."

Her eyes flicked back to his.

He was not wrong.

This, she felt. Deep in her bones.

Deep in the scars she'd spent too long chasing.

She'd been foolish, having any faith in Sam. Having faith in any of them, really. Because what had they brought, but disappointment and pain.

They'd used her.

Fletcher, to play out his fantasy of humanity.

Sam, to slip Clark information.

"Fine," she found herself saying, palms pressing into her damp cheeks, willing the tears away. "What if you're right. What if all this is true, and...what is it that I stand to gain? Trusting you?"

A wicked grin spread across his face, eyes sparking to life. "A city, my dear, the likes of which you've yet begun to imagine."

SAM

It was necessary.

That was what he told himself, turning over the cream envelope.

Cherried wax had been spilled across the pointed flap, a generically calligraphed S.A. coming into relief when he pulled the seal away. *They will hunt her,* he'd been told. *I do not know when and I do not know how, but eventually, they will come for her.*

And when they do, they will kill her.

But who.

Who wanted Elsie dead.

Fletcher's not even supposed to be here, she'd shrugged, Elsie's own confession as she'd sat curled beneath the blanket on Sam's sofa.

No.

No, he damn well wasn't.

Eyes damp, Sam sniffed, slumping back into the cafe chair, tossing the envelope atop the polished tabletop.

Fletcher was nice enough. The boy unquestionably had a good head on his shoulders. He was thoughtful. Quiet. Kind, too, far beyond what Percy had been.

And he wasn't worth her life.

But it was Fletcher.

Fletcher.

Elsie was precocious and witty, and Teddy was sweet-hearted and gentle, and he loved them both, and it had been utterly wonderful, having someone else join their little ensemble, someone who could tell the difference between the Fieldlande '82, with the oaky aftertaste and rousing tannins, and a Winter Reach '84, with the fruity lightness one would expect of such a mellow red. Someone who appreciated a proper table setting, who noticed when the napkins were folded fancy for special occasions, who took each meal as a vivid exploration of palate instead of merely the sustaining of body.

A friend.

The word hit him hard.

Elsie, he'd always thought of more as a sister than anything else. A spunky, wild little sister. And Teddy...well, *fiancé* had been a word he'd been hoping to use for a while, now.

But Fletcher was a friend. A good friend.

He was everything to Elsie, that much was plain.

And she was everything to him.

Clark's words echoed loudly in Sam's memory.

They will kill her.

They will hunt her, they will find her, and they will kill her.

Unless you bring this to me, she will die.

Maybe not today. Maybe not tomorrow.

But she will die, Sam. That, I promise.

And who better to hunt a back-water bastard than a warrior singing her praises from every proverbial roof-top.

Eyes tearing up, he blew out a breath, fingers drumming against the table. The thought made him feel sick. Tendrils of cold, oily shame were curling in his gut at the unspoken accusation.

That Fletcher—his friend, Fletcher, Elsie's lover, Fletcher—would use her, toy with her feelings, draw her out...and for what?

No.

No, he'd been here for nigh on six months. If he was going to make a move, he'd have done it already. And he certainly wouldn't have shown his hand. Anyone could see the wary distance in Elsie's eyes. It was the same look one might find in a cornered cat—dangerous. Like she could bolt, at any moment, if he gave her cause. Fletcher ate with them, talked with them, laughed with them, wrapped his arm around Elsie as she nestled into his shoulder on the sofa, and if he'd been hoping to make a strike in Elsie's direction, he'd certainly had his window.

The question remained.

If it isn't Fletcher—and it can't be him—who is after Elsie?

"Mr. Alderton?" A child's voice drew him from his melancholia with a start.

Chim was lingering by the table, staring at him, unblinking, head cocked to the side. "Mr. Alderton, is something wrong?"

"I, uh..." He straightened up, swallowing. And paused.

She'd already boosted herself up onto the chair across from him, had, in fact, already gestured the waiter over, and was, as she waited, turning over the teacup before her, pouring all the contents of the creamer therein. "Is it the dockman from the store this morning?"

"What dockma—oh, no," he muttered, watching her heap spoonful after spoonful of sugar into her filled-to-the-brim cup of heavy cream. "No...no, it wasn't that. I received some rather disappointing news today,

135

that's all."

She rested the spoon with dainty elegance against her saucer, and with her pinky out, lifted up the cup, taking a delicate sip of her sugared cream. "Well, buck up, buttercup," she nodded, smacking her lips.

"Buck up, buttercup," he echoed. His eyes flicked to hers. "My mom used to say that."

"Mine, too," she said softly. "It never really worked."

"No. But it was nice hearing it, all the same."

Quiet fell between them, the cafe still in the mid-afternoon lull.

"What would you do," Sam said, breaking the silence after a long moment, "if someone told you, you had to betray the people you love to save their life?"

She shrugged. "I'd eat whoever told me that, probably."

"Eat them," he asked, an incredulous smile tugging on his lips.

"You asked." She took another slurping sip of cream.

He glanced across the table once more, his own cup—of tea, not cream—long abandoned and cold, a thin film already long since formed across the top. Then, rising, he shook his head, grinning. "Eat them...I admit, I've heard worse advice. You, um..." He paused, straightening his lapels. "You said your mom used to tell you to buck up. She doesn't? Anymore?"

Her eyes were inky and unwavering on him as she laid her small hands neatly in her lap. "The dead are quiet here."

"You have a place to stay though? That's safe, warm?"

She gave a curt nod.

"But if you didn't, you'd know to tell Teddy or me?"

"There's no need to worry, Mr. Alderton," Chim grinned, flashing her pearly whites. "I told you. If anyone bothers me too much, I'll just gobble them right up."

~ • ~

Eat them.

Sam envied the irreverence of childhood.

His eyes trailed the cracks between the cobblestone path, following the jarring pattern of the grayish stones. He'd run these paths as a little boy, when they'd still tolerated such childish outbursts of joy.

Of course, he'd been taken with the idea of being a gentleman, he recalled. He'd wanted so desperately to prove he wasn't like the other sons of whores. To prove he'd been worth the gamble.

Anymore, though, he spent most of his time trying to prove he was still the little boy that flouted the authority of the nursery governess and ran defiant down the garden trails.

He'd tried to be that boy, when he'd met Teddy. Carefree and light and full of adventure. Teddy had seen through it at once, naturally, but he'd never minded, that Sam wanted to be someone else.

I don't know who I am. He'd found himself leaning on a split-rail fence in the most exquisitely expensive black suit money could buy, overdressed for the barnyard where Teddy stood, scattering corn for the chickens. Three months of seventeen had seen his first kiss, breathless in the meadow. His second kiss, beneath the rose arbor of the introduction ball. And hell. Unimaginable hell.

Well, who do you want to be, Teddy had murmured, a half-thoughtless remark as he dipped his hand into the pail, sweet split corn running through his fingertips.

My mother's son.

Teddy'd paused, sea-blue eyes flicking over, darkened in the fading light. *What was her name,* he'd asked softly. *If you don't mind.*

Rebeca. Rebeca Alderton.

Teddy had pursed his lips, giving a *well, there you have it* kind of shrug.

137

So, that's who he was. Sam Alderton.

And Sam Alderton looked out for those he loved. He would go to the ends of the world, fight to the death, tear the universe apart, if it meant they stayed safe and happy.

His pace was reluctant, finding the carriage house.

I am a good man.

I am a good man.

I am a good man.

And I am doing this for her.

He gave a soft touch to the envelope in his breast pocket.

He kept it near his heart.

Like Elsie.

Closing his eyes, he took a deep breath.

This is the last time.

Not the first time he'd made that promise to himself at the carriage house door.

He raised his fist to knock.

And paused.

Voices—a voice, really—drifted through the door, wary, half-shaken, the Commissioner's slick tenor smoothing out quick consolations.

Clark had company.

ELSIE

"Hope is the refuge of the living."

~from 'The Advice of The Long-Dead' and Other Essays

"Take care, love," Clark said softly, giving her elbow a squeeze. "We'll talk again soon."

Nodding, she watched as he closed the door to the carriage house with a soft click, the snap of a lock following close behind.

It must've been hours she'd been in there, because the sun had long since disappeared beyond the horizon.

A city.

She was death, cold and dark and ended even before she'd begun.

He was a merchant.

And he peddled life. A chance to start over, to make something better.

To be something better.

A quick glance around, to get her bearings, eyes straining against the night—

She drew a sharp inhale, her step back reflexive.

Leaning against the brick, hands stuffed in his pockets, Sam was watching her.

Shadowed.

Waiting.

His expression was somber. Mournful, even.

He pushed himself off the wall, and with a couple shuffled half-steps, the light from the windows bled across his face.

Across his still-damp cheeks.

"Elsie—"

Turning on her heel, she didn't wait to hear the rest.

TEDDY

"Right and wrong. It's all just guesswork in the end, a game none of us can win."

~Adrian Lynch

Elsie was not difficult to spot, on the wrought-iron bench bathed in cold light.

Snowflakes were beginning to drift down from the darkened sky, fat and slow as they waddled down, down, down to the ground, soaking up the sounds of the world.

Teddy had always loved the smell of snow.

The way the air was just *clean,* the hint of wood-burning stoves lingering across the top of it all, smoky and warm.

She must've been there a while, he realized. Her black hair was undone in waves down her shoulders, her back flecked with glistening white, her eyes vacant, even as her face was streaked with tears.

"El?"

Her head snapped up, her sharp inhale puncturing the night.

But her surprise was short-lived as he sank down beside her, and she dissolved, leaning her head on his shoulder, chest heaving renewed sobs.

"Sam told me what happened," he murmured quietly, drawing her in close. He brushed a kiss across her forehead, squeezing her shoulders—a universal bandage for broken hearts. Even in the winter, she smelled vaguely like roses. Some perfume, or something, that Sam had given her when she'd turned sixteen that she'd managed to ration thus far.

Sniffling, she dared a glance up in his direction. "Did he tell you he's a—a lying—lying sonofa—"

I was at Clark's. I overheard him talking to El, of all people—Teddy, he's making promises to her he can't keep! He was talking as if he—he knew her mother, and she was drinking it up!

Of course, why he'd been at Clark's—presumably to get his job back, but he hadn't outright said—

"And Fletcher, h-h-h-he's...well, it's done—" She was cut off by her own coughing, a half-sob still working its way in.

A hell of a night.

He'd checked the lodge, first—and found Fletcher's note, second. *Going home. Love you, El.*

And she didn't need that tonight. Another good-bye. Not after having a falling out with Sam—about what, Teddy was still fuzzy on the details.

"I don't want to go back." Her voice was a whisper buried in his coat. "I can't, Teddy. I can't go crawling h-home—"

"Sam said you're still welcome to stay with us. With him, I suppose," he amended. It wasn't his apartment. Wasn't his life, as much as he pretended it might be.

"With that motherfuc—

"He said," Teddy cut in over the top, "he'll keep to the sewing room, while you're there."

A lie.

But if Sam knew what was good for him, he'd oblige, anyway, lest he find himself on the receiving end of that damned knife he'd stuck her

142

with in the first place.

She swallowed, pressing the tears from her swollen eyes. Not a no.

"El?"

"What," she breathed.

"What did he tell you? About...your mom? Sam didn't say what he heard. Just that Clark made some, er, rather grandiloquent promises."

She was quiet for a long moment. "He told me a lot of things. That she was brave. And strong. And that she—she loved me—" Her voice broke, dissolving once more.

It'd be enough to break anyone's heart.

Elsie had come with snow and death.

Tessa had been cold and buried not two days when he'd awoken to a screaming baby sister. Their eldest brother, Tom—he'd hated Elsie. And maybe it'd drifted towards something akin to apathy, even passing fondness, through the years, but there was always resentment in his blue-gray eyes when he looked at her, a sort of *why can't you be her* sort of look.

Their parents did what was usually done, when a bag of gold and a merchant's bastard ended up on someone's doorstep—though the attempt to pass her off as Marlene's natural-born child, a little Solstice surprise, was somewhat marred by the almost complete disinterest in the baby girl.

Now Teddy, he'd been sort of fascinated by her. That she wasn't Marlene's had been plain enough, so there was a mystery, right there. And she cried—a lot—and he had a knack for helping, so eventually he'd just scooped her up, as best as his eight-year-old self could, and she'd settled down, and that was that.

It'd always been the two of them.

And it was odd, now, sitting here with her on that wrought-iron bench beyond the darkened bookstore, the bench that they'd sat on hundreds of times, sharing sweetrolls and tears and hugs and stories, because it was just the two of them again.

The thought wasn't comforting.

Just the two of them, and hadn't those been such sad times.

Just the two of them, because there'd been no other choice, nobody else looking out for either of them. Just the two of them, and right now, it meant there'd been loss, loss of love, loss of comfort, loss of a fragile trust so delicate it'd been forged with fractures.

"Tell you what," he murmured, rubbing her arm with a gloved hand, "let's go. There's dinner waiting, and hot tea."

"At Sam's."

"Yeah."

She scoffed, pulling away, shaking her head in disdain. "So, you're still with him. He told you what happened, and you're still—"

"What do you want me to do, El?" he sighed, rising. "I'm not about to leave him because you two had a spat—"

"It isn't a spat, it's betrayal—"

"Look, I don't know what's going on with you two, but you have no right to ask me to walk just because he decided—no, no, I'm not doing this. I'm not fighting with you, El. And I'm not breaking up with Sam. You have a problem with him, you march right into that apartment and *tell him*. He has been your friend for nine years. He has dragged you out of gods-know-how-bad of places, he has fed you, he has clothed you, he has loved you, and you know what," he added, hitting his stride, "at the very least, I think he deserves a piece of your mind. You at least owe him that." Holding out his hand, he raised an eyebrow, challenging her to refute him.

Glowering, she took his hand, pulling herself up.

A small victory, he supposed.

One he was praying he wouldn't regret.

144

CHIM

"Leave no stone unturned, and no debt unpaid."

~Dryadic Proverb, from the Book of Adagic Texts

Chim strolled idly by the dock, popping another piece of candy in her mouth. The Master was a fool. And she lived to for the Game. That, and sweets.

The man at the store had been very fun. Much funner than the others.

Not that she'd been planning to pay for the bag of sweets. Oh, no. She'd had an excellent story cooked up. There'd have been tears, pleading, a tale about a crippled mother and an unemployed father, a sick baby brother...

But he'd played the Game better. Had happily given her the candy before she'd even realized the Game had begun. All in all, a brilliantly strategized round.

The least she could do, really, was pay him back.

~ • ~

The dockman had been tough, Chim mulled, picking a piece of gristle from between her teeth. Though the decades-long marinate in cheap ale had certainly helped.

Belching, she rose, smoothing out her blood-stained smock. It was a pity. She'd liked the white one. But she was such a messy eater.

With care, she unfolded the brown bag of candy, pulling a mint from the assortment of sweets—there was nothing worse than having dockman on her breath all night.

The minty sweetness began dissolving on her tongue, and she resumed her stroll by the harbor. One dockman for a bag of sweets.

Not a bad price. Not a bad price at all.

TEDDY

*"I kept her in the pages of books, in the sound of the
leaves through the trees, in the songs we sung as children,
and deep in my heart, where I hoped she might finally be
safe."*

~Theodore Alderton

That night, Teddy dreamed of his sister.

~ • ~

"Shh!" Tessa was giggling through the admonition, though, squirming beneath the blanket as she lay in between them.

"You're the one who should *shh*," Tom whispered, and he was grinning, head propped up on his hand. "They're gonna hear you!"

She looked at Teddy, her laughing eyes glittering in the moon, *the moon like milk*, he remembered they'd called it, the way it poured into the window, cold and fresh, and her fingers found his ribs, tickling with the dexterity only little sisters could possess. He stifled his laugh in the pillow, but not before letting out a shriek of surprise.

Their giggles faded, eventually, and Tessa's small arm had settled around his waist, Tom's arm around them both, the three of them huddled together in the cold of winter.

It felt so good, soaking in the warmth, knowing that beyond the blanket was an unrelenting chill, but beneath it, they were safe.

His hand was around Tessa's, her skin hot.

Hot...and sticky.

Something was wrong.

"Tess," he whispered, shaking her shoulder.

Her eyes were wide, shining in the moonlight, empty blue wells.

The bed was soaking wet, the warmth fading as something dark leeched into the pillowcase, into the sheets, into the blanket, into his skin, and there was no laughter on her face, now, nothing but terror. "Tessa," he said, and he could hear his voice, scared, young, as he shook her shoulders. "Tess, wake up!"

Darkness coated his hands, glistening—blood—and she wasn't waking up, he realized with a jolt, wasn't doing anything but laying there, her tiny little body jolting, shivering—

"Tess!" He was screaming, now, tears hot as she convulsed, and he was trying to hold her still, cradle her in his arms until—

Until he could fix her. He could fix her.

A knack for helping out, but he'd seen what happened when people got hurt, he knew he could do more than help them, and he could help her too, if he tried hard enough.

His shaking palm was pressing against the gouge deep within her skull, trying to stem the waterfall. There should've been that spark, when his skin hit hers, that rush through his veins, the fire, the heat, the prickling deep within his fingers—

He could hear it, Sam's machine, and he tried to picture it, whirring away where his heart should be, stringing that Thread through the hole

148

in her head, but she was disintegrating.

Falling to pieces in his arms.

Fading, until there'd be nothing left.

Already, her face was blurring, like it'd been for years, her features contorted with time and pain, and there were just little bits of her hanging on. Her brownish-red curls, brushing what might've been rosy cheeks, but he didn't know, couldn't see—

Blue eyes melting into his own until they were simply his, dead in the mirror, and she was all he could ever see—

His fingertips were searing, and nothing was happening, nothing, burning and cramping and pins-and-needles and nothing—

~ • ~

He awoke as he always did, when he dreamed of Tess.

A flare of prickling sparks against his skin where someone had touched him.

Sam. Sam, with worried eyes and his low, honey voice.

And tears.

So many tears.

THE FIRES

I find myself reflecting on the essence of the flame.

Warmth. Comfort. Destruction. Revenge. Retribution.
Grief. Victory. Warning. Light.

It can be a symbol for the passion sparked in our hearts,
a rallying point of an angry crowd, the rising of the sun,
the crumbling of the familiar.

It can cleanse the earth. It can destroy the earth.

And I think the complication of the flame, really, is that
it is never simply one of these things, so much as all of
them, all at once.

~SAM ALDERTON,
EXCERPT FROM A LETTER DATED NOVEMBER 2ND

THE BEAST

"There are few things so dangerous in this world as the hope of faith."

~from 'The Advice of The Long-Dead' and Other Essays

She had been perfection.

Her fear had been juicy, ripe, full of the hope of decades yet lived, deep with just enough years to embed within her a terrible, frightful, wonderful, delectable comprehension of worldly terrors.

She *had* been perfection.

But as with them all, it'd run stale, just before the end.

"Don't know why he's dumpin'em here," the Muscle muttered, tossing her over his shoulder like a bushel of wheat, "people've been askin' questions..."

The Beast only growled, bristling at the doubt. To question the drawing of fear through blood was to question life itself. It was to stare into the face of a god and see nothing but imperfection, it was—

"'Course, it's prolly too much work, haulin'em somewhere else— though it's winter, prolly wouldn't start to stink. Prolly jus' freeze."

The problem with the Muscle was that he was too dumb to be afraid. Convenient, in this line of work, the Beast supposed. But difficult when it came to discipline.

"It's like I keep sayin', though," the Muscle carried on, boots scuffing the cobblestones with plodding steps, "too many questions an' we'll be movin' camp before the fortnight—"

The Beast gave a snapping snarl at the Muscle's ankles. He lacked the proper fear.

And there was no question, the Master should have made the Muscle afraid.

The gods did not fear the curses of ants scuttling before the rain. But they would fear the Master.

The Master lived to serve the Blood. He would harness the gods themselves. He would unlock the passageway and release the relic from this world, heralding in a new dawn.

A new, fearful dawn.

TEDDY

"They tower above us, unmoving. But given the test of time, they, too, will wear away to nothing. An echo of their grandeur, and so, the mountains fade."

~from 'The Advice of The Long-Dead' and Other Essays

The weeks had worn him down.

And today had been no different than the last fourteen.

Elsie would awake, cold fury in her green eyes.

Sam would awake, cinnamon eyes dead.

And they would sit across the table in silence.

Glaring.

Until Teddy sat down, and they'd eat, and drink tea, and he'd force out a few words.

And they'd both force a few words back at him. But never to each other.

Sam would retreat to the sewing room.

And Elsie—he didn't really know where she went, during the day.

She was never there when he got home.

One thing he knew, though, was that she didn't spend her days with Fletcher.

He knew this because Fletcher had taken to loitering in the store, investigative duties permitting.

Fletcher didn't stay away long.

A couple nights at home. Probably good for him, really. It sounded like he saw his family. Who knew, though.

He didn't really talk about it much.

He talked a lot about Elsie, at first.

And after he'd talked about her until there was nothing else to say, he talked about everything else.

Caelaymnis.

His sister, Alva.

His brother, Augustus.

His other sister, Cam, who was four years older, and he used to get along with, but didn't, anymore.

How he'd been different, and he thought he was maybe more human than Drada, but he didn't know how that was possible, except the Praequintelyas might've had a human in their line, once, a millennia ago, so maybe that was it.

And after Teddy'd listened and worked and stocked and rung up customers and listened some more, they'd lock up and leave.

Sam cooked dinner, mostly. Idle time didn't suit him, oddly.

Teddy had sort of imagined he'd fall back on his merchanted pastimes, like watercolor or cards or hell, even smoking, but he didn't.

It seemed like he mostly just sat.

Thinking.

But he'd cook dinner, and Elsie'd show up, cheeks flushed from the cold, and she'd glare at Sam for his eavesdropping, and she'd glare at Fletcher for not knowing how to tell a disbelieving young woman with a very sharp knife that he was a mountain elf, and she'd glare at Teddy for letting Sam and Fletcher sit at the table with them, and then she'd curl up in the far corner of the couch, eyes fixed at the same point on the same page of the same book, pretending not to listen to the quiet conversation, because she was too stubborn to give in yet too lonely to leave.

And Sam would sit in his armchair, as far away from her as possible, giving her frequent glances, trying to catch her eye as they talked.

And Fletcher would sit on the far end of the sofa, staring at his hands, listening.

And Teddy would sit in front of the fire on the hearth rug, half-reading—half-escaping, more like—and half-talking, until he could barely keep his eyes open, and he'd sink into a hot bath, or else fall into bed, to do it all again the next day.

And anymore, he was just a mountain.

Distant and cold with rockface still, encased in stone and rubble and roots, beyond where living souls could see.

The lock clattered shut with a snap, keys jingling as Teddy stuffed them in his coat pocket.

Gas lights flickered in the corners of his eyes, egging the world to spin a bit faster, the town around him melting into a place that mountains didn't know.

He should go home.

His boot slipped off the slicked curb, jarring his bones.

He should pay attention.

A tavern door opened, a rush of tobacco and ale burning his nose.

His stomach turned, nauseous, but he didn't feel it, not really, because this wasn't his body, walking down the sidewalk.

It couldn't be.

He was a mountain.

Mountain, mountain, mountain...

That wasn't right.

Someone else was a mountain. Not him, though.

He was not a mountain.

He was not immovable and strong.

He did not withstand the battering.

In the barrage, this, he knew.

They'd taken everything, it felt like, today.

Every flicker of personality.

He was playful, sometimes, that's what Sam had said.

You. Are. Playful.

Even the thought didn't stick in the slant.

He wasn't anything.

He had died, the day she had.

This much, he knew.

No.

You.

Are.

Alive.

A jolt hit him square in the chest, knocking the breath from his lungs and he caught himself against the brick wall. There was something caustic in the air, burning away the town, making his eyes water, and he blinked back the sting, sucking down mouthfuls of the crisp air.

And it hit him again.

You.

Are.

Alive.

He stumbled back, clinging to the wall, clutching his chest stinging with—with what, exactly?

Panting, his gaze flitted up and down the street.

Nothing.

Alive.

It barreled into him again, and his eyes snapped shut, a sharp inhale echoing in the night. Something crackled, hot stone—

His palms had singed the brick.

He jerked his hands from the wall in shock, trying to catch his breath, something like embers fizzling out beneath his gaze, a pleasant heat still lingering in his fingertips. Bile was biting at his throat as he glanced at the dusky street, ignored by the passersby. His knees were shaking, he realized—with adrenaline or fear, it was hard to tell.

"Alive," he whispered to the night, trying to catch his breath. Some days it didn't feel like it. Some days he was just a mountain—

Alive, it echoed back, threatening sparks beneath his skin. *You are alive.*

Listen to me, it seemed to say. *Go.*

It was tugging on him, he realized, pulling him forward, not just from the rubble and wreckage of who they'd told him he was, but down the street.

His feet were moving, his lungs drawing in the crystalline air carried on the roaring wind. The stars above glittered behind their gossamer clouds, and his movements were deliberate, focused, each step a promise. He moved through the saunterers, idly winding their way home, their tired eyes glazed, cracked only with the lucky grins of friends passing by, cracked with *grab a drink and a bite,* cracked like ribs and the medicine was time.

This, he could do.

He could mend.

Heal.

Help them, help them all—

No. He had to focus.

A call willed him down the street, the very Thread within him tying him to the hurting of another—

161

He wouldn't have seen them, if the Thread hadn't pulled him down the alley.

Elsie's shadowed silhouette, though, was unmistakable, the crouched figure beside her undeniably Fletcher. And the slumped form against the garbage pails—

His chest was tight, and he jogged the last few steps, needing to move, needing to see, needing to make sure it wasn't Sam—

A woman with eyes wide and glassy with fever and fear was hunched against the wall, and it took one look to see she had hemorrhaged—

Knees smarting as he hit the pavement, his fingers brushed her hair aside, checking for a pulse, scanning her up and down, trying to find the source of the bleeding. A faint quiver kissed his fingertips, the spark against her skin sending a shudder through her freezing limbs.

Alive but drowning, fluid rattling in her lungs as she tried to suck down another uneven breath.

"It's alright," he soothed, his voice oddly calm as he shrugged off his coat, "we're gonna help you, it's gonna be alright…"

She tried to grip the coat, to pull it around her more.

He found her hand, cold and raw—

The Thread recoiled violently. It—he—could see the tears, the rips, the cuts, could see what needed mending, and it was all of it, *all of it* was disintegrating before his eyes, dark and unnatural. This was not a slipped paring knife or a scraped knee on the gravel. It was slick and oily, a frozen wasteland of disbelonging, sludge in her veins where blood ought to be, blood that had retreated, finding solace in the slants between the cobblestones.

He had been too late.

There is no tear that can't be mended. That was what Sam said. *No cuts that cannot be fixed.*

No wounds that will not heal.

162

But even he couldn't fix her threadbare heart. There was nothing to push through the veins.

There was no room for a mouthful of air.

He felt it, when she died.

It was a shock wave, resonating through the Thread and deep into his heart.

He did not know her.

But he would miss her, all the same.

Violence had cradled them all, from birth to the grave. It had pressed him against cold stone walls in fear, had held him bruised and broken, and anymore, he could not extricate himself from the way cowards marked them all with fear.

It is Tessa all over again. Helpless and afraid.

Falling back onto his heels, he let his hands drop—hands coated in her blood, he realized, stinging cold as the wind nipped at them.

Something warm and heavy was being set gently onto his shoulders, and Sam was crouching down beside him, running a soft hand against his damp cheek, and he realized his eyes were flooded with tears for the woman he would never meet.

He pushed himself up, Sam's hand around his arm, pulling him up. "H-here, I d-d-don't want—"

"Just take it," Sam breathed, eyes darting for a split-second to the coat around Teddy's shoulders.

Threading shaking hands through the sleeves, his breath was frosting in the air, taunting them all.

Why.

Why were they all here.

Together. Elsie, and Sam, and—

And Fletcher.

He met the Drada's gaze—elven, unmistakably, even in the dim-lit

163

alley, lit—

Teddy did a double-take. What he'd taken for a sconced light flickering in the wind wasn't a lamp at all, but a shimmering orb, hanging gently over the body, casting a dim light across her.

"I didn't know you were a Healer," Fletcher said quietly.

I just have a knack for helping. That's what he'd meant to say. But the words got caught in his throat.

Just a knack.

Just nothing.

Because she was gone.

ELSIE

"What was birthed in the ashes of her fire, none could
say. Mortals worshiped it. The gods feared it. And even
the light of the stars could not rival it. From death it was
borne, and death, it would bear. Such is the word."

~Emilyon Dresada, 'Sermons'

"She has to burn." Fletcher's soft voice split the air, and Elsie ripped her eyes away from her brother, pale and shaking, his hands frozen in helpless grasp, painted with the woman's blood.

It felt wrong, being spurred to action so quickly. But four and one, loitering—it was bound to draw attention, and even in the shady quarter, it'd be difficult to explain away the bleeding body heaped against the garbage bins.

Already, Fletcher was stooping down, threading his arm beneath her shoulders with heartbreaking gentleness, his other coming deftly beneath her knees.

He wasn't a strong man. Still, he seemed to lift her small frame with ease, her head falling limply back as he rose, her arm sliding off her chest to dangle towards the ground with his movement as Teddy's coat sloughed off into the pile of rubbish.

And for a split-second, a spark of jealously flared in Elsie's heart.

The way he cradled her in his arms, the way he drew her so near his chest, his fingers digging into her, only his white knuckles betraying the strain, and it was pathetic, to envy the dead.

But she did, anyway.

He wasn't the bulking mass of a warrior the tales boasted that he ought to be.

He'd never whisk her off her feet, in illness or romance, it made no difference, because he wasn't a strong man, and she wasn't that tiny little thing he'd scooped up a moment before from the alley refuse, and she wondered if he wished she was like the dead woman, thin and delicate and *dead, dead, dead, I wouldn't be surprised if he wished you DEAD*—

And he was gone.

Vanished, in a whorl of mist and sparks, he'd left nothing but the darkened alley.

Teddy's eyes were fixed on the blood-soaked refuse nested around where the woman had been, the crumpled newspapers and rotting food now nothing more than a darkened splotch. Then, with shivering breaths frosting in the dark, his canvas shoes ground against the grit as he took a hesitant step, then another.

Bending over, he gingerly picked his coat from the mess.

~•~

Teddy had clung to the coat, only relinquishing it to quickly clean his hands, watching Elsie do the same, and Sam, and he seemed to be thinking what they were feeling, namely, that the hot water did very little, in the end.

How did it come to this.

She knew, objectively, how they had arrived here.

She'd seen Fletcher, moving purposefully down the street.

He hadn't been coming for her, though.

Even if that's what she'd been hoping.

He'd paused for a split-second, pain in his eyes. He nodded down the alley, and she'd known, too, that there'd been another one.

That he'd felt a tripwire snap, or else, had heard something as he'd patrolled the streets.

She knew that, in spite of her anger, she'd followed Fletcher into the alley, because this investigation somehow overtook her resentment.

For all his lies, he was trying to stop a very, very bad person.

Teddy tossed the dishrag aside, moving to wash his hands once more, but Sam stopped him, putting a hand against his cheek, eyes worried. "You're warm."

Teddy made a small noise of protest, and Sam let his hand fall.

Elsie knew, too, that Sam had stepped out for something. Cigarettes. A bottle of wine. Some merchant bullshit he couldn't live without.

Or worse, he'd left the apartment with the specific idea of seeing Teddy.

Of walking him home.

And it wasn't fucking fair.

He had *betrayed* her.

He wasn't supposed to be kind and loving like that.

And yet, like her, he had followed his companion down an alley, getting more than he bargained for.

Beyond it all, it'd been shadows, pulling them together.

Tendrils of death, bringing them all forth.

And now, in Sam's apartment, Elsie watched the haze of mist on the welcome mat, glaring.

"Sorry," Fletcher breathed, eyes catching her before turning to Sam, then to the floor, his face flushed with something beyond cold. "I—I didn't mean—well, I-I did, I just…nobody—I—"

"What's wrong," Teddy frowned, looking panicked.

Elsie turned for her coat, tossed haphazardly on the back of a dining chair. "It's unacceptable to evanesce directly into a residence," she snipped, an answer to her brother's query and a reprimand, all at once. He had no business acting like he had a right to be here. "It's a gross violation of privacy, presuming you're welcome whenever you fancy."

"Sorry," Fletcher echoed again.

"It's fine," Sam muttered, hand on the small of Teddy's back as he ushered his companion to the door.

Elsie ground her teeth, swallowing a retort, because a moment later, the three of them were gone.

Gone, to the wherever-it-was-you-burned-them place.

The silent minutes ticked away.

And she did not relish being alone.

As with every parting, Elsie couldn't say whether Fletcher'd come back or not, but that was sort of a lie, because he always came back.

This time was no exception.

You sonofabitch—

"Shall we," he edged, offering his hand, misty haze still fading from where it swirled about his boots.

Her weeks of staunch resentment had undone any resistance she'd built to the stomach-twisting sensation of being torn apart as the world dissolved before them, and bile was biting at the back of her throat as the shadows of an unfamiliar glade pieced themselves together before her light-tainted eyes.

Deep breaths did little. The air was thin—too thin, she realized, straining to push the blooming lights from her eyes even as cold air filled her lungs.

And before them, mountains.

Beneath the starlight, they sat, cragged and majestic, great stalwart guardians before the pines, sending long moon-shadows pouring down into the valleys.

If she'd had any breath left, they'd have taken it away.

And for a moment, she forgot to be angry.

It came back quick enough, though, with one glance at the whitewood pyre. Teddy was tucking his coat around the limp form, and even in the darkness, she could see his cheeks were streaked with dampness.

A nudge on her arm, and she started, head snapping to Fletcher, a retort on her tongue, but he preempted her admonition.

"Alva," he murmured.

"What..." But her voice trailed off as she squinted through the darkness to the figure behind the pyre.

And a moment later, the glade was a blinding wash of white.

The heat was stifling, even some thirty feet back, the distance growing as she edged further away. A sharp crack split the night, a great spiral of sparks released from a vein—not of sap, though, she realized. It couldn't be, those blood-red whorls hurling to the sky with vicious ferocity.

The sickening stench of burning meat filled the air, sumptuous and fetid. It sent her stomach churning anew—

crrrACK

Another burst, this time darker, like a fist-full of rubies glowing against the navy sky.

She was going to be sick.

She felt it, lurking from the moment they'd evanesced into this gods-forsaken glen—

The gods have not forsaken it, a voice admonished.

A voice, it took her a moment to realize, that did not belong to her.

169

Her feet were ready to move, she was going to be ill, violently ill, when that same voice, that same beautiful, sweet, bird-like voice filled the glen.

More than the glen.

Filled her.

And her mind stilled. Her heart fluttered to a quiet rhythm, and the air—it was enough. The frigid breeze against her back, the raging inferno against her face, they became a balance, and for a moment, the world was sort of beautiful.

May the fire release your soul from the confines of your mortal body.

It did, Elsie thought, watching the blue-white flames licking the logs.

Who had she been, before she'd been ashes?

Pain.

She had been pain.

And it was a better fate, to become embers in the night than refuse in the street. A better fate than to remain the discarded shell, than the weapon of weak men.

Better to be embers than scars.

May the light of the gods lead you safely to the afterlife.

What a light it was, blazing towards the heavens, columns of flame growing, growing—

And she blinked, and the world was dark.

It took her a moment to realize the fire had vanished, that she'd been left light-blinded by the pyre. She squeezed her eyes shut, the way Teddy used to tell her, when she was a little girl and he'd blow out the lamp beside her bed, and *one two three four five six seven eight nine* until she could see through the dark once more.

The pyre was gone.

Not even charred earth and smoldering ashes remained.

Who'd she been, before she'd been fire. A better question, perhaps.

170

Delicate hands were withdrawing from beneath the figure's cloak, pulling back the hood as they stepped across the patch of ghostly moon-bathed grass where the pyre had burned moments before. Blonde curls cascaded down, eyes flashing as a whisper of color twirled at the hem of the black shroud, a gown that did not belong in such a mournful place.

She was making for Fletcher, meeting him with a hug—a hug given on tip-toes, and even then, her head didn't clear his chin.

But her name...her name was a rumble beneath the earth.

Alva.

SAM

"And the frigid winter whipped through the trees,
whispering all the words we thought existed only in the
darkest corners of our minds."

~from 'The Advice of The Long-Dead' and Other Essays

He found Teddy leaning against the kitchen counter, arms crossed, vacant ocean eyes staring out the darkened window.

"Hon?"

But the soft word fell pathetically to the tile floor, unheard.

A few quiet steps, though, and Sam had broken his stare, coming to stand before him. And quietly, he edged closer, hands gently finding Teddy's waist as he straddled Teddy's stockinged feet with his own, until at last, the touch seemed to awaken something in Teddy, the brilliant blue eyes registering him at last.

With a sigh, he drew Sam in, arms holding him close to his chest.

Four inches between them, each one conspired and carved for a perfect fit.

~•~

Retreating to the apartment, a small wake had manifested in Sam's living room. A bottle of wine had been passed around—a very fine Warken, heavy, with faintly nutty undertones and a deep warmth that seemed to reach into ones bones—a hot, baked cheese with fig and water crackers on the coffee table.

But where remembrances should've been, they could offer nothing.

Alva had, apropos of an abundance of empty chairs, sank delicately onto the floor, her burnt-rose gown spreading like melted candies around her, glistening with something more than the exquisite weave of choice satin. It moved where she moved—moved how she moved would've perhaps been a better description, though, Sam thought, eying the dress from his armchair.

There was vivacious youth about her, with her curling hair, tied half-back with a slender pink ribbon, her small frame setting him, for once, in the role of only second-shortest in their little ensemble.

And yet, there was one inescapable word about her.

Dangerous.

"I don't understand," Elsie muttered, running her finger around the rim of the wine glass, making it hum and whine, the way she always did when there was a question to be answered. "Why leave her alive? It's cruel, for one, and she might've let something slip about who did this to her."

"She wouldn't've." Teddy's voice was soft, eyes falling down as he left the rest unspoken. *Not in her condition.*

Sam's gaze flitted to the pale burgundy wine, legs drawling in long streams down the glass from where he'd taken a sip, tannins still weighty on his tongue. "This is an odd question," he began softly, swirling the wine, watching a faint sediment stirring at the bottom, "but blood magic...what they are collecting is her blood, no? Transformed, mutilated, yes, but it's still what's running through her veins? So, forget leaving her alive—why leave her bleeding in the street? Fletcher, you said yourself that's why they burn. Why not completely exsanguinate them? It's...wasteful."

"Ah, a keen, if not rather morbid, observation," Alva remarked, taking a rather ill-timed taste from her glass. "Allow me to pose a counter-query. When collecting cream, why only skim from the top?"

Teddy frowned. "Because that's...where the cream is. The rest is just milk."

"Precisely. What remains, after they've taken what is ripe, is an increasingly watered variant of the first harvest. The cream from the top, the first pressing of oil, it is...potent. I, too, find it worrying, to the highest degree, that so much has been discarded."

"It means whatever they're using it for has to be something big, something powerful," Fletcher put in at last. Legs crossed in the Elsie-adjacent corner of the sofa, his eyes flicked at regular intervals to her singing cup, fingers still dancing across the rim in idle circles.

"Something big—like what," Sam asked, unable to stop the question.

And Alva paused, goblet half-way to her lips, her eyes flicking to meet his. They were glowing in the low light, the lamp catching them, and she seemed a cat, preening before the fire. "It could be anything. Blood brings power—and if the scripts are to be believed, blood brought us the gods, too."

"The gods?" Teddy asked softly.

"Long ago," Alva nodded, her voice almost a song once more, "in a time before remembering, there was no Life and Death. There simply was. Memory is long, but it is not forever, and as the creatures of the world forgot, the world was unmade in fire and terror. But the flame would remind them of their folly, and in the light of destruction, the world was remade. Such was the way of things. But Life was lurking, in the fire and the blood, hand-in-hand with Death, and as the world once more crumbled, they seized their chance. They breathed life into the creatures of the world, only to watch them die. And so, the world was empty, and Life and Death were alone.

"The nothingness left in the wake of the massacre, though, proved unnerving. Perhaps, they reasoned, it had been a mistake to leave nothing but the void, not when the two of them remained.

"But where Life wanted light and shelter, Death only wanted the darkened cold. *Should we not offer a second start to the world,* Life reasoned. *We are the ones who have stripped it bare; it is fitting to restore it.* But Death was unrelenting. *We have torn existence from the mountain tops and ocean floors. It is time we pay our penance.*

"Where once was love, there remained nothing but resentment and mistrust. Some say it was Death that struck the first blow, knowing it would come for Life, in the end. Others say Life moved first, cutting down the only opponent it had known in that void existence. But all agree that the blood of both was spilled. And in the blood, the creating.

"Life and Death fought so viciously, they ripped through this world and into the next. From the blood spilled in the battle of Life and Death, so came the gods, swarming like flies to honey. They pulled the warring gods apart, and beaten and bruised, Death and Life found a truce. Some say that together, they drank from a font of peace to seal the pact. Others say they bartered their own blood.

"We believe Death and Life struck a trade, trying to balance the world. For Death, the allowance to walk amongst the living, to see what beauty she would claim, in the end. For Life..." She snickered, taking a sip of wine. "Life was given a coin from the coffers of Death herself. A threat, some argue, that she would break the vow and claim him, in the end. A mercy, others said, for even the gods cannot live forever. I say it was a gift, though. Life gave his sister a remarkable chance—the chance to find something worth living for. Death gifted her brother with the same. The ability to love something enough, he could give his life for it. And so, the balance is maintained."

"A remarkable story," Sam sighed. He glanced to Fletcher. If gods could spring forth from blood...

Sam lost himself in his own thoughts, only drawn forth again by a disgruntled sound from El.

"Ugh." Elsie's fingers were still circling the rim of her wine glass, conflict burgeoning.

Fletcher tensed. "I just—will you stop that," he snapped, whirling on Elsie.

Her fingers darted away from the lip of the wine goblet, the whirring hum falling silent as she shot him a glare. "Don't you dare—"

"I have asked you not to do that—"

"It didn't seem to bother Alva," she snipped, setting the glass on the coffee table, stem wobbling precariously as she rose.

"I *asked* you, Elsie, I *asked* you not to—to make them sing—"

Sam eyed them warily, making to rise. "Hold up, I'm sure she didn't mean—"

"Shut up," Teddy muttered, catching his arm, pulling him back down into the armchair.

His intervention came too late.

"Oh, so once again, I find *Sam Carson* intervening," she snarled, turning on him with clenched fists. The first words she'd said to him in weeks. "That's just *perfect—*"

"El, I—"

"I am *done.*" A dozen long steps, and she was yanking her coat from the hook, the unpleasant sound of straining stitches ripping as she did so.

Teddy was on his feet, following. "Elsie—"

"Don't," she glared, jamming on her coat. "If I wanted to be berated by a pair of sniveling cowards too buried in their own-self interest to see past their navel, I'd have stayed home!"

The walls of the apartment gave an ominous rattle as she slammed the door behind her.

Alva was on her feet a moment later. "I think," she said softly, "that is my cue to leave, as well." Drifting towards the mat, she gave them a courteous nod before vanishing, leaving nothing but mist in her wake.

Swearing, Teddy sank back down.

"I should go, too," Fletcher muttered, turning for the coat rack.

"Don't you dare go chasing after her," Teddy bit, giving him an icy stare. "You're liable to end up with a knife in your gut if you go after her right now. Give her time. She'll cool off."

Unlikely advice.

Elsie was an inferno.

And she'd been burning for weeks.

ELSIE

"Ah, what is sweeter than just desserts?"

-from 'The Advice of The Long-Dead' and Other Essays

The cold light of the farmhouse windows met her like a bitter old friend, waiting in the dark.

Go baaaack, the hinges whined, door echoing the sentiment as she slammed it closed. *Go baaaACK.*

Acrid tea, brewed from a corroding kettle and icy water pushed to steaming on the cast-iron stove, and musings of ill-faith about the reliability of fellow living souls, carried Elsie to her straw-stuffed mattress and stupid, no-good, lying lamp that promised warmth but never gave it.

Perhaps...it was time.

The floorboard beneath her writing desk popped up with a sharp *thud* from her fist.

It wasn't much, what she'd managed to stash in the fraying burlap pouch. Extra coppers that came from Teddy, but that really came from Sam, because it was an impossible idea that the middle Mirabeau son would support his drunkard-of-a-father and spendthrift-of-a-mother, not to mention his kid sister, on the salary eeked out in that place. That whole thing, the thing where Sam put extra silvers in Teddy's bag and they pretended like he didn't, that'd been going on a while.

But most of the weight jangling in her hand had come from Percy.

Well.

That was a lie.

It was her doing, those gold pieces. His idea, at the start, but he didn't possess the wits really required in this day and age for honest-to-goodness thieving.

Nor, had it turned out, did he possess a benefactor with pockets to pay off the mercenaries, which, now that she thought about it, didn't reflect terribly kindly on her credentials as a sticky-fingered pastry princess.

Yes. Yes, it was time to go. Time for Princess Pastry to pack it up.

At least for a little while.

She had to get out of this mess, with Clark.

A city, he'd told her time and again.

The likes of which you've yet begun to imagine.

Maybe she'd try to find it, eventually, the city he talked about. Find the place that called her home.

And do what, Elsie?

It is delicate, Clark had simpered, leaning back in his arm chair.

In spite of herself, she'd returned to the carriage house. Again. And again. And again.

We cannot simply waltz in, heads held high, and expect anything but a quick death. There is maneuvering. Petitions to be made, alliances to be forged, threats to be delivered. We will pull your ascent from the hands of our enemies. Slowly. Painfully. And in the meantime, he'd frowned, looking her up and down, *there is work to do.*

That was when he'd invited her for dinner last week.

There is work to do. Are you hungry? Come, dine with my family.

179

She quickly realized he hadn't meant there was work to do, in that they should be strategizing.

He'd meant she was *unrefined.* She didn't look the part of an heiress. Elsie had thought she could probably tolerate a night of manners and etiquette if it meant dining on the rich foods laid at the Carson table.

One foot over the threshold of that marble foyer, though, and she'd regretted the sick curiosity that'd dragged her towards the gilded dining room. It hadn't been dinner. It'd been a finishing lesson.

She'd heard Sam talk about his sisters over the years. She knew that at twenty-four, he outstripped Cele by barely a year, and Minna by three. She knew Cele had been a relentless torturer, their feuds extending to anything and everything, from boys to the birthrights, and that their early adolescence had been marked by fierce competition on the battleground of elaborate fetes. She knew that Minna had developed her sister's enthusiasm, if not necessarily her talent, for torturing their adopted bastard brother, and her efforts, though often childish and unsuccessful, had once resulted in an unfortunate incident involving some heavy-whipped cream and a freshly-dressed Sam.

Even still, Elsie had more or less been expecting to find allies at the table. As if they shared something, now. A title. A position. Hell, even a blood-curdling dislike of Sam.

Minna had been all flushed cheeks and giggles at her father's chastisement as Elsie picked gingerly at the tender morsels of red meat, feeling sick. *Rude.*

But not rude enough, it seemed, to warrant more than a side-long glance from Clark as he'd snipped at Elsie. *Dab, love, dab,* he'd sighed, watching her wipe the corners of her mouth with the napkin.

She'd raised an eyebrow in question, half an inch from leaving. That was when she'd still kind of wanted the city, though. The one beyond imagining.

Lest you smudge your painted lips, Cele had put in, not bothering to look up.

I...don't paint my lips.

Clark had given his wife a knowing look, clicking his tongue. *Not yet, love. Not yet.*

Dessert had been the final straw.

Strawberries and cream atop a sinful chocolate torte, so rich it melted right on her tongue.

And what had they done, but leave it just out of reach.

You...don't eat it, Minna had snickered, one arm draped elegantly across the back of her chair.

Sure enough, she'd looked up, and their desserts were untouched, only the sweet wine, thick and pungent, sipped gingerly in quiet conversation.

Elsie had pushed back her chair, tossing her napkin on the table, and scooping up the half-eaten dessert atop the gold-rimmed porcelain plate, silver fork stuck unceremoniously in the center of the cake, she left.

Fuck the city.

All she wanted was to eat her cake in peace.

Now, tonight, her fight with Fletcher had led her back to the panic stash beneath the floorboards. Elsie rose, tucking the burlap pouch into her satchel, fingers brushing the scarf-wrapped plate she'd stowed last week. It'd turned into a sort of trophy—and with gold inlays, she could probably get at least a silver stack for it, if she really wanted.

They'd've thought it was funny. Teddy. And...and Sam.

Her brother would've been a silent mess of laughter, and she knew he'd have been driven to tears of amusement. Sam would clap her on the back, tell her it was a job well-done, and he'd've turned for the pantry, the idea of dessert still swimming in his head, and as he pulled out a cake or cookies or those tiny little chilled tarts he loved from the bakery down the street, together, they would've aired their grievances.

Sam probably would've been doubly amused, she thought, sinking down onto the edge of the bed. Knowing that Clark had tried to twist her into something—someone—she wasn't, and Elsie hadn't taken his bullshit.

Or, at least, the old Sam would've been proud. The one who hadn't written those letters. Who hadn't played spy to Clark all these years.

Not the one that betrayed her.

Her eyes drifted to the note tacked above her bed, nailed there by a ten-year-old girl with a book full of too-long words. Elsie was all memories tonight.

Don't give up, just yet.

Keep asking those questions, and you'll get there.

It'd been tucked in the cover of the book—her book, the book she'd never have been able to afford—and held at the counter, the day after she'd accosted the merchant boy in the back of the bookstore. The day after she'd met Sam.

It was sort of funny, because she'd read through Sam's letters time and time again, the ones handed over to Clark, by Clark, and not once, did he mention the bookstore. The damn things didn't even start until she'd known Sam for the better part of a year. Until after she'd been arrested for stealing that roll.

She'd first met Sam in the bookstore—had held him up, told him to stand and deliver whatever information he'd had, when she'd asked him to define the words she'd never even heard of before—and it hadn't just been that. Ten years old, and he'd been fifteen, and he'd seen her for the child she was. He'd hardly known her for ten minutes, didn't even know her name, and he'd seen her, waiting at the storefront window for Teddy. He must've known that she was afraid of the dark. Afraid to walk the six blocks over to find her brother, alone, a child on the streets of Taylor Town.

That had been the start of it all.

The real start.

Eight months later, when he'd pulled her out of the debtor's cells, when the letters started—gods, it was difficult to be furious at those moments.

Whatever else he'd done, Sam had looked after them both, after that.

Eight months after they'd met, and by all rights, he hardly knew them, beyond the afternoons in the bookstore, or else the afternoons that morphed into hanging out at the general store, Sam tossing the occasional half-copper in the till so Elsie could have a stick of candy, talking all the while with Teddy about books and the weather and what it was like, living on a farm, and parties and dresses and anything else that those two could possibly think of.

But those months had proved enough, because he'd pulled her out of the debtor's cells, and he must've realized they'd been starving, because there was always food, after that.

And Clark...

You've known my son for nine years, and not once did you question why the charge of the Commissioner—the heir to the district, heir to the Guild, even— would befriend a poor little farm girl. You never stopped to wonder, and now, in your hands, you hold the answer to a question you were too naive to even ask.

He assumed it was Sam, who approached Elsie. He assumed that even for her uncouth naivete, she'd know better than to reach beyond her station.

He assumed wrong.

Then, too, there was the matter of the gap. Why withhold eight months' worth of letters? If the aim was to guard her, to gather a steady stream of information about the one who'd inherit the city beyond

183

imagining, it seemed ill-advised to willingly forego additional intelligence. And Sam—he'd never been the heir to the district. Rumors flew viciously, but he was a bastard.

This district was Cele's.

There was only one reasonable explanation.

Sam hadn't told Clark.

If Elsie were to wager, she'd put her entire stash of grifted gold—and that damnable cake plate, too—on the card that said Sam's duties as courier-spy had begun the night he'd pulled her from the debtor's prison. What better opportunity to position Sam as her savior?

Why then? Why that night?

For reasons she could not understand, Sam had cordoned off those eight months prior—and she could only assume Clark had not pressed for them, if he knew about them at all.

A small slice of privacy.

What if, another thought edged, *Clark already had those eight months.*

And the realization dawned on her.

Sam probably hadn't been the first spy.

If she truly was the heir to a city beyond imagining…

Sam had simply been an opportunity.

He'd been used, too.

A means to an end.

And that made it so much harder to be angry, which was frustrating, because she prided herself on being well-practiced at the feeling. But it also made her that much more mistrusting of those who came before. Who else had betrayed her?

Elsie let the satchel sink off her shoulder and onto the bed, and closing her eyes, she sighed.

Perhaps this…this wasn't the moment to run. Reconciling with Sam wasn't her first choice, but he might be able to name his predecessors.

"What are you doing?"

The pernicious tone of a little girl cut through the air, and Elsie started violently, whirling.

Atop the desk, the kobalde.

"You," Elsie hissed, darting forward on instinct, grabbing for the little she-demon.

But Chim disappeared, and Elsie was left grasping at air, a memory of an inky black column the only evidence she hadn't been alone.

"You can't get me," the little voice simpered. Elsie's head snapped to the shadow stepping into the moonlight beneath the window, and the kobalde was giggling as she smoothed out her smock. "Not unless I want to get got."

You can't and Elsie lunged again, Chim was nothing but smoke in the dark. "This isn't a gods-damned game—"

"It is always a game," the kobalde challenged, lingering by the bedroom door, finger trailing at the handle. "Going somewhere?"

"None of your *gods-damned* business—"

"It is *always* my business, the comings and goings of a girl like you." Her eyes were inked-out, shining wells of black. "You shouldn't be out, on a night like this."

"Leave—"

But the kobalde snapped her fingers, and the words were cut off.

Coiling up her arms, down her legs, around her middle, twisting, twisting, rope curled like morning glory vines, binding her tight. Elsie was squirming, fighting them off, muffled cries for help rendered useless by the rough gag worked between her biting teeth, and panic was rising, deep and insidious.

She was trapped.

AUGUSTUS

*"Morality is dreadfully exhausting. For once, wouldn't it
be fun to be wicked and well-rested?"*

~Alva Praequintelya

Dark had fallen, and Augustus paced the Western Gate, vial clenched in
his fist.

Collected as the Master had instructed.

Ruby Tears. Called so, because that was where they bled first. From
the eyes. Little red droplets, trailing down cheeks, potent and fresh.

And after it'd been collected, he'd sought solace in the gods.

They gave their blood, through the vessel, and Augustus repaid them
with sweat and prayers. He had hiked the Dagger, the great looming
peak that pierced the sky, refusing food and water as he cleansed himself
through the exertion. He had bathed in the font of the temple, had
anointed himself in oil and ice. He had prayed, prayed until his knees
were stinging on the alter steps, prayed until his bones were locked in
the form of penance, and then, he had prayed some more.

He'd prayed to the Ender. To the Trickster. To Winter, and to
Wisdom. To the Healer. To Order, to Summer, to the Sun itself.

Now, forgiven, he waited.

The Master moved silently down the border, the only sound the padding beast panting and growling at his side. Cloaked, no face was to be seen—but that was to be expected. Such magics as the Master knew were forbidden, and even a transient practitioner had to be wary.

The silver threads of Augustus's own insignia gleamed in the moonlight.

A reluctant partnership, the Master and the General.

Loyalty before amity.

And make no mistake, it was loyalty that drove him here. He had watched good men and women and *ro* die at the hands of a ruthless enemy hoping to bleed the Drada dry.

Well, the humans had an expression.

Fight fire with fire.

Or, in this case, blood with blood.

This was the only answer.

"You have it," the Master drawled, joining Augustus by the gate.

Augustus gave a curt nod, uncurling his fingers to offer the vial. The Master took it, uncorking the stopper with an easy flick of his thumb, and holding it before his darkened face, he inhaled deeply. "Oh, very good," he murmured, voice intoxicated, "very good indeed, love. This will do." Turning, a single finger beckoned Augustus through the dark. "Come."

TEDDY

It was a loud thud from the hallway beyond that drew Teddy's attention.

Of course, the neighbors upstairs were unmercifully heavy-footed, and across the hall, they'd just had a baby, and gods, the screaming—but this, this was the sound of someone hitting the landing below with the weight of a body behind it.

With an exasperated scoff, he closed his eyes, and leaning his head back against the tile, he let himself sink down into the steaming water of the bath.

"I've been thinking."

Teddy pried open his eyes, glaring at Sam as he stood before the sink, a tiny jar of what looked like orange jelly balanced precariously on the edge. Sam's eyes were fixed intensely on his own reflection as he scrubbed the jelly into his face with his fingertips, the movements painstaking, his concentration palpable.

"What the hell is that?" Teddy demanded.

"Sugar scrub. Marjorie's recommendation, from the shop—of

course, she says it'll take ten years off—"

"Oh, gods above, Sam, you're twenty-four, you take ten years off—"

"It's just something to get this gods-damned ash off my face," he snipped, shooting Teddy a look in the mirror. "Pardon me for not wanting to finish the evening with the essence of burned woman, and if it takes Marjorie's scrub to do, then so be it."

Teddy frowned, watching as Sam turned on the tap, splashing his face clean. "So?" he asked hollowly as Sam reached for a towel.

"So, what?"

"Did it work?"

Sam inhaled deeply, running a hand along his jawline. "I dunno." His gaze flicked to Teddy, grimacing. "I smell like a tangerine. A very smoky tangerine." Rolling his eyes, he re-capped the tin, tossing it with derision into the drawer. His blonde hair was still damp from the bath he'd already taken, his tan skin still red from where he'd scrubbed it raw, and he seemed to take his tangerine failing as surrender, leaning instead against the counter, looking rather dejected.

It wasn't the first body Sam had found dead in an alley, and the first had been his mother, so it wasn't hard to find the parallel.

And as for Teddy, it wasn't the only blood he'd gotten on his hands.

Maybe his guilt had been written across his face, because Sam was scrutinizing him with crossed arms, eyes dark. "It wasn't your fault, you know," he said quietly.

"I know." His eyes drifted across the colored bottles lining the lip of the tub, their perfumed oil making the air heavy and thick with lavender and eucalyptus. "I keep telling myself that," he went on, sitting up, water sploshing against the side of the tub, "that I did everything, that her death was the—the act of a coward, that it isn't on my hands, and I...don't think I will ever really believe that, Sam."

"I wasn't talking about the girl in the ally."

"Yeah, well," Teddy mumbled, fist hitting the surface of the water with resignation, "neither was I."

It'd been weeks, and he hadn't been able to shake the dream.

The sweetness of the start. The bitter end.

Nothing about how Tess died was right.

For their faults, they'd adored that little girl, Marlene and Gregory. Her death had broken them both into apathetic squalor, though, and he couldn't remember a single tear being shed after she left.

She'd died, and their family had, too. Slowly. Painfully. The beginning of a very long end.

Abandoning the tub, he rose, stepping onto the mat. He yanked a towel from the rack, glaring at nothing in particular. "Well. Anyway," he muttered under his breath, trying to snap himself out of memory. It wouldn't do to lose himself in melancholy again. Not when the Thread had found the warpath in that regard, apparently—an unpleasant development, one he could've certainly gone without.

At the thought, the Thread nudged him, almost like it was *offended.*
Healer.

Fletcher'd used that word, in the ally.

I didn't know you were a Healer.

Well, Teddy thought sardonically, *neither did I, Fletcher. Neither did I.*

"Anyway?" Sam edged, raising an eyebrow.

"You said you were thinking?"

"Oh." Sam's expression of displeasure melted, shoulders relaxing slightly. "Yeah, I was thinking, this evening exempted, that the apartment's starting to feel a little crowded. And then..." He paused, fiddling with his hands. "There's the matter of work."

Work, and the slowly draining accounts.

"We haven't really talked about it," Sam went on, glancing down at the floor, "but I...I don't think it's likely I'll be able to find work in the district again. Mulligan's was a long-shot from the start, and—and it's done, now. The lease here is up next month, and I wouldn't be surprised to find we're not able to renegotiate, either. And I keep thinking about what a big place the world is. About all the places we haven't seen, places we don't even know exist—"

A loud knock shattered through the apartment, cutting him off.

Frowning, Teddy tugged the belt around the dressing robe tight, following Sam down the hall, a billow of steam from the bathing room at his heels.

"Two in the gods-damned morning..." Sam yanked the door open, glaring.

And froze.

Chim was standing politely at the threshold, hands laced behind her back, red hood tilted back. Her perfectly girlish curls were askew, her usually bright pinafore apron wrinkled and smudged with dirt—though beyond this, she seemed in high spirits, flashing them both a wide smile. "Good evening," she beamed, bouncing on her toes with excitement.

But Teddy's eyes had fallen in disbelief to the parcel—or rather, person—in tow.

Elsie was on the floor, leaning against the corridor wall, scowling. She'd been gagged, a great mass of rope stuffed in her mouth, her hands tied behind her back, her ankles bound.

Sam was already across the hall, kneeling beside her, deft fingers undoing the gag amid her muffled protestations. "El, please—"

"No, shut up—it's her," she snapped, grimacing as he let the rope fall. "It's her! Get her!"

"Are you hurt?" Teddy's fingers were shaking as he tried to loose the bit about her ankles, but the knot had been pulled impossibly tight—

"Ugh! Get her, you moron! She—"

"Well, that's quite rude," Chim remarked, watching them from

191

where she leaned lazily against the door frame. "I find time in my *very busy* schedule to step in and *rescue* you, and—"

Sam shooed Teddy's hands away with a scoff, turning to make quick work of the bindings.

"Rescue? This isn't how you rescue people!" Elsie retorted, tone more exasperated than anything else. "That's a basic principle of rescuing people! You don't kidnap them—"

Teddy was waving them both off, running a hand through his hair as he glanced between them. "Okay, El just—what happened?"

"I was *trying* to tell you! *She* kidnapped me!"

"You," he muttered, turning for Chim.

"Yes, her!" Elsie cut in, moving for Sam to reach the bindings behind her back. "It's her! She's the kobalde!"

TEDDY

"Burn. Burn unceasingly, unendingly, burn until all that remains is the charred earth, fertile, ready to begin again."

~from 'The Advice of The Long-Dead' and Other Essays

"Kobalde," Teddy echoed, staring at Chim.

The little girl merely plucked the bag of candies from her pocket, and began fishing around inside.

"Just—get—will you hurry up," Elsie snapped, glaring over her shoulder at Sam, "since neither of you'll—"

"I told you. You can't get me if I don't want to get got," Chim frowned, examining a piece of candy against the flickering wall sconce of the hall.

"Everything alright out here?" A rather stout woman was peering out of the door several apartments down, her hair in rolling papers, surveying the chaos in the hall with something between interest and annoyance.

"Yes, Mrs. Hughes," Sam muttered, releasing the rope from Elsie's wrists, and beginning to coil it quickly in his hands. "Nothing to see here, simply the usual hubbub..."

"Well, hush!"

Her door slammed, sconces rattling, and Teddy pulled his robe a little tighter, face heating.

Elsie made a grab for Chim—

She vanished.

Actually *vanished,* nothing left but a hint of the black vapor she'd been swallowed up into.

A high-pitched giggle echoed from within the apartment a moment later. "Well, come on," Chim was laughing, bouncing up and down on Sam's sofa, clapping her hands with glee. "It isn't a game if nobody else plays!"

"Okay, you—come on," Teddy muttered, hand on Elsie, moving her towards the apartment.

Elsie was rubbing her wrists, moving to lurk in the entry way, shooting dirty looks at Chim, who'd taken to wandering with great curiosity about the apartment, touching anything and everything vaguely of interest. "You're being awfully calm about this," Elsie snipped to Teddy under her breath, never taking her eyes off the kobalde.

"You've come back with worse," he bit back, tucking a strand of hair behind her ear.

"She kidnapped me—"

"Oh, quite untrue," Chim mused, touching the knick-knacks on one of the shelves. She picked up a small music box, finding the key beneath it, and a moment later, sweet music chimed up, tinny and warm, gears clicking in time to the tune. "See, she was about to run away—"

"Not true!" Elsie snapped.

"Elsie," Teddy sighed, exasperated, "seriously? Again?"

"I wasn't!" His sister's eyes were wide on him, anger falling away for just a moment as she summoned a look of innocence.

"You didn't let me finish," Chim whined, pouting.

194

Sam quirked an eyebrow, gesturing her to go on. "Then finish."

"She was *gonna* run away, which would have been okay, but she started looking at the *plate,* and she got all *sad* and *mopey,* and I had no choice but to tie her up, because otherwise she was going to stay," Chim finished.

"What's so wrong with her staying," Teddy breathed, already having a dozen answers to why she was better off out of the farmhouse.

Chim started fidgeting with her smock, looking around the apartment. "It's gonna be full of chaos. Chaos and fire."

~ • ~

Teddy strode quickly down the packed dirt road, scanning the horizon for any sign of arson.

But the night was dark and cold, the only light visible the warm windows of Butterfly Ridge.

"I don't see anything," Sam said quietly, half-jogging to keep up with Teddy's steps. In the glow of moon and windows, his cheeks were flushed, his eyes wide and alert.

Elsie shot Sam a glare, but aimed her words at her brother. "The demon was lying."

A distinct possibility, but one Teddy had found improbable. But the threat had pulled to the surface guilt that had been simmering for a while.

It had been months since Teddy had been home, *really home,* as in, slept in his bed, ate with his parents, home. He hadn't meant to stay away so long—but one night at Sam's turned into two, and before he realized it, a week had gone by, and suddenly the lie of *I'll go home tomorrow night* had turned into *maybe sometime next week* which in turn became *well, I'll simply drop off 'salary'* and here he was.

195

"If this is trickery," Sam muttered to Teddy, "are we walking back to town?"

"I...don't know. Probably." Teddy winced a little, glancing to Elsie.

"Don't look at me," she snipped, "if I had a fancy feather bed, I wouldn't stay there either. Even if I had to share that bed with a *liar—*"

"Elsie, please—"

But Teddy's chastisement was cut off by a loud explosion, a great fiery column rising to the midnight sky from beyond the edge of the village. A jolt of adrenaline and panic made his heart drop, and for a moment, all he could do was stare as dread overtook him.

His footfalls felt too soft against the earth, his pace too helpless.

Screams began to fill the air, a bell ringing, and as he neared, he could see great plumes of smoke billowing up from—

"No." Teddy whispered the word, knees beginning to shake as he watched their farmhouse consumed by flames. "No!"

A couple of the neighbors had gotten there first and were shooing Bells, the Mirabeau's ever-stubborn cow, out the gate, the chickens already fleeing from the now-catching barn.

He didn't know what to do.

I have a knack for helping and I am so fucking helpless—

The door was consumed with fire, the roof already falling in—

Sam caught up, out of breath, hand on his shoulder. "Oh, fuck— Teddy, I'm so sorry..."

"What do I do?" He looked to Sam, feeling feverish. "Sam, what do I do?"

But Sam just shook his head, eyes sad.

The panic wouldn't abate.

Be a mountain, be a mountain, be a mountain, because mountains did not have anxiety attacks, he could be cold and still and painless—

The Thread recoiled at the thought, sending a rush of hot, prickling magic through him, making him feel even more ill.

"Hey!" Someone was pointing at Elsie and Teddy. "Hey, there's the other two—the kids are okay!"

"Oh, thank the gods," Linette, one of their closer neighbors, was murmuring, and she was making her way to where they stood, as close as they could be to the burning without themselves catching fire. "Someone was running about here—damn kids getting drunk, kept screeching about her." She nodded to Elsie.

"What'd they say," Elsie breathed, brow knit in confusion and anger.

Linette looked sad, giving Elsie a sympathetic sigh. "They called you...the Heiress of Death. I'm sorry, sweetie, it...comes with the territory."

Teddy felt nauseous, watching Elsie's face fall. She was the bastard, likely the bastard of a merchant, and he could only assume, based on Linette's accounting, a vandal had taken the taunt too far.

Exhaling, he wrapped an arm around Elsie, holding her tight, and he realized he was crying.

Pursing her lips, Linette looked back to the fire. "Hope your parents got out alright."

They didn't, it turned out.

The more Teddy watched the blaze, the more he began to feel hot and shaky and sick and like he couldn't breathe, anxiety squeezing tighter and tighter around his ribs with each inhale of the cold, smoky air.

"Yeah," someone called out at last, when the house was nothing more than smoldering remains, "they...they were in there."

He hadn't felt them die, though they surely had.

Where the Thread had given a soft, sad quiver when the girl in the alley died, it had chosen now to wrap around him tightly, making his joints ache and his muscles burn.

Tom was making for him, now, Tom, who had clearly been dragged out of the tavern for this, who looked plainly like this was nothing more than an inconvenience—

"So, Mom and Dad," Tom began hollowly, gesturing to the house.

Teddy ran a hand through his hair, palm brushing against his forehead beaded with feverish sweat. But words wouldn't come.

"You look like shit. You should go home."

Teddy's eyes skirted the wreckage, tracing where it'd all been. *Why didn't I go back sooner. I hated it, but I never got to say goodbye.*

They were gone.

Marlene and Gregory Mirabeau.

Mom and Dad.

Gone.

I am a mountain.

The Thread recoiled at the thought, thrashing into his chest, and he'd've fallen over, if he hadn't been able to lean into Elsie on the pretense of a hug.

"Teddy, you're sick, we need to go home—"

Home, smoldering as the hint of dawn was peering resentfully over the horizon.

Home, smoke and ash in the air.

Home, and it was gone, all of it, gone, the hungry nights, the cold nights, the happy nights where the books were enough, the hurting nights of broken ribs, the tender nights where his mother would kiss his forehead and squeeze his cheek and tell him he'd done good picking Sam, the lonely nights where he'd sit at the table with his father and they wouldn't say a word, the nights when he and Elsie had toasted bread over the roaring fire, the fire that burned them all, took them all, all his nights he'd ever had.

It didn't matter that his home was somewhere else, now.

He was dizzy, dissociative and fevered and sick. His knees buckled, Elsie taking a staggering step back, her arms around him, now, shouldering his weight.

He was burning up.

His feet were reluctant to hold the ground.

Elsie said something, then, soft and gentle, cold fingers brushing his cheek. Her eyes were flooded, too, he noticed, pale light cresting the edge of the world.

His gaze flicked to Tom, moving for the charred remains of the farmhouse.

No, please, not now, I'm not ready—

Tom was gesturing to a couple of onlookers, buddies of his, his low, hollow voice asking for a hand—

Teddy's throat was tight, his body hot, too hot, and he could not bear to watch them poke and prod the blackened planks with toes of boots and half-burned lumber.

His heart was racing uncomfortably fast behind his ribs, frenetically pounding an escape, and the world was getting darker again, darker and hotter, burning—

"El...Elsie," he stumbled, her name clumsy on his lips. He was clutching her coat where he'd wrapped his arm around her waist, leaning heavily against her. But it didn't matter, because he was falling, slipping towards the cool earth beneath, slipping away, away, away.

His knees hit the packed dirt, and there was a tremor, through his bones or in the ground, he could not say.

Sam was helping to pull him back to standing, and they were walking, but he didn't want to go.

Walking, and he should stay and help.

Help.

Help.

FLETCHER

"Love does not afford uncrossed lines."

~Sam Alderton

He had heard a whisper of the fire burning.

One foot into the street, and he'd tasted the soot.

And when he'd seen the ashes for himself in the early morning light, he found himself searching for the sound that'd carried him this far. Wherever Elsie was, though, he told himself it was too far for the beating beneath her ribcage to reach his ears.

That didn't stop him from hearing it, all the same.

Da-dum. Da-dum. Da-dum.

The wreckage reeked of more than match and tinder.

You did this, you did this, you did this.

Fletcher's worry nearly overtook him, that somehow, his presence here, his involvement in her life, had finally reached the tipping point. What if whoever was at the center of the investigation, this—this *Master,* what if they had realized he was onto them? What if this was retribution, what if—

"Vandals," he heard someone say, "vandals, chasing that poor bastard girl, I heard someone call her Death's Little Heiress, so cruel..."

Elsie was a bastard—likely a merchant's bastard, according to her, dropped on the doorstep of the Mirabeaus with a bag of coin, and striding through the dwindling crowd, the whispers made Fletcher's heart hurt with worry.

Why would vandals be chasing Elsie?

The Master is a merchant, we're increasingly sure of that—if Elsie is a bastard of a merchant, is he coming for her next?

What does Death's Little Heiress mean?

The Mirabeau farmhouse was nothing more than a burned and blackened pile of rubble.

Elsie had forbidden him from coming to this place.

Forbidden him from meeting the once-parents, now dead and covered in patchwork quilts, half in the ditch.

That must've been her eldest brother, Tom, lingering by the bodies of her not-parents. He was stockier than Teddy, his skin looking rather wan and yellow, the stubble of more than a few nights scratching noisily against his fingertips as he scratched his jawline, frowning at the rubble.

Another one, forbidden.

"Pardon." Fletcher's voice was hoarse in the smoky air, his tenor pushed higher with nerves.

Her brother turned, jerked from thought.

"I—I'm sorry, but El…" Fletcher trailed off, unable to finish the thought.

She wasn't gone. He could hear it, she wasn't, wasn't, wasn't—

"Left already," the brother said gruffly, tossing a hand down the road towards town. "Ted's sick, she an' Sam took'im home. You're Thatcher?"

He tried—and failed—to hide the look of relief he knew was written across his face. "Fletcher. I'm, uh, sorry for your…your loss," he muttered, turning, "it's…sorry." Whatever words he'd meant to say fell flat as he left the brother. Sleepless nights and endless worry had left his

201

mind devoid of any Vernacular words he usually held close, leaving nothing but the flowing Dradic words of his youth and home.

Relief bit at the heels of his awkwardness, though, as he made his way back towards town. Thank the gods Elsie had not been in that house.

He'd snapped, last night, and he'd never have forgiven himself if their argument had driven her to a funeral pyre.

As it stood, though, this was another nightmare for her to remember.

But she'd sent the wine glass singing, the crystal trembling, shaking, screaming with each pass of her dampened fingers against the rim, the pitch wavering as the wine tilted precariously, dropping by uncomfortably obscure increments as she sipped it away, and it'd set his skin afire. His hands had been shaking, his head throbbing, and whatever ground they'd gained in their silent game had been lost to the searing pain from between his ears.

She knew, too. He'd *asked* her not to make them sing, and she'd done it anyway, not giving a damn that the sound had been eating him alive.

About one thing, his brother was right.

Humans could be cruel.

~ • ~

Fletcher stood before the golden *401* of Sam's apartment, the tremors of his fist against the door still rippling through the wood. Inside, a faucet was running. Someone was pacing—Elsie, if he gauged correctly, her soft foot-falls so opposite of the heel-striking humans lodged above him in the Merchant's Quarter. Sheets rustled, and someone let out a groan, of pain or relief, he couldn't tell.

Still, his brother's words clung to him.

Humans could be cruel.

Fletcher hadn't been there a year ago, when humans had been cruel and an elven patrol found Augustus, half-dead, drained for the sake of blood magic in the Woodshades. A Sentinel, Fletcher had been buried in intelligence reports at a border post to the east, devoid of human life. Or any life, for that matter. Nobody cared for the eastern border.

No, all the action was to the west. The human settlements, with their raiding parties and their production rings and their subsistence farmland that, most years, produced so little it was a wonder they tended it at all.

Word had been sent, and he'd found Augustus with the medics in the compound infirmary. He'd refused to be moved to the palace.

But beyond that, he'd returned an empty shell. His pale eyes had remained distant, his jaw clenched in silence as he stared at the ceiling, lost somewhere else.

Augustus never came back from that place. Not really.

Humans could be so cruel.

The problem was, though, his people were no better.

My people.

They weren't his people, not in any true sense.

The door opened, and Elsie gave a sharp inhale, eyes widening. She'd been crying, but knowing her, probably pretending she hadn't been. Her dark braid was falling apart at the ends, strands flying out in anarchistic fits, the sleeves of her tunic pushed up to her elbows. "Fletcher." His name was uncomfortably soft on her lips, soaked deep with warning.

"I saw," he managed, and her brow creased—not in disapproval, though, he realized.

In pain.

Wordlessly, she beckoned him inside. "Teddy—"

"It's enough to make anyone ill," he mumbled, trying to drown out the conversation from the back of the apartment.

My mother, Teddy was saying from the bedroom, and Fletcher tried

203

to block out the private words.

"You talked to Tom." Elsie sniffed, wiping her eyes, and she almost looked like she was going to start crying again.

You're just numb, right now— Sam was offering words of comfort to Teddy, and it was hard to focus, with the two conversations happening at once.

It was an effort to rip the words through the din, and Fletcher pinched the bridge of his nose, headache rising again. "El..."

"Elsie!" Sam's voice was sharp with worry, cutting down the hall, and something was wrong, very, very wrong. The sounds of conversation had died into gritting teeth and a shivering bed frame, and he could sense it, the tempestuous quiver of unmistakable power hanging in the air, caustic and sterile, magic gone awry.

This was not the illness of grief or shock. It was something much more dangerous.

Perhaps Teddy mended cuts and scrapes.

But this, the unmistakable sounds of one violently ill, this, too, was the work of a Healer.

SAM

*"In his heart, there lay turmoil so vast that it shook the
seats of the gods themselves, one word left in the wake of
the tremor. Listen."*

~from 'The Advice of The Long-Dead' and Other Essays

Sitting in bed, curtains drawn against the rising sun, Teddy watched with
a look of dismay as Sam rung out a damp cloth over the bathing room
sink. "I told you. I'm fine."

Sam glanced over, raising an eyebrow. "Mm-hmm." Then, shaking
out the rag, folding it into a neat rectangle, he came to perch on the edge
of the bed. "Lean back."

Reluctantly, Teddy sank back into the pillows, not sparing Sam an
eye-roll that would've made El proud. But as Sam pressed the cool cloth
against his forehead, a sigh of relief escaped Teddy's lips, his eyelids
fluttering closed.

He was burning up.

The blankets had been kicked back, his thin cotton shirt already
soaked with sweat.

"So," Sam said softly, blotting Teddy's pale skin with care, "do you
want to talk about it?"

"Do I want to talk about how I just watched my older brother pull my parents' burned bodies from what's left of my home," he echoed. Ocean eyes blinked open, bleary and bleak. "No. No, I really don't."

Little flecks of soot were bleeding into the white cloth, smudging gray and black across Teddy's already ashen cheeks. "I remember when they took my mom," Sam said softly, working the marks from his lover's skin. They'd talked about it—in nine years, how could they not—but it was different, now.

They shared the loss.

He wasn't the garden path boy running to his best friend. Not anymore. Every shred of innocence was gone.

"I..." Sam let his hand fall to the bed, cloth forgotten. "Hon, I—I have so much, right now, I wish I could say. And it's all wrong, but...it's alright, not to feel a damn thing right now. It's okay to be numb, or—or buried in hard facts. But please, Teddy. Don't tell me that you're fine. You don't have to be crying on the floor, or—or collapsed in the road, to not be fine. You can be laying here, quiet inside, and still be not fine. It is allowed, you know."

"I know," Teddy whispered, letting his eyes close.

A long quiet sat between them.

"We will get through this. Not—not just today, I mean," Sam went on quietly, "but...but all..." He trailed off, panic rising as he watched even breaths replaced with jolted, shallow ones, Teddy unhearing, seemingly plunged into unwaking nightmare.

~ • ~

"Teddy!"

But crumpled on the bed, furrowed brow welling with beads of moisture, skin flushed with fever, he would not wake.

"Come on, hon," Sam begged over Teddy's unconscious groans. He didn't want his voice to be so desperate. Didn't want the fear to edge in any further.

Just a nightmare. Just a nightmare.

But people woke up from nightmares.

What they didn't do was slip into unconsciousness, shivering and drenched in sweat.

"Teddy, please! Wake up!" Elsie's eyes were starting to swim, her knuckles white as she gripped his shoulder, shaking his limp body with dangerous ferocity. "Theodore! Now!" Like using his full name would somehow snap him from whatever hell he'd clearly slipped into.

His hair was dark with dampness, and he was tossing and turning from some unseen enemy, taking in the rasping breaths, sharp and irregular, racing heart pounding frantically beneath—

Like embers beneath his skin.

Like there'd been something ignited, deep inside.

But this was not the beautiful fire of poets and dreamers.

"What's wrong with him," Elsie whispered, her hand shaking as she pushed the tears from her cheeks. "Sam." Her voice was louder, fear masquerading as anger and blame. "What's wrong with him?"

An accusation, like this was Sam's fault.

Teddy's hand was hot, too-close-to-the-fire as Sam brushed his fingers against it once more, and he'd read the lines in a book, once, words that were the closest to prayer he had.

I will pull you back from death.

I cannot live without you, and so I pull you back to keep on living.

A pathetic relinquishment of his own agency.

But they were so true. So gods-damned true.

Amid the convulsions, a whorl of sparks crackled up in a rush of ozone where their skin collided.

Hot in Sam's veins, prickling deep into his palm, it burned oh so sweetly, knocking the breath from his lungs like it did *every damn time* but this time was different, this time wasn't a paring knife that slipped in distraction, a bruised elbow collided with a door frame, a jagged rock slicing his leg with delicious ferocity.

The memory was vivid in this moment of panic.

Let me take a look, Teddy had murmured, hands steady as Sam had winced, grimacing at the streams of red staining his calf, and Sam was seizing at the flood of memories rushing in the wake of doubt, youthful memories of that hot summer day by the river so many years ago.

Let me take a look and what he'd really meant was *I care that you're hurting, and I will stop it, if I can.*

Let me take a look and I will always be here to hold your hand, to help you up when you fall down.

Let me take a look and we are it, you and I.

Sam hoped that memory would not be all he had.

The catalyst of touch that let sparks of Teddy's familiar healing fly was enough, it seemed.

Enough to bring Teddy back from whatever hell he'd found.

Blue eyes flew open, locked on Sam's, wide with terror and brimming with tears, and Teddy's chest was heaving, fingers digging deep into Sam's hand. "No, no, no..."

Sam damned his own voice for breaking as he cradled Teddy's damp cheek in his shaking hand, thumbing away the tears with soft sweeps. "You're okay, it's all okay, I promise, everything—everything's going to be fine..." But even as he said it, he watched Teddy's panicked eyes, tears welling in his own.

And he worried it wasn't true.

THE BEST LAID

PLANS

It is disheartening, watching everything crumbling.

I don't even know why I'm still writing these letters.
Habit, maybe. Writing these letters to no one.

I suppose it's my own way of trying to convince myself
that everything will be alright. That these letters can be
something more than treachery.

My heart tells me that I did this for her. But some deep
instinct in my gut says I did this for me, too. That I was
not prepared to face the fall of refusal.

Such, I suppose, are the plans of mortals.

~SAM ALDERTON,
EXCERPT FROM A LETTER DATED NOVEMBER 12TH

ELSIE

"Shit. Shit, shit, shit—" Elsie paced the living room floor, arms wrapped tight around her body, trying to stave off the deep panic still overflowing in her chest. It was difficult to focus, her eyes unable to pause, to take in less than everything, falling in at her, all at once. But she had to be calm, she couldn't let Teddy see her panicking—

"El?"

"Shit!" She started violently, heart slamming itself into her ribcage.

Fletcher was lingering at the threshold of the hallway, and she couldn't recall him ever being quite so *still*. It only unnerved her that much more.

"You—you have to do something," she snapped in a half-whisper. "What even was that? What the hell just happened? I—you—"

"There is a captain in my unit who is a field medic," Fletcher interjected, his gentle voice even and calm, "and did a rotation in the settlements—"

"Then go! Go get them!" she snapped.

He gave her a curt nod. Then, in a swirl of shimmering mist, he was gone.

A little more pacing and a lot more swearing, and once she was able to find adequate calm in the empty living room, Elsie turned down the hall once more. She found her brother sitting on the edge of the bed, looking like he might be sick.

Teddy blew out a breath, dry shirt limply in hand, already crushed as he braced his fists against the bed, like he was going to make to rise.

"Fletcher...went to get a medic," Elsie offered tentatively, folding her arms across her chest as she leaned against the wardrobe.

His eyes snapped up. "I do not need—"

Sam scoffed. "Hon, you—"

"I know what happened," he hissed, turning on Sam. "I was *there*, I gods-damned know..." His voice trailed off, brow furrowing. Then, pressing his eyes closed, he let another deep exhale out. "Sorry. I just...I don't think that's necessary. I'm fine."

"Well, it's three-to-one," she muttered.

"Oh, lovely, so *now* you're chummy with those two—"

"Shut up." But her eyes flicked to Sam, all the same.

He met her gaze, giving her an almost imperceptible nod of approval. "A medic is a good call," he said softly.

Elsie looked down, face heating. Even in spite of the anger she still nursed, his approval made her feel warm and proud.

They both just wanted Teddy to be okay.

~•~

A field medic.

Elsie's tired mind had conjured up fairy tale pictures, and still, Captain Isa Mirestva was not what she'd expected.

214

Watching the warrior sink kindly down on the edge of the bed, a bright, friendly smile dancing across their face, she had the distinct impression that the small apartment would simply not contain the swaggering confidence. Isa had obviously been pulled from the middle of something—the gray uniformed jacket had been tossed lazily on, half the diagonal buttons, cold and silver, left hanging loosely open. The accompanying gray trousers had been tucked into scuffed black boots almost up to the captain's knee.

Isa's entire being seemed to say *fuck authority* in a way Elsie found immensely satisfying.

"I am afraid," Isa was grinning, voice accented with an unfamiliar cadence, "that human abilities are not my, ah, area of expertise. Now, get one of your friends to slice you open in the mess hall..."

Elsie snickered, drawing a pillow into her chest as she sat catty-corner at the foot of the bed. It was difficult to nurse the feeling of resentment amid the banter.

Isa's dark eyes flicked up to hers, sparkling. "Are you volunteering? I've heard you're rather quick with a blade, Miss Elsie—but then again, the Commander desperately loves to brag." The Drada turned back to Teddy, fingers now deftly taking a pulse, gaze searching. "Light-headed? Blurred vision? Nauseous?"

"No," her brother said quietly, faint amusement at the corners of his mouth.

Elsie was awash in pride. *Fletcher brags about me?*

"And are you a practitioner, Mister Mirabeau?" Isa inquired.

Teddy gave the captain a quizzical look.

"Can you control it," Fletcher interjected from where he was leaning on the door frame, arms folded in thoughtful study. "Conjure a lucent, or—or heal in any capacity?"

"Well, I..."

It's not nothing now, is it, Teddy, Elsie thought sardonically, watching him squirm. The denial ran far and deep—in them both, if she was being honest, at least until she'd seen Fletcher for what he was.

"He can," Sam offered into the stumbling pause, glancing inquisitively at Teddy. "At least, a little bit. Right?"

"A little," Teddy confessed, voice hoarse.

Isa nodded, turning Teddy's hand over, palm up, the captain's own hand musing above his. Teddy gave a sharp inhale, and Elsie gripped the downy pillow tighter, searching him—

The shimmering motes between their hands caught her eye. Where before, there'd been a chaotic spray of lights and haze, this was a quiet spiral, full of order, ease.

"It is a travesty, I think," Isa smiled softly, eyes following the motes, "that these skills are not beloved within your realm. You seem fine. If I were to wager, I'd say it's the equivalent of..." The captain glanced to Fletcher. *"Amdormvitae?"*

"Er, sleep-walking, I think," Fletcher muttered.

"Sleep-walking, then." Isa's eyes met Teddy's, preempting the question so clearly carved in the azure. "I cannot speak of your people, but in my experience, magic can sometimes be a bit...badly behaved, I suppose. A bit aggressive. Some find that burning off a bit of magic now and then can curb the proclivity for trouble. For a human, it's a bit unorthodox, traditionally speaking, but this should help."

Teddy's brows were furrowed in concentration, a look Elsie hadn't seen him wear since his days at the schoolhouse. "Traditionally speaking?"

"You're not like us. Your magic is not an endless font. Should you deplete the well, it'd need time to fill again, so to speak."

"That's what you're doing, though. Burning it off?"

Isa gave a small nod. "Nice and slow."

Teddy loosed a small breath, tilting his head back against the headboard, eyes never leaving the stream of shimmers drifting peacefully up from his palm.

Quiet filled the bedroom—and in its wake, a question, nipping at Elsie's tongue.

"He's not supposed to be here." She'd blurted it out, unable to take her eyes off the captain, coaxing the swirls from her brother's palm. "Sorry—Fletcher, though. He said he was defying orders to be here. Aren't you going to get in trouble, too? For being here, for—for coming to help?"

Isa glanced up, eyes dark, shoulders tense, despite the jovial tone. "I have friends in high places."

TEDDY

"Healer, mend thyself."

~Unknown

It was like draining a bathtub with a teaspoon.

Except the bathtub was sort of endless, and the water was angry, and there was an audience of onlookers, watching the tub drain.

Teddy let out a sigh, watching stitches of magic being pumped out through the palm of his hand, even spirals of Thread dissolving up, vaporizing before they reached Isa's. It would've felt nice, probably, to let it all go, if there hadn't been a void in the wake of the release, a void slowly filling with a mass of conflicting feelings, each one stronger than the next.

"Not to impose," Isa asked, glancing to Sam, and then to Elsie, "but a cup of tea tends to be my fallback prescription. A cup of chamomile for our Healer would do a world of good."

Elsie frowned, giving Sam an expectant look.

Rising, he gave a quiet scoff. "Come on."

"It doesn't take two," she mumbled, crossing her arms.

Oh, for fucks sake, El. "I think the captain meant for you both to go."

Teddy could feel her seething as he let his eyes close. The bed gave slightly as she rose, though, and he heard her storming down the hall, the bathing room door closing angrily behind her. Sam's lips brushed his forehead a moment later, muttered complaints thinly veiled as apologies still audible under his breath as he left them.

"Do I want to know what happened with those two?" Isa asked, voice dripping with amusement.

Teddy opened his eyes, guilt swallowing up the relief of the empty room. "No. Probably not."

"But I think perhaps you should tell me, anyway." The captain's eyes were glittering in the lamp light, smile faltering. "I appreciate that you have been through a harrowing ordeal this evening," Isa went on softly. "Far beyond what the others can imagine, I suspect, and far beyond what you might confide in them. Love, in all its glory, sometimes remains a burden."

"It isn't...I'm not really in the mood to talk. No offense."

"None taken," Isa shrugged. "I take it you're itching for another incident, then. That's fine. Your choice."

"Excuse me?"

"You're untrained. You have no concept of your abilities, so your emotions dictate their use. Someone gets hurt, you have a core reaction, deep in your gut, and your powers kick in. And this time, you're the one that's hurt. But there's no cuts or bruises to heal, because this is where you're hurting," Isa nodded, tapping their chest. "Your heart. Except the problem is, Healers don't mend hearts. They fix broken bodies. Thus, it overwhelms you"

Teddy looked away, eyes starting to sting. "So, that's what it was, then."

Even now, he felt the Thread coiling, ready to strike, his skin growing hot where Isa worked the magic from him. It'd been a friend, once. And now it was tearing him apart.

"Elsie's pissed because the district Commissioner said he knew who her mother was," Teddy said softly, staring out the darkened window. "And Sam was the Commissioner's ward. They had a falling out, and— and he's been after Sam for a while, now, on and off, so Sam went to go talk to him, and he overheard the Commissioner talking to El. He was concerned the Commissioner was just using her, and she got up in arms about it. I..." He trailed off, shaking his head. "I think there's something else going on. But they've been pretty closeted about whatever went down."

"That must be difficult," Isa said softly, "watching two people you love dearly go after one another."

"Honestly, it'd be fine, if she'd just fucking get over Fletcher."

"Tell me how you really feel, then."

"Sorry," he muttered, glancing back. "They're driving me insane, though. You're Drada. You tell me he could've walked up to that woman and given her any semblance of the truth. And it doesn't matter, because if it hadn't been that, she'd've found another reason to push him away. I watched her do the same thing over and over again. Any semblance of a real connection, and she's gone."

It was like the dam was starting to crack.

He hadn't realized how stifled the flow from his palm had been, until that moment. Through the din of the thrashing Thread, he was starting to feel the tug, drawing the well up, up, up, until it was left swirling in the air, shimmering out to nothing.

An open faucet instead of a teaspoon.

"And I can't imagine trying to navigate that after last night," Isa went on, dark eyes intense as they met his own. "Finding so much death, and still, it's you that has to be the buffer between them all."

Sinking down into the pillow, Teddy let out a sigh. "It's not even that

I mind being a—a buffer, or whatever. I just...how am I supposed to feel? They're gone, and it was too much, watching Tom..." He swallowed, fighting back the bile at the back of his throat. "One moment, I'm torn up. I—I'm never going to see them. Never going to go home for dinner, or... The next, though, I'm relieved, because I'm never going to see them again." His eyes were tearing as he looked away again, his words hardly a whisper. "My father is never going to take the board to me again. My mother is never going to shatter what little pieces of joy we found, never going to scream our hearts away. And it's really hard to be sad about that. Especially when I think that—that they found more peace on the side of that road than they ever had when they were alive."

"And that was the second pyre, I think, you found last night," Isa prodded.

"Gods, I—that was just Tessa. Tessa, all over again." His cheeks were wet, now, streaks of cold running down his hot skin. "It has been twenty gods-damned years, and I am still killing myself over that girl. And it's so simple, to Sam and El. It wasn't my fault. So, I should let it go."

"But it's always different, looking from the outside."

"They don't understand that it was my fault. They are so ready to write her death off as something that doesn't belong to me, when it does. It was mine, as—as much as it w-was hers, and it should've been me, too, burning in that—that house, tonight," he whispered, shaking his head. The room was soaked in tears, and he was grateful, so guiltily grateful, for the solitude. For space to simply feel.

"No matter the conflict between your sister and your lover, though, you can rest assured that neither of them would wish the same," Isa said quietly, fingers coaxing up the bright web of motes with casual ease. "It is apparent they care deeply for you. They would, I have no doubt, go to great lengths to ensure you are getting what you need, if you were brave enough to tell them. So what is it, Theodore? What is it that you need, today?"

What do I need

He didn't seem to be able to stop the tears, an unrelenting, silent flow down his cheeks. Isa pursed their lips in sympathy, digging a handkerchief out of a trouser pocket with a spare hand.

It was soft against his skin, pale gray, like everything else about the Dradan aesthetic, as far as he could tell.

What do I need

In the wake of the question, as his magic burned away, Teddy let himself sink deep into memory.

~ • ~

The night he'd first kissed Sam, he'd found Chloe waiting for him afterwards, like they'd promised.

Sam called it the night he'd kissed the wrong boy, who'd been the right boy in the end.

And that was all well and good, but to Teddy, it'd begun an intense, internal conflict.

Chloe had waiting, leaning against her father's barn in that sweet lavender gown that hugged her form tight, dancing lightly around her ankles, the first hint the heavy dresses of winter were to be stuffed back into storage. A handful of months, that'd been all, and he knew she was the one.

He was going to marry Chloe Thompson.

It'd been rash and instinctive, his kiss with Sam in the meadow, and it was easy to dismiss.

A few days before his introduction, and Sam had been a nervous wreck, dreaming of his fairy tale. *It has to be perfect,* he'd fussed nervously, plucking blades of grass to shred them in his manicured

222

fingertips. *And I've never kissed a boy, so it's going to be a disaster.*

I could kiss you, Teddy had teased, stretched out on the grass. *Then you'd be an old pro by the time you got to the ball.*

You would do that? Sam's voice had been serious, his eyes molten.

More than would. He *did.*

They'd laughed it off, albeit sort of awkwardly, because it'd kindled something between them, something that was impossible to ignore.

He'd thought a lot about what it was he needed after that. The question would invariably creep into his mind, too, when he'd fight with Chloe, when the vicious words between them brought out an animalistic anger in them both, feral and destructive, because in those moments, it felt like Sam would've been a better ally.

Sam never yelled at him for scraping up enough coppers to buy the wrong birthday present.

Sam never minded when Elsie tagged along.

Sam never cared that he cried, sometimes, because life had promised a hell of a lot more than it gave him.

What do you need?

That'd been a question asked time and again in the school house as his hand met the air for the millionth time.

He'd been thirteen when Elsie started walking with him into town to go to school. Walking wasn't precisely the right word for it—she'd been four, nearly five, so he and Tom took turns carrying her most of the time. She was too young to be there, by all rights, but Marlene had gotten tired of her by then, and Mrs. Henderson didn't mind, anyway. El'd been supposed to sit up front, with the youngest ones, but Mrs. Henderson, too, had looked the other way when she'd refused to budge from between her brothers.

He remembered working through an arithmetic book—Tom's—at sixteen. Elsie was sick, and nobody said anything as she dozed, fevered, on the bench beside him, head resting in her arms atop the desk. She'd been up all night, and so he had, too, and there wasn't any breakfast for them that morning, and there wouldn't be any dinner for him, either, because when he had to choose—and he'd had to choose quite often—it was always her who'd eat.

What do you need, Mrs. Henderson had asked, head inclined to the side as she swept back to look over his shoulder.

He'd wanted to tell her that they needed something to eat. That they needed some sleep. That he needed medicine for his little sister.

And now, here he was.

Elsie might have been royally pissed. But she was well-fed. Warm. Safe, now. Loved, dearly and deeply, even if she didn't want to accept it. And Sam was hurting, but it was difficult, too, to be upset about Clark pushing him further away.

But what do I need.

SAM

"The simple act of prayer can mend the soul. It is not that the gods are listening—or, if they are, that they particularly care. It is simply the belief that you are not alone, and that...that is a powerful tool."

~Alva Praequintelya

Sam's hands moved through the motions, thought they weren't his own.

Tea in the basket. Water in the kettle. Match to the burner. Kettle on the stove. Cups on the counter.

He moved, until he could move no longer. Until his eyes stung with saltwater and the world was bleeding, a watercolor memory.

"You know, he—he was laying there, and I thought, *this might be it,*" Sam said hoarsely, hands braced on the edge of the sink. "That might've been the time we had. And he's fine. But in that moment, I went to pray? Only, there was no one to pray to. We—we talk about these gods, but when it mattered, what..." He shook his head. "All I wanted was one fucking prayer, and I had nothing."

The kettle began to spit and whistle, clanking against the grate. He pulled it from the heat, clicking off the burner, a wash of steam billowing up as he filled the tea pot.

Even now, he could feel the phantom burs in his hand where he'd touched his lover.

One prayer.

One prayer, because Teddy had almost died.

One prayer, because Elsie had almost burned.

She should've been in that farmhouse tonight, save for the grace of Chim.

They will find her.

And they will kill her.

He'd refused to hand over the letters, and she'd almost been a third, beneath the quilts on the side of the road.

That was what Clark had threatened, wasn't it? That she was going to die...but the letters, these letters would've done nothing.

They'd've warned of Fletcher—her ally, despite what she claimed. They'd've told many things.

But not of a moment's anger, the slamming of a door, not until it was too late.

Whoever had set the fire had been watching.

They knew.

They followed.

The thought terrified him, because soon, they would realize they failed.

"I, um..." Fletcher trailed off, evidently at a loss. Brows knitted, he was leaning against the counter, banished by awkward imposition when Sam had been sent for tea, vainly hoping to steal a moment to catch his breath.

A boy, trailing after me like a little dog.

He regretted the thought instantly. It belonged to a bitter tart, angry at his lost monopoly of heartbreak.

Swallowing, Fletcher put a tentative hand on Sam's shoulder. Then, with a soft exhale, he closed his eyes. "Gods below," he breathed, "cast up these words. Find our brother in the depths. Cora, cutter of threads, stay your hand. Lucia, trickster, show your mercy. Stell, cold-hearted, give your warmth. Hadri, in the night, light your lamp. These be the words" —*Cora Lucia Stell Hadri Cora Lucia Stell Hadri Cora Lucia Stell Hadri*— "Gods above, cast down these words. Find our brother in the heights. Asa, bind the wounds. Natali, give shelter from the storms. Ignata, calm the fray. Kiran, restore the day" —*Asa Natali Ignata Kiran Asa Natali Ignata Kiran Asa Natali Ignata Kiran*— "These be the words."

Sam repeated the names in his head, for the reckoning.

The kitchen was silent, and Fletcher let his hand drop. "I don't know if they listen," he said softly. "Or if they even exist."

Sam's eyes fell to the five cups on the counter. "I don't think that's really the point."

They were quiet for a long moment.

"Can I ask you something?" Fletcher paused, hazel eyes tentatively probing. "Teddy...after the fit," he asked hesitantly, arms folded across his body, moving in tight little palpitations back and forth, "he kept saying something about Tessa. Who is she?"

"Tessa," Sam sighed, rubbing the roped muscles strung tight on the back of his neck, "was his little sister. She was six, he was seven, and she fell." *She was six, he was seven, and she was pushed.* "Hit her head on the corner of the dining table. It was a long shot, taking her to see a physician, but they did. An hour in the cold—skull cracked—and she made it into town. Even still, it wasn't a hopeful prognosis, but the physician was willing to work on her, and with time, money, maybe..." He trailed off, shaking his head. "They couldn't even buy her back off the examination table. I don't know how familiar you are with the nuances of our little district, but the Guild has a price for everything. She was kept as collateral."

"What happened to her," Fletcher edged, too much false hope in his eyes. "She didn't..."

"A death certificate was delivered to their door the next day, and a notice to which public grave plot she'd been buried in." Sam returned to the tea, the rich reddish-brown brew long oversteeped. "Teddy blames himself. He's got a talent for healing, as you've obviously seen. And he's got a singularly kind heart, of which I believe Tessa still holds the most of. I do not believe a day goes by when he does not miss her more badly than any of us can imagine."

"He—he was a kid, there was nothing he could've done..."

Sam tossed the steaming leaves into the bin, the basket clattering against the sink. "Guilt doesn't discriminate, Fletcher. We're all victims. And now his parents..."

An uncomfortably familiar rap of *rat tat-tat-tat* against the front door interrupted Sam, making him start.

The clawing of a caracara.

A chill swept down his spine, unpleasant and cold.

Impossible.

It was impossible, that he'd come here.

But here, he'd come.

Clark Carson was waiting at the threshold as Sam pulled the door open, knuckles white against the brass handle as he tried to hide the shaking.

"My deepest condolences," Clark said, voice dark as he pushed past Sam, not bothering to wait for an invitation. "I came the moment I heard, naturally—our young friend, she remains intact?"

"El's fine," Sam muttered warily, glancing down the hallway.

Clark's sigh of relief was palpable as he ran a finger across the rim of his top hat before tipping it off, eyes skirting the room. His gaze landed on the sketch set on a bookcase shelf, framed beneath silver and glass.

It'd been from ages ago. Sam had sketched it, a portrait of he and Teddy laughing together, arms around each other's waists, testing the waters of romance—and a new set of coloring pencils. Teddy had paused on that page of the sketch book as they'd flipped through it together, curled on the sofa and armed with wine and conversation. He'd loved it, he said, the moment he saw it. *Like I loved you.*

When Clark's eyes flicked back to Sam's, they were full of fury. "I'm waiting."

"For what?"

"You know what for," Clark snapped, glaring. "You cannot possibly believe that last night was a coincidence." In the wake of his voice, the apartment had gone eerily still.

They were listening.

"What was in them," Sam asked softly.

"Pardon?"

"What was in the letters," he echoed again, voice nothing more than a whisper, "that would've saved her?"

A little game he'd been playing since they'd seen the rubble. *What, oh what, would those letters have done.* Not a damn thing.

"I will not indulge your rhetorical lines of questioning. Hypotheticals are the refuge of the weak—"

"Nothing," Sam breathed, cutting him off. "There was nothing. Do you know why, Clark? Because she wasn't even supposed to be there, last night—"

"I am protecting her best interests."

"The way you protected mine?"

"Yes, as it so happens—"

"No," Sam hissed, "no, you are *not* a hero. You do not get to come into my home, our home, trumpeting your own moral high ground. *You're* the one that gave her that damnable locket. You might as well have put a target on her back, if any of what you've said is true—"

Clark's beady eyes were narrowed, fists clenched in anger so finely veiled as he walked the streets, so expertly tucked away as he laughed and drank and smoked away his nights, so impossible to deny when his little flocks flew away, and all that remained was the two of them.

It was the same look, carved now across his face, that he'd borne, finding Sam and Mattie in the garden.

Disgust, that Sam thought he might belong to another.

And beyond that, lethal envy.

"It was her birthright. She is of age, now, and though others may be too paralyzed to act, I am not—"

"You are a degenerate thug," Sam growled, crossing his arms tightly across his chest. "You are not welcome here. I bought your line once, Clark, when I thought you could've really done something for her. It's time to move on."

"You have overstepped for the last time—"

"I have kept your secrets, Clark. But I have no qualms divulging if you don't leave her alone—"

"You—oh, this is precious. Are you trying to blackmail me?"

"If that is what it takes to discredit you, to get them to see you for who you are, *to keep her out of your way,* then so be it." Sam's chest was tight, his words breathless as they cut the air.

"And what then," Clark asked softly, his voice sinking to a deadly timbre. His eyes were burning, something salacious bored deep into those dark pits as he took a step towards Sam. "What will they say, when you tell them you sought comfort in the arms of your mentor? That, in the throes of adolescence, in a world unfamiliar, I simply helped *guide* you into manhood? You know such accusations cannot stand."

"I—You overestimate your position—"

"Our fellow merchants will side with their Commissioner," he pressed, a vindictive smile starting to curl at the corners of his mouth. "And as for everyone else...well. It isn't me, they'll be calling a degenerate."

"They will see you for who you are—"

"Then they will see a powerful man, who does not cow to the baseless threats of lesser men!"

"You cannot—"

"I can!" Clark was glaring again, knuckles white as he gripped the rim of his hat. "Do as you wish, Sam. Spread your vicious rumors. Cling to your morality, *love,* and tell me of its steadfastness in your waking hours, when it is all that remains of the life you wanted! And I promise you, it is all that will remain." Words still hanging in the air, he turned on his heel for the door.

"You can't," Sam echoed, voice soft. A whispered cry.

He would not be defeated. He would not bow to these threats. Not again. Not when it had cost so much already.

"You," Clark snapped, shooting a foul look over his shoulder, "are an impertinent fool! I am the master of this Valley. I do as I please!"

Sam swallowed hard, eyes stinging as he pressed a shaking fist to his lips, trying to steady himself.

The master of the Valley.

FLETCHER

"Never doubt your instincts. They're why we've survived this long, and they're going to be what gets you through."

~Adrian Lynch

Loyalty before amity.

Maybe they weren't such different things, in the end.

He saw his reflection in the kitchen window in the split second before he moved.

The soft, two-button tunic, like the kind that Teddy liked, cotton and casual. The furrowed brows over his mother's eyes. He might've passed for a human, if they hadn't bothered to look for the tipped ears poking through his messy, dark blonde hair.

He could remember the first time he'd made an arrest. It had been two years ago, and he'd been in a freshly-pressed cadet's uniform, boots still shining, fresh from the box.

His striped socks would have to do, this time.

"Commissioner Carson." Fletcher stepped across the threshold of the kitchen, crossing the dining room in a few quick paces. Magic was flaring in his wrists as he sent an unseen wall between Clark and the door, the Commissioner's hand hitting solid air as he moved for the handle.

Another flick of his hand, and the Commissioner was walled in completely.

Clark's fist hit the shield in frustration, teeth baring. "What—"

"You've as good as admitted to killing those pastries," Fletcher cut in, and he found his shoulders thrown back a little more, found an invisible string pulling him up a little taller. "The charges against you are as follows: the illegal operation of a production ring, resulting in the deaths of nine known persons, the interaction and employment of persons of known dangerous magics, the assault of an officer of Caelaymnic law with such persons, the attempt of bodily harm against the royal family of Caelaymnis, and..." He glanced back to Elsie, lingering at the back of the hallway. To Sam, eyes glistening, arms held tight to his chest. Then back to Clark. "And the knowing and willful assault of a human within the sequestered borders known as Aerdela." A charge—willful assault of a human—that was intended to protect the humans from any rogue Drada who sought to exact vengeance against humans, never mind that the folks living in the bounds of Aerdela had no part, or even awareness, of what their Woodshade cousins did. But there was no reason it couldn't be used to protect the humans from themselves, too.

"On whose authority," Clark snarled, his chest heaving. His hands were pressed against the shield, like it might give way, his breaths panicked and fast.

Someone didn't like enclosed spaces.

"On the authority of the Senate, Council, and Crown of the Dradan Territory of Caelaymnis."

Clark had burrowed into his breast-pocket, slamming a slip of paper against the wall, shimmering faintly as the sun edged toward the entryway where he stood, trapped. "Release me."

"You confessed."

"Curious, what those letters might've said," Clark snapped instead, eyes flicking to Sam. "You are a fool, boy! You are meddling in things you know nothing of—"

But Fletcher's eyes were flying across the sprawling script curled across the parchment beneath his hand. *Under the provisional charter, Chancellor Margaret Faulise hereby grants political immunity to the friend and ally of the Hidden City, Commissioner Clark Carson, bringing him for all intents and purposes beneath the govern of justice that reigns within the City—*

"Chancellor Faulise is no longer in power," Fletcher muttered, scanning the rest of the letter, "this is void, under new leadership..."

"It is *not*. I assure you that Regent Chancellor Vaupellum has ratified the ruling, now release me!"

Fletcher turned, finding Elsie's gaze from deep within the hall. "I'll be back," he said softly. "I promise."

And snapping down the walls of the shield, he grabbed the Commissioner's arm, and the world dissolved into a swirl of lights.

~ • ~

"You *arrested* the Commissioner!" Augustus slammed his hands on the desk, the legs whining against the floor as the whole thing went askew. "What is *wrong* with you, Fletcher? This is an embarrassment! Father is meeting with the Chancellor, trying to smooth over your diplomatic fumbling—"

"It wasn't fumbling," Fletcher muttered, not meeting his brother's gaze.

The general's office was stark, minimal and gray, just like the rest of the compound. A fireplace, the massive desk, littered with neat stacks of parchment, each little thing in its place—until he'd nearly shoved it across the room in his fury.

A pen was rolling slowly across the wood, clicking and clacking until it rolled right off the edge, hitting the floor with a satisfying *ki-tak clack-clack.*

"It wasn't fumbling," Augustus echoed, growling the words through gritted teeth. "Are you not *listening* to what I've just said—"

"He as good as confessed."

"No, he damn well didn't! You were so desperate to make an arrest, you would've arrested your own lover, if she'd said the same!"

"He said he was the master—"

"It is a *common Vernacular phrase,* Fletcher! He is the master of the Valley—he runs the gods-damned place! Hell, he runs all of Aerdela! You stuck your nose into your little family spat, and you've made a grand little diplomatic incident for all of us!" Augustus scoffed, kicking his chair as he straightened. "I've let him go."

"You can't—"

"I have let him go," Augustus snarled, glaring. His angry breaths swallowed up the words as he paused, eyes unblinking on Fletcher's. And when he spoke again, his voice was deathly quiet. "You haven't made an arrest in nearly a year."

"No. Sir," he added, not wishing to test the limits anymore.

Augustus slid a piece of paper from the now-collapsing stack, eyes falling to the swirls across the page. "Your arrest record before today was unblemished. A flawless conviction rate."

"Yes, sir."

His eyes flicked up, pale and flashing. "You were sure about this. Why."

"I...don't have a reason," Fletcher mumbled, stuffing his hands in his pockets, eying the floor. "It was a hunch."

"A hunch. What's that?"

The Vernacular word had slipped through his lips without a second thought, and he felt his face heating. "A guess. A feeling in your heart, so strong, you can't fight it." Love was kind of like a hunch, now that he thought about it. Maybe lots of things were hunches. Hunger. Exhaustion. Happiness. Relief.

Augustus blew out a breath, eyes flicking about the room. "I don't have a choice in releasing him," he said, after a long moment. "He *does* have diplomatic immunity, and his Advocate has been quite clear that it is not within our authority to proceed with indictment. *However.*" He paused. "If you are able to dredge something up, any shred of physical evidence he's actually running a production ring, I will be right there with you as you bring him in."

He glanced up, hardly believing the words. "You're serious? The— the censures, and—"

"Fletcher, you disobeyed a direct order and disappeared to a human settlement for six months. I believe in this cause, but what else was I supposed to do?" Augustus shrugged, tossing the arrest record aside. "His release is only going to bolster his confidence. The Commissioner believes he can hide behind Vaupellum's edict, and as far as he's aware, our government has no interest in pursuing this further. Father is busy plying him with apologies as we speak. But even still, you don't have much time." His eyes flicked to Fletcher's. "You need anything," he said softly, "anything at all—you tell me. Our resources are yours."

ELSIE

"Nobody ever asks the wolf why he wore the sheep's skin—they just assume it's because he was a greedy bastard looking for a cheap shot at dinner. Maybe he was just doing the best he knew how with the tools he was given. And at the end of the day, isn't that all any of us are trying to do?"

~C.H. Williams, 'Memoirs'

Verbose silence filled the apartment as Elsie watched Fletcher and Clark vanish.

Her eyes were damp, the cold bleeding through her sweater as she leaned against the hallway wall, just beyond sight.

The draft was a relief against her burning cheeks, and she stole the quiet, blinking back tears. Then, pushing herself off the wall, she met the living room.

"Sam?"

His head snapped over, dark eyes wide under furrowed brows.

"Elsie."

Her name seemed to eviscerate him.

Gutted. Right there, on the carpet, for all to see.

Another handful of ripped-out pages.

It sort of felt like walking out of the debtors cells, finding him there.

If that's what it takes to keep her out of your way.

"Sam," she echoed again, reaching a tentative hand brushing against his arm, "are...are you okay?"

Maybe that's what it'd taken.

Maybe she'd needed to see it with her own eyes. Witness him, standing an impossible line.

He didn't say anything as he met her gaze, brown eyes watery. He only shook his head, jaw clenched tight.

It was a bitter-sweet hug, the one she found after that.

One she didn't want to have to give.

One, though, she was glad she did.

~ • ~

The morning waned into early afternoon, and it was odd, finding a truce with Sam.

Teddy was sleeping comfortably, Isa said, though Elsie and Sam couldn't verify this first-hand, as they'd both been banned from the bedroom. Elsie had been left to her corner of the sofa, her tired body trying to draw in as much of the heat from the half-hearted fire as she could.

"Here." Sam's low voice interrupted her thoughts, and she glanced up to see him offering a steaming cup of tea. "It's a bit strong, if that's alright."

Warmth soaking into her fingertips, a wash of heat met her lips, the familiar cinnamon of distilled brandy burning her tongue. Her eyes flicked to his as he sank down beside her, nursing a cup of his own. "Thanks," she whispered, watching the tiny smile tug on his lips at the word.

238

There's a sick kind of solace, finding someone hurting worse than you.

Like pain could be freedom.

At least, that's what they'd been told.

When did you age, Sam Alderton? It was yesterday, and you were fifteen.

It'd been so easy, starting to cut him out.

Except that it wasn't, not really, not when it came down to it, the action itself of carving him out of her heart.

That was what people like Clark did, with their spun words, though. They wanted her to cut out all the good. They acted like right and wrong were indisputable facts, as if there were the winners and the losers, except there were no winners here, only good kids in bad situations trying to prove they were worth something more than spit on the sidewalk.

There was no right, there was no wrong, there was only the surviving.

The making of it all to the next day on the thought that if they could get through this next challenge, it'd all get better.

The willing surrender of self and others, in the hope that maybe this time, it wouldn't be that bad.

"I think about the first one a lot," she said softly, giving him a nudge with her elbow. "The first letter. What happened, with the, uh, the mercenaries, and the roll, and everything. I don't think we ever...we never really talked about it. Afterwards."

"Wasn't much to say," he murmured, taking a sip of tea.

"He told you I was there."

"It...was after dinner, and he pulled me into the carriage house. Didn't say a word. Just handed me your intake form and tossed me a velvet money bag. And when I got back, he told me he needed someone to keep an eye on you. That your life was on the line." He sighed, closing his eyes. "Elsie, I am so sorry—"

"I'm still mad at you."

He opened his eyes once more, shards of cinnamon sugar, tired and dull. "As you have every right to be. But I hope that doesn't preclude our friendship."

She gave him a side-long glance. "I suppose it doesn't," she said hesitantly. "And...you didn't want me dead, so that's a point in your favor, I guess."

Sam gave a quiet laugh, and she felt a reluctant smile lurking on her lips as she eyed him with mock wariness.

"He told me I should've been suspicious," Elsie went on, drawing the throw a little closer. "A merchant's heir shouldn't have wanted to befriend me. But that...wasn't quite right. It didn't sound like he knew about the bookstore. And you—you're not an heir. You're a bastard. Just like me. I don't know what he was planning, or what he told you, but it—it seemed like even then, you sort of knew you weren't going to inherit his empire. He wouldn't have let you, not when he treated you like you were disposable."

"I'm not," Sam said softly. "Like you, I mean."

She only shrugged.

She felt his arm against hers, a soft nudge where words failed.

"About Teddy," she went on, a moment later. "I...I'm not ready, Sam. I'm not ready to lose him."

"He'll be alright," Sam nodded quietly, "you heard Isa—"

"That's not what I mean. I'm not ready for him to stop being my brother. A-and I'm not ready for him and you to—to...I didn't tell him," she stumbled, eyes stinging. "You know I didn't tell him what you did, and I know you didn't tell him what you heard, and maybe...maybe he has a right to know, but I'm not ready. That life, that—that city, I'm not ready, Sam, I can't do it, I don't—who am I, even? More than a name, a family, a city, I haven't even—haven't even—" She broke off, at a loss.

Haven't even lived.

"It was a sweet thought," she whispered, after a moment. "The things he told me."

There was a barrage of words waiting on her tongue, a barrage that didn't come.

"It..." Sam dropped his voice, leaning in, his breath warm against her ear, his words hardly audible. "That place is still rightfully yours." There was defiance in his voice, challenging her submission.

Maybe it was hers. Maybe not.

It depended on what Clark had stood to gain by telling her the truth.

Or by feeding her those delicious lies.

She leaned her head back, wishing Isa hadn't banished them from keeping vigil. "Sam?"

"Hmm?"

"I need to tell you something."

"Oh?" His voice dipped up with soft intrigue.

"I...took something." Sitting up, she tugged her satchel into her lap from where it'd been heaped carelessly on the floor.

"I hate to break this to you," he warned, watching her warily, "but I believe my sway with the Commissioner's mercenaries may be waning..."

Snickering, she shook her head, pulling the bundled scarf from her bag, tossing it into his lap. "Just open it."

An indelible smile was tugging at his lips as he unearthed the dessert plate, holding it up to the light.

"And it came with chocolate cake, too," she grinned, heart starting to lighten.

"Brilliant," he whispered, running a finger around the gold rim, a bright smile dancing across his face. His gaze flicked to hers, sparking in the sun, a sun that didn't seem quite so treacherous reflected in his eyes. "I missed you, El. Thievery and all."

TEDDY

Teddy blinked back the haze of dreamless sleep to find the bedroom bathed in uncertain light, neither dawn nor dusk.

His body was stiff, like he'd lain unmoving for hours, and his joints were reluctant as he stretched, trying to shake the cloud from his groggy thoughts.

The room was quiet.

He was alone.

Alone, save for the tired Thread, curled dormant in exhaustion deep inside.

His muscles ached as he rolled out of bed, burning with fatigue.

The Thread stirred—not in the fury it'd known, though, pent up and angry.

It moved in apology and regret.

He put a hand on his chest, like he'd be able to feel the Thread, hot and sleepy, buried somewhere beneath his heart.

It was tempting, to crawl back beneath the blankets, to let sleep take him again.

A disgruntled growl from his stomach, though, demanded a meal—and gods knew how long he'd been out for. For all he knew, he'd slept away days.

Even so, he paused in the doorway to the hall, not relishing what fresh hell he'd find those three to have released in his absence.

But it was quiet voices, Elsie and Sam's, that met him.

"...I dunno, it's not a small task, bringing him in," Sam was speculating, legs tucked beneath him as he sat beside Elsie, one throw tossed over the both of them.

"He's been gone nearly six hours, how long does it take to toss someone in...hey!" Elsie's eyes flicked past Sam, a bright smile lighting up her face as she threw back the blanket, rising to meet him. "How're you feeling?"

"Er, fine," Teddy mumbled, ruffling his hair, watching them both. "And...you both seem..."

Sam gave a small nod, an easy smile on his lips. "Better."

Collapsing into the armchair, taking the cup of tea Elsie pressed into his hands, he loosed a breath, fighting off the disorientation, not aided by the lingering light-headedness. "What time is it?"

"Nearly six," Sam offered.

"In the morning?"

"In the evening."

"What day is it?"

"The same day as it was when you dozed off. You've been out most of the day, but it's still Thursday."

"Isa?"

"Left," Elsie chimed in. "A few hours ago. Said you needed some rest, but you're gonna be fine."

"Fletcher?"

"In Caelaymnis with Clark."

"I'm sorry, *what?*" Teddy was glaring at his sister, certain he'd misheard.

"It's true," Sam said quietly. "Clark came by, because of the fire, and—well, things got heated. He as good as confessed to running the ring, so Fletcher arrested him."

Leaning back into the armchair, Teddy shook his head, a hint of a smile tugging at his lips all the same. "Gods. Sick for one afternoon, and I miss out on all the fun."

"Believe me," Elsie muttered, falling back down beside Sam, "it's more fun on this side of it."

Sam raised his teacup. "Here, here. I'll drink to that."

"Arrested." His limbs felt heavy, disinclined to do more than sit limply as he turned the word over on his tongue. "That's—I mean, that's incredible—"

"No. It isn't."

Fletcher's voice was sharp from behind them.

Lingering in the doorway, a few stray motes still fizzling out from where he'd evanesced onto the mat, Fletcher was dressed in a sharp gray uniform, an almost startling contrast to his typical attire. Boots polished, silver buttons gleaming from hip to shoulder, a black cloak had been pinned at the epaulets, tipped ears skirting a thin silver circlet hidden in his hair.

"Fletch—"

"He was detained," Fletcher muttered, snapping off the cloak and tossing it haphazardly on the floor, the circlet following, "for all of twenty minutes, before my father was kissing his gods-damned boots, apologizing for the misunderstanding."

A look of painful disbelief washed across Sam's face. "He's not—"

"Back home, safe and sound at Carson Manor."

244

FLETCHER

"Hold close. Don't let go. Not now, not ever, do you understand?"

~from 'The Advice of The Long-Dead' and Other Essays

Da-dum. Da-dum. Da-dum.

Elsie was staring at him from the opposite end of the sofa, and Fletcher loosed a breath, pressing his eyes closed as he took in her sounds.

The quiet rush of air in her lungs, meted out in slow, deliberate inhalations, an echo of forced calm.

The dull pitch of the slender gold chain against her neck, her mother's locket buried beneath the knit gray sweater.

The whine of her fingers in her pitch-black hair, twirling the braid with idle frustration.

The *swish* of cotton-on-leather as she tucked a leg beneath her, pulling the other knee close to her chest—her favorite way to sit when there was pouting to be done.

When he opened his eyes again, there was a bit of clarity to the screaming world.

The apartment door opened, Sam returning. *Going to have a smoke,* he'd mumbled, distant, and he'd been gone for the better part of an hour.

"You're back," Teddy edged, piercing blue eyes fixed on Sam and only Sam. His body was tense, locked between the impetus to rise and the desire to stay where he had settled beside his sister.

Sam's necktie was hanging limply over his shoulder, the top buttons of his tunic already undone as he tossed the suitcoat on the dining table. "I'm back," he muttered, turning for the kitchen. The acrid smell of tobacco followed him, soaked into his person, and Fletcher had listened to the crackling drag of cigarettes from the street below for three quarters of an hour.

After news of Clark's release, though, it seemed there had been little else for Sam to do but try and steady his shaking hands with cigarette after cigarette.

Sam reappeared from the kitchen a moment later, a frosted bottle of reluctant topaz liquid tucked in the crook of his elbow, four crystalline cups in hand.

"Good idea," Elsie said darkly as she stole a glare at Fletcher.

And to his surprise, she held his gaze, her green eyes storming.

Sluggish dollops of the chilled liquor were being doled out over the sound of quiet explanation, and he was lost, lost in a forest of green and emerald mines and rolling plains of spring and splatters of paint on a gallery canvas, where words were just sounds and it took every ounce of his being, every fiber of strength, just to stay there in the beyond of her stare.

Her lips were moving the shape of his name, the sound of her irritated voice rolling across the air in rhythmic hesitation.

"Sorry," he managed at last, ripping his eyes from hers to find the world as he'd left it.

He'd have drowned in those eyes, though, if time were no matter.

246

Sam passed him a cool glass of whiskey, the condensation catching sweetly on Fletcher's fingertips as he murmured quiet thanks.

Teddy watched tentatively, curled beneath the blanket. He'd been dozing, on and off, waiting for Sam—but not before a few choice words.

I love you both, he'd sighed, eyes distant. *But this is such bullshit. Either get out of here and have it out with each other, once and for all, or just—just move on.*

Elsie had straightened, glaring. *But—*

Take it somewhere else, or let it go. I can't deal with this right now, though. I just...can't.

It'd felt wrong, after that, to linger, so Fletcher had retreated back to the kitchen, idly letting the magic curl into his fingertips.

The cooling pot of tea on the counter had proved an alluring distraction from the mourning siblings, sharing their grief.

He had closed his eyes, feeling the room.

His hands met the air, weaving together the thin strands of magic, letting it blossom out, a sigh of relief as it encircled the chocolate-brown pot.

Now, the fun could begin.

With practiced hands, he coaxed a column of air within the shell, hugging it close to the tea pot between the secondary membranes of magic. The trick wasn't the column that clung near the pot, though, drawing tighter and tighter as he compressed it down, building a shield around the porcelain, not unlike the one that'd held the Commissioner. It was tricky, yes, watching the curves and bends, elsewise the pot was liable to shatter, but the real trick to it was the easy weave holding a wide berth around the whole thing.

It didn't much matter how much heat he'd make, if the insulation didn't work.

There'd been a smile on his lips as he'd drawn the column of air tighter, tighter, tighter, until with a wash of mist, he'd evanesced it gone, a faint draft of chilled air lurking over his shoulder where he'd dissolved the column.

And when steam began curling from the spout, he'd turned the whole thing around, setting to cooling it once more.

Needless to say, it'd been a credit to Elsie's patience, finding a solid block of ice inside the kettle when she'd come, at last, to fetch a cup. Still, though, they'd been feigning peace well enough, not really exchanging any words, per say, but finding an amiable patter, nevertheless.

Not really caring for another visit to Caelaymnis—one had been sufficient, for that day—he'd shed his uniform in favor of Teddy's borrowed clothes. The gray coat and polished boots had been donned hastily, and at Augustus's snapping—*you look like a gods-damned human, Fletcher, put some clothes on*—and it'd been a good call, seeing as he'd been dragged before their father and dressed down before the Council.

It'd been an unintentional mercy, leaving the specifics of his punishment to Augustus.

The cracking of firewood overtook him, a snap of sap sending a spray of sparks pinging into the grate, and Fletcher was snapped from his thoughts back to the present.

"To the best laid plans," Elsie murmured, eyes lingering on the amber contents of her crystalline glass.

"To the love of family when they fail," Teddy added softly, putting his arm around her, drawing her close.

"To friends that stand the line," Sam nodded to Fletcher.

Their eyes were on him, and Elsie was watching him expectantly, eyebrow raised.

"To..." But there were only the words of his people drifting through his mind. *"Apoticaeum defuespes,"* he mumbled, face flushing.

A half-smile was lurking on Elsie's lips as she found his gaze again.

"That's lovely," she whispered, cocking her head to the side. "What does it mean?"

"To failed poetic expectations."

The room was filled with laughter as they raised their glasses, and he watched her take a sip of whiskey.

July had clung to Elsie, sticky and hot, and the *sh-flick* of her turning pages rolled like thunder through the clouds blossoming over a distant mountain home. It had been a hopeless refuge, the wrought-iron bench by the gurgling fountain. Hot wind had kissed the sweat-curled hair pulled back into a messy bun, ringing like wind-chimes, and her peach cotton dress, he remembered, had matched the baked earth beneath them.

He hadn't known her name, then.

Hadn't known anything, except that something was happening between them, something he did not quite understand, something terrifying and dangerous and exhilarating and electrifying, something that made him almost shake with undiluted happiness.

She told him later he'd been staring.

That was why she'd looked up.

Staring as he'd walked down the shaded path, winding his way back through the park, the vision of a bloodied corpse stained across his eyes, and she had been *so fucking alive,* with the perpetual *da-dum, da-dum, da-dum* that had called him through the streets, the resounding cry of *I am here, I am alive, and you have to listen* getting him drunk on summer love.

He walked by her twenty-three times.

Twenty-three days watching her eyes flick up from her book as she slayed those hot afternoons away, hiding from a world that didn't want her.

Twenty-three days, and it was about to be twenty-four, except that day, she didn't have a book, because she was waiting for him, one arm resting lazily on the back of the iron bench, her legs crossed beneath that white summer dress, embroidered with the smell of grass and sweat, and maybe he'd have kept walking, but his feet knew better than to leave her, and somehow, he'd been sitting next to her, asking if she'd finished her book, if that was why she had arrived empty-handed, and she'd laughed quietly, brushing a strand of hair behind her ear, saying no, no that wasn't why she wasn't reading right now, she was just curious, curious about the boy that took the time to smile, and *I'm Elsie, by the way, Elsie Mirabeau,* and that was when he loved her.

In July.

On the bench by the fountain.

ELSIE

*"May your soul know peace, may your heart be at rest,
and may you finally know tranquility in the sweet arms
of Death."*

~*Dradan Funeral Prayer*

One look. One gods-damned look from that insufferable elf, coupled with the booze, and Elsie had to excuse herself.

The cold water bit her cheeks, her breath catching in her throat as the bathing room tap gushed proto-ice into her still-cupped hands.

Another splash across her tired face, and the faucet squealed to a halt as Elsie yanked the fluffed hand-towel from the rod, burying her face into the soft fibers.

The overindulgent scent of lavender and lemon tickled her nose. It made her vaguely drowsy, a recall of nights stolen away in Sam's apartment, of nights *safe, safe, safe.*

Fucking Clark.

Eyes flitting across the accoutrements scattered on the countertop, she sighed.

Of course, Clark had stuck his greedy little fingers into dark magics. He'd wrung the Valley empty, sucked every last copper from the drying teat, and of course it wouldn't have been enough.

Of course, he'd have walked free.

A soft tap on the half-open door interrupted her thoughts.

"What," she muttered, tossing the now-crumpled hand towel towards the hamper, not bothering to see who'd come calling.

"Can we talk?"

"Fine." She folded her arms tightly across her body, waiting.

Fletcher exhaled deeply, the door closing with a soft click as he leaned back against it. The pale teal tunic pushed his eyes to the border of blue, a storming sea, the ship-wrecked flecks of brown all that was left of what they'd been before.

Human.

And he was all but, standing there before her.

Even with her hands balled to angry fists, crammed against her ribs, she was acutely aware of the empty space between her fingers. The space she wanted his to be.

"I'm sorry," he said quietly, his voice little more than a whisper humming off the tiles.

"For what," she growled.

His eyes flicked to hers. "Do you really think I came in here to deliver half-apologies? For *lying,* Elsie. I'm sorry I lied."

"You admit it, then."

"Yes. I—it was pointed out to me," he went on hesitantly, "that while I thought I wasn't...culpable, because I hadn't said the words—hadn't expressly claimed to be one of your people—but given the circumstances, it was advantageous for me to appear human, and...and such a deception is lying by omission."

Elsie could hear her brother in his words, Teddy's phrases twirling and turning as Fletcher strung them together.

"Look. I wish I could say I would do it better, if I could do it again.

But honestly, Elsie, I have no idea what the right answer is. How do you walk up to someone you want to love and bare your soul?" His voice was drenched in desperation, an actor without lines trembling before the crowd, terrified of forgetting the obsolete little play-act drama of their life to the maddening night.

Her fingernails relented their excavation of her palms, daggers drawn for a fight.

She'd brought knives to a negotiation.

"You…" The word hung between them, and he was waiting for an answer that would never come.

She let her arms fall.

"I don't know," she said softly, and the ten-by-ten was a mausoleum of surrender-white tile.

But there were no mourners.

Only the dead-on-their-feet, looking for some rest.

Her reluctant fingers found his, warm and sweet, a reflection of a smile on his lips, and he pulled her into him as he leaned against the door. She let herself melt, his hands on her hips, and she buried her face in the crook of his soft neck, letting her arms rest cradled between their thudding heartbeats, pulsing into her skin.

"I love you," he murmured, and his breath was warm, his lips brushing across the rounded tip of her ear, sending a cascade of pleasant shivers down her spine.

Her guard was down, the sentries were gone, the gates were open and this, this was what it was like, to be buried alive.

They'd taken the underworld for themselves, for their damnable sinner souls, fuck the godful, left up above, with their piety and suffering, because death was life, life was death, magic was ordinary, the ordinary was magic, and the whole gods-damned world was upside down in Sam's bathing room.

His skin was a whisper of salt on her sweet kisses, the finest confection. "Love you, too," she whispered, so soft she couldn't even hear the words, but he did, he heard them, because he gave a small inhalation, drawing her closer, like he'd hold her, and her words, until the bitter end.

She wanted to gorge on those salt-caramel kisses.

Her fingers had found the collar of his tunic, had gripped the stiff cotton tight until it gave beneath her hold, a starchy, crinkled mess. "Do you know," she asked breathlessly in between the barrage, "what it is I want most, right now, in this very moment?"

"No." His voice was low, hushed with reverential longing. He'd found her waistline beneath the sweater, fingers drifting against the bare skin, and she gave way, leaning in, the softest sound of *more, more, more* on his lips.

To draw him beneath the sheets.

To yield the mausoleum, to forsake the ice, and simply be, as they had been, before.

In the sweet, human months of summer. In the wide-eyed seven days of autumn.

One brilliant winter night.

To unravel.

To remake.

Now, though, fatigue was pressing heavy on her shoulders, her eyes burning with wakefulness known for too long.

A coy smile was tugging at the corners of her mouth as she moved to meet his eye-line. "What I want, Fletcher, more than anything in the world, is some gods-damned *sleep.*"

Bright laughter dissolved them, and she caught a glance of them in the mirror, red-faced and giggling.

The sound had shattered the mausoleum.

SAM

Elsie had excused herself, Fletcher following, and Sam had the utmost confidence they had gone to quietly bicker until Fletcher had left, laughing, and Elsie gathered her things, making to follow.

The timepiece on the mantle boasted a quarter past two in the morning, and Teddy had drawn his sister into a long hug, bidding her good night before padding off to bed.

"El, wait." Sam gave her a wave to hold on as he went to rifle through the writing desk.

I am a good man.

I am a good man.

I am a good man.

But, Sam thought, good men didn't betray the people they loved.

It wasn't a betrayal. It couldn't be. Because Sam Alderton wouldn't do that. He was a good man.

Sam Carson might, though.

Sam Carson had been persuaded into doing a lot of things that Sam Alderton wouldn't do. Had kept a lot of secrets Sam Alderton would have refused to.

He turned the thick envelope over once, and then, lips pursed, handed it over. "It belongs to you," he said softly, watching Elsie split the seal. "I had no right to it."

Over six months of letters to Clark, gathered and held in the breast pocket of his coats day in and day out as he'd dared himself to turn them over, failing each time.

The letters he would've delivered to Clark, if he hadn't overheard them both in the carriage house.

If he hadn't realized he, too, had been betrayed.

Her brow knit as she skimmed the pages, expression unreadable.

"I did take the liberty of adding something at the end. Something I found notable."

She turned to the last page, a soft *oh* on her lips as her shoulders sank down. "She is fierce," Elsie read, hardly audible over the crackling fire, "fierce, and unapologetic. These are enviable traits, for they mean she does not compromise. She does not allow her moral integrity to be twisted, the way mine has, nor does she accept anything less than the respect she deserves. It is…" Her voice broke, and she shook her head, swallowing. "It is my duty," she went on, eyes watering, "to fight for her. For all of them. For their right to trust, and for their right to be loved, without fear, and without pain."

They were victims.

All of them.

Tendrils of fire licked the logs with succulent tongues, and Sam sent a silent prayer to the heavens.

To Cora and Lucia and Stell and Hadri and Asa and Natali and Ignata and Kiran.

Let us both survive this love.

And gods, did Sam love her.

Not romantically. Never romantically, in spite of Clark's intentions.

He'd indulged the thought, when he'd been young and stupid, and even then, it'd been absurd.

It could protect her, he could recall thinking, *having my wedding band.* And yet, it was the pastries that had fallen first. How naive, he'd been. Ready to condemn them both in the name of righteousness.

But nevertheless, he loved her fiercely. And it had been love at first sight, no matter what the critics said.

Such a tired trope, misused by the arrogant poet, misunderstood by the dimwitted reader.

And still, Sam had loved Elsie from the moment they'd met. Quick, wise beyond her years, she'd been unabashedly kind, the sort of kindness that took courage beyond reckoning.

"Oh, Sam." She pulled him into a hug, the pages still clutched in her hand.

"I meant it," he whispered, holding her tight. "I will fight for you, El. You're not alone."

CHIM

*"The best games we play are the ones we know not, for
when given the rules, it is in our nature to break them."*

~Dryadic Proverb, from the Book of Adagic Texts

Elsie had been saved, Teddy had been warned, and the hunt was now afoot for the arsonists who set the farmhouse alight.

They called themselves Factionists, which Chim thought was very funny, because mortals loved to name themselves things that sounded important.

A fine game of chase, this made.

The point of chase, Chim often had to remind her fellow kobalde, was not to win a prize, like it was with swapsies or hide-and-seek. The point was to capture.

Elsie had not been good at chase. She'd been captured by Chim almost immediately.

The Factionists were not very good at chase, either. They were no-good rumor-mongers, and as such were very loud.

Their screams were very loud too, when Chim got them.

A three-course meal, fit for a vengeful demon girl. Silly men, all of them, and they tasted of smoke and incompetence.

But they had some interesting things to say, before they'd been gotten entirely. They said that Elsie was the heiress of Death, and that was a curious thing, for they hadn't been the only ones circulating rumors of such things.

The Faulise family had long claimed ties to Cora, God of Death, and if they were true, it meant that they were allied with the other gods of the Below, and that included Chaos.

And Chaos meant Chim.

AUGUSTUS

"Peace. Only a moment, and even then, it was fleeting.
But it was peace, all the same."

~Elizabeth Clement Faulise

The hot water of the barracks showers pummeled the aching muscles screaming in his neck, his back, his hips, and Augustus closed his eyes, letting the steaming barrage douse his sweat-soaked hair as he worked the soap with his tired fingers.

It was empty, this time of night, as a rule.

Empty, save for the soft drag of leather-soled boots against the damp floor.

A smile was curling on his lips as he pushed his doused hair back, blinking the water from his eyes. He knew that soft-footed swagger.

"I'm back," Isa grinned, fingers making deft work of the slanted buttons across their coat. "Your future sister is absolutely charming, by the way."

"She won't be my sister," he mused idly, "not if I can help it." Rubbing his shoulder, he drank in Isa, lingering by the bench a few paces from the open stall.

Exquisite.

"Don't think there's much to be done, lover." Isa pulled the boots off, tossing them aside before letting the gray trousers fall easily down. "The heart wants what it wants."

And what his brother's wanted, it seemed, was that human girl amidst their ranks. Not completely useless, Augustus supposed. Maybe, in a world where the peace with the Woodshades had held, she would've been welcome.

The Commissioner, running a ring of his own.

The Master had sought Augustus out, and together, they were working *here*, in Caelaymnis, to enact the divine transformation of blood to magic to quell the Woodshade conflicts. Fletcher had been chasing the ghosts of this investigation for months, though, and Augustus couldn't risk him being right.

He couldn't risk Aerdela finding blood magic. They were starved of magics, and that made them desperate.

So Augustus would go. He'd meet them all, put on a diplomatic face, indulge his brother's whims, answer the request for additional force for the seizure of the grounds.

He wasn't exactly sure what he'd do, just yet, but the accusation of blood magic in Aerdela could no longer be brushed off over a brotherly spat. Already, Augustus had gone to the furthest reaches to wipe that scourge from the settlements beyond Caelaymnis, risking his own immortal soul. That risk had brought the first victories his people had seen in a long time. *Only this once,* he promised himself, dosing his own warriors. *Only this. No more. No less.* There'd been no other choice.

The Woodshades weren't content with what they themselves could do. They weren't content to Heal. To rend ice and fire and stone in isolation.

They wanted more.

They wanted the undefinable magic of the elves. They wanted to fold the fabric of the universe to traverse the world, to bring light, to shape not only their ice and fire and stone but to bring nature itself to heel.

All Augustus had done was taken back what was his.

A professional blood magic ring could seize and transform magics beyond most mortals.

If production rings were spreading through humanity, from the backwoods settlements towards the heart of Aerdela itself, if this proclivity for illegal magics was becoming common place...he had to act.

The simple fact of the matter remained: the Master had been correct to assert that Caelaymnis, with their devotion to the gods and their mystics and their care of magic, could safely play host to a small production ring as a last-ditch effort to stop the Woodshades.

Anything else was unacceptable.

Augustus reached for the bar of soap balanced precariously on the ledge. "What was wrong with the brother?" A morbid curiosity.

"Nothing. It's the same old story," Isa shrugged. "These humans don't know what they are. Don't know what they can do. And some of them can't contain it. Her brother's uncontained in more ways than one," they grinned, miming two scars across their chest.

Augustus huffed a laugh. "Good for him."

"Quite." Isa's eyes sparkled, and Augustus's resentment eased, seeing their delight.

Standing there, bathed in the lucent-light, the pale-yellow binding gently hugged their strong chest, a soft outline of breasts beneath the traditional cloth where they'd been bound not to flatness, lest the ribs crack at the strain, but simply to what Isa, with a sparkle in their eyes, always called *out-of-the-way-ness*. Tight undershorts clung mercilessly to perfect hips, taunting, the body sculpted not of hard lines and intense musculature, but rather the tone of one who knew how to move. The top half of the captain's sleek, dark hair had been tied in a tight knot, the rest shaved low, in the traditional style, fierce and elegant and lethal, all at once.

Isa was not only uncontained, unrestricted by the confines of their birth, but they were also *ro*.

From the ancient myth, Rho.

A rare star, escaped from the heavens, destined to walk amongst the mortals to flee the gods. Devastatingly beautiful, the mortals vied for Rho. A prized wife, kings proclaimed. A coveted husband, queens demanded. But Rho laughed, for the mortals did not understand.

Ro. To be neither. To be both.

To be defined only by the soul.

To shine true to the heart, to bring forth a true self that shone so bright mere mortals would have to shield their eyes.

The elves believed in the stars, above all else. That in death, a soul could be set into the cosmos, that in life, the stars sang prophecies. Rho was not the only one. For as many stars lay above, there were those who'd take their names and stories from the sky. Endless names, endless ways of being, for the stars knew no limits.

It made a mortal radiant, following the paths of stars.

To be radiantly uncontained.

This was an honor, above all else, to see the *ro* as such. Coming undone.

Isa's gaze was idle, practiced fingers winding the swath of yellow into a neat roll.

The pinnacle of trust and sacred vow, a promise not to err, as the gods first had. A promise not to contain the *ro* within their gods-granted flesh.

"Well, you're back, now," Augustus murmured softly as Isa joined him beneath the water. Lacing his fingers through theirs, Augustus sighed. Isa's hands were strong, callused, like his own, from years of training. Perfect.

"I'm back," the *ro* agreed quietly.

It was a gentle dance, the one they danced.

Head resting on his shoulder, Isa let out a deep breath.

Augustus pulled their locked hands to his chest, wrapping his other arm around their waist.

And they let the water take them both.

RISA

*"There are admittedly few problems I've been unable to
solve with an insane amount of arrogance, some sharp
words, and the ability to win a staring contest.
Remember that."*

~Risa Barrett

Risa was sitting lazily in a desk chair, one leg crossed nonchalantly over
the other, eyes staring unblinkingly at the man across the table.

It was, in truth, a favorite pastime, bringing arrogant pricks like him
to heel.

And yet, that insidious bastard wouldn't look away.

"Ms. Barrett, you'll pardon the impropriety, but I fail to understand
why you are even being included in these talks at all. This petition, my
aides have explained, is due to be answered by the Chancellor himself."

"Mr. Carson." Her fingers were steepled before her, poised for the
attack.

"Commissioner Carson," he corrected.

"Mr. Carson," she repeated, not looking away. "What you elect to do
within the confines of Aerdela is your business. But what you're
proposing comes under direct jurisdiction of the Hidden City. A trade
agreement with Caelaymnis? What are you even planning on exporting?

All they can offer is illegal to trade within the confines of the Quad—the treaty is abundantly clear on this matter. The trading of magical goods is strictly prohibited beyond the boundaries laid forth."

He ground his teeth, seedy black eyes narrowed. "You are contradicting your own agreement. Chancellor Faulise—"

"Is no longer the Chancellor," Risa interjected. "Nor has she been for some time. This argument is tired, Mr. Carson. The Guild has taken this matter up time and time again. How many more rejections do you require? Because frankly, this" —she gestured vaguely across the desk— "this is a waste of everyone's time."

Gods, to watch him simmer.

Adrian slid a note towards her, accompanied by a severe look. With deft fingers, she flipped it up, glancing at it before folding it up neatly and tucking it in her portfolio.

Don't play with your food, Risa.

"Look." She sighed, a bit disappointed. "I'm well aware that Chancellor Faulise had her recommendations—recommendations you know we support, otherwise you wouldn't be wasting your time here. But there's nothing we can do. The law is the law, and unless the Guild wishes to be cut off from the City, you will abide by it. And you will not get your way by petitioning Vaupellum into submission. He's already looking for an excuse to choke off Aerdela. You don't need to give him any more reasons."

"If you are looking to take action, I suggest continuing to work the unanimous vote within the Guild," Adrian suggested, eyebrow raised. "Unity among the Commissioners sends a stronger message than burying His Excellency in kindling."

Clark Carson rose, fingertips resting on the tabletop. "I will, of course, abide by the laws of the City. The last thing the Guild wishes is to be cut off from our cousins to the north. But if I might say, this place?"

He scoffed. "It's gone to shit since Maggie left."

"We know," Adrian nodded, sighing as he scooped up the papers in front of him. "Believe me, we all know."

With no small amount of disdain, the Commissioner pulled his suitcoat on, brushing off the lapels with disgust before turning.

"Commissioner?"

Adrian was on his feet, dark eyes boring into Clark's back.

Glancing over his shoulder with disinterest, fingers on the doorknob, Clark paused.

"Aren't you forgetting something?"

"No," he said softly, a whisper of sardonic amusement on his face. "No, I don't believe I am. Now, it's been a long day, on account of being *arrested,* so if you'll excuse me—"

A glacial snap.

The Commissioner had promised letters. Records of the girl's every movement, an inventory of her hopefully still-ordinary life.

And he'd delivered them consistently for years.

Until now.

Whorls of frost curled across the mahogany table, geometric designs skittering with frenzied creaks and groans up the windows. The air was ice in Risa's lungs, and she let a devious smile curl on her lips.

"Cut the bullshit." Glittering crystals of ice clung to Adrian's dark tan skin, his breath steaming in the make-shift snow globe. "You come in here, demanding we stick our necks out for the sake of your coffers, and you bring nothing in return? Ten gods-damned years, and you still think you can fuck with me? Where's the fucking dossier, Clark?"

~•~

Buried far below the marble library lay quiet rows of dust-gatherers,

Archivists skittered about, wary of the intruder, the occasional pair of eyes squinting from their corners of history.

Risa could not take her eyes from the single wrought-iron lock, ensconced in a tomb of shining glass.

"Kiran's Cornerstone." Adrian's voice tumbled quietly through the dark, and amid the scuff of shoes on marble, he joined her beside the pedestal. "I thought I might find you here."

Why such a relic had been consigned to a glorified basement was beyond her. Some Factionist political agenda, probably.

He'd meant to open it, someday, so the stories said. To open the slender barred gates that had long-since been ripped out, replaced with impenetrable stone towering high around the city.

"This place was supposed to be a refuge," she said softly.

"It still is."

"For who, though, Adrian? Clark's right. This place is going to shit. Faulise—"

"Was before your time," Adrian cautioned, voice low.

"No, Chancellor Faulise *was* my time. She was *my* era, *my* salvation," Risa bit back. "That raid on the tunnels? Children died! Margaret Faulise would've never signed off on an operation that compromised anyone with a right to set foot inside these walls!"

"Risa—"

"We promised *solace!*"

Her words rang through the archives, the echoes betraying her for what she was.

A Rescindant.

A terrorist, the Factionist-leaning papers had called them. Had called her, indirectly, by association with the Rescindants.

But they were simply fighting for the sanctuary that had been promised, before the gates had been barred. They were fighting for the humans left behind. The ones stranded, sinking into depravity in their isolation, humans like the ones in the so-called Woodshade settlements beyond Caelaymnis. The humans cordoned off in Aerdela, condemned to forget magic, even as it ran in their veins.

"And when they say that solace is not a sweet-treat to be handed out on street corners?" Adrian's voice was soft in the ringing quiet. "You will prove them wrong."

She brushed the tears of anger from her cheeks, refusing to turn her gaze from the behemoth lock before them. "But?"

"But nothing. Now get out of here. Go have a drink. Cry over Lea, because I know she broke your heart. Scream about the missing dossier. And then prove them wrong, Risa. Prove them all wrong."

THE PROMISES

Our investigation has taken a disturbing turn.

Regardless of the events that transpired in Caelaymnis, I remain convinced of the Commissioner's guilt. He has grown restless, having risen to the heights of the Guild. What he's planning to do with the magic he's wrung out of the pastries, I do not know—a siege has been suggested, or perhaps a grab for land. Personally, my bets lay with trade.

There are more than a few who'd sell their soul—and everything they own—for bottled magic.

For the moment, though, I believe we have a plan to bring him down.

I have often said there are few things that cannot be cured with a bit of dancing.

~SAM ALDERTON,
EXCERPT FROM A LETTER DATED NOVEMBER 30TH

TEDDY

"Warm companionship, unconditional kindness, and
perhaps a hot cup of tea—I think that's all anyone's
really looking for in the world."

~Sam Alderton

Sugar laced the air, carried into the still-chilly apartment on the steaming cups of sweetpear tea and the shining glaze being drizzled gently across rows of hot muffins stacked on grated cooling racks, and there was a faint smile on Sam's lips as he dipped the spoon into the bowl for another pass, the sleeves of his button-up tunic rolled past his elbows, waistcoat and cravat left abandoned cold in the wardrobe.

Teddy paused at the threshold of the kitchen, raising an eyebrow as he glanced back to double-check the mantle clock.

Eight in the morning.

Early, for a tart with nowhere to go.

"I know, I know," Sam grinned not taking his eyes from the ribbons of glaze. "You don't have to make a thing of it."

"Who, me?" Coming behind him, Teddy wrapped his arms around Sam's waist, brushing a quiet kiss against his neck, witch-hazel and lemon still lingering faintly against the smooth skin. "So, shaved and baking before mid-morning—what's the occasion?"

"No occasion."

"You, Mr. Alderton," he snickered, nestling his face in Sam's shoulder, "are a terrible liar." And closing his eyes, he waited, a smile on his lips.

But the quiet laugh, the small witticism—they never came.

"Maybe," Sam said quietly, letting the spoon down on the edge of the bowl with a gentle clink. "I...have been doing a lot of thinking, these last few days."

Not exactly the shocking revelation his low caramel voice hinted it was.

Squirming out of Teddy's hold, his brown eyes were fiery. "There is something I need to do. For all of us, for this town—but I can't do it by myself."

"What do you need," Teddy offered softly. "Anything, Sam, anything at all—"

"You. I need *you.*"

Those words, and Sam's hands were around his own, soft and strong and warm and he'd memorized them long ago, every line, every turn, every callus, every bend.

"I have known you for nine years, now," Sam was saying, and he was leading up to something, a playful spark in his eyes, a hint of mischief turning up the corners of his mouth, and, "you've always been my best friend, there's not a moment that went by when I didn't feel completely loved by you," and *why is my heart pounding, why can't I breathe,* but the tightness in his chest was so sweet, the air trickling in so pure, unadulterated elation, and, "four years companions, and there is nothing, Teddy, nothing in the world that feels as right as you and I."

"Sam—"

His cinnamon eyes were molten in the morning light, the sun

incarnate. "I know, now, how I need to move forward. And I don't want to face it without making sure you know how dear you are, how deeply I hold you in my heart. Which leads me to muffins."

"Muffins," Teddy echoed hoarsely.

"Muffins," Sam smiled.

And he paused.

"I thought," he said softly, sinking down onto one knee, "you might want a quiet breakfast, after I ask you to marry me."

ELSIE

"Loving someone doesn't mean you immediately know their soul or understand the darkest corners of their mind. Rather, to love someone is to hope that eventually, you will."

~Elizabeth Clement Faulise

"I don't understand Sam," Fletcher muttered, scooping up an armful of papers off the desk in the lodge. "I don't think you said a dozen words to me in as many days, but now we reconcile, he kicks us out?"

Snickering, Elsie tossed the blankets back, dangling her legs over the side of the bed, daring herself to let her feet meet the chilly floor.

"What's so funny?" He dropped the stack onto the sofa, eyes narrowing on her. "What do you know?"

"Nothing," she snickered, padding towards the bathing room. "All he said was that we're banned from the apartment until dinner."

Abandoning the mess of parchment, the sheets spilled towards the hearth rug with soft little *flit-flit-flits,* chaos giving way to tiny paper avalanches lilting over the leather sofa. Fletcher paid the mess of papers no mind, though, frowning as he followed her. "Until dinner? He's not mad?"

"Gods, no." She snagged a tangle as she combed out her hair over the sink, watching him over her shoulder in the mirror. "He was grinning like a fool. He didn't say anything directly, of course, but I think he's actually going to propose."

Fletcher's brow softened, eyes finding hers through the reflection. "Oh. And you are..." He trailed off, waiting.

"Happy," she prompted. Sending the comb clattering across the counter, she pulled her hair back into a quick knot at the nape of her neck, strands already breaking free in tiny little frizzed rebellions. "It's about damn time. They've been pining over each other for longer than either one would care to admit."

He only nodded thoughtfully, taking a step to join her on the rug. His fingers trailed her waistline, and he rested his head softly on her shoulder, studying them both.

Theirs was a quiet peace.

One, she knew, built on the pretending of it all.

"I think," she said softly, lifting his hands away from her hips, "I'm gonna take a bath before we go." Still early, they wouldn't be expected in Caelaymis—gods, she was actually going to see it, Caelaymnis!—for another few hours, and the tub—and the tap for hot water—was calling.

"Can...I...join you?" His words were hesitant as his body tensed for an attack, a wince already growing in his tightening shoulders as he took a step back.

Coward.

She eyed him, smile faltering.

It wasn't like he hadn't seen her naked before.

"No." The word was soft on her lips, and she swallowed, watching him. "I just...need some space." A way of saying that since she'd watched them all burn, she'd been burning, too.

His touch left her skin on fire, like the capsaicin salve made from hot peppers and oil she used when her cycle sent her back aching. Only, instead of reluctant, slightly singed relief, she only found pain.

It'd taken her more than a moment to recognize that the skin-on-skin of the two of them hurt. He was so gentle, and she was so gods-damned hungry for touch after weeks of starving, and they'd lain there, in his bed at the lodge, and he'd carefully threaded his hand beneath her shirt, wrapping his arm around her middle and drawing her in close, and there had been an undeniable—and markedly uncomfortable—burning where he touched.

Magic—that'd been her first thought.

It wasn't, though. Maybe it'd have been easier if it was, because then there'd be a reason. But it didn't feel like the prickling sensation of knitting flesh and bone she knew from Teddy, and when she'd held the lucents, touched the shields...they were smooth, and vaguely warm, and nothing more, and that meant something inside had simply broken, and that was that.

She couldn't touch him anymore.

"You can stay, though," she amended, watching him turn for the door. "If you want. The company would be nice." Better than being alone with her thoughts, miserable as they'd turned. It was easier, thinking about her brother, and the wedding Sam would make all of Aerdela remember.

Or she could think about Caelaymnis—that was nice, too.

She wouldn't see much, Fletcher had regretfully promised. By all rights, she wasn't even allowed inside, though she'd been assured that, as she'd be in company of a pair of princes, they'd overlook the rules this time. Even still, though, the idea of seeing a slice of the compound Fletcher had resentfully described as they lay curled together in the dark of night, seeing a bit of his life...

"A proposal." Fletcher sank down on the edge of the tub, fiddling with the taps as Elsie stood lost in her thoughts, leaning on the counter. "You're okay with Sam marrying your brother? After everything?" The side-long glance told her what she'd already suspected.

He'd overheard Clark's demand for the letters, had, then, put it together, what Sam had been doing.

Spying.

"Because he chronicled my life for the better part of nine years so that Clark-fucking-Carson could have the only printing of the Story of Elsie Mirabeau: A Novel by Sam Alderton?" she mused.

"Something like that."

Elsie shrugged. It had felt like a betrayal, until it didn't anymore.

She knew Sam had been chasing his own scars. And knowing what they were didn't change what he'd done.

Just another welcome-mat confession to go unpunished. The merchants took what they wanted, this, she knew—and yet there had been a thin line in her mind, one she must've surely known they'd cross.

When page-rippers gave commands, the books had to follow.

Such was the ink-and-parchment life.

To live in the lines of another's book, or else, die between the spaces of their own.

Elsie sighed, folding her arms across her chest as she watched Fletcher feeding a thin stream of soap into the bath she hadn't asked him to draw. "Sam did what he had to, to survive," she said softly, watching a plume of bubbles meet the water. "Any of us would've done the same."

He raised an eyebrow, nodding as he watched the water. "True," he muttered. "Very true."

"You don't have a problem with him, now, do you?"

He shook his head. "I like Sam. He never makes me feel...out of place."

Sam was welcoming, that was to be sure. He was never one to harp on distinctions.

Her fingers skimmed the top of the soapy water, testing the temperature before undressing.

Hot, like fire.

The bubbles crunched uncomfortably beneath her hand as she dipped it below the surface, the water pressing in painfully tight, threatening to pull her down. She grimaced, withdrawing, wiping the suds on the nearby towel.

What is wrong with me?

"On second thought, I'm good," she muttered. It was too bad. Delicious tendrils of steam were curling from the tub, beckoning her cold body in.

She would settle for the warm rays of sun falling on her shoulders across the divan beneath the window, even if she had to evict the pile of Fletcher's clothes that had nested there in the weeks she'd left it vacant.

Fletcher's eyes were hunks of jade and honey as they found hers, his brows furrowed. "Everything okay?"

No.

No, clearly everything was not okay.

She'd watched Teddy shaking and sweating, sickened with his own magic. Their parents—not even really her parents—were dead, something she'd hardly given a second thought to, because they were never hers, and she never belonged to them, except nineteen years couldn't just be erased with charcoal and flame, no matter what she wanted, and it was the fire that became the page-ripper, now, making her skin endlessly burn.

And that wasn't even the half of it. Fletcher might know that Sam played the courier-spy, but even now, she had her secrets, secrets there was no choice to keep.

Even if it didn't put his life on the line, even if the Factionists—whoever they even were—wouldn't have extinguished her and anyone perceived to be her ally, she wasn't ready for that conversation.

Hey. So. You know how you're, like, a prince, but it's fine, because you're the third child, and you can't inherit unless basically everyone dies?

Yeah. Well.

I outrank you.

An heiress to a city beyond imagining and her Dradan prince.

As if there wasn't enough to deal with.

There were more pressing matters, though, for the time being, than the sugar-spun tales of a merchant page-ripper—tales she couldn't even be sure were true, anymore, tales she feared were more true than she dared to dream.

"Everything's fine," she lied softly, turning to leave the bathing room.

They would end Clark.

They would find the evidence, some key thing that would link him inextricably to the production ring, and *they would end him.*

Everything else was icing.

"I know I'm going to regret this," Fletcher said warily, following, "but if you're not feeling well, you are under no obligation—"

She whirled on him, glaring with incredulity. "And miss seeing your home? I think not."

TEDDY

"There is much mythology concerning the danger of inherited rings. Some corrupt. Some grant absolute power. Some warrant invisibility. And some...some boast love, stronger than even the gods themselves believed."

-from 'The Advice of The Long-Dead' and Other Essays

Teddy's hand was shaking in Sam's, cinnamon eyes staring up at him, a soft smile like sunshine warming the room.

Yes, tell him yes, you idiot!

"When," was all he managed, swallowing hard.

"I rather thought the breakfast would follow the proposal, but if you're opposed to the order—"

A smile was tugging on his lips as he scoffed, holding on as Sam pulled himself to standing.

"Oh, you meant the *wedding,*" Sam snickered, brushing a kiss across his cheek. "Well, spring would be lovely—it's a bit fast, pulling it all together, but I don't much fancy waiting."

If he was being honest with himself, he didn't fancy waiting, either.

If.

Two days ago, he'd been spasming in the bedroom, soaked in sweat and shattered by the Thread. And with a simple question, Isa had unveiled the problem that'd driven it to feral frenzy.

What do you need.

A question he'd asked himself again and again and again until he could start to grasp at a sort of vague kind of answer.

One moment, it'd just be sleep. All he'd want to do is close his eyes and rest.

One moment, it was food—food he kept forgetting to eat, in the days of recovery that followed.

But mostly, it was Sam.

He just wanted Sam.

Loving arms to hold him while he grieved for parents he didn't realize he loved so deeply. A honey voice to soothe, to sing, to laugh.

Sam.

"What about now?" He was worrying his cuticles, his soft voice hanging tentative in the air.

"Pardon?"

"What if we did it now. Got married right here, in this kitchen," he breathed, letting the words flow. *What do you need.* "Before breakfast."

Sam let out a long breath, laughing quietly as he drew Teddy in. "Oh-ho, El would quite literally murder you. Me, too."

"I told you not to give her that knife. This one's on you, my dear." Teddy closed his eyes, let himself get lost in the smell of starched linen he'd long come to associate with his companion. "They'd never even have to know."

"We could make it up to them," Sam offered.

"That's exactly it. Do this now, just for us," Teddy whispered. "We could still have a party in the spring."

"Make it a whole thing, with the flowers, and the dancing..."

"And they'd be happy, and we'd be happy—"

"We've got ribbon, twine, and candles," Sam muttered, eyes drifting up to the ceiling as he mentally checked off the items, "rings, though...that might be a bit of a problem, in that we don't have them, and if we did, they wouldn't go un...unnoticed..."

Teddy drew back, finding Sam's vacant eyes. "What," he frowned. "I know that look, Sam, what—"

Something sparked across his face, and he withdrew, snapping his fingers as he turned on his heel. "I've got it. Teddy, I've got it," he called, retreating down the hall, disappearing into the sewing room. "Put on your best tunic, love. We're getting married."

~ • ~

The heavens had stilled, sky frozen in eternal morning, and the sheets were impossibly cocooned around them both, not-warm-enough wrappings of thin linen, but the blankets had been kicked unceremoniously off the foot of the bed, too far to warrant the expedition to retrieve them.

Propped up on an elbow, legs inextricably tangled together, Teddy's smile was indelible.

Indelible like us.

His fingers traced the soft skin of Sam's jawline up, up, up, to run through his silken hair, and he leaned in for another lingering kiss. The encroaching chill, the betrayal of a fire neglected for a more enduring source of warmth, had nothing on their flushed skin, burning where it touched, chilled where embrace had failed.

"Husband," Sam murmured, eyes deep. His dark lashes caught the sun, tiny sprays of light, his breath laced with sugar and bread.

Perfection.

A glint of yellow caught the sun, and Teddy's fingers trailed the thin chain down to the ring on Sam's collarbone, a thin circle of woven gold, braided together to form a wedding band, before finding its pair hanging about his own neck.

Unconventional.

Discrete.

"You'd never mentioned your mother had married," he said softly.

Sam sighed, a half-smile dancing on his lips. "She didn't. Not until after I was born, anyway." His voice was warm, like caramel, sinking into the space between them with gentle ease. "I think she would have approved," he said softly, letting his hand rest atop Teddy's where it sat on his chest. "Him too, I suppose. I don't...I don't remember him. But she always said he had a wry sense of humor. I think they'd have liked the idea of such a thing."

It was a beautiful thing, too.

Standing over the kitchen sink, his hand clasped around Sam's, his voice clear as he'd wound the pale ribbon around their fists, whispering the words.

I am yours, and you are mine,
And with this ribbon, now to bind,
Hearts and hands and hearth and home,
For ne'ermore I have to roam.

He'd imagined himself teary-eyed, with quaking words, the day he wed.

But they'd bound the candles in twine, and let them burn, and it had been calm that filled him, the sort of serenity that took a person when they did something rash and thoughtless and hasty and completely, utterly right.

Giving Teddy's fingers a gentle squeeze, there was reluctance on his lips as Sam moved, unraveling the sheet that held them pressed together.

"No," Teddy groaned with mock displeasure, hand trailing lazily after Sam's as he rose from the bed, "stay..." His begging dissolved into quiet laughter, though, as Sam paused, watching him with amusement. *That is rather the point in all this,* Sam's look seemed to say. *The staying of it all.*

A promise, to be sure.

But it was more than that.

It was an unspoken question for reassurance.

Don't leave me. Don't leave my mangled heart.

There'd already been too much leaving, more than plenty for a lifetime, to Teddy's thinking. There was no sea so rough, no war so brutal, no drought so dry, no pain so real, that they couldn't see it through together. No, there'd be no leaving.

Husband.

Sam was tugging on his undershorts, eyes flitting about the room. The pressed tunic lay crumpled somewhere—the hallway, maybe? Teddy couldn't remember where his fingers had almost torn the buttons off in a breathless flurry, and it was better this way, anyway, shedding their clothes and their worries, all at once.

"So, what is it," Teddy asked softly, drawing Sam's pillow to his chest, eyes unwavering. *Husband.* "This thing, you said you have to do, that you can't face alone."

Gods know what I can't face alone.

A funeral, for one.

Sam's knuckles went white against the wardrobe door. He said nothing. One reluctantly carameled glance, and he sighed, turning for the chest of drawers, extracting a simple box, plastered with the garish paper of the boutiques. "For you," he breathed, eyes finding Teddy's, coming to sink down beside him on the feather bed.

Teddy pushed himself to sitting, pillow on his lap, taking the gilded parcel with a quizzical look. Sam only waved him off, shaking his head in unmistakable self-disdain.

And lifting off the lid, it became clear why.

A mask sat atop a cushion of blackvanilla satin, encrusted with sapphires, adorned with exotic feathers of deep turquoise and expansive iridescent purples. The box had been soaked in the smell of rotting citrus, sickeningly sweet and decadent, and he searched for the crisp, clean air he'd been gulping down amid hushed moans not ten minutes ago.

"I would like you to accompany me," Sam said quietly, hand trailing Teddy's shoulder. "As my fiancé, publicly."

"It..."

But the words caught in his throat.

A lovely piece.

An abhorrent piece.

His eyes flicked to Sam.

A piece to make the Commissioner fall.

ELSIE

*"There is nothing so exhilarating as finding your feet
somewhere they don't belong."*

-from 'The Advice of The Long-Dead' and Other Essays

Her stomach was roiling as her feet found cold, smooth stone, and the whisper of winter air kissed her cheeks beneath the hood.

The difference between cloaked and coated seemed a handful of letters in her mind.

She felt sinister, beneath the black swath pinned about her neck. It fell low over her face, concealing her features, shielding her from prying eyes and the biting wind in one stroke.

A few gray buildings sat in the basin-of-an-encampment, a little bowl of stepped complexes and graveled paths.

The compound.

Where Fletcher had spent the last four years training and studying and fighting and earning the insignia now visible on the sleeve of his right arm, two blackened bars running parallel to a stream of curling script—what she assumed to be a single letter, though she could not read it.

Their pace was quick, only a stray Drada here and there passing them by. Where the rest were, she could not say, though the emptiness gave the compound an ominous feeling, like that of a graveyard.

With each step, she conjured up memories of calm. It was a tactic her brother had used, whispering sweet memories to her in moments of panic, and it was at least worth a shot, trying to replicate it now.

Finding the kittens in the barn. Gods, she'd loved those kittens. Teddy had come in from the barnyard, cheeks still red from the cold, grinning, and it didn't matter that she'd still been in pajamas, because he'd picked her up and carried her outside, her toes bare and wiggling in the crisp spring air, and he'd shown her the mewling creatures, in the hay. The first crop of barn cats she'd try to tame.

The Drada passing by seemed to pay her no mind. She wasn't the only cloaked figure skirting the grounds, and everyone else seemed to be decidedly in a rush to get somewhere.

A whisper reached her ears, and she realized someone had called out a greeting to Fletcher, putting a hand in the air. His murmured reply must've been loud, to their ears—he could hear her heart, he'd said, three blocks away—but the unfamiliar words washed over her ears almost unnoticed.

Eating sweets with Teddy and Sam on a chilled spring night. She remembered Sam tossing his cravat aside with shocking irreverence, his waistcoat following before he'd crawled onto the big bed in the boys' room, leaning back against the wall with far more exasperation than she thought one should have at seventeen. She didn't remember where the sweets had come from. Only that Sam's introduction hadn't gone well, that Teddy had a huge fight with Chloe, his then-companion, and Elsie was simply glad not to be alone.

Fletcher ushered her into a side-building, down a long hall, through a stark corridor, and Elsie was nearly breathless as Fletcher pushed open the heavy door.

A massive Drada lurked behind a desk, arms crossed, jaw clenched. Bulky, he loomed a head above her, his eyes shards of pale forest. His uniform was nearly identical to Fletcher's, with the exception of the insignia, and the look of worn-down-ness about the fabric. If she touched it, it'd probably be soft from wear.

Tilting her hood back and shedding the cloak, she glanced to Fletcher.

"This," he sighed, gesturing to the man behind the desk, "is my brother. General Augustus Praequintelya. General, this is Elsie Mirabeau."

Elsie offered him a hand. "It's nice to meet you."

Augustus only frowned—it hadn't seemed possible for his face to frown any more, but there it went, all the same, frowning away—and with the air of someone who'd stepped in dung, he eyed her outstretched hand.

"You're supposed to shake it," she edged, the words tumbling out of her mouth before she could stop them. Who knew. Maybe the Drada did things differently. Isolated in their mountains for six-hundred years, there was no reason to believe they'd know human custom.

Eyes narrowing, his gaze flicked back to hers. Then, reaching out his hand, he took hers, gripping it tight. "I am well aware of human customs."

He was wary.

She liked that.

"I don't think you are," she shrugged, not breaking his gaze, or the handshake. "Most people say 'it's nice to meet you, too,' right there. Or 'how've you been,' if you're feeling casual."

"I think I have done my part of extending a cordial welcome. Your presence here is not permitted, and yet, here you stand." He cocked his head to the side. "Not in a prison cell."

"It's bad form to arrest your brother's companion. But if I'd known it was protocol, we'd've hung on to Isa a little longer."

A tiny smile cracked across his face as she released the grip, and his gaze flicked across her shoulder. "I like her. You said you found a human, I thought you'd dredged up some sugary wench. I didn't know you found a fighter."

Elsie glanced back over her shoulder to see Fletcher, grinning as he leaned against the wall, arms crossed.

"I like her, too," he said softly.

~ • ~

Clustered around the desk, a handful of Drada studied the rough sketch of Taylor Town, a haphazard drawing of the Carson estate thrown aside for the moment.

"The problem is the eastern line," a plump strawberry blonde woman was saying, her accent thick as she ran a finger down the map. She'd been dipping between the Caelaymnic words and Vernacular for the better part of an hour, Elsie catching strands of meaning along the way. "It isn't blockaded."

Mia Siddeus was bubbly, bright, and completely deadly.

The former two, Elsie could attest to—the latter, even Augustus seemed to acknowledge with almost reverential awe.

"There's going to be runners, Captain. It's the nature of the beast." The infamous Rodion Kastarae. A strapping Commander with dusky skin like nutmeg and deep velvet eyes, his loose curls of shining black hair had been pulled back with a strap of cloth as he studied the plan.

Isa was lingering beside Elsie, watching them all with amusement. "If anyone asked me—"

"They didn't," Augustus and Mia cut in together.

"Why can't you just shield the border?" Elsie's eyes flicked to Fletcher, standing on the other side of the table. "That's what you did when you took him in the first time, right? Why not do that, only bigger?"

"It's too much focus," he mumbled. His gaze held on the tabletop, unrelenting. He'd said remarkably little, in the time since they'd been here, despite this allegedly being his command.

"Our magic is tied to us," Isa explained, picking up where Fletcher had left off. "You can't just cast something and leave it. There's a—a bond, between you and the magic, connecting you, like—

"Like a thread," Elsie offered.

"Exactly. If it breaks, the bond is severed, and the magic doesn't work anymore. So, you could cast a shield that big—but it'd take all your focus to keep it up, and unless you maintained constant awareness of every inch of the shield, which is realistically impossible, there'd be these gaping holes, rendering it useless anyway."

"Sorry, but...it's just a sort of membrane, isn't it? Couldn't you still cast it pretty wide, even if it doesn't cover the whole thing?"

"Well...it isn't just a membrane." All eyes were on Isa, now. "A shield for this purpose is just a wall of densely packed air," the captain went on. "Our magic—the membrane, if you will—is what holds it together. We don't just conjure up a barrier made solely of our magic."

"Why not?"

Isa sighed, dark eyes meeting hers in thoughtful contemplation. Then, holding out a hand, they said, "Give me a gold piece."

"I don't have one."

"Then make one."

"I can't."

"Why not," Isa pushed, raising an eyebrow.

"I don't have the gold, or—or a forge, or the stamp, or any of it."

"Now, what if I asked you for a gold piece, but instead of you needing to make one, you could just take it from somewhere else? A coin purse, or my pocket, or what have you."

Elsie's face heated guiltily as she nodded her understanding.

"It's easier to use the tools you have instead of trying to remake them at every turn," Isa said, a smile tugging at their lips. "We *could* work a shield of just magic. But it would be small and concentrated. Trying to block a blow of magic is harder than just stopping a person. Instead of using magic to shape magic, though, we can spread ourselves further by borrowing the elements this world has given us."

"A membrane blanketed around something else," Elsie put forth. "Like…like watering down booze to make it last."

Augustus's eyes flicked to Elsie's, his expression unreadable. "An apt, if not rather depressing analogy."

"Even with Mia's…spicy shield," Isa frowned, "we don't have a good chance of shielding the boarder."

"Spicy?" Elsie whispered under her breath, confused.

Snickering, Mia held a palm outstretched.

Elsie had to do a double take, watching the lightning storm summoned into the small hand, crackling and hissing.

"Family gift," Mia challenged, flashing a bright smile.

The gift of lightning in her fingers.

And in the blink of an eye, it was gone again, and Isa gave a small *so there* kind of shrug.

"That's it." Fletcher's voice was soft, at last breaking his study of the table map. "Elsie figured it out. She's right, we need a shield."

Augustus heaved a sigh, thrusting a finger at his lover. "Were you not just *listening* to them? Isa already explained this, Fletch—"

"Shield the warehouse."

"That's great, if you want to wait three weeks to starve them out."

"Try three minutes," Fletcher pressed, shaking his head. "Just bleed the air out of inside. We can pack a shield so dense a person can't get through—why not air, too?"

A look of understanding dawned across Augustus's face, eyes lighting. "Knock them unconscious. There's not even a fight...I don't see why it couldn't be done, but you've got three days, and that's still a massive shield if you're going to pack it so dense—"

"Plenty of time," Rodion interjected jovially, clapping Fletcher on the back. "He can learn."

"It also depends on whether your friend can get you in," Augustus pressed on, running an anxious hand through his dirty blonde hair. "Your plan doesn't account for any mercenaries outside the warehouse. If they come from the manor house, or if the Commissioner gets wind of what's happening and tries to make a run for it—the last thing we need is him running off to the City with another botched arrest attempt—"

"He'll get us in." Elsie felt a swell of pride in her heart, saying the words.

I will fight for you. That's what Sam had said.

She'd been meaning to burn the letters he'd given her. Even without the last page, a written confession of his own misdeeds, she'd have kept them, though.

Reading them, it felt like she'd forgotten how to live.

He'd chronicled every pain. Every hurt. Every joy. Every smile, every laugh, every good day she'd had in the last six months.

Her life, in ink and parchment.

SAM

"Call me simple, but I've always fancied the best
introduction a quick and unremarkable one."

~*Theodore Alderton*

On the stoop of the massive buttercream house, Sam waited.

Beneath the blue silk cravat, beneath the pressed tunic, hidden beneath the undershirt, the ring atop his collarbone, quivering in time with his heart.

He wouldn't have bothered to drag the cravat from the wardrobe and noose it around his neck, wouldn't have bothered to dust off the charcoal jacket, except that those things mattered, here.

Of course, waiting on the doormat of a merchant's house wasn't how he'd imagined he'd start their honeymoon.

It would've been the ocean. Or else, a library somewhere, where he could've paid a fortune to have the thing locked up for a week, and he'd watch his husband—Sam's heart skipped a beat—buried in a stack of books, reveling in the quiet peace of tomes.

They would've been married a year ago, if Sam had saved enough to get a house on the merchant's edge of the district. That was when their dreams had been different, though.

That was when they were going to fill their house with children and

Sam was going to spin out gowns from a shop of his own and Teddy was going to spend his days baking pies and loving their babies and Elsie would be coming and going as she pleased from the apartment he'd wanted to bequeath to her, when they'd moved on to greater things.

He had to find a way to tell her what they'd done.

Stowing the ring beneath his fussy clothes was one thing. But Teddy was going to have a hell of a time keeping that gold chain hidden beneath the thin tunics he wore.

Married in a kitchen as November died.

It sounded like the kind of wedding Sam Carson would've hated.

And the kind that Sam Alderton adored.

You'll get your lace. His words to Desi were still ringing in his ears.

The rich wood of the sewing box was stained golden and puzzled together, tiny bands of sunlight-soaked panels holding the mother-of-pearl starburst inset. Held at his side, it'd been a faithful companion at Mulligan's, and hardly touched in the weeks since he'd left.

She'd be getting lace, alright.

"Ah. Mr. Alderton." A rather dour looking man, aging and gray, pulled open the door, beckoning him in.

A squeal of excitement, though, cut off any semblance of courtesy, as a flurry of crinoline and pink swirled around the corner. "Sam!" A young woman threw her arms around him, kissing each cheek in turn before planting a jovially exuberant and very innocent one right on his lips.

"Des," he grinned, returning a half-hug with his free arm. "The weeks have kept you well?"

"Oh, gods, no! Sam, my dress—thank the gods you've come, it's the most horrendous—but why have you come?" Her eyes were wide, affected concern written beautifully across her face.

"To see my favorite client, of course," he offered kindly, and nodding to his sewing box, added, "and make some casual amendments, lest a certain young woman find herself wanting at her introduction."

~ • ~

Sunlight bathed the drawing room, and Desi stood valiantly beneath the mass of jewels and silk, watching Sam work the hem.

They'd given her lace, alright—but not the fine weave she'd likely wanted, spun on the Coastal Reach. It'd been a rough Warken pattern, wretchedly floral and coarsely stitched in without a second thought.

"I had a suspicion that I was needed," Sam mused, kneeling on the carpet, pinning a gorgeously woven *Raspberry Harvest* pattern lace to the hem. True to its name, the deep burgundy drew out the pale pink of the gown, the pattern nothing more than delicate twirls, tasseled at regular intervals. "Seamsters can sense these things, you know—when there is a crisis of lace."

Desi giggled, her mother giving a quiet laugh from the corner. "It is fortunate you came to call," Lora remarked, working herself on a spot of embroidery. "Everyone is simply distraught at that fool Mrs. Mulligan, and right before the introductions, too. It is quite the scandal, Sam—though I'm sure you've heard."

"It is no fault of Mrs. Mulligan, I assure you," he muttered, glancing up.

Lora pursed her lips. "We know, love. We know. And rest assured, on this matter, we cannot find solidarity with our Commissioner."

Sam gave a slight dip of his head in gratitude before returning to his work. "A lovely sentiment. Though," he sighed, "these things do happen. My only regret is that I won't get to see sweet Desi here meet society."

Desi's shriek of dismay shook the room. "What? Sam, you have to be there! You *promised!*"

299

"I wasn't invited, hon. But you'll be marvelous—"

"He didn't even *invite you?*"

"Forget it, Des, I shouldn't have even brought it up—"

"Mama, fetch the proofs from my stationary desk, this is *absurd,*" Desi fussed, nearly falling off the stool in her distress, catching herself with a hand on Sam's shoulder as she was inclined to do at least once a fitting.

"Love, you don't have to do that," he murmured, trying to keep the smile out of his voice. Rising, he abandoned the hem to her flustered movements, making instead for the sewing box on a nearby end table. His fingers traced the places where it'd been worn down to streaks of white, never to be refinished. The click of the latch, the resistant whistle of the hinges, and it didn't matter how long it'd been, he knew the contents better than he knew himself.

A spool of purple thread, a needle stuffed messily beneath the layers, half-threaded. A thimble, once too big for his fingers, but she'd let him wear it all the same, that cratered little tin hat. A pin cushion, once pink but now faded, speckled with little brown stains he'd memorized long ago, and if he breathed it in long enough, held it close, turned the grainy little pillow over in his hands enough, he could still smell it, the lavender buried deep inside the shell. A tattered corner of dotted cotton, happy pastel-blue circles woven in the yellowing cloth, the disintegrating fibers catching on his callused fingertips.

Careful, Sammy.

A voice, sweetened like wine in his memory.

Your daddy gave this to me, she'd smiled, tucking a strand of curling honey hair behind her ear, and he tried to remember what color her eyes had been, but they'd only been a reflection of flame as they'd sat, huddled on the hearth rug of that dingy one-room flat. *And do you know what, Sammy? There's no tear,* she'd say, taking out the spool, *no tear that can't be mended. Remember that, sweet.*

"No tear," he echoed under his breath, drawing the lid shut with a sigh. *I've got more than a few tears that need mending, Mom. I wish you were here to fix them.*

I am fine. I am dealing with it.

He didn't really know if he was. Not really.

Teddy helped.

They'd tumbled into each other, hurting in their own ways. And in a twisted kind of way, it'd been beautiful. They'd loved not because of the pain, but in spite of it. When they had bared their souls, what remained was raw resilience.

"Oh! Oh gods, now I can meet him!" Desi squealed, in a tizzy about the possibility of at last meeting the boy who'd won Sam Alderton's heart. "The boy! Everyone—oh, *gods,* Sam, *everyone* talks about him, but it'll be me, bringing him out! Ooo, we're going to meet *Teddy!"*

"I am afraid he is a rather private person—"

"Please, Sam? *Please?* You have to bring him!"

"I shall be sure to pass the invitation along," he reassured her, watching her fret and fuss in front of the mirror, skirts rustling playfully, "though he is quite introverted—he elects to spend many an evening with his sister—"

"Then bring her, too!" Desi was almost quivering with excitement, her face flushed a deep rose. "Bring her, she—oh, a ball, she'll be splendidly excited—"

"I don't doubt you're right. Now, if you're quite finished, *hold still,"* Sam snickered, shooing her back atop the stool. The silk was smooth beneath his fingertips as he straightened the skirt, eying the half-done hem. *One more.* "It'll be her first ball, you know—her companion has been simply dying to take her out dancing—"

"She never met society?" Desi's mouth had fallen slightly open, eyes wide.

"Des, sweet, Sam's companion is a farmer's son, remember," Lora warned softly. Sweeping back from the writing desk, stack of stationary in hand and armed with a fountain pen, she gave her daughter a look of dismay. "They don't meet society the way we do."

"Well, not the *same* society, *obviously*, but the farmers are still a *society!* Don't they have that—that festival, or what have you?"

"The festival is a disastrously fun excuse to drink and dance," Sam offered. "It's hardly an introduction ball, though."

"You've *been!* Oh, how charming—"

Lora scoffed. "Des—"

"Oh, right, *gods,* I nearly lost track—four, yes?" She glanced down at Sam in question. "Is that right? You, and—and Teddy, and his sister, and his sister's companion?"

"Truly, there is no need to make waves over such things—"

A bright smile blossomed across her face. "It's settled, then! Four invitations to my introduction ball, Sam, and I will *not* take no for an answer!"

"I didn't think you would," he grinned, setting to work once more.

AUGUSTUS

"There is life in the blood—this, we universally
acknowledge. Where there is life, there are lies, and too,
heartbreak and hope."
-from 'The Advice of The Long-Dead' and Other Essays

Arms braced on the desk, Augustus's eyes were fixed unseeing at the map spread across it.

Hours of planning, strategizing, and his thoughts had at last drifted away from the task at hand.

Last night had brought another attack against the city walls, and with it, more death, more destruction, and more desperation.

The Master's contributions had dropped death tolls into the single digits. It'd given Augustus's own men a fighting chance against the Woodshades, a chance to wrench what was more or less a victory from the hands of the humans addled by the blood magic.

A single drop on the tongue of each warrior.

One Ruby Tear, and the humans had found the virulence of their attack weakened.

To take the blood was to take the magic. The humans had done as much—they'd taken elven blood, taken what little bits of Dradan magic they could scrape up from the sacrifice, and taken the Caelaymnic troops with insurmountable force. This, what Augustus did with the Master...it put them on even footing. Nothing more. Nothing less.

They would quell the uprising in the settlements. Pinch out the production rings in Aerdela.

And at the end of it all, they would retake their kingdom.

"What happened there?"

Elsie's voice drew him from his thoughts, and he glanced up.

She wasn't what he'd expected.

Tall. Gorgeously tall, with shining black hair the color of Isa's—except Isa's was straight, truthfully a little limp, when it wasn't kept in the tight knot—but nevertheless, Elsie's wild mane, barely contained, seemed to pair well with her wickedly sharp tongue and the almost demanding tone to her voice.

He raised an eyebrow. "Excuse me?"

"There," she said quietly, finger gently trailing towards his bare forearms. "What happened?"

Fool. He'd pushed up his sleeves thoughtlessly. Everyone else knew the story, knew better than to ask, and of course, she couldn't simply leave it alone.

He jerked his arm away, and she started, flinching, like the movement was the precursor to a blow. His eyes locked on hers, an admonition on his tongue...

And yet, it wouldn't come.

Fletcher once said he got lost in Elsie's eyes. There was truth in that, to be sure.

Staring into them was like staring into the face of Death herself.

"It's personal."

"May I?" Elsie was gesturing to his arm. To see the scars, he realized. Maybe that was something that humans did. Gawk at each other's scars, poking and prodding until everyone was thoroughly fucked up.

Ama always did say there was a human in the Praequintelya line.

That had to be why he held out his arm, not breaking her gaze. Some inherited stupidity from a round-eared moron ages ago.

"Ouch," she muttered, eyes following the lines up from his wrists to where they disappeared beneath the wrinkled gray sleeves clustered at his elbows. Gingerly, the tip of her finger brushed across the band of them, like she was strumming a sinewy, purpled, skin-stretched band of lute strings. "My brother's a Healer. I bet he'd try and help, if you wanted him to look. These look pretty fresh, I imagine he'd be able to fix them."

"I know what he is. And there's nothing he can do." Augustus pushed his sleeve back down, turning away.

"It's kind of funny, isn't it. How we chase scars. Like we don't deserve to be unmarked, or something."

"It isn't a matter of deserving," he countered. *Don't even engage with her. This isn't any of her business.*

"But it is. If you thought you deserved a chance to get better, you'd let Teddy take a look—"

He turned on his heel, glaring. "You don't think I had the best medics in Caelaymnis to try and fix this? I am a prince. A general of the Royal Army. I had Drada crawling all the way from Thallassas trying to help, and you know what? It wasn't a matter of deserving, because none of them could do a *gods-damned thing!* These scars? They'll never fade. I will have them for the rest of my life, because some piece of shit human decided to cut me open, and the last thing I need is some half-baked healer running his filthy hands all over me, reminding me that I am marked, and there is nothing anyone can do about it!"

If she was shaken by his reprimand, though, she didn't show it.

She merely pursed her lips, and with a quiet sigh, returned to the study of the maps across the desk.

"That's it?" His voice reeked of desperation for a clash. Isa would've taunted him for it, would've turned his furious hunger into something approaching salaciousness.

But as it stood, her expression was placid, uninterested in the spar.

If she was going to fight, it'd clearly be on her terms.

That, he could respect.

He loosed a breath, rolling his neck.

"You alright?" she asked, not glancing up.

Augustus said nothing, pacing the length of the desk, trying to siphon off the agitation.

"I was being kind, you know," Elsie sighed. "They looked painful, and...well, you're a general. The others—they respect you. You're their leader. They're not about to fuss over some scratches. It's terrible, being in pain simply because nobody has taken the time to ask if you need help."

"Look, what I said about your brother—"

"He is inexperienced," she shrugged, straightening up, at last meeting his gaze. "You're not wrong." She paused, tucking a strand of hair behind her ear, her mouth slightly open, like she'd caught a slew of words just before they left her lips. "I am sorry that happened to you. Page-rippers are cruel."

His fingers were poised on the desk as he took a curious step towards where she lingered, on the other side. "What did you call them?"

"Page-rippers," she said softly. "People who rip out pages of the story you're trying to tell."

Augustus gave a derisive snort, rolling his eyes as he retreated to the fireplace. Night was beginning to fall in the compound, an insidious chill encroaching in the stone office. *Page-ripper.*

A delicate way of describing what had been a brutal, bloody affair.

And yet, not inaccurate.

He recalled awaking in the compound infirmary, on that too-small cot strapped with itchy, white sheets, and it'd been Isa, sitting worriedly in the rickety wooden chair beside him. The *ro's* dark eyes had been tearful, meeting Augustus's.

Isa didn't understand this kind of hurt.

Augustus's father had simply been dismayed that his son had been captured and drained. He hadn't even bothered to see Augustus, beyond the requisite visit for the sake of publicity, to show Caelaymnis he could not condone the actions of the Woodshades. Cam, too, had done well, seeming the grieving sister—and Heir Apparent—as she played nursemaid for all of an hour at his bedside.

Fletcher, at least, had the sense to bring their mother to visit. Not that she'd even recognized her sons, but it'd been a small comfort, listening to her incoherent stories and feeling the touch of her hand in his, at least for a little bit. Alva, too, had paid a visit, for as long of one as the mystics permitted—though that they granted her reprieve from sequester as a novice in the Conclave at all was merciful.

Floods of others came, too, held beyond the infirmary by the medics and their aides as he recuperated.

Of all the words of comfort he'd been given, though, all the apologies, all the platitudes...

Page-ripper.

The office door opened with a shivering squeal of the hinges, Fletcher appearing, out of breath and discomposed. "Father—"

"Mystic's tit—now?" Swearing, he moved on instinct, sweeping not to move the map aside, but for the cloak tossed across the back of the chair behind his desk. She couldn't be caught here. He was on thin ice, as it was, with his father, the illustrious King Bowyer, breathing down Augustus's neck about every gods-damned movement on the plateaus, and Fletcher was one misstep away from landing in a cell.

In a smooth movement, he snapped the cloak across her shoulders, eliciting a fiery glare and a smack on the hand as Elsie moved to pin the broach herself, scowling.

Maybe Isa was right.

Maybe she'd be alright, as a sister.

"Until next," he nodded, snapping his boots together, throwing his shoulders to attention, and he could've sworn there was mischief in her emerald eyes as she pulled up the hood.

They were out the door in a heartbeat.

It took seconds to clear the maps, and Augustus was right behind, except where they'd turned right, making for a side-exit, he'd veered left to intercept Bowyer. Light-footed as she might be, the king would recognize a heavy-breathing human in the strict silence of the compound corridors.

A few days' time, though, and this would all be behind them.

The Master had promised him the blood of one marked by Death herself, and against such a force, the Woodshades would be no match.

Salvation through the gods, through Death.

He just had to find her, first.

Had to find Death's Little Heiress.

RISA

"Let them toast the victory, thinking they have won the war, for the battle has not yet begun."

~Adrian Lynch

Bouncing on the balls of her feet, Risa was a fighter at the edge of the ring. Her blue advocate's robes jostled against her pressed trousers, whispered cheers of an imagined crowd, and her eyes were on the closed mahogany doors, sleek in the evening light.

"Ready?" Adrian was coming up behind her, clapping a hand on her back.

She rolled her shoulders back, nodding. "Ready."

And for a moment, the world stilled.

She found his dark eyes, icy and familiar, his masked smile, dangerous and cold.

This was their ritual.

"You are strong," he said quietly, turning for the door, words said as much for her benefit as his.

"Fiery and unstoppable." There was a chill in her voice, a promise of hellfire.

"You are power."

She flexed her hands, drawing heat back into her fingertips. "A force to be reckoned with."

"You are goodness."

"Worthy and pure." A smile was curling on her lips, now, devious and vengeful, and she was ready, ready to fight the good fight, to take names, to go until she could go no longer.

"You are light," Adrian intoned with resolution, already moving for the opening door.

Risa's heels snapped across the granite as she tilted her chin a little higher, pulled her own sort of ice from deep inside. *You are strong, you are power, you are goodness, you are light,* and she exhaled deeply, striding for the carved set of chairs set behind a matching desk.

You will not be extinguished.

And when they tell you you're nothing but a foolish girl dreaming of the impossible?

You prove them wrong.

Draped in a garish set of white robes, embroidered with the symbols of the city, Regent Luminary Chancellor Vaupellum was smirking with self-satisfaction from what was, for all intents and purposes, a carved wooden throne some distance from the rostrum. Behind him lingered Ingrit, the pathetic little creature who'd been plopped into the Adjudicant Chancellorship and bore a look of eternal confusion, broken only by undying reverentialism when his eyes found Vaupellum.

Strange bedfellows, indeed.

"The session," Vaupellum drawled, not deigning to meet Risa's gaze, "has come to order." With an indolent wave, he scooped Ingrit to attention.

From just beyond her periphery, she could feel a pair of eyes boring beneath her skin.

"The matter on the table stands as such," Ingrit twaddled on. He gave the affect, she thought with some amusement, of a rather over-plump mouse stuffed into an ill-fitted bed-sheet. Vaupellum had treated his pet to a set of those crisp, white robes he'd yanked unceremoniously from the annals—but if he'd thought the attire would lend credibility to his skeezy little mouse-man, his hopes had been painfully misplaced. "This is a provisional hearing of the Aerdelaean Revisionary Request to review the charter proposition regarding the re-negotiation of trade allowances between our esteemed City and the independent territory of Aerdela, comprising nine autonomous districts represented by a Guild of Merchants, present and accounted today. As is customary, we will hear from Advocation for the Guild first."

You are strength, you are power, you are goodness, you are light.

Adrian's eyes met hers, and he gave her a slight nod.

A third-year Resident with qualies almost in sight, she was expected to litigate her last six months independent of her advisor.

In one hundred and eighty days, she would sit her qualifying exams.

But today, she'd make them regret setting the case in her hands.

Today, she'd prove them wrong.

"Advocate?" Vaupellum was eying her with condescension, gesturing her forward with two fingers, as if she were a feral dog he was trying to coax inside. "I do believe that would be you, no? Do you have an opening statement prepared?"

Risa rose slowly.

Her movements, though, were not of hesitation.

They were of a predator, lying in wait.

Not breaking his gaze, she took the rostrum.

You are strength, you are power, you are goodness, you are light.

And she was back in the bathing room, staring herself down in the mirror as she'd said the words again and again all week, staring into her eyes, *his* eyes. The eyes of her brother, worlds away. Her fingers brushed the smooth polished wood, stained black, and she owned the moment, steadying herself, unblinking.

Against the grain of the wood, her fingertips sparked, and it was difficult not to smile.

What would he have said, if he could see her now.

Would he be proud, like a brother should be.

She liked to think so.

It was moments like these when she pretended she was talking to him. That these words, they were the only ones that he got to hear. That these sentences were his only taste of her, that in these sentences, she had to make him understand, make him see her world with the clarity of polished crystal.

"I appear," she began, "in defense of the charter upon which this City was built." Her voice cut through the room, and she heard shuffling and shifting as everyone sat up a little straighter and this, this was her chance to show him who she was. "Make no mistake, Chancellor. That is the only thing I defend today. I do not represent the interest of the Guild and the districts they covet. I do not represent any of the vying political factions within this City of our own, with their partisan agendas and power-plays. I represent nothing more than the founding doctrine that swore to provide refuge to humankind, the doctrine that swore blood be no decider, when the right to sanctuary lay at stake, the doctrine that vowed above all else to preserve the peace inherent in the hearts of humans. And today, in light of the majority vote from within the Guild, I will prove that this doctrine—our doctrine—is not being fulfilled, within the City and without. Beyond our moral duty to our kin, I will demonstrate our unwavering legal obligation to intercede, and at last bring Aerdela into the fold."

Ingrit only glowered, shooing her away from the rostrum.

Swallowing a smile, she turned on her heel, daring a glance at the men congregated in haphazard chairs directly behind her desk.

The blue-eyed, blonde-haired sausage that was Commissioner Johannsen looked acutely uncomfortable, Commissioner Fieldson, too, with his fussy little face smooshed into a grimace.

Only Clark Carson, with his smug little rat eyes, looked utterly unconcerned.

He shouldn't even be here. It was no wonder he'd taken to licking Maggie's proverbial boots, though, when it'd been her legislation that let him through the gates.

Subjects of litigation, her infamous address went, *have an inalienable right—nay, an obligation—to face the music.*

Perhaps.

But it felt a little like playing with fire and praying it didn't burn the City down.

"Thank you, Advocate Barrett," Vaupellum sighed, rising. "The issue on the table remains the question of whether or not to expand the current trade agreement. As it stands, limited quantities of rudimentary medical supplies are permitted to be distributed across Aerdela in exchange for rations of basic staples provided by the vast agricultural districts therein. The proposed modification would expand the definition of 'rudimentary supplies.' Further, it would also allow the infusion of various recreational supplies, including art and literature, from the City into Aerdela itself. Lastly, some—including Advocate Barrett—argue the expansion includes granting the right of territory to Aerdela, bringing them into the fold, as she says. This would dissolve the Treaty and allows the dissemination of culture—including magic— freely and without inhibition across the continent. Let us begin."

~ • ~

"Risa—"

"NO!" Her breath was steaming in venomous plumes on the night air, tears freezing to her cheeks, and she had failed, failed her City, failed her mentor, failed everything that they'd been working for years, and none of it mattered, because she'd failed him, failed him worse than any of the rest put together.

"You cannot win them all—"

"But this was the one that mattered!"

Her voice shattered the alley behind the Chancery, and Adrian was quiet, leaning against the brick wall, arms folded across his advocate's robes.

"This was the one that mattered," she echoed damply, face hot as she pushed back her coppery hair, fallen in soft curls from the knot it'd been barely contained in not ten minutes ago.

Petition denied.

Ooh, those words...they crawled beneath her skin. They pissed her off, made her work that much harder, but then—

And, upon additional review, the Chancellorship will further revoke current allotments to the standing agreement. Medical supplies are suspended until further notice.

Her plan—their plan, hers and Adrian's—it'd been a carefully laid set of causal events.

Get the unanimous vote.

Well, they hadn't, they'd only managed to get a 7-2 majority, and that'd been a gamble, as it was.

But the vote wasn't supposed to matter, not really, because the City was a refuge.

Until the Regent Chancellor, in his mighty wisdom, had uprooted any efforts to bring Aerdela back into the fold, and Risa was staring, now, not down a darkened alley, but down the truth that crept to the edge of her nightmares, the reality that she had been running from deep within the Archive basements.

The City didn't want Aerdela.

Which meant *he* was gone.

The one she practiced speeches to in the mirror.

The one with eyes like hers.

Really gone.

He would never know her world. And she would never return to his.

Unless—

"I want to tunnel-run."

Adrian's head snapped up, his brow furrowing. "You want to what?"

It was a small chance.

A hopeless chance.

That he would find the tunnels, find his way to the City, but there were a lot of runners waiting for someone on the outside, Asher included.

"I heard Asher talking about it, last night. He—he lost a medic," she said, pressing the tears from her eyes with the heel of her hand. "He's short-handed. What we're doing, Adrian? It isn't enough. We're moving backwards, and you know I can't just stand here, watching them take, and take, and take."

She half-expected to see frost curling at his fingertips, to feel those glacial eyes chastising her for reckless abandon.

Instead, he pushed himself up off the wall, exhaling deeply, nodding in thoughtful contemplation. "Well, I'll talk to Asher. I think you're an excellent candidate, for one—of course, gods forbid someone tell Asher what to do, stubborn jackass—but I agree. This is not the time to lay down and lick our wounds."

The affirmation made her eyes water, and sniffling, she turned her back to him.

"Risa."

There was ice crunching under foot, and his hand was on her shoulder, not cold.

Not warm, but...

She wondered if he felt it, too.

How it bled the cold from her bones, when he touched her.

"I know this was personal for you," he said quietly. "And I know you're grieving more than a bad hearing."

"I just...I want to go home."

"I think that's an excellent idea. Nerene and Roger—"

"No. I want to go *home*, Adrian." Her words hung in the air, defeated. "Not forever. Not even for very long. Just..."

"You know any contact with you makes them a target," Adrian murmured in a hushed voice. He was doing his best to be reassuring, probably. But his words only stung. "Especially without the most recent dossier, we're running in the dark."

"What about eyes," she pressed, and she knew she was barely treading water, grasping at sodden straws. "What if we put eyes on Clark. You know he's not going to take this lying down, and it'd be a chance— I mean, at least peripherally—to see..."

Adrian's hand fell from her shoulder, his sigh hissing disdainfully in the night.

And she listened as his footsteps faded into the black, listened as the sounds of the City overtook her.

Home, supposedly.

Home, after the tunnels.

ELSIE

"We often exempt our love from the oddities of daily life, as if it is something that resumes when the difficult parts are done. It makes me believe we know neither love nor loyalty."

~Theodore Alderton

Clustered around the dining table, the wine flowed with ease as merry conversation filled the air of Sam's apartment. Empty plates lay heaped in the sink, forgotten in the revelry, a half-eaten cake of strawberry and vanilla sitting at the center of the table, each of them in turn promising they couldn't possibly eat another bite, only to go back for another slice.

It'd been a successful day of scheming—and it seemed, as far as Elsie could tell, that Sam's proposal went off without a hitch.

"Well, I, for one, don't know what took you so long," Elsie remarked, raising an eyebrow as she edged her fork towards the cake, forgoing any ceremony altogether. "I told Fletch, it's been ages coming, whether you admit it or not." She shoved the oversized bite in, almost instantly regretting it, the sugary paste dissolving with sickening speed across her tongue, making her too-full stomach churn.

Didn't matter.

Worth it.

"What're you thinking for the wedding?" Fletcher asked, head tilted to the side, studying them both. "As I'm given to understand it, human celebrations vary drastically from our own. I remember when my eldest sister wed—of course, there was all the pomp and frill of your typical ceremony, but it was a bit longer, too, as she's the Heir Apparent."

Sam narrowed his eyes, a look of wry amusement on his lips. "How long is longer to you, Fletcher?"

"Another thirty minutes, maybe? So, three hours, beginning to end."

"Three—are you kidding me?" Teddy snickered, shaking his head. "That's absurd."

Fletcher merely pursed his lips, nodding his agreement.

Valley ways were simpler. An easy binding, and that was it. Say the vows, burn the candle, and really, it could be done in ten minutes, if there was a rush.

Elsie had never seen herself swearing the vows.

But if she did, she'd drag it out. If they were going to watch her stand up and tie herself off anyway, they'd get a hell of a show.

Sam gave a side-long glance to Teddy, still considering the question. "We talked about spring," he said slowly, and Teddy nodded, grinning. "Though as to the specifics of where and who—I mean, it only just happened this morning."

"I always imagined trees, just in bloom," Teddy mused. "Dunno why. Maybe 'cause we don't even have any flowering trees here. At least, not the right sort. I think I read it in a book, once, though. Flowers, perfuming the air, and whatnot, it always sounded very romantic to me."

Elsie snorted into her wine, coughing. "I—I know that one. Seemed to feature a girl in a white dress, didn't it?"

"Girl in a white dress, boy in a white vest," he shrugged, giving Sam a boyish smile. "I always thought that tale could've done with a rewrite."

"You could get married in Thallassas," Fletcher interjected, leaning forward.

"And that is," Sam prompted, eyes lingering on Teddy for a long moment before flitting back to Fletcher.

"A Dradan island in the southeast sea. Thallassas in the spring is beautiful, though," he carried on, "there's nectar trees, blossoming along the coastline, and the ocean—it's pure turquoise, and as clear as glass. Rodion's like a brother to me, I imagine his father, the Magister, would be happy to preside. 'Course, that'd mean a rather extensive guest-list..."

"That sounds beautiful," Teddy agreed, leaning back in his chair.

"Agreed," Sam added, "though I should mention that the Magister's services won't be needed. Our weddings don't include a presider."

"You...marry yourselves?"

"It's an old tradition. Goes back to when most of Aerdela was young. It was impractical to go all the way back east to find a Commissioner to marry you, not when you had fields to tend and work to be done. You know old saying—*if you want something done right, do it yourself?* Legend has it, it started with Aerdelean weddings."

Teddy rolled his eyes, snickering. "Anyway..." He shook his head, sparing Sam one final look of disdainful amusement before glancing back to Elsie. He said nothing, though, as he held her gaze, his smile fading somewhat.

There were words poised on his lips, that much, she could see.

But whatever they were, though, they were lost when Sam rose, pushing back his chair. "I suppose that is enough wedding nonsense for the moment," he said, scooping up the picked-to-death cake, turning for the kitchen.

He didn't need to say the rest.

He didn't need to tell them there was work to be done.

319

"Four invitations." Sam tossed four pearlescent envelopes onto the coffee table before falling down beside Teddy on the sofa. "You and I, of course," he nodded, threading an arm around Teddy's waist, settling in. "One for El...and one for Augustus."

"Good, good..." Fletcher was pacing the hearth rug, eyes distant, like they'd been in the general's office.

Curled in what was usually Sam's armchair, Elsie drew her knees to her chest, watching the boys with quiet disinterest.

Caelaymnis had been surreal.

It'd at least been nice, seeing Isa again. One familiar face—one she knew she got along with.

She'd been so ready to hate Augustus on behalf of his brother.

And it was true, that he was brusk. Abrupt. Sort of rude, if she read a little too much into his sharp tone. Two minutes, though, was all it'd taken, and she wouldn't have minded, staying a little longer. It was admittedly easy to see why he didn't get on with Fletcher, why the two might come to clash every so often—Fletcher could be frustratingly dense about some things, wickedly clever about others, and Augustus seemed to refuse excuse for either.

Even so, he wasn't half bad. Not really.

"I don't doubt the masquerade's a distraction," Sam mused, his caramel voice bringing her back to the living room. "Is it enough, though?"

A plan, forged in the scant few days of Teddy's recovery, in the wake of Clark's failed arrest. Sam had been skirting around the idea, hesitant, promising nothing, beyond that he'd find a way to get into the manor.

Now, with the invitations sitting on the coffee table, he'd come through.

I will fight for you.

Fletcher nodded thoughtfully, rolling his question over. "I believe it's enough. It's, in truth, more of a distraction for the Commissioner than his mercenaries. Augustus was quick to point out they'll be busy patrolling the manor house, but there's nothing to stop them from letting slip that the production facility's under attack."

"And you're sure it's on the estate?" Elsie asked, unconvinced.

"Mia and Rodion have been reporting heavy traffic in and out of a far corner of the estate to a heavily guarded warehouse. There's more than a few unsavory creatures amongst his ranks, too, from what they're telling me." Eyes flicking to Elsie, he resumed the steady pace of the creaking wooden floor. "The plan," he went on, worrying his hands, "is this. El and Sam, your job is to distract Clark. Head off the mercenaries, and keep him too busy to care what may or may not be happening beyond the boundaries of the manor house."

"Should be easy," Sam offered, craning one-handed across Teddy to tug the throw over both of them. "There's intrigue galore to be had, arriving with a fiancé on my arm, and that doesn't even broach what El and I can bring, with his nonsense about her mother, and whatnot."

If it was really nonsense.

Elsie spared a look to Sam, who didn't return the glance.

It could be more than a distraction. Something could be two things at once.

Maybe they'd pull his attention from the raid happening beyond the house—and maybe they'd pull some information from him, too.

The two of them together, maybe they could bully something more substantial from him—like what the information in the letters was guarding her against. What threat was so immense, that a woman of sound resources and judgment had willingly left her infant child in a back-district farmhouse. What details Sam might've seen, woven into

321

Elsie's life, details Clark was so keen to capture.

"Augustus will be close, acting as guard and officer, to make the arrest, when the moment comes. He can't apprehend Clark initially, but he'll be playing the role of El's...escort, so as not to draw attention," Fletcher remarked bitterly, grimacing. "Meanwhile, myself, Rodion, Mia, and Isa will take the facility. If all goes according to plan, it should be swift and silent."

"And me," Teddy prompted, looking underwhelmed. No matter how much he'd gushed about the engagement, there was no way he'd appreciate being toted about as a token oddity, the requisite rags-to-riches of every fairy tale. He'd do it, though, Elsie thought, watching him. He'd do it for Sam. For Fletcher. For her. He lived too much of his life for other people.

"Help with Clark, and when he's been detained, help with the facility," Fletcher said quietly. "There's no telling how many are still in holding, or what kind of shape they're in. You'll play aide to Isa, triaging and treating anyone who needs it."

The mantle clock chimed nine.

With a sigh, Fletcher at last abandoned his patrol of the floor, turning to brush a kiss across Elsie's cheek. "I have to go."

She could see the discomfort in his eyes, that this plan weighed so heavily on his adaptiveness. His abilities, from her perspective, were quick, practiced—but nobody would've ever said Fletcher rolled well with the punches.

If he couldn't sequester the facility—doubtless a heavily warded facility—in suffocating isolation, there'd be bloodshed, and lots of it. So, Fletcher had to master the sequestering of the facility. And that meant logging hours with his brother in the training hall at the Caelaymnic compound.

"I'll see you at the lodge," she murmured, giving his fingers a squeeze before rising herself. "More wine?"

"Sounds lovely," Sam grinned, nestling in closer to Teddy.

Elsie smiled. At least for the moment, things were alright.

AUGUSTUS

"Great are the men that challenge the gods, and dust are those who defy them."

~*Anscip Xavishia, Insidiae in the Coalition*

"Something on your mind?"

Cam's soprano voice cut through the soft clip-clop of hooves, and a pair of flashing eyes met Augustus as he glanced to the rider beside him.

Even on a casual patrol through the pines to the northwest of the city, she looked regal. Her almost platinum hair was slicked back into a severe knot, an easy circlet atop it, dropping a single teardrop sapphire onto her delicate forehead. That was where any real elegance ended, though.

Beneath the dark cloak, her glistening silver tunic was belted with a swath of cord, as was the traditional style. On most, it was a friendly look, giving an almost quaint appearance to the Drada dwelling in these mountains.

On Cam, it was terrifying. Augustus himself had always been left with the vague impression that if he really pissed her off, she'd have happily garroted him with the belt without displacing a single hair beneath her circlet.

She remained, though, his sister and his confidant.

Blood ran thicker than the impending fear of a good garroting.

The gentle padding of Valoxus had done little to soothe his troubled thoughts tonight.

A few hours prior had found Augustus in the Master's company. In the streets of an unfamiliar little settlement buried in oceans of prairie and scraggled trees sucking down what little water ran through the arid desert of grass before it crashed into the massive river, the river he knew cut through Aerdela like a scythe.

Nobody had given the Master a second glance, strolling down the Valley avenues.

He belonged there.

I don't have time for games, Augustus had growled, leaning against the brick shop, trying not to breathe in the stink of tobacco and piss. Humans were filthy creatures.

She will come, the Master mused.

The one marked with gold.

The one marked by Death herself.

At last, the Master's finger had drifted up, pointing across the street. *There. That is the one. That's the little heiress. That's the descendant of Death.*

A girl with hair as black as the night, and eyes like emeralds.

A girl, who even then, had been turning something gold over in her fingertips once, twice, before tucking it back beneath her navy coat.

And now, there was a choice.

Cut down the humans besieging Caelaymnis once and for all. End the assaults, end the bloodshed, end the pyres that seemed to light the sky every gods-damned night.

Or let the violence continue.

I solved your little mystery, brother, Augustus thought bitterly, nudging Valoxus forward. The Master's work had taken him into the Valley.

325

Fletcher had been right, there was blood magic here. But Augustus's own fears had been unfounded—it wasn't Aerdela, amassing magic. It was the Master, invoking the power of the gods. And that changed everything.

It made sense. The first of the Ruby Tears had to come from somewhere, while they had waited for the batch brewing in Cam's cellars to ripen. Before that Woodshade scum had cried those first drops, while Augustus had still been marked with the bruises of lightning, while Epherias's pyre still smoked, the Master had bequeathed to him a taste of the forthcoming victory.

It would've been hopeful, seeing the girl in the street.

The girl that had to die.

Hopeful, if he hadn't known her. Talked to her. Become rather fond of her, in the few hours they'd shared.

One life for thousands.

Tactically, it was a sound decision.

She was the heiress to powers only gods could dream of, and in her veins, old magic begging to be awakened. Her blood would bring a victory devoid of death. Her sacrifice would bring a stop to the violence spilling from the Woodshades.

The Master said she was the only daughter of Cora.

The only daughter of Death.

Such drivel, he'd thought, had been the stuff of legends. The gods were not to be mocked, painted as impulsive interlopers sharing the beds of humans—and yet, the Master had not been wrong, in his direction to administer the Ruby Tears on the tongue of each warrior, to wrench their magic back from the grip of the Woodshade humans who'd so wrongfully stolen it, and so, perhaps in this, he was not wrong, either.

Perhaps it *was* that the gods had imbued within their descendants a gift to mortals.

A gift that would save Caelaymnis.

Tomorrow, Augustus had intended to don a waistcoat and cravat so beloved in Aerdela in the name of chasing blood magic from these boarders. But this was not the Woodshades. This was not a mad dash for magic from people starved of it for too long.

The Master was in control, here, and he knew the power he wielded. Knew it, honored it, and understood that Caelaymnis needed it.

And so, tomorrow, he would abandon his brother.

He would abandon his lover, his friends, the soldiers under his command.

But he would not abandon his city.

Loyalty before amity.

"Father is a fool, parading about these victories against the Woodshades as though they were his own," Cam remarked with a look of disgust.

"He is a fool for holding fast to his sentiments," Augustus muttered, glancing back to the towering spire, hardly visible through the trees. Even in the dark, it shown brightly, marking the temple of the gods at the center of the city. He would cleanse himself doubly, for her sacrifice.

"Does he think shattering the treaty will do anything but bring violence? And not to mention the hungry, the sick—anyone demanding the mysticism of the Drada be harnessed for their own good."

"Not when the City refuses to do the same," he agreed, pushing Elsie from his thoughts. It did not do to dwell. "They increase their protections, and we are supposed to open our gates to the flood of humans they have abandoned? I think not."

"Things will be different, when I have his seat. Cormalum assures me I will have Senate support, when we move." A glint of silver flashed in the moonlight, her circlet shining as she spared him a glance. "Father can spout his open-walled nonsense from the inside of a cell for all I care. What he plays at is treason."

So is plotting to overthrow the king.

Not that he'd dare counter with the remark, even as a joke, for she would not take it as such.

At least her husband, the illustrious Senator Cormalum, had guaranteed backing. Now that had been a powerful match, the Heir Apparent and a Senator. A guaranteed control of the politicians scurrying about the rostrum steps, and an honorary title for one of inconsequential bloodlines—few of peasant birth could boast of being Senator and Titled Prince.

Augustus would win his victory for the city.

He would see his sister crowned Queen.

And it would all begin with the arrest of Elsie Mirabeau.

RISA

"Who are you, when things get hard? Will you fight for
them, as much as you're fighting for yourself? Or will you
turn and run? They're fond of saying 'right' and 'easy'
are not the same, but I wonder how easy it must feel,
knowing you've abandoned them in their hour of need."
~Adrian Lynch

Prove them wrong.

This place was a refuge. *A solace for your winters,* that was the carving above the Chancery. *Fuel for your fires. An ocean for your tributary. And bandages, for your wounds.*

From the founding doctrine, and quoted in the treaty that had raised the City and sealed the walls.

In the cavernous sewer, frozen and putrid, Asher's face was all shadow. But even so, she didn't have to see the carved disdain across his brow to feel his disapproval.

Tunnel runs were dangerous.

And a novice runner like her was a liability.

But each team needed a medic, and the latest casualties had left an unfortunately opportunistic vacancy, one Risa had been happy to fill.

The straps of her knapsack bit into her shoulders through the thick wool coat. She shifted the weight, the scrape of her rubber-soled boot through the sludge beneath ringing gritty through the empty shaft.

"Shh," Asher hissed, sending a wave of goosebumps prickling up her neck.

Twenty years a tunnel runner, and she trusted his reprimand. He hadn't made it this far by being careless.

Slowly, in the distance, the sound of the angry ocean began to seep towards them, with it, iced water that could cover their heads, when all was said and done.

So started the clock.

Brine filled her nose as the roar grew louder, someone down the line unleashing the cover of the storm.

Freezing water up to their ankles, now, soaking mercilessly through the layers, and Asher's voice was another cresting wave. "Move."

Her hand swept down the slimy brick wall, boots splashing through the onslaught as they ran towards the flood. A sharp right, the tunnel narrowed, and it was up to her calves, her blood crystallizing, her breath catching as it frosted in the night.

Keep going.

There were only three, waiting at the junction. A man, a worryingly quiet bundle in his arms, and a little girl, blue lips quivering with tears, her rasping cries thick with mucus.

"Dose her," Asher muttered, pulling the little girl out of the water and scooping her onto his hip. She was a rag doll in his arms, her struggling limbs and hyperventallic cries useless in the cold.

Risa, though, had already popped the cork from the vial. A few murmured comforts, and the girl downed it in one shuddering gulp.

She was silent a moment later.

Asher only gave the motionless bundle a quick side-long glance before turning to leave.

Water mid-thigh, and Risa was the last to follow, shooing the man and his bunch of blankets before her down the tunnel. The current dragged against her numb legs, ate away at the ground beneath her, and if she fell, they would never know. Never see. Never turn back and try to find her. And she would be alone.

Rescindant, the water seemed to hiss.

Rescindant.

This part, she remembered from when she was a girl.

Rising out of the water, ready for the relief of dry land, only to find the biting air was merciless.

The staircase seemed to rise forever, her heavy, feelingless feet plodding against grated iron, and there was breathless urgency as her water-soaked lungs strained against the wet clothes, sucking the heat from her with frightening rapidity.

And she was alive. Her muscles were burning as a shout echoed from behind them—so close, gods, they were so fucking close—

A concussive shock rippled through the underground, flecks of dirt raining down. The man in front of her stopped dead, clutching the bundle of blankets to his chest, petrified, shaking, because how far had he come? How much had he risked, what had he lost that made this look so gods-damned glorious, what made him drag his infant child across gods only knew how many miles to plunge through the icy sewer, praying that there'd be a tomorrow for them both—

"Go," she snapped, fury in her voice, and he jolted into movement.

She could see it, the faint crack of light beyond as Factionist flares erupted to life behind them.

Solace.

~•~

Risa had never been very good at letting go.

Her grudges, to hear Nerene tell it, had been notorious as a child. And she obsessed, too—*allegedly*—would find any detail, regardless of how small, and allow it to consume her, devour her, tear her apart until she could see nothing beyond her own fanatic worship of minutia.

But above the infatuations, the fixations, the relentless compulsions that ground away the patience of anyone within earshot, Risa had found that nothing hurt quite so much as the letting go of a goodbye.

She hadn't really known any of them, tonight. Hadn't known the little girl wrapped in blankets, sucking down hot chocolates, giggling with an aunt who'd come through the tunnels the year before, Elementals, the both of them, from the north, with ties to the City that might've reached back before the walls. Before the wars.

Nor had she really known the man, smiling quietly as he bounced the cooing baby on his knee—alive and well, thank the gods. A Healer, hedging bets that this place of refuge was more than just a rumor. A father, hoping his talents were not the fatal affliction his wife had accused, that he had not damaged their baby girl with whatever lay coiled in his veins.

And it still stung, all the same, knowing she'd never see any of them again.

Asher, for all he claimed to be a hardened man, salted with age and experience, still looked a little teary-eyed when they'd parted ways.

Do you ever wonder what happens to them? Everyone you've brought in? It'd probably been an improper question. Propriety, though, had never stopped her.

I do, he'd replied.

She'd been surprised that he excused his staunch stoicism for an answer.

No complaints, though. And no remarks, either—chalk it up to expert interrogating skills, and call it a day.

I do wonder. It would be good, some days, I think, to see what a second lease on life looks like. But that is too much happiness for such a bitter old man. It isn't my lot to know. And there's always you, kiddo.

Risa had been the exception.

Forget that Nerene and Roger knew Asher from way back, that they were all of them Resindants, that anarchy ran in the blood of them all.

She liked to think it was because she refused to say goodbye.

He had carried her through the tunnels just like that girl tonight—except that was before they'd started dosing the kids, before tunnel running was a lethal marathon—and he'd carried her right on up to the front door of Nerene and Roger Barrett, right on up the carpeted stairs of their house by the sea, right into that abhorrently pink-and-white little room they'd painstakingly decorated for the little girl they'd wanted so badly, and when he'd gone to set her down on the bed by the window, she'd death-gripped his neck, like she had the moment he'd scooped her up, and refused to let go.

She'd done enough letting go, by then.

Asher, she'd learn later, had lost his brother. He'd lost his sister-in-law, and he'd lost his niece, and his nephew, and his parents, and his wife, too, and he wasn't terribly keen on letting go, either, in a sort of reclusive and bitter almost-uncle sort of way.

With a sigh of exasperation, Risa tossed a wax-paper bag down on her desk, slumping into the leather armchair.

The Chancery was cold and deserted and worlds better than her stupid little apartment where stupid Lea should've been waiting with her stupid *you were supposed to be home at ten* and *let me fix you a bite* and it'd been a stupid, stupid, stupid mistake, letting that girl go, and Lea was needy and selfish and she'd cared, she'd cared that Risa ran herself ragged, she'd cared that Risa was beating herself up over every damnable failure, she *cared*—

No. No, she wasn't going to do this.

The rough-textured numbers on the drawer lock moved silently, clicking open with a quick *0302* and she tossed the file onto her desk, fanning the papers out.

Elizabeth.

No last name, of course. Not that she needed it. No description, no age, no address, no indication of where she'd been left, and it was odd, seeing someone's life laid out, not really knowing who they were.

A bright young girl, this chapter of the dossier began. The handwriting was elegantly neat, with loops and curls that only someone from the Guild would've taken the time to craft.

She is taken with her books, and the idea that there is simply more. Unafraid and utterly resilient, I believe defiance is in her blood. Even under arrest for blatant thievery, her spirits remained unhindered.

Risa snickered, thumbing through the stack of parchment. Sam was a character. She'd been tossed the file three years prior, expecting clinical descriptions, only to find the waxing poeticism of one determined to chronicle life with all the artistic liberties they could muster.

She adores her brother, another read. *Not a moment goes by when I see them willingly parted. He is defensive of her every move, and she of his—should one be slighted, the other would end the offender without batting an eye. A formidable team, the pair of them.*

Did he know, she often wondered. Did he know how much of himself he'd betrayed.

Her brother recently fell ill, as have many in the district. It seemed to be a small thing, brought on with the changing season. His absence from his place of employ led me to escort her home that evening, for which I rightfully received much admonishment on her part. I believe, though, her sustained lecture was, in part, in jest—my aim, it seemed, in accompanying her, was written on my sleeve.

The dilapidation of conditions was disheartening. Wind easily cut through the drafty walls, the pantry was painfully bare—though I knew their home before, my visits remained during warmer months, when time was spent in the cool glade by the river. Where their parents had gone, I do not know, but she had managed a watery, albeit hot, soup whilst I stoked the dying fire, trying to warm him with threadbare blankets.

I confess her denial of the gravity of his illness, and my own concern. I stayed, to see him through the night.

The most recent dossier sat atop them all, penned some six months ago.

There is happy news, I believe, on her behalf, though her reluctance to—

"Risa?"

She started violently, head snapping up as papers scattered in alarm across the floor. "What the fuck, Adrian," she muttered angrily, stooping to collect the spilled file, "lurking on the threshold at two-fucking-o'clock in the gods-damned morning—"

"You have a correspondence, I was going to leave it on your...desk..." He trailed off, envelope forgotten in his hand, brows furrowing. "What happened to your hand?"

335

Her eyes flicked to the blood caked to the back of her hand, creeping down her wrist in several dark lines, dried and crusting in the cold air. "Had a run with Asher. Meant to clean it up, I just..."

"You just...decided you'd get a little work done first?" Adrian scoffed, snatching up the waxy parcel abandoned on the corner of her desk, extracting the bottle of emollient and roll of bandages.

"It was a long night, okay? Leave it be—"

"And you're supposed to be a Healer." He'd pulled up a chair adjacent to her, uncorking the vial before taking her hand in his, and slowly, he let the thick, purple salve drip down into the cut.

It wasn't worth the fight, she thought, leaning back in her chair, her fingers limp in his. She was too tired to die on this pathetic hill of poor self-care.

"I can see," he murmured, tearing off a piece of cotton bandaging, "why you weren't fond of study at the Institute."

Watching him work the flakes of blood from her hand with gentle sweeps, she raised an eyebrow. "Oh?"

"My understanding is that training for one with your talents typically involves, oh, I don't know...actually *healing.*"

"I was never pent-up enough, or powerful enough, to mend myself," she said dully.

His dark eyes flicked up to hers. The irony hadn't been lost on him, it seemed.

"I was always painfully resentful of the Healers," he offered softly, after a long moment. He'd returned to work, binding her chilled hand rather messily with a clean swath of cotton. "They wore their talents for the world to see. A sort of moralistic badge of honor."

"Yeah. Well. Bully for them."

He gave a soft chuckle, tying off the bandage. Then, a smile still lingering at the corners of his lips, he laced their fingers together, letting his eyes close.

And deep in her bones, she felt it.

To describe it as burning, as heat, as delicious warmth...it wasn't right.

It was the absence of cold.

And in its absence, herself.

That deep ice that'd bled into her veins wading waist-deep through sewers of freezing saltwater was, at last, seeking refuge elsewhere—in him, as he siphoned it away, leaving her tired body to find some semblance of warmth once more.

A master of the ice.

"Thanks," she said softly, watching his eyes open once more.

He gave her fingers as squeeze before letting go. "Anytime. Just don't tell the Healers," he teased, as an afterthought. "They'd tell me to stop meddling with things beyond my ken." Rising with some effort, he tapped the envelope on her desk. "Speaking of..."

The parchment gave beneath her fingers as she tore into the letter, grimacing at the familiar scrawl atop a gilded card.

MS. Theresa Barrett is cordially invited

"Oh, you have to be fucking kidding me..." Turning the card over, her eyes flew across the chicken scratch on the back.

You will find, in attendance, Clark's handwriting read, and she could almost hear his salacious drawl, see his smirking grimace of satisfaction, *You will find, in attendance, the last dossier.*

ELSIE

*"There is nothing so unnerving as returning to a place
familiar, and seeing how much you've changed."*

~Risa Barrett

The first sugared flakes of snow were beginning to drift gently down beyond the frosting windowpanes as the world at last relented to winter, and Elsie sat with her head in her hands, entranced as she watched the magic filling Sam's apartment from her seat in the dining room. Wave after wave of brilliant little motes were sent whirling in tiny little puffs, her brother's eyes flaring with concentration, Fletcher occasionally murmuring some inaudible instruction, moving every now and then to guide a wave of sparks with a soft gesture of his hand until they coalesced into a humming little swarm of merry light.

"It's...ugh, come on," Teddy was muttering, flexing his fingers as he sat cross-legged on the sofa. An unseen breeze seemed to ripple through the motes, drawing them into a hazy cloud—that was until, with vivacious rebellion, one flew violently from the pack, burning out like an ember from the hearth as it finished its chaotic arc through the air.

A quiet snicker of delight escaped Elsie's upturned lips and her brother glanced over, a smile dancing in his eyes.

There was no terror in his gaze. Nothing but brilliant determination, and a sort of peace she didn't know if she'd ever really seen.

"Good," Fletcher nodded, and Teddy's eyes snapped back to the task at hand. "Don't be afraid to coax it with a physical gesture, like you did that last time. Shaping a lucent can be quite abstract, and I often find pairing it with a tactile movement immensely helpful."

Exhaling deeply, her brother nodded, shaking out his hand before starting again.

She could've watched them all night. Had, in fact, watched them for hours as they worked every evening after dinner. It was a funny kind of new normal, magic in the living room.

There was a smile tugging at Sam's lips as she joined him by the sink. Grabbing a dishtowel, she plucked a still-steaming plate from the stack of dripping dishes and began to dry.

"So," she began idly. "Tomorrow." As if it was just another day.

"Tomorrow," he echoed, smile faltering somewhat. But he said nothing else as quiet fell between them, the sound of soapy dishes and the squeal of her cloth against porcelain overtaking the conversation.

Only when a stack of dried dishes sat gleaming on the countertop and Sam had plunked the baking dish into the soapy water with a quiet *thunk* did he break the silence.

"Not to be untoward," he asked in an undertone, hands braced on the edge of the sink as he met her gaze, "but can I ask you something, El?"

She nodded, leaning against the counter.

"Did you go back often? To the farmhouse?"

"No. Not since Fletcher," she said simply. It'd been a fracturing point. And it didn't matter. They hadn't wanted her there, she hadn't wanted to be there...and now they were ashes in the ground.

Occasionally, they'd sent half-baked regrets of her absence from

Tom to Teddy, and from Teddy to herself. But it was mutually acknowledged that they were nothing more than the lines to be said at the given moment, and in time, the feigned concern would fade to mutual animosity, then to distant memory, and eventually, to nothing.

Like they'd never even existed.

"When...do you know the last time Teddy went back?" The question had been poised on her lips, a thought snapped forward in the spur of the moment.

Sam glanced at her before fishing the pan from the sink. "It'd been a bit. Couple months, maybe?"

"Not that they were fussed," she put it, straightening up to hoist the stack of plates into the cupboard.

"Oh, gods, no," he agreed.

"He could be bedding down with a rabid dog, and they wouldn't have said a peep, so long as it had a healthy inheritance."

Snickering, Sam shook his head. "True. Rest their souls, it's very true."

Elsie's fingers lingered on the ridged handle of the cabinet as she gave him a side-long look. "Why did you ask about me going home?"

"Just...thinking," he mumbled, eyes focused on the task of scrubbing brown-melted cheese and baked-on potato from the glass dish. "Thinking about going back to the places we were raised."

In her mind, he was always taller. It was the fault of memories, she mused, that stretched him out. They made him a bit older, too. But he'd hit five-and-a-half feet and stuck, something almost petite lurking distantly behind his well-muscled body.

"So." She watched as he rinsed the suds from the dish, his hands red from the hot water, the sleeves of his tunic rolled up past his elbows to reveal tanned forearms. "Tomorrow. A gods-damned ball."

He passed the dish to her before pulling a cloth from the stack, drying his hands. "Tomorrow," he agreed softly. Then, with a grin, he beckoned her to follow. "C'mon. One last gown fitting before your grand debut."

THE MASKS

Traditionally hosted by the district Commissioner, an introduction is the single most important moment in the life of every merchant's child. It is a moment of becoming. Becoming eligible. Becoming an adult. Becoming who it is you truly wish to be.

It is with eager anticipation that I hope this is a night of becoming, not only for young Desdemona, but for us, as well.

If all goes as planned, this will be a night I become free.

~SAM ALDERTON,
EXCERPT FROM A LETTER DATED DECEMBER 3RD

TEDDY

"Behind the mask, who truly be,
Behind the mask, you truly see."

~Emilyon Dresada, 'Child's Chant' from 'Collected
Dradan Poetry'

Long ago, in a time before recollection, there had been a child who'd fallen through a mirrored meadow lake. It'd been enchanted, or so the tales said, and instead of drowning, the child found a grotesque carnival of the unimaginable, delightful and frightening, all at once. No earthly bounds constricted the realms beneath the glassy surface, leaving it a barren canvas upon which only the gods could paint a picture, both terrible and fantastical.

The carriage jostled to a stop, and Teddy swallowed hard, his throat burning with the taste of polished leather seats and saccharine vanilla hangings.

Through the lacy windows lay the manor, set aglow against the burgeoning twilight.

His personal mirrored meadow lake.

Already, Sam had taken the plunge, stepping onto the smooth walk, a brilliant smile sketched across his lips—a smile that did not reach his molten cinnamon eyes buried inside the scarlet-rubied mask. He offered a hand, and Teddy took it, willing his jellied legs to work.

The chilled air was perfumed with the stench of anise and orange, the whole manor transformed—presumably transformed, he supposed, from Sam's vague recountings—into a glittering palatial monstrosity, the walkway decked with swaths of shimmering white satin, patterned lanterns throwing out bursts of textured light against the pale stone walk, great sparkling spheres illuminated from within suspended in an arbor above them, scattered in between the thin paper snowflakes drifting lazily from ribbon in the whispered breeze.

He was frozen where he stood, hand closed tightly around Sam's.

Whatever else it was below this glassy surface, it was hellishly beautiful.

"Shall we," Sam prompted softly, giving Teddy's fingers a squeeze. Even his voice had changed. The edges of his words had been squared off, any lilt that betrayed his birth choked out of the air.

Teddy gave a small nod, eyes flickering back as his heart heaved into motion once more.

Fashionably late, that's what they were. Only a few pastries lingered, the distant ringing of conversation echoing from somewhere unseen as they crossed into the marbled foyer. And it was better this way, he had to remind himself. The more eyes that could linger on the two of them, the fewer that might stray where they ought not to.

Even still, there was a haughty sort of confidence about Sam.

He would revel, tonight, in the falling of the Commissioner, revel like one first tasting freedom.

Summiting the landing, Teddy caught a reflection of a man glinting back at him in a garish mirror against the damask wallpaper.

Lingering a handful of inches above Sam, the man was slender, with reddish-brown hair that'd been tamed in a side-part, smooth and soft and already betraying the tousled frame it usually held. A silken vest sat beneath a black suit, a deep purple cravat beneath that, dotted with a glimmering silver pin that matched cufflinks peering out on crisp-white sleeves, and he looked, to Teddy's eyes, a painting. A surreal painting— one Sam might've conjured in his adolescence, if he'd been asked to paint himself a husband at fifteen.

The man in the mirror reached up to touch the sapphire mask, and Teddy felt his own hand brush against the feathered temple, felt the settling of felt against his hot skin beneath.

Sam was offering an arm, now, a booming voice echoing beyond the doors cracking open like some horrendously encrusted egg, shrouded in paint and jewels and bearing flocks of pastries within, and their names almost ripped him from himself, hearing them scattered down the grand staircase now flowing down before them.

"Master Samuel Carson" —*no, no, no, that isn't right, everyone thinks he's Samuel, but he's just Sam, it isn't short for anything, and he's Alderton, they got it all wrong*— "and Theodore Mirabeau" —*so empty, it's so empty, Master for the Commissioners and their families, Mister for the rest of the Merchants, and then there's just me, it's just me, empty, empty empty*—

You are not empty.

He could feel the stitches prickling in his chest, angry to be bottled in his blood when they ought to have been floating in his palm.

You are alive.

He had to remember to breathe as they took the first step down together, and he couldn't recall so many eyes ever watching him.

Crystal chandeliers threw the ballroom floor into the light of a sugar-spun fever dream, the wild colors and diamond teeth the makings of some sort of dessert-cart menagerie, only here, beneath the lake, it'd be the pastries and the tarts that gobbled them all down.

Another step.

He had a tight grip on Sam's arm, fingers digging into the suit coat fabric, and Sam—Sam's snowy smile was white, bright as he waved—actually waved—and Teddy realized there was applause rippling through the crowd beneath them, cheering—

Painted faces were gawking, bedecked fingers pointing—pointing at him, he realized, salacious grins sparking with hunger.

And another step. He could do this. Was doing this.

His eyes scanned the crowd, searching—

There she was.

Her deep green gown clung to her like a second skin before flaring out below her hips, belted in a single row of black diamonds Sam had carefully set by hand the night before.

Elsie was grinning, arms folded across her chest, eyes caught in the emerald mask.

She felt miles away.

But seeing her—it helped.

He forced a small smile, eyes not drifting from the back of the ballroom.

A silver-masked man, a head-and-a-half over El, lingered uncomfortably close at her side.

Augustus.

The suit did little to conceal the lethality about his movements. If anyone took notice of him, though, it didn't show—whether this wasn't so much Augustus's discretion as his imposing physique, Teddy could only speculate.

Beyond the garden hedges were the rest.

Rodion, with his mop of curly black hair, his boyish face, his rich mahogany skin that seemed to radiate warmth.

Mia, with her cropped strawberry-blonde hair and her almost impenetrable accent, so thick it verged on unintelligible.

350

Isa, walking somewhere between definition itself, ready to mend whatever waited beyond the production facility walls.

Teddy ripped his eyes from Elsie and Augustus as he met the ballroom with Sam.

The others had their work.

And he and Sam, they had theirs.

The eyes of Commissioner Clark Carson were needles from beneath the pearlescent mask as he murmured something to the chittering little desserts clustered around. Tittering, they scattered, and Teddy was left with the distinct impression of roaches skittering away at the strike of a match.

Sam paused under the pretense of straightening Teddy's cravat. "Well," he breathed, and there was a faint smile of reassurance lingering on his lips. "That's our invitation." His eyes flicked up, some cynical amusement deep in the brown. "I suppose, after nine years, it's rather time I introduced you."

"I think we could've made it a nice round ten, and I wouldn't have complained," Teddy said hoarsely, glancing over his shoulder.

Sam's smile faltered as he brushed a speck of dust from the spotless lapel. "In another life, maybe. So it goes, though, that this," he quoted, "this be the river we're destined to sail."

"Your authors wouldn't've been so complacent if they'd had to talk to Clark."

"No," Sam sighed, taking Teddy's arm as he plastered an artificially cheerful smile on once more, beginning to steer them towards the Commissioner's vacant patch of ballroom. "But it's the best we've got at the moment."

Books and tea and we're going to stay locked in this damn apartment, just the two of us, for days, Sam had promised that morning, as dawn had crept steadily on and they'd lain beneath the sheets, passing the moments of a sleepless night. *And we won't say a word. I'll paint you in kisses, and you'll understand.*

He clung to that promise, now, watching one last time as Sam betrayed himself.

FLETCHER

"It is nature not to see the trap until it is sprung, lest traps we would not call them."

~Dryadic Proverb, from the Book of Adagic Texts

Whispers of mercenaries rippled across the grounds, heavy boots clodding across dampened soil, ripping great chunks from the muddy earth with squelching disregard as they stomped through the night.

Eyes pressed closed, Fletcher let the calamity overtake him, fill him, become him.

This, he knew.

Snakes of magic, unfamiliar and warning, came across the hissing grass, an echo of unbelonging.

The Commissioner had a keen taste for talent, talent he ought not've known, talent that ended not with the kobalde in the brambles. Employ of thugs like these wasn't unheard of, in the depths of the wild, where the treaty did not reach and all sorts of sordid creatures roamed unchecked, pillaging as they went. Here, though, where the humans had been cordoned off from magic, where the greatest threat wasn't the formidable beasts from the shadows but overdue taxes and mismatched finery...

No, there was only one reason the Commissioner would find use for such unsavory types.

Wood groaned, a door slamming shut to the sound of bloodied promises, lest posts they abandon.

A round dozen.

Outnumbered three-to-one.

If he could not do this, blood would be shed, and he could not guarantee none of it would be Dradan.

Fletcher exhaled, letting his shoulders fall down.

And with the snap of his wrists, he encased the warehouse. *Just like the teapot.*

It was a careful play of pressures, draining the air from the shield, and he reveled in the rush of air burning against his skin, the sensation of utter satisfaction of crafting something new with his own two hands, something practiced in the dead of night as Elsie slept, in the training hall under Augustus's watchful tutelage, with every waking breath.

He was air, packed tightly between the membranous wall of magic.

He was nothing, a calm void inside the warehouse, spreading silently into lungs now choking on what little air they'd wrung out in their sputtering breaths.

He was the grass that hissed, he was the dark stars singing, he was the gritty earth sighing beneath his boots, he was everything, and nothing, and it was freedom.

His eyes snapped open as the last body hit the floor, unmoving.

Done.

A faint smile was tugging on his lips, and there was a rush of pride deep in his chest as the wall fell, a rush of air quelling the vacuum within in one chilled gust. This was not the beluae, a victim of careless distraction, snarling beast though it'd been.

"Move."

Rodion clapped him on the back, grinning like an idiot before jogging forward, and with Mia's help, pulled open the warehouse door with a bone-chilling *screeeeeetch*, and breathless, Fletcher stopped a few feet out from the threshold.

No. No, no, no, no, no—

Swearing, he gave an angry swat of the air, furious.

There was no victory here.

RISA

"Bitter are the meetings of our childhood, for they
remind us of times we wish were simpler."

-from 'The Advice of The Long-Dead' and Other Essays

Any sense of victory sparked by returning home to the Valley remained somewhat overshadowed by the overtly dubious means by which Risa had arrived.

Ideally, it wouldn't have been by extortion. *Appear, and you'll get the dossier.* Appear, get the dossier, and the Rescindants could go on protecting the girl in their charge with the information therein.

Then, too—ideally—she wouldn't have been sequestered to the curio-cabinet manor, the frozen, fairy tale relic on a bluff above the town, stuffed into a moth-balled gown dragged reluctantly from a trunk of theater costumes.

But home was home, even if she couldn't see it from within the manor, and none of that really mattered, anyway, because she was here for one thing, and one thing alone, on that, Adrian had been painfully clear.

The dossier would not collect itself.

The Commissioner wasn't difficult to spot, nursing a snifter of brandy.

"Charming little shindig, Clark," Risa remarked dryly, purple dress *whishing* as she came to a stop at his elbow, displacing a stuffed-suit doll in the little circle of adoration he'd no doubt summoned to soothe his perpetually ruffled feathers.

She wasn't a sadistic woman.

But watching him squirm through her painted mask—his buggy little eyes bulging, his thin little lips pressing into an impenetrable line—a wave of chills left her arms covered in goosebumps of satisfaction. "Commissioner," he corrected stiffly, the refrain another verse in their eternal give-and-take of *Mr.-no-it's-Commissioner-no-its—*

"Oh, you," she simpered, draping her fingers on his arm with an air of jovial fondness. "I've told you, there's no need to call me Commissioner. Ms. Barrett will do just fine."

Laughter—suspiciously authentic and a bit too robust to be feigned—rippled through the tight circle.

Clark, it seemed, wasn't amused.

"You'll excuse us," he snipped to the adoration, hand already on her elbow, dragging her away, "my...associate...odd sense of humor..."

"Odd? I'd say brilliant—"

His glare snapped into place, tone shifting from familial embarrassment to utter outrage as he took refuge in the shadow of a towering pillar, sculpted to perfection from the sweetest butter-marble. "They say discretion is the better part of valor..."

"Well, mercifully for you, *Clark*, I'm not a heroine, I'm Adrian's lackey on an errand," she bit back, smile faltering. "Where's the dossier?"

It suited him, the opulent mask hiding his crows-feet skin, home to the coal she'd come to know so well. Beneath the Chancery lights, bright and unforgiving, he had looked old, worn, a corn-husk doll painted pretty but fraying all the same. But there was room to hide, here, beneath the warm cascade of chandeliers. Room to obfuscate.

"Patience, patience, all in good time…

"She doesn't have time, Clark. Every minute we're running in the dark, we risk losing her, and if we lose her, you can guaran-gods-damned-tee that I will make sure you're begging on the streets—"

"Hush, love." Clark was nodding to the grand staircase, a half-smile now playing at his thin lips. "All in good time."

Her eyes flicked to the top of the staircase.

A small piece of good news, at least.

"Master Samuel Carson…"

A rush of silence fell across the buzzing bees below as a man in a ruby mask stepped onto the carpeted landing, a dazzling smile greeting them all.

It's Sam, not Samuel. That much, he'd been clear on, the one and only—time they'd met.

If Clark could not deliver the dossier, at least he could bring forth its author. Not quite enough to forgive his sins.

Close, though.

A fine young thing was draped across Sam's arm, too. The man seemed to have the good sense to look slightly alarmed, though, glancing about the ballroom—

"…and Theodore Mirabeau."

Risa froze.

Him.

It was *him.*

She couldn't seem to rip her eyes away.

"Ah," Clark simpered, his breath in her ear. "So lovely, isn't it? To see such a familiar face."

It wasn't familiar, though.

Hidden beneath that shining sapphire mask, it was hard to tell, but nothing about it was the way she remembered. He'd been a child, then, so there was that—but he'd grown up different.

Skinny.

His shining chestnut hair was hers, though, his eyes almost inseparable from their jeweled encasement—

"Theresa, love," Clark was saying, his hand on her elbow, and she forced herself to blink that blue-eyed boy back, because somehow he was there, right there, standing in front of her— "You know Teddy? It is Teddy, isn't it," Clark mused, cocking his head to the side, studying the boy. "And of course, I am Commissioner Carson, though I daresay Sam has filled your ear with such tid-bits, already—and Sam, you remember Risa?"

A whirlwind introduction if she'd seen one, and it left her reeling.

Sam. The dossier.

And *him.*

"Pleasure seeing you again," Sam nodded, offering her his hand. "I imagine it isn't recreation that brings you back to the manor?"

"Nor does it bring you, Sam, don't be coy," Clark mused.

Sam, though, ignored the remark, his eyes looking past Clark and glittering with mischief as he beckoned someone forward. "El, love," he murmured, brushing a kiss across the cheek of a dark-haired woman in an emerald gown, "excellent of you to come...this is Risa Barrett, a mutual friend of Clark and myself. Risa, this is Elizabeth Mirabeau, Teddy's sister." His eyes locked on hers, molten.

And with deafening realization, she saw.

It's her.

~ • ~

Risa blinked, trying to clear her head, because the whole world had gone off-kilter.

She'd been knocking back champagnes, safe in Clark's little dollhouse, because hadn't that been the condition? Hadn't Adrian said there was to be no contact with the girl, much less that blue-eyed boy now standing before them? And Adrian was right, unequivocally right, because one breath of Rescindancy in that dilapidated little farmhouse, one whisper that the political persuasion was bleeding through this back-water district, and they were dead, all of them. The girl. The blue-eyed boy. All of them.

They conspired to release a flood of magic, her and Adrian and all the rest, and the girl—Elizabeth—she was supposed to be safely tucked away until the time was right, stowed away from any whispers of influence from the City, away from suspicion.

No.

She had lost herself to the story she spun to keep her life a little more hopeful, so that she could believe enough to fight on, and *get a grip, Risa!*

"You're...his sister," Risa echoed, not bothering to take the girl's hand.

Sam had authored the dossier. Sam, who fully confessed on those pages to falling in love with the brother of the girl he was supposed to be watching, the brother who was standing there, right now, only it wasn't some back-district fling, it was Teddy Mirabeau.

Until this moment, it'd been *her brother*. *She* and *her brother* were inseparably close. *She* and *her brother* would venture to the river on hot summer days. Others, more distant, were gifted initials, but clearly, the anonymity had been pressed, lest the dossier fall into the wrong hands.

Until now. When it all fell to shit.

Fuck Clark.

This was all his fault, and *mother below,* did it hurt like a sonofabitch, so close and so *fucking far,* and she wanted to rip that mask off *her*

360

brother's stupid face, his stupid, beautiful, all-grown-up face to see, really see who he'd become.

Him.

The one that had chased her dreams.

The one that pushed her into waking.

The one that Sam loved, and his life had been sitting on her desk for years, now, hers for the taking.

He was the one who'd been sick, that winter. He was the one, inseparable from Elizabeth, her unwavering friend, her protective brother.

Adoptive brother. *Adoptive.* Like the word could wedge a space for Risa between Teddy and Elizabeth.

She adores her brother

Oh, that much was clear, watching her lingering close to him, his eyes darting often back to her.

Risa had found far more than a dossier in attendance.

She'd found the girl who'd taken her place.

You wanted a report, Clark's eyes seemed to say, flicking to hers. *You got it.*

He was a gods-damned fool, bringing her here.

"A pleasure, Elizabeth," Risa smiled, the name bitter on her tongue. *Mask of ice.* "Sam's told me a good deal of you, naturally—excellent to put a face with the name." Lies, all of it lies.

The whole thing stank of Clark's interference, too, that motherfucker.

Coincidences.

As if.

They were all just pawns in his scheming, little puzzle pieces being shuffled around the boards, even her, even the notorious Theresa Barrett, who brought men like him to heel, who made men like him think twice before fucking with her, even she had been used.

Traded, more like.

Just another bargaining chip for Mr. Clark Carson to hedge his bets on.

"You'll excuse us," Elizabeth said quietly, glancing to Teddy before her eyes found Risa's. "I, um...things weren't left well, with Clark and Sam and I, and we really must unravel it, but...could we talk?"

Risa held her gaze for a long moment.

She was jealous of those emerald eyes.

Emerald eyes that had twenty years of Teddy, all to herself.

If there'd been a better guardian for such a girl, though, Risa couldn't have thought of one.

Teddy was everything a brother should've been, if her memories—and the dossier—served true.

"Yes. I think we should," Risa said coolly, looking her over.

But Elizabeth lingered another moment, even as Clark and Sam moved around the ballroom edge, making for the exit. "Sam...told you all about me." She leaned in, and her fingers brushed on Risa's elbow as she moved to whisper in her ear. "Did you read his letters, too? Do...do you know who I am?"

In anyone else, the words would've been a threat.

Elizabeth spoke them, though, with trepidation.

She knew.

She fucking knew.

Risa's gaze fell to Elsie's long neck, to the golden chain dipping down into the bodice.

Oh, Cora below.

Clark, you sonofabitch, what have you done?

He was planning her ascension.

There was unmistakable worry in the girl's eyes as she watched Risa.

362

"We'll talk," Risa nodded, softening. "I promise."

With that, the girl turned, a faint smile on her lips as she left, and Risa was left standing with her brother, stuck like a bug in the sugary trap Clark had sprung.

ELSIE

A few quick steps, and Elsie had caught up with Sam as he trailed reluctantly behind Clark. She spared a glance back, first to Risa and Teddy, and then to Augustus, where he had been left brooding at the edge of the ballroom. His eyes flashed, locking on hers, and he gave her a small nod of reassurance to signal he'd follow at a distance.

"Risa and Teddy aren't coming?" Sam muttered, offering her his arm as Elsie joined him.

She took it reluctantly. "Apparently not. You didn't mention anyone else was reading the letters." It was a strain, to keep her tone low—and she couldn't fight the reflex to reach for the smooth bone handle of the switchblade, even now, tucked into the pocket of her emerald dress.

She might very well look the part of the pastry. But it wouldn't be a sugared cream filling they'd find, if they took a bite.

"I didn't know anyone else *was* reading them," Sam breathed, glancing up at her.

"She said you told her *all about me?*"

"Okay, that was clearly her way of saying she'd read the letters—which I didn't know about—he must've had them copied out—"

"Clearly? You went behind my back once," she bit back under her breath, "so pardon me for being concerned when the man who will talk for hours about anything under the gods-forsaken sun hasn't mentioned an associate who knows my life story."

Sam gave a small sigh of exasperation, pace slowing slightly as they followed the Commissioner. "Apologies for not mentioning every secretary I've met during my time at the manor house," he snarked stiffly, tone chilled. "In case you haven't noticed, he tends to be involved with a rather unsavory crowd—"

"You seemed to remember her just fine tonight—"

"Because he'd already introduced her to me again by the time you managed to drag yourself away from Augustus—"

"And what is that supposed to mean?"

His arm flexed with frustration beneath her fingers. "It means," he said slowly through gritted teeth, "that I am stressed, Elsie, and I am not dealing with it particularly well."

Her fingers were digging into him, she realized, nails biting into the sleeve of his coat as they strolled down the gilded corridor, the Commissioner more than a few paces ahead.

Not dealing with stress particularly well seemed to be a theme for the evening.

"Yeah, well. Me neither," she grumbled, relaxing her grip. "Where're we going?" She'd been trying—and failing—to keep a mental map of where they'd woven through the hallways.

"Carriage house," Sam whispered, an uneasy edge to his tone. "He doesn't conduct business in the house." His eyes flicked to hers. "What did you tell Risa, before you left?"

"That I wanted a word with her. She said she'd wait around."

If everything went according to plan, the partygoers wouldn't even know their Commissioner had fallen until the revelry died of its own accord.

"That bodes well, I suppose," Sam mulled. "Don't know many of his associates who'd willingly agree to linger, especially at the behest of..."

"Of a bastard?" she offered.

"I was going to say, of anyone who's not the Commissioner himself. But you're not wrong. And on a quick note," he added hastily, watching as Clark glanced back over his shoulder, "it seems to me a bit of bickering might make for an interesting knot to unravel, if you follow."

"What are you two gossiping about, back there?" Clark fell back to match their pace, seedy eyes pecking them apart with an insidious gaze. "I suppose I shan't complain, though, finding my two sweetlings as thick as thieves. I take it you have reconciled your differences?"

Elsie raised an eyebrow. "I thought Sam wasn't to be trusted."

"Oh, that doesn't mean you can't be the dearest of friends."

"It is rather a prerequisite, to my understanding," Sam muttered.

Elsie gave a derisive snort, looking away.

"You disagree?" Sam challenged.

"I think it's amusing that you're going on about trust, when you're not the one who was betrayed," she snarked, earning an approving look from the Commissioner—and a look of hurt from Sam.

Oh, but he was.

Clark had betrayed him, as much as any of them.

She held Sam's cinnamon eyes.

His expression was one of flawless apology as they found hers. He understood, she saw, why the words were coming so easily to her. He understood that in spite of their reconciliation, his actions still cut her deep. Or, at least, she hoped he understood.

Clark put a hand on Sam's back, running it in a few brisk strokes

366

between his shoulders. "Learning well, isn't she?"

Sam only frowned, shaking off Clark's hand with irritation.

The noise from the ballroom was at last beginning to fade as they stepped into a thoroughly over-wintered garden, and she found herself holding on to Sam a little tighter, savoring the radiating warmth clinging to his suit coat.

It felt wrong, coming back to the carriage house at all, much less draped like a pastry on the arm of a tart.

Suddenly, she had a thousand questions she wished she would've asked.

Why were you even at the carriage house that night?

Why did you wait for me, even hearing what you heard?

Did you know he was going to betray you, in the end?

The carriage house was unchanged.

Warm, soaked in bourbon and firewood.

"I confess," Clark simpered, sinking down in an armchair, "I was pleasantly surprised when Lora informed me you'd begun making house-calls."

Sam exchanged a dark look with Elsie, bracing his hands on the back of the leather sofa, puckered and polished. "And I suppose you find it very clever, inviting Theresa here."

Smart. See if he could draw the information out. See precisely how much they could wring from him before he fell.

"Oh, far more clever than you realize, love. But I haven't got all night." His smile faltered as he glanced between them. "What's this about?"

"We've talked it over," Elsie said quietly, perching on the edge of the sofa, finding his gaze. "Sam and I. And I'm ready."

367

TEDDY

"Tragedy is the prerequisite of healing."

~Dradan Proverb

Teddy's sister.

Sam's told me all about you.

To love, to really love, was to trust.

And it was a decision, in that moment, watching Sam and Elsie disappear into the crowd, arm in arm.

A decision to trust his husband.

Even so, he couldn't help but wonder how the *hell* Sam knew one of Clark's associates well enough to tell them all about Elsie.

"So, how—how do you know Sam, again," he asked quietly, glancing back to Risa.

Nine years hanging about with Sam, and he'd learned enough to know that Risa didn't belong here. Her purple gown hung off her, a veritable sheath of a thing, so unlike the puffed pastries encompassing them, and her sleek chestnut hair had been rolled elegantly back, almost quaintly simplistic in comparison to the others about her.

"We're acquaintances from a few years back." Her eyes lingered on his, a fierce shade of blue. "It is lovely to meet you," she added, nothing more than an afterthought. "Sam speaks quite highly of you."

Funny. He hasn't said a word about you.

Teddy wracked his memories, suddenly doubtful.

Take a nice girl with you, he could remember naively telling Sam as his best friend had spilled his worries over Mattie and the introduction.

I don't fancy girls. You know that, Sam had retorted with a frown. *But I've never kissed a boy, so it's going to be a disaster.*

I could kiss you, Teddy had put forth. *Then you'd be an old pro by the time you got to the ball.*

And when they'd kissed, and Sam had grinned, gushing about how brilliant his first kiss with a boy had been, and how pleased he was that it'd been his best friend.

Teddy exhaled.

Insecurity wasn't a good look on him, Elsie had remarked once. She was right, of course, this pang of jealousy was absurd.

"So, the companion of Sam Carson," Risa mused, looking him up and down.

"Alderton," Teddy corrected in a mumble, "and husba—fiancé."

A small smile was dancing in her eyes, now, as she folded her arms across her chest. "A bit eager, there, are we? Did you almost call him your husband?"

"Meant to say husband-to-be," he lied, face heating.

Her eyes narrowed.

She didn't buy it, not for a hot second.

"M'kay, then. So, what does the husband-to-be of the infamous Sam Alderton do, when he's not confusing the facts," she prodded, her voice playful.

"Shop clerk." He barely muttered the words as he stuffed his hands in his pockets, looking down.

369

"Oh."

He glanced up, meeting her surprised expression. "Oh?"

"You don't help out on the farm?"

"Oh. No," he swallowed, the Thread awakening, a tangled knot in his tight chest. "No, it—it wasn't ever really enough for me, or—or them." Not that it mattered anyway. All that was gone, now. "What about you?"

Risa sucked her teeth, eying him with skepticism. "Sam tell you what was going on with your sister?"

"With Elsie? Yeah," he lied. "Yeah, they, um...they told me everything."

What the hell are you doing?

You know they're lying to you, part of him seemed to say.

But it's none of your business. Leave it alone, you're only going to get hurt, prying where you shouldn't. All you'd have to do is ask Sam, and he'd lay it all out. You know that. And that's why you haven't asked him, because you know it's gonna hurt. So stop it. Stop it this instant.

She seemed to sense the fib, though. "Mm-hmm. Well, I advise the Commissioner on legal regulation. Compliance, that sort of thing."

"You're an advocate," he pushed, hedging his bets.

An infectious smile split across her face, a quiet laugh on her lips. "Yeah. Yeah, I'm an advocate," she sighed, running her hand reflexively across her already-smooth hair.

"Not the one that defended Clark in the recent, er, situation?"

"Oh, gods—no," she snickered, shoulders relaxing. "I can't believe you heard about that. No, that would've been my advisor, Adrian—and if by defend, you mean reluctantly drag a screaming Commissioner out of a Caelaymnic cell whilst trying to hide any sort of regret that the Chancellor made him fish that skeez out of there, then yes, I suppose he did technically defend Clark. Though 'rescue him from his own incompetence' might be a better way to put it."

"Sorry, but...you think he's actually innocent?"

"I think he's actually a self-serving sonofabitch. He knows we'll bust his balls for that kind of bullshit. The Guild may be autonomous, and protected by the Treaty, but there's a limit, even to that kind of freedom."

They should've been reassuring words.

But her confidence in them stirred something uneasy in his gut.

She was shrewd, offering an unapologetic analysis of the Commissioner to a veritable stranger, not seeming to care if he got wind of it or not.

He shook the doubts from his mind, watching her toss back the dregs of champagne.

He didn't know her.

She didn't know him.

There was no reason to preach the innocence of Clark Carson based on the words of a woman who had fully admitted to giving him counsel.

"Did I say something to upset you?" Risa was watching him, almost unblinking.

It was unnerving, the way she read him like an open book.

"No," he edged slowly, "I...I guess I'm just not convinced he's innocent."

She pursed her lips. "Being innocent and being not guilty are two very different things. What—"

Her words were cut off, though, as a gut-ripping snap of thunder shook the room, the tinkling of glass following the groan of metal and the resounding crash.

There, in the center of the ballroom, a chandelier had come crashing to the floor, sending wax and crystal everywhere.

Move.

The air was caustic, sterile, as he dodged the pastries, moving for the scene. Someone was screaming, disconcerted murmurs filling the room—

His breath caught in his throat, looking at the wreckage.

Pinned beneath the massive chandelier was a young woman, her pale pink gown already blossoming with blood where a metal shaft had pierced her gut, had sheered through her arm, had left her face an unrecognizable, bloodied mess. His hands were shaking as he pushed forward, finding the Thread, summoning it with every ounce of anger and grief and regret and sorrow and pain he could find.

He recognized that gown.

It was one of Sam's.

He felt a pulse—weak, but there—and it was only when he took a single breath to steady himself that he realized Risa was kneeling beside him, hands hovering across her body like the girl was a fire, and Risa was warming her fingertips.

"Go on," she muttered, eyes flicking briefly to his. "Get to work."

Another Healer.

He'd found another Healer.

ELSIE

"And in burst the knight, ready to save the damsel. There was one problem, though.

The damsel didn't want to be saved."

~from 'The Advice of The Long-Dead' and Other Essays

"You're ready." Clark raised an eyebrow, crossing his legs. "And you truly expect me to believe this? That after you both tried to have me arrested, you come back, ready to reconcile, as if nothing whatsoever has happened?"

Doesn't matter, doesn't matter, just keep him here, keep him busy—

"I had nothing to do with—"

Elsie's words were cut off as a young boy in a secretary's suit slammed the door open, breathless as he moved to whisper something inaudible in Clark's ear, the Commissioner's expression growing darker with each passing second.

"What business could possibly be so urgent," Sam pressed, frowning, "to warrant this kind of—"

"Silence!" Clark was on his feet, snapping his fingers at the secretary, some unspoken command between them. "I am through! I am through with this—this childish insubordination! You bring a chandelier down? And what purpose, do you think, this serves?"

Elsie was glaring, making to rise. "A—what?" A falling chandelier hadn't been part of any plan she knew of.

But already, a hulking monstrosity of a man was waddling through the door, a pair of skinny things at his heels.

Mercenaries.

A breath, and one of them had snatched her up, the others taking Sam.

"Stop it," she struggled, trying to break free. "No—"

It was useless, though.

She was eleven again, and he might as well be kicking her roll into the street. Only this time, Sam wasn't going to be there to save her.

"Bind their hands," Clark snapped. "I don't have time for deviants."

Panic was rising, her skin burning beneath the manacles. "Augustus—Fletcher!" She was screaming, throat ripping raw in the sound, but if he could hear her heart beating from three blocks away, then he was damn well going to hear her yelling his name from wherever he had to be—

"Can it," her mercenary growled.

"Augustus—"

His hand met her face, stinging, something salty and warm meeting her tongue as her lip began to bleed.

"No!" Sam's voice cracked through the room. It'd taken both of the skinny ones to hold him back, and his eyes were swimming as they found hers. "Don't you dare touch her—"

Augustus's growl cut through the chaos. *"Enough."*

Elsie pressed her eyes closed, thanking the gods above and below.

He'd heard.

Augustus had heard.

The grubby hands on her bare arms fell away, and there were tears of relief on her cheeks, watching him own the carriage house.

"More fucking Drada!" Clark was walled in again, seething, his mercenaries trapped behind shields of the same shimmering mirage-y membrane she'd watched Fletcher summon before the Commissioner not a week earlier.

"Sam, are you—*oof.*" She collided with an unseen wall, making for him.

"El!" He was shaking his head, eyes flooding. "El, run!" His fists met the wall, furious, a look of unmistakable pain carved deep into his face as the mercenaries yanked him back once more. "Elsie—"

She turned, coming face-to-face with Augustus.

It was his eyes, cold and unfeeling, that betrayed him first.

"What're you doing," she warned, backing into the invisible wall, panic starting to rise once more. "Augustus—"

A heartbeat, and he was dragging her towards the door, unperturbed by the kick to the shins, the elbow to the gut she tried—and failed—to deliver, and she was screaming, screaming, praying someone would hear her.

Lingering in the threshold, he pressed a finger to her lips, drawing it away as she gnashed her teeth, aiming for the flesh.

"Hush," he crooned, atop her protestations. "Hush, darling."

"What are you doing—let me go!"

"I cannot. You are essential to the Master—"

"I knew it!" she shrieked, glaring tearfully at Clark, "I knew it was you, I knew this—this was too good—"

There were words on Clark's lips, though, his brows furrowed as he shouted something over the din.

Fight. Back.

"Fight back!"

What the—

"Don't let him take you!" Any trace of anger in the Commissioner's voice had faded, nothing but command in its wake. "Elsie, fight back!"

It was useless, though, in that stupid dress.

Clinging tight to her body, she wasn't going anywhere. A silk prison. Nothing more.

"Don't you *dare* give up," Clark yelled, hands pressed against the wall. "Not now, not when it matters—"

His words dissolved as the world faded to black, lost in the dimming swirl of lights.

She was gone.

FLETCHER

"Power comes in all sort of packages. Little girls with bleeding heads, tiny babies with golden trinkets, affected letters of an angsty adolescent...and yes, love, it even comes in tins of salve."

~Commissioner Clark Carson

"Oh, Stell's ice," Rodion swore, eyes darting inside the darkened warehouse.

Row after row of iron shelving filled the enormous depot, craning high into the rafters. The mercenaries lay toppled in the dirt—still breathing, but unconscious, at least for the moment.

"Siddeus, round up the mercenaries," Fletcher muttered, waving a hand to the nearest, a rather stout man reeking of alcohol. "Put them...anywhere out of the way." Then, taking a step forward, he crossed the threshold.

The shelves were lined with bandages. Salves. Tonics. Ointments. Contraceptives. Poultices. Teas, medicinal herbs, braces—

"He's been hording medical supplies?" Isa mused, picking up a nearby tin. "And ours, too, from the looks of it."

Fletcher gestured to them to toss the tin, and he caught it, glancing at the label.

The swirled script across the front was unquestionably Dradan.

He'd heaped salve identical to this on more than a few cuts and scrapes over the years.

"Mirestva, Kastarae, secure the warehouse. Make sure it's what it appears to be," he muttered, turning on his heel. "I need to find the general."

SAM

*"He told a truth so outrageous, it had to be a lie. If only
it had been so simple."*

~*Sam Alderton*

A swirl of emerald, a hazy mist, and Elsie was gone.

And with her, the barriers that had kept the Commissioner at bay.

"You fool!" Clark was fuming, teeth grinding as he turned on Sam. "You have brought her death! Do you understand what you have done? I warned you that she was wanted dead. I told you they would find her, but did you think to listen? *No!*"

"If you had stopped playing your games—"

"Games? I could not have been more clear, you stupid boy! And yet, you were content, watching her fall in with the likes of—of *them*, because *you knew best!*"

She wouldn't die.

She couldn't.

It was a simple impossibility.

He had promised to fight for her. And yet, she'd been taken, and what had he done, but pound his fists against an unmoving wall, terror overtaking him as he'd watched Augustus rip her away.

There was so much time still left between them, him and El.

So much gods-damned *life*.

"What are you doing?" Clark squawked, and Sam started, heart churning out ashen beats with embered determination. It took him a moment to realize Clark was snapping at the mercenaries, waving them off. "Go after them, you imbeciles! Go!"

Relief, painful and resentful, swept across him as their grip fell away, and Sam turned to follow. He had to find Fletcher. Warn him.

A hand, though, caught his chest, beady eyes finding his own. "Not. You."

~ • ~

"I could've had an empire, with her," Clark snarled, pushing Sam back. "She could've been everything. And you have signed her death warrant, Sam Alderton. You, and you alone."

He caught himself against the sofa, knees starting to shake.

Cora Lucia Stell Hadri

"Just like your whore of a mother. Uncompromising." Clark took a step forward, cracking his neck.

"She wasn't a whore," Sam breathed, and he wasn't the boy in the garden paths, running wild and carefree, not anymore, because Clark had killed that little boy long ago. "She did what she had to do."

"As did I, until you interfered!"

Taking a step back, Sam's chest was tight, panic nipping at his heels. "You paraded her about—"

"I dared to give her what those cowards couldn't! Look me in the eyes, love, and tell me she didn't have a right to know who she was. Tell me, from that lonely view atop your hill of morality, Sam, that she was better off not knowing she would inherit a kingdom!"

380

Sam's back hit the wall, a jolt ringing through his body at the shock. Trapped.

He was trapped.

His head was pounding, ears ringing with the sound of his own ashen heart as Clark took one last step forward.

Clark's breath was hot, heavy with allspice to cover the taste of tobacco and brandy. His finger came to rest square in the middle of Sam's chest, lain with sickening gentleness atop the silk waistcoat. "You," he whispered, voice drenched in depravity.

A single word. A threat, a curse, a promise, all at once.

And with a scoff of derision, Clark let his hand fall, retreating in anger to the armchair behind his desk.

Sam pressed his eyes closed, tears clinging to his lashes before falling reluctantly down his hot face.

Cora Lucia Stell Hadri Asa Natali Ignata Kiran

That first summer he'd known Elsie and Teddy, that summer nine years ago, the summer that felt a lifetime ago—that summer had been hot. Stiflingly hot, unbearably, unlivably hot, and even with his sleeves rolled up, his cravat and waistcoat stuffed into his satchel, he was sure he'd die of heatstroke, when all was said and done.

Elsie, at ten, had looked like a wilted leaf, collapsed beneath the shady maple, beads of sweat making her hair curl viciously. Teddy, at eighteen, on the other hand, simply looked like he melted. Just a pool of blue and copper, stretched out in the grass beside his sister.

The books lay abandoned. They were fodder for cooler imaginations and fuel for chillier days.

River, Elsie had sighed, her young voice almost resigned to the inevitability of the seemingly nonsense word.

River, Teddy had agreed, pushing himself to sitting.

They'd both looked at Sam in question, as if he'd have known why it was they'd settled on the one-word conversation.

What, he'd frowned, too hot to pretend to be polite.

Do you want to go down to the river with us?

And do what, he remembered asking. He more or less pretended that his senses had been dulled by the oven-of-a-heat-front moving through, scorching farmland and wits alike, because it seemed better than admitting that he hadn't fathomed the river useful for anything other than shipping goods and generally currying the errands of merchants wise enough to own the riverfront.

Snickering, Teddy had rolled his eyes, pulling him up. *Come on.*

There'd been something thrilling, shedding his heavy clothes on the riverbank and stripping down to undershorts. His skin had soaked in the hot rays of sun beating down upon them, and he'd been sure he was going to burn to a crisp, exposed to the elements like nothing more than the base-born bastard he was.

The river rocks had been slick against his rebelliously bare feet, the cold water delicious against the heat of the day, and...

And the rush of what he'd felt was almost enough to carry him away.

That afternoon, he'd *felt* like he was sixteen, rebellious and wild and carefree.

He'd watched Elsie blossom into the child it seemed like she never quite got to be, hurling her stones into the river with a dangerous grin.

And when he'd made a misstep, he had watched as Teddy seemed to make a lifetime's worth of hurts vanish with the soft touch of his hand.

Sam could recall sitting in the sweet clover grasses, letting the roar of the river overtake him as he idly ran a hand up and down his leg, searching for some evidence of the fall. But all he'd found was the straggly dark hairs of an adolescent boy, coarse on his sandy golden skin.

So, there'd been nothing left to do but lay back, drying in the sun as he watched the puffed white clouds against the cerulean sky, safe in the comfort that no hurt could find him there, that pain could not reach them by the muddy river eddy, that for the first time since he'd left his mother's cold, stiff arms in the alley so many memories ago, he had found a little slice of peace.

RISA

*"It seemed so malicious. So cruel. It was only at the end
of it all, though, that they were the actions of someone
who, above all else, wanted to be stopped."*

~Risa Barrett

"Easy," Risa muttered, glancing over to Teddy. The girl's limp form on
the marble was warm beneath her hands, some life lingering reluctantly
in her yet. "You go too far, they'll start asking questions you can't answer.
Go from the inside out. Leave the superficial stuff."

His eyes flicked up. "I did."

Mask tossed gods knew where, hands bloodied from packing the
wounds, he looked young.

Young and tired.

Bloodied hands, quiet voice...

That brought back some unpleasant memories.

She let the tendrils of magic reach out, searching for the pain, the
cuts, the hemorrhage...

He'd done it, alright. It'd been chaotic, the magic flooding in spurts,
but he'd managed to mend the massive hole deep in her gut, at least
enough, for the moment. Mended, and no sign of burn-out—he had a

knack for this, no question.

Risa had been left to tend to what was left of the girl's arm.

Which, after binding and healing and no small amount of prayer, would be nothing.

There were simply some wounds too deep to heal.

But the girl would live, and that was a victory, anyway.

Blankets had been piled beneath her on the marble, a make-shift hospital on the ballroom floor. Someone had brought hot water and bandages and a bottle of alcohol, and the floor was littered, now, with discarded rags and slops of pinkish water, sprinkled with tiny pieces of crystal and finery, a most macabre little cupcake.

It hadn't taken long for mercenaries to start shooing the gawkers away, thank the gods, and the room was quieting as the crowd began to thin. A few of them had helped lift the chandelier, at least enough to pull the girl out, and someone had held her shrieking mother back as her daughter spilled blood, violent and red, across the white ballroom floor. They'd worked quickly, though, magic tearing through the girl. A cruor tonic, some rest, and she would recover.

"You," Risa beckoned, waving one of the waitstaff forward as she rose. "She's stable enough to be moved, but not very far. Find her a quiet place to rest, and see if you can't dredge up a physician or six from the carrion still in the foyer." They'd do nothing more than sterilize and bandage—but mercifully, that would be enough, for the moment, until she could send for a medic's pack from the City.

A commotion from one of the garden side-doors drew her attention as the serving girl skittered away.

"Back—you can't come in here—"

But a man in a peculiar gray suit was pushing past the mercenary, anyway, glaring as he made a beeline for the chandelier.

Risa scoffed, wiping her hands on a damp rag as she strode to meet him.

A Drada.

His ears might've been filed down to rounded tips, his build stockier, his teeth suspiciously dull, his fingers so un-claw-like, and yet, the uniform was unmistakable.

Commander.

"Look, I don't know what you're doing here," she snarled, "but Caelaymnis needs to back the fuck off—"

It was like he didn't even see her.

He would've walked through her, if she hadn't side-stepped him in their little game of chicken.

"What am I, fucking invisible—"

"What the hell happened here," he snapped, taking one of Teddy's bloody hands to help him up.

"No idea," Teddy sighed. "One minute, everything seemed fine, the next, this." His tired eyes flicked to Risa. "Theresa, meet Fletcher. Fletcher, Risa. She knows Sam...or something."

Lovely. Just lovely. This evening had been unraveling with stupendous speed, and so why wouldn't it have met this wretched little climax on the bloody ballroom floor?

Well, now you know how he knew about Clark's little arrest.

Because his buddy, there, had been the one to arrest him.

His Royal Highness seemed to be content to ignore the introduction. "Teddy, where's the others?"

"Excuse me," Risa cut in, crossing her arms. She would not be brushed aside.

Fletcher turned, scowling. "And you are?"

"Someone with a vested interest in why Caelaymnis has a military presence at an adolescent's introduction ball," she hissed, taking a step forward.

"We, unlike the City, are content to continue enforcing the terms of the Accords, as you have so blatantly failed to do so!"

"This is about the blood magic?" she demanded in a half-whisper, shooting an incredulous glare at Teddy. *Couldn't just keep your head down, could you. Couldn't just be the sweet little boy you were when I left.*

Teddy gave her a helpless shrug, brow knit. "Look, I told you, I don't believe he's innocent—"

"We don't have time for this," Fletcher cut in, eyes on Teddy. "There's a problem."

Risa scoffed. "Don't keep us in suspense, Highness."

"This business does not concern you," he muttered, moving back as a pair of servants approached, stretcher in tow.

"Look." She lowered her voice, eyes finding his with burning intensity. *Make your case.* "If you stirred this whole debacle up after that abysmal first arrest, you either have a death-wish or proof. Believe me when I say that either way, I'm happy. If he's involved in something shady, and the Chancellor is asking my advisor to smooth things over with your people, I need to know. And if you're hell-bent on sending your career careening into a flaming pile of garbage, that's fine with me, too. I'm an advocate. Either way, I can help."

Fletcher's eyes flashed, his hand tapping uneven rhythms against his leg as he studied her. "Fine." He glanced back to the girl. "We were supposed to raid a secret warehouse on the eastern border of the estate. I had intelligence that that's where the production facility was being housed."

"But you didn't find it."

"We found the warehouse," he said, dropping his voice to a barely audible whisper. "It was chalked full of medical supplies. From Caelaymnis, of all places."

"Oh, mother—are you fucking kidding me," Risa demanded, letting the rag fall, forgotten on the tile. "Medical supplies?"

That fucker.

Clark had signed an agreement with Caelaymnis.

Vaupellum had cut him off, and so he'd signed a black-market trade agreement. For medical supplies.

Some bind.

Either enforce the Treaty or let the district die.

He had her up against a wall the whole time, and he knew it.

Her fingers found the pin holding the chignon in place, and tugging it loose with exasperation, let her hair fall. "Okay," she muttered, running her fingers through the loose strands to soothe her aching head. "Okay, what was the game plan, here?"

"I have to find Augustus."

"I saw him follow Clark and them out," Teddy said, scooping up the abandoned rag from the floor, beginning to work it over his own fingertips.

"They were going for the carriage house, it's where he...hold up." Risa shot a look to Fletcher, the realization dawning on her.

Sam knows Teddy through Elsie, Elsie and Fletcher...

Oh, shit.

The little heiress had found herself quite the match.

"What," Teddy asked softly.

But her eyes had already flicked to the massive man sauntering down the grand staircase, a general's insignia on his breast. "That the 'Augustus' you're looking for?"

Fletcher looked thoroughly unnerved, though, watching his brother descend down the steps.

Not that she could blame him.

She only knew the youngest Praequintelya son by name, and that, only because it was her job to know. The general, though...

She knew him by reputation long before she'd been an advocate.

"Sir," Fletcher began, "the warehouse—"

Augustus cut him off, a letter outstretched in his hand.

Not a letter, she realized.

An order of arrest.

FLETCHER

*"We are all traitors. Every last one of us. We have
forsaken the gods, and they have forsaken us, and there is
no honor, anymore, nothing but sinners and blasphemers
and those simply too tired to fight anymore. You wanted
the truth. There it is."*

~Augustus Praequintelya

"What is this," Fletcher glared, snatching the parchment from
Augustus's hand, nearly shredding it open.

Something was wrong.

He should've been able to hear it, thrumming away.

But in the quiet of the night, the stillness struck in the wake of
tragedy, he could hear nothing.

He split the wax, eyes flying across the order.

BY MANDATE OF SENATE, COUNCIL, AND CROWN, WE HEREBY
ISSUE THE ORDER OF ARREST FOR ONE ELIZABETH MIRABEAU,
UNDER CHARGES OF HIGH TREASON, CASUAL DELINQUENCY AGAINST
THE REALM—

"You arrested her?" Fletcher snarled, throwing the parchment aside,
magic curling in his fingertips. "I don't—what the hell were you

thinking? Have you lost your gods-damned mind?"

"Have you?" Augustus replied coolly. "Defending a traitor with such fervor?" His voice was placid, flat and unfeeling, his eyes nearly unseeing.

The way they'd been when he'd come back.

After they'd tried to drain him.

It was with that same sort of indifferent disregard, now, that Augustus looked him over, not seeing a brother, a friend, even another soldier, but only an enemy, an enemy with an agenda that did not suit the general's whim.

They had killed him, Fletcher decided. They'd killed him, when they'd drained him in the highlands.

It'd been a ghost that he'd found, this last week. He'd found the ghost of his brother in the halls of the compound, an echo of the spirit of who he'd been, and it had moved on.

Leaving him with this.

"Clark—"

"Is of no consequence to the realm," Augustus remarked. "Lying little girls, on the other hand—"

Fletcher turned, fury rising. *Lying little girls—*

Whirling without warning, he sent a lucent flying towards Augustus, fiery and angry.

"Tsk, tsk. Temper, little brother," he murmured, deflecting it with ease.

"What is your problem? Four days ago, you were laughing it up with her, and now, you've arrested her? You've lost your mind!"

"Do you know whose bed you've been sharing, brother dearest? Did you know she has a criminal record nearly a mile long? She has picked and plucked from every street cart in the district, broken into every shop on the boulevard, stolen everything from stale bread to diamonds!

She nearly murdered a man, Fletcher, and you've been fucking her without a second thought. It is time to face the facts. She saw your crown, and she made a grab for it. A heist to top them all."

Something was clawing at his chest, raw and bitter, sucking the air from his lungs, sparking magic in his palms.

"Don't," Fletcher breathed, eyes smarting. "Don't talk about her that way."

She was Elsie.

She was sweet and good and kind and honest and she saw beauty in the world, saw hope, saw life where she had no right to see it.

She was the one he would've married, if she'd have ever wanted that, but she didn't. She didn't want the ring or the crown or the titles or anything but a soft little kitten and a quiet little cottage and a life where she could stop hurting and actually start living.

"I only speak the truth. If you can't bear to hear it, then perhaps you should've chosen a less...destructive companion."

This—this had taken their petty competition to new depths, using Fletcher's own mission to get Elsie alone, to toss her in a cell, all a pathetic play for dominance.

The lucent that flew through the air wasn't the warning shot the first had been.

This one had been made to kill.

Augustus sent a shield deflecting the blow—barely. Another, and Fletcher had nicked his brother's leg, undiluted anger, cold and hateful, fueling the precision.

With the third lucent, though, the general had sent another shield rising, except this time, it was Fletcher who was trapped, trapped with his lucent quivering in agitation, itching for the fight, trapped in the humming walls of magic.

"I am warning you," Augustus growled. "Do not test me, Fletcher.

This isn't a path you wish to go down."

"I hope you *die!*" There were tears in his eyes as he sent the lucent futilely against the wall, feeling it fizzle out before it'd hardly left his hand.

"Fletcher Praequintelya—"

"—I hope you die, I hope you rot in hell, I hope you pay for this—"

"—you are under arrest for the violation of an Issue of Aegis, for contamination of the sequestered territory known as Aerdela, and for the threat of death, real and attempted, against a member of the reigning royal family."

The air was thin, refusing to stick in his lungs—

Bleeding out.

Augustus was bleeding the air from the shield.

"You..." But Fletcher couldn't finish the words, spots beginning to speckle his vision as he slid to his knees.

The only meaningful training sessions he'd ever found with his brother, crafting this trick, and what had Augustus done but turn it against him.

The world was tunneling, and he knew it was a matter of seconds, now, before it went black altogether.

He turned his thoughts to Elsie.

At least if they'd both been arrested, they'd find each other again in the cells.

She was so beautiful tonight, in that gown.

A beautiful, wily, wickedly smart, unapologetically proud thief.

And he loved her for all of it.

Sins, and all.

THE MASTERS

She is gone.

Risa fights for her, every day. Teddy mourns. I am told that Fletcher's friends are working for answers, too, though I cannot say I trust them, after what has happened.

As for me, I visit Desi, some days, so as not to feel so useless. The rest can fight, and there is nothing that I bring, at least not now.

Clark is useless—and innocent of nothing more than subverting the bad end of a trade agreement that would've left the Valley half-dead.

And still, she is gone.

~SAM ALDERTON,
EXCERPT FROM A LETTER DATED DECEMBER 21ST

CHIM

"Truth from the mouths of babes, for they witness all."

~ Dradan Proverb

Chaos called and Chim answered, and she was *livid* that she had missed the party.

Especially one with such varied and violent guests.

As the masquerade dwindled, the air rich with blood and abduction, Chim stomped through the halls. Sometimes chaos had a way of taking advantage, and it was rude that it had taken advantage when Chim had been otherwise occupied, because this was *not* the sort of chaos she'd had in mind.

To ease her upset, Chim had taken to rifling through drawers and poking about in rooms with locked doors and eavesdropping on conversations she ought not to have been eavesdropping on.

"A faulty chain, that's what they're saying." The Master's voice was hushed, through the halls. "Poor thing. And now they are saying that girl is missing? The one Clark's taken an interest in?"

Chim paused, peering around the corner, listening to his lies.

There was no way the chandelier could be an accident. That was one of the rules, that when you crammed a lot of dastardly people into one house, one of two things happened: either a chandelier would be dropped on a rival, or an apparent stranger would be revealed as a long-lost family member, and Chim couldn't say she was aware of the latter happening.

"I should go." The Master gave a courteous nod to the would-be-Commissioner, maybe the soon-to-be Commissioner if the current one didn't come back from the interrogations.

Of course, the Master would be going.

"On your marks," Chim whispered to herself, "get set...go!"

In charcoal swirls, she vanished, trailing the Master. Elsie had been betrayed. A nice bit of discord, well-executed, but alas, Miss Elsie was on the side of Death, and that meant she was on the side of all gods Below.

That meant she was an ally.

Thus began Chim's game of hide-and-seek.

ELSIE

Bound and gagged, Elsie was kneeling on a sinfully soft hearth rug, the fire crackling wickedly behind her.

A great beast lurked in the shadows, heavy exhalations bringing snorting growls, wet and blood-curdling across the room.

At last, the etiolate rose from the armchair.

His skin was a translucent sheet of white, delicate and pale. His snow-colored hair was slicked back across the top, sides sheered close. The pale gray waned charcoal against the lightness of it all, and he seemed, to her, drained of color.

Save for the eyes.

The color of apples, ready to pick beneath the flaming leaves of fall. The color of a sunset, setting the sky alight.

The color of blood.

"Remarkable," he mused, squatting before her, head cocked to the side. "You are made in her likeness, this, I knew, and yet...remarkable."

The silk cords against her skin were hot, so slick she should've been able to slip them, and yet—

"You wish to escape," the etiolate continued, rising once more. The corner of his lips were curling upward, watching her expression. "I know you, love. I know your deepest desires, your secret wants, what you, above all else, crave most in this world and beyond. I am Anscip Xavishia. It is my business to know."

She had struggled. She had screamed. She had fought.

And she'd still been torn out of her emerald dress, shoved into a cotton shift, and tossed onto the hearth rug for this—this *creature* to devour.

"I am an Insidiae," Anscip said, stopper clinking against the vat of liquor, leaning back against the bar to watch her with lustful red eyes.

Stop it, stop it, stop it, get out of my head—

He gave a quiet laugh. "I'm not reading your mind, love. I'm not one of those parlor-trick Listeners, pretending to peruse the mind as if it's a book to be read. I told you. I am Insidiae. Your darkest urges, your most passionate desires...they belong to me. Every. Last. One."

The beast was stirring, now, stretching, arching its spiked back.

It was a monstrous thing.

Horrifying, the mangy fur, clumped and matted, clung to the creature, and with a snarling snort, its fangs flashed in the firelight, dripping and dangerous.

A barghest.

The words itself seemed to send her mind into a panicked frenzy, fear consuming all rational thought, and all sense of fight or flight had been overwhelmed with one command, one edict, one unbreakable rule that she couldn't seem to not follow.

Freeze.

The impetus to statue-stillness was petrifying.

Anscip snapped his fingers, and the beast hissed, retreating back into the dark.

"It knows," the Insidiae snickered, returning to the armchair. "It can smell the death in your veins." Reaching for the silver bell on the side-table, he gave it a ring, the echo tinkling innocently through the room, and a moment later, a door opened.

Augustus.

His expression was empty as he watched her struggling against the bonds.

"Take her," Anscip was saying, gesturing with boredom to Elsie, "and be careful. Not one drop of blood comes from her body, not one cut, one nick, one scrape, one splinter, or this is for naught." He glanced up at the general. "When she bleeds—and mark me, she will bleed—it will be from our draught of fear, that is to say, from the dhacrym, and nothing else."

SAM

"Ah, the caracara—a majestic bird of prey. Notorious carrion, their off-spring are vicious, having even been known to fling each other from the nest for fear of self-predation."

-from 'The Advice of The Long-Dead' and Other Essays,
'A Natural History of the Unnatural: A Memoir'

Sam left the carriage house, utter loss and panic circling like carrion, but it was only carnage that welcomed him back to the manor. He could not track magic across the miles, could not chase Elsie in the mist of golden motes. He could not heal, and a seamster's sutures were not what Desi needed anymore.

But he could boss people around, and that was exactly what he'd been doing when, coming around the corner of the second floor corridor, Sam was met with a pair of black coal eyes and a delicate foot, tapping with furious delay beneath a hearty layer of crinoline.

Celeste Carson.

"How dare you," she snarled, arms crossed as she watched him with hateful fury.

"What now?"

"You have the audacity to detain Father, conveniently stepping up to 'take care of things' in his absence? What the hell kind of bullshit is that?"

"*I* didn't detain anyone," he snapped back, turning down the hall. "It's his own foolish meddling that's gotten him into trouble, and pardon me that you were nowhere to be found. I had a ballroom of servants, bleary-eyed and frightened after witnessing a fight, a foyer of guests that refuse to leave, and a band of mercenaries chomping at the bit to toss anyone who looks at them wrong into the debtor's prison by the harbor. What did you expect me to do, Cele? Sit back and wait for you whilst everything went to hell?"

"It's pathetic, staging these accusations against him to take his place—"

He turned on his heel, glaring. "Excuse me?"

"You heard me," she hissed. "You're angry that this is *my* district, that it'll be *me* stepping up when Father dies, that it'll be *me* binding ribbon with Mattie, that you're left with nothing but your pathetic little back-district farm boy!"

"He is my *husband,* which is more than you can say about Mattie," he snapped back.

Cele's scowl faltered, realization dawning in her eyes. "What did you say?"

"Nothing," he muttered darkly, turning to leave.

She caught his arm. "Sam—"

He shook her grip off, making for the staircase. "Leave it be, Cele. I don't want your damn district. You want to step in and deal with this mess? Be my guest."

"That's...it?" she said, disappointment in her voice.

Sam glanced over his shoulder as he hit the first step, watching her fingertips lingering on the balustrade. "I didn't ask to be here," he said quietly. "I didn't ask for any of this. And I thought a part of me still wanted it, but..." He shook his head. "I don't. This isn't my life. It's yours."

His eyes drifted down the stairs, to the figures waiting at the bottom.

"Sam?"

He caught Cele's stare. "What."

She sighed, the corners of her mouth twitching. "Congratulations."

~ • ~

He found the lot of them in the mercifully emptied foyer.

"Our people have scoured every inch of the estate," Risa murmured in a low voice, eyes flicking up to where Cele was watching from the floor above, fingertips poised delicately on the railing. "Nothing."

"Nothing," Sam echoed in disbelief.

"Look. The evidence against him was circumstantial, at best. I know your relationship with Clark has been strained, and gods know he's not an honest man, but I think what Fletcher was keying in on were simply his movements as he brought in the medical supplies. Secrecy, heavy traffic—unusual traffic, for the districts...it's a mistake anyone could make." Risa was tying her chestnut curls back into a messy bun. "Believe me," she muttered, "nothing would bring me more pleasure than nailing his ass to the wall. But if he didn't do it, he didn't do it."

"Seconded." Rodion was sauntering through the side-door, Mia a few steps behind.

"We...searched," Mia said thickly. "*Enate.*"

"Nothing," Rodion echoed dully, giving her a lingering side-long glance.

Sam exhaled deeply, massaging his neck. And it was Cele, he found himself watching, Cele in her scarlet gown, with her dark curls pinned back.

Today was not her day to step into Clark's place.

"Not that I don't love standing in silence in a foyer," Risa remarked dryly, annoyed, "but with that crisis out of the way, we need to move on. We need to focus on getting Elsie—and Fletcher—out of Caelaymnis. Adrian's already there, but I'm due in the city in..." She plucked Sam's pocket watch from his waistcoat without so much as a second thought. "...soon. Let's move this party somewhere else, shall we?"

"The prison is—is very nice," Mia said knowingly, patting Sam's shoulder.

"Our cells are very comfortable," Rodion cut in. "Very, er...civil. Soft bed, fresh food and water, heated, and very clean..."

"Well, I, for one, don't care how comfortably she's sitting," Risa snapped, handing the watch back to Sam. "She's still in a prison cell. And I'm going to get her out."

FLETCHER

*"There is nothing more brave than a friend who speaks
the truth."*

~Elizabeth Clement Faulise

Ten by ten and deafening silence.

That was what Fletcher had been afforded.

A military cot in the corner, strapped with starched white linens and an itchy woolen blanket, a facility behind a partition, and a little stone ledge, where sat a plate of now-cold winterbean soup, a crumbling cornbutter muffin, and a tall glass of clear water.

The silvered bars of the prison cell were thin, no bigger than his little finger, strung together with hardly an inch between them, and yet they pulled at his magic something horrid, leeching him of just enough to make sure he stayed tethered. He watched the grated hallway pass back and forth, back and forth, as he paced the bars, hand tapping almost violently against his thigh as he walked. There'd be no evanescing out.

His military garb had been traded for a simple tunic and trousers, the rough linen clawing at his skin.

Arrested.

He had been *arrested*.

And he'd been expecting to find Elsie in this corridor, too, had been expecting to find anyone at all, but the only thing that had greeted him were two stone-faced guards, disinclined to words as they'd thrown him in the cell.

He recognized Rodion's steps at last echoing off the stone, and the Commander's boyishly round face appeared a moment later, frowning.

"Elsie—"

"I haven't been to see her yet," Rodion cut in, putting a hand up to silence him. "I have news, and you're not going to like it."

Gritting his teeth, Fletcher swore, turning.

"Our search was thorough—some people from the City looked, too, and nobody found a damn thing."

"You let humans from the City conduct a search?"

"Yes," Rodion warned, "and before you start, yes, it was a joint effort, no, there was nothing suspicious on their part, no, I don't think they're culpable in a conspiracy to hide a production ring, and yes, I think your obsession has carried you too far. Into a prison cell, namely."

"They are tied inextricably to his interests—"

"Fletcher. Listen to me." Leaning against the bars, Rodion looked weary, his deep brown eyes cupped by dark circles. "You need to let this thing with Clark go. You have bigger issues to deal with, here, than a Commissioner buying black-market bandages. Your brother has arrested Elsie on charges of *treason.*"

"He sabotaged a raid—"

"No! There was nothing to raid, Fletcher! He didn't sabotage anything, because there was nothing to sabotage!"

"Get out!" Pacing like a caged animal, his chest was tight, breaths coming in short, angry intakes. "I don't need this right now, I don't need you here, explaining to me how I fouled this up, explaining how I have once more messed something up in a catastrophically irreversible way and simply can't see it! So, get out."

Because that was all it had been.

Another failure in twenty years of failing, again, and again, and again.

He'd almost destroyed his relationship with Elsie, he'd spent six months investigating only to arrest the wrong man, he'd raided a warehouse of flipping bandages, and now this, this was the crowning jewel of his fucked-up-ness.

Elsie, accused of high treason.

Proof of how unwilling he'd been to leave her be.

That was the proof of his love.

A prison cell.

Rodion loosed a breath, letting go of the bars with the cascading sheer of skin-on-polished-metal. "None of this is your fault, Fletcher. And I'm not trying to blame you for what happened. I'm just asking you, for your own sake, to be realistic."

Collapsing against the cool wall, Fletcher let himself slide to the floor. "Sometimes, it's like—like everyone else has this window to what the world looks like. And you're all looking at the same thing. Except me." He let his head fall into his hands, cradling his pounding temples beneath sharp nails. "The one I'm looking through, the curtains are half-drawn and the pane's all dirty. And everyone gets so mad when I can't see what they're seeing, and they think I'm not trying, that—that I could just open the curtains, or clean the window, or something, but it's not like that. I'm stuck with the window I was born with."

Swearing, Rodion scuffed his boot across the floor.

Somewhere in the distance, a bell-tower was ringing, signaling first meal on the compound.

"I'm being an ass," Rodion said quietly, after a moment. "I'm sorry."

"It's fine. You—you're right. Elsie is sitting somewhere in here, facing charges of treason and gods know what else, and I'm busy obsessing over a tart a thousand miles away. I just...I don't know if I'm ready to eyeball

410

those sounds yet."

Rodion gave a quiet chuckle. "You're not ready to what?"

"Eyeball...sounds?" He gave Rodion a side-long glance. "That's not right, is it? It's something Elsie used to say..."

"I think the expression you're looking for is *face the music.*" Still snickering, Rodion sat down, crossing his legs as he watched Fletcher through the bars. "She's quite a woman, isn't she," he said softly, eyes sparking.

That didn't even begin to cover it.

"She doesn't care what my window looks like," Fletcher breathed, tilting his head back against the cell wall. "She doesn't care what's outside at all. Everyone's looking out their windows, and she's the only one that sees the house they're all trapped in."

"You know, it—it's funny, that even now, I can almost hear your brother trying to set you straight?"

Fletcher rolled his head to the side to look at Rodion. "Yeah?"

"Yeah. And..." He shrugged. "I think he'd probably say you're wrong. I think he'd tell you that your window isn't dirty, or curtained, it's just that you're...I, dunno, seeing a view that nobody else can. They're all staring at a mountain, and you've got an ocean vista, so of course, when you say you see waves, they think you're wrong."

"You think I was onto something with Clark?"

"Maybe. Maybe not. What I do think, though, is that it's easier to dwell on the Commissioner, than face the fact that the person you love is facing a death-sentence because of charges your brother brought about. But," Rodion continued, pushing himself to standing, brushing off his fatigues, "she will be roaming these halls a free woman before the day is out, if I have anything to say about it. Anything you want me to relay?"

"Just that I love her. And I'm sorry." So gods-damned sorry.

RISA

"I often find my best decisions are made impulsively.
Come to find out, it's a family trait."

~Risa Barrett

Risa's gaze lingered on the sketch, framed in silver, and sitting quiet on the bookshelf in the living room of Sam's apartment.

Teddy, laughing, his arm around Sam.

Her own blue eyes stuck behind the glass.

"Here you are," Sam said quietly, joining her behind the sofa, steaming mug in hand. "One cup of tea." Sleeves of the button-up tunic rolled to his elbows, top button loosed when the cravat and waistcoat had been abandoned, he seemed a far cry from the stuffy young man she'd taken him for three years ago.

"Thanks."

Go home. Take a shower. Get out of this gods-damned dress.

I am home, another, louder voice seemed to say.

Adrian would be expecting her in Caelaymnis.

Careful.

They had to be so careful.

One wrong move, and the Factionists would converge.

They had to play this casual. Like it was no big deal. Like they'd just been in the neighborhood, and while they were there, they'd swing by and check on the human so publicly arrested, and if they felt like it, maybe they'd do something for her.

Not like they'd be fighting tooth-and-nail to pull her from the prison.

Tonight had proved that she was already two steps behind. She and Adrian had been working towards unification when Clark had the young heiress and was planning a reunion of his own. If the Factionists caught wind of who Elsie was, they would strike up their usual attempts at assassination.

The Factionists were dangerous. They'd been known to burn down the homes of their opposition—and gods only know what they'd do, if they realized who Elsie was. They might be a rag-tag band of conservative extremists, but their conviction had proved a deadly and dangerous weapon.

Risa's gaze lingered on a sketch sitting on the bookshelf as she took a sip of tea. This, being here, standing in their apartment, in the middle of their lives—it was landing in the middle of a book she'd been memorizing for the last three years.

"I remember when you drew this," she said softly. "You said it was the first time you'd been able to really see his eyes, and when you looked, you saw your own reflection in the blue."

Sam sighed, scooping up the frame to study the drawing. "It's so strange," he said slowly, voice low. "Thinking about a student, in a library somewhere, memorizing such trivialities."

"That's just it, though. They weren't trivial, otherwise you wouldn't have included them."

"I was young, and stupid, and there were many things I wouldn't have done, if I'd spared any of it a second thought."

"Ah. You've stumbled across the motto for the life of Risa Barrett," she snickered, cradling her tea to her lips.

He gave a quiet snort, setting the picture frame back on the shelf. "Ah. Well, she sounds like a person I look forward to getting to know."

"Who is it, you want to get to know?" Teddy was coming down the hall, drying his hair and sporting a change of fresh—and decidedly casual—clothes. An easy tunic, soft, with two buttons at the top, and simple canvas trousers...

Yeah. That was him.

"I was saying I'd like to get to know Risa," Sam said.

"I thought you knew each other," Teddy frowned, towel forgotten in his hand, damp hair standing almost on-end.

"We met once, in passing, when Adrian was introducing me to the cases we maintained," Risa explained. "Part of our job is to act as a buffer between the Commissioner and the Chancellor, and regulate some of the minor requests."

"Funny. I guess I hadn't explicitly realized the Guild was aware of the City. I mean, Clark—I sort of took him for the exception..."

"I certainly didn't know," Sam mumbled, glancing to Teddy.

Their shared glance was enough to know the words were rightly believed.

As far as young Sam had known, Risa was an advisor, ordinary and un-magic.

"Aware may not be the right word for it. Clark excepted, they look the other way, and we let them go about their business unimpeded." The mantle clock chimed, and Risa sighed. "I should go. I..." She trailed off, eyes lingering on Teddy.

I'm not ready to say goodbye.

She'd never been good at letting go.

You can rationalize anything, Adrian once told her. *That's our power, as advocates. We can make ourselves believe any lie. And we must believe it, Risa.*

How do we fight this fight, knowing the truth?

"Come with me." The words had slipped out of her mouth before she could stop them. "Teddy, come with me to Caelaymnis. You—you can visit Elsie. I imagine seeing a familiar face would do her a world of good right now, and seeing as Fletcher can't—and you can testify to her character, if we need, and—"

"Yes," he breathed, eyes sparkling, a smile tugging at his lips. "Yes, that would be wonderful. It—is it allowed?"

"I'm an advocate, and...well, it isn't not allowed..."

He looked to Sam. "What do you think?"

"I think she'd be ecstatic, seeing you there," Sam said softly, his eyes flicking to Risa.

"That's it, then. I will. When—you said you had to go now?"

"To go home, to change. Give me ten minutes, and I'll meet you here," she grinned, fishing for the whaynedisc in her pocket.

"I—I don't understand," Teddy frowned, taking an anxious step forward, "how—ten minutes?"

Risa flicked the whaynedisc up into the air, glass glinting as she caught it like a coin. "Worst kept secret of the Hidden City. Why should the Drada have all the fun, evanescing like they do?"

"You're a—a Healer—"

"Don't have to be something special to use the disc." She grinned, taking a step back towards the door. "It's what we do, Teddy. We find the loopholes."

She wouldn't be leaving him behind.

Not this time.

ELSIE

The sound of water drip, drip, dripping filled the tiny stone cell, each reverberation louder than the last. Raspy breathing roared in Elsie's ears—her own. It had to be her own. And the pounding, drums, drums deep in the prison, the fibers of her very being stretched thin across the rim, pounding relentlessly—

Her fingers gripped her skin, slick with sweat, her cold, clammy skin, where the beads should've frozen into drops but they rolled, rolled, rolled, rolled beneath her skin, making it crawl like skittering little beetles in the dark—

Aching, aching, aching, why did she hurt so much, like her bones were stinging with an impact and yet she sat there, unmoving, because each movement tugged at her seams, and if another stitch was ripped she'd come undone, undone completely—

Terror had grabbed her by the shoulders, that was why her body ached, had shaken her back and forth, banging her head into the stone wall, forcing up every memory, every pain, every hurt, every doubt—

"Why?" Fletcher's voice echoed through the cell, and she didn't remember him being there, but there he was, and she was crying, crying, clawing at herself, trying to crawl out of her skin and into the pages of her books, because maybe then she'd be at peace—

"Why did you betray me?" He was crying, angry, his fist slamming into the wall, and it terrified her—

"You lied! You lied, lied, lied," he screeched, stomping his foot in time with the words, a sadistic song and dance for the amusement of her broken heart, "and I can't believe I ever loved you—"

Her scream pierced the air, because it was true, true, true, he had never loved her, never, how could he, and she knew not to trust him, that she'd let him in too fast, loved too quickly, fallen so hard that there was nothing, consumed, that's what she'd been, consumed by her undying need for approval—

And she would write him away, but the panic was crawling in, crawling under her skin, making her writhe with the doubts unspoken, a gravedigger unearthing the rotting corpse of who she might've been.

A shovel struck the vein, found the cache, struck it rich with the feelings in the box—put it in the box, put it in the box, put it in the box, that was what he'd taught her, because they were weaknesses and what happened to the weak but they'd failed to survive and it was her.

She had failed.

These feelings—this fear—would undo her.

AUGUSTUS

"More pleasant to eat the veal, than to slaughter the calf."

~Dryadic Proverb, from the Book of Adagic Texts

Arms folded across his chest, Augustus waited, watching her through the bars on the heavy iron door.

Her shoulders jerked at odd intervals, her muttered arguments with the shadows interspersed with tearful screams as she clawed her own skin, staring at phantoms brought forth from the darkest depths of her own imagining.

It would take time for the Ruby Tears to fall. Days, perhaps weeks, even, but it didn't matter.

He would wait.

One drop of her sweet Ruby Tears, one drop on the tongue of each warrior, and they, too, would walk with Death. Not as victims, though. Not this time.

This time, Death would be a warrior amongst them, and one by one, the Woodshade settlements would fall.

In her delusions, she mumbled into existence names Augustus did not know, conjuring people she must've loved or feared in a different life.

There was a boy, Percy. He'd tried to rape her, so she'd stabbed him, that much he knew from the town archives his aide had rummaged through, in search of her malfeasance.

There was her brother, the one she loved. There was her other brother, the one she loved, but who didn't love her back. Her friend, the one who loved her brother, and loved her, too, a mother, a father, a girlhood companion, a neighbor, a teacher, and yet, it was Percy, who stuck in the recesses of his mind.

She was a fighter.

Augustus had been a fighter, once, too.

He'd been a fighter, swaggering into the stables with all the arrogance of barely-twenty. He'd been a fighter, slinging his leg atop a freshly groomed Valoxus, the warhorse's coat shining like onyx in the small winter sun.

He'd been a fighter right up until the moment he'd seen the encampment.

In that moment, there'd been a decision. Go back for aid, and risk losing the camp, or take the camp with the three cadets riding patrols with him.

A scraggled old man had been hunched over a fire, his fur ear flaps almost frozen to his head, his beard a forest of icicles. It hadn't been a pot of soup he'd been warming atop the campfire, though.

The Woodshade humans were sick.

Their minds were twisted, addled by magic that wasn't theirs, and so they would take the blood, storing it in massive clay vats until it could be distilled, boiled down, spiced with herbs and sacrificial meats, fermented, and bottled. It was not the pure burgundy tears the Master cultivated, where the body itself housed the change, lest the magic seep from the blood as it drained.

419

The magic of the Woodshades was crude. Old.

And lethal.

One by one, he watched as they drained the cadets, like lambs for the slaughter. It had taken days for them to die, bleeding out and freezing in the heavy spring snows.

The Woodshades had taken the horses, too, save Valoxus, who remained a fighter, even after everything. He'd put a dinner-plate hoof through a man's chest when they'd converged, humans skittering out from their lean-to village in the trees. They'd managed to pull Augustus down, but Valoxus bolted.

It'd been Valoxus at the side of the Commander who'd found them. Him. Not them, because they had all died.

Him.

Valoxus had been devoid of a rider, refusing to be mounted, refusing to be stabled, and so they'd had no choice but to bring the stubborn beast along.

You fight well, he could recall the old man saying.

In time, he'd come to realize, that was why he'd been taken.

They didn't want the weaklings, separated from the herd. They didn't want the vulnerable or the sick or the old, because they saw there was no pride in taking down easy prey, no victory in seizing those already half-way to falling, no use in blood so craven.

They came only for the fighters.

As if there is strength from taking down someone so strong.

He shook the thought unbidden from his mind.

The time for doubts had long since passed, and he would not sell his kingdom down the river for the life of one girl.

Even if she was a fighter like him.

TEDDY

"Funny, how the world works. To venture a thousand miles but to find a familiar face—that, I think, is the sweetest kind of irony."

~Theodore Alderton

The bitter late afternoon wind of Caelaymnis was all ice and pine, and Teddy shoved his hands a little deeper in his coat pockets, trying to stave off the chill, just as he'd done every day for the last seven days.

Knit cap pulled low, scarf wrapped nearly to the point of strangling, he shot a side-long glance at Risa, looking perfectly content to stroll down the freezing avenue in nothing more than a stylish woolen coat and a pair of thin ivory gloves.

Ms. Mirabeau is too dangerous to be held in the compound, or even in the palace, a Senator had admonished once again, impatient as they had been kept in their office with Risa's demands. *Even if I knew where she was being held, I cannot disclose it. It is a matter of safety.*

That was the line. That she was too dangerous. That her offenses had been too egregious, that her knowledge of magic and Caelaymnis made her a threat.

And once again, he would have to deliver the news to Fletcher. The news that Elsie was yet unfound, that Teddy had once again failed as her brother, failed to stand between her and an unpleasant and painful world.

He shivered, the cold cutting deep. "Risa?"

"Hmm?"

"Have you ever been to Thallassas?"

"I have," she said coyly, a smile on her lips. Her blue eyes sparkled in the early evening light as she spared him a playful glance. "Dreaming of warmer shores?"

"Something like that," he muttered. Not that Caelaymnis wouldn't have been lovely in the summer—the cool mountain air would've been a pleasant change from the stifling Valley heat—but it was difficult to appreciate the impressive vista with the ever-looming threat of death-by-ice.

The streets would've been a welcome distraction, too, if it hadn't been for the bitter temperatures that had plunged Caelaymnis into a veritable icebox.

As it was, though, he spared nothing more than a glance into the window of the weaver's shop, a massive loom propped in front of the glass for the passers-by to see. A woman on a stool sat in observation, her fingers strumming the air like a harp, watching as the shuttle dipped and dived through the threads, leaving in its wake a half-finished tapestry of otherworldly yellows and greens.

A week in the City of Lights, stomping down the familiar path to the cells day in and day out, and he found himself watching as a picture took shape across the loom, worked with unseen dexterity by the loomstress.

It was hopeful, in a quiet sort of way. Like even amid the futility and frustration, it was still possible to create.

"It's too bad Sam isn't here," Teddy remarked, voice muffled through the scarf. *Too bad my husband isn't with me.* That's what he'd wanted to say.

"A brother trying to find his sister, they can overlook," Risa sighed. "Beyond that, though, and we're pushing our luck."

The limestone steps descending into the cell block beneath the military compound came too quickly. Through a thick, plated door, and another, down the barren corridor, through yet another door, and they were stopped by the same old guard, reeking of juniper mints, who took their bundlings and bags, whose rough hands gave an indelicate search for contraband, and then through a silver, grated door, Teddy had found the cells once more.

His stomach was an uncomfortable knot that had nothing to do with the silver grating that barred the rows of curiously empty cells.

Seven times, he'd had to bring bad news, and each day, it only got worse.

Fletcher sat on the small bed, back against the wall and knees tucked to his chest, his perpetual motion back and forth kicking into gear once more at the sight of them. "El?"

Teddy shook his head.

There'd been no sign of her.

No record of her being held within the compound prison, no trace of her as Risa had walked row after row of cells, not a whisper of where she might've gone from Rodion or Isa or Mia or anyone else, for that matter.

Save for the blood-soaked order sitting on Risa's desk, not a shred of evidence existed that she'd even been taken.

Arms folded tightly across his chest, wishing the warden hadn't snapped in broken Vernacular to take off the woolen sweater, Teddy noted the tray of untouched food still sitting on the ledge. "You have to eat."

"I'm not hungry."

423

Teddy raised an eyebrow, pulling the sleeves of his tunic further down his wrists, as if the extra half-inch would be the difference between freezing and not. It was hard to blame Fletcher's loss of appetite, though, in this place.

How do you hold a prisoner that can bend the fabric of the world to their whim.

Something Teddy had not truthfully considered until he'd crossed the prison threshold.

It was like getting punched in the gut.

His ribs ached.

He couldn't breathe.

Even now, the Thread guttered feebly, sputtering as it was leached away.

Whatever Isa had done, drawing his magic from the palm of his hand up and away, easing the overflow, the prison seemed to execute the trick tenfold.

It was the bars.

Set into the stone, encasing them all, the blackish-gray rods criss-crossing back and forth were greedy, stealing what they could from anyone inside.

"What," Fletcher frowned, glancing between them. "I told you, I'm not hungry."

"You're a gods-damn liar," Risa cut in, rubbing her hands together as she approached the grate, heels clacking against the stone. "Choke it down, Highness. No use withering away."

They'd gone through the same thing yesterday, of course. And the day before that. And the day before that one, too.

Glowering, Fletcher rolled off the bed, shuffling towards the bowl of soup. He'd learned quick not to go head-to-head with Risa—even if it meant forcing down winterbean soup.

424

Not that Teddy could blame him for refusing the paste-of-a-soup, either. It seemed to be a popular staple, eateries offering their own variant, each claiming to be the oldest or most authentic or the most revered by whatever patron mystic frequented the shop, and it was truly remarkable, really, it was, to find so many different flavors of bland. A city where anything might be possible, where looms wove themselves and the streets were lit not with lamps but with lucents, and nobody had thought to just add a pinch of salt to their winterbean soup.

"Today's Council session was a bust." Risa was watching Fletcher pick gingerly at the bowl of mush, her eyes icy. "Her, uh, colorful recreational activities haven't exactly been endearing."

"Though 'endearing' is a matter of opinion," Teddy put in, thinking back. "Sam always found her pastimes rather charming."

The first time, it'd been an act of desperation.

'Course, it wasn't like anyone had bothered to tell him, not until his burgeoning friendship with Sam had been on the verge of collapse. It wasn't like he'd had a choice—he'd searched the streets, the bookstore, the fountain, all her favorite haunts, and the pair of them were nowhere to be found until Sam strolled into the store two hours past when he'd been due with El, talking about how he'd lost track of time. Two weeks of silence, and they'd finally had it out with each other, yelling at each other in the back room of the store, and what did Sam do but let slip what'd really happened.

It was a hell of a lot easier to forgive him after that.

Elsie seemed to sense, at least to a certain degree, that her secret had been spilled, but she seemed content to play innocent for her big brother, and he wasn't about to go stirring things up when really, she'd just been hungry, and there'd been no harm done, anyway.

Sam always seemed to be a little proud of her, rebelling against the district, even if it'd been sort of futile in the end—though there was an undeniable poetic justice to padding the prison ledgers with the Commissioner's own funds.

Their visit with Fletcher went the way they always did. They talked about the unwillingness of anyone to cooperate, the oddity that nobody seemed to be able to find her, the murmured hopes that she was alright, wherever she was, the unspoken petrifying fear that she wasn't. They reminisced about her, relived the masquerade for the hundredth time, and at the end, bid each other goodnight, praying they'd wake up to find her home.

~ • ~

Stepping into the night, leaving Fletcher and the juniper guard and the limestones steps behind, it was clear, why they called it the City of Lights.

Great streaks of purple and green blanketed the stars, illuminating the snow-capped peaks in an other-worldly light, and it almost made the bone-snapping chill worth it, walking with Risa beneath the ribbons in the sky.

The moon was beginning to crest, too, and waxing full, the streets of Caelaymnis were hardly in need of their lucent-lamps, glowing soft in the snow-spritzed mist, shadows cast instead by the beams of cold light funneled down the mountain slopes.

"The moon like milk," Teddy whispered under his breath, a reflex as he watched the world leeched of color.

"What?"

He glanced to Risa, the corners of his mouth twitching up. "The moon like milk. It's just this stupid thing from when I was a kid. The moon like milk, the sun like honey..."

Risa gave a quiet half-laugh, her eyes tracing the basin edges.

The moon like milk, the sun like honey, and rain to wash you free,
Bless this table, bless this hearth, and great the bounty be.

"It is funny, the way those silly things worm their way into your brain," Risa was saying, running her fingers through her hair. "You go along, thinking yourself grown up, and a moment later, you've got a childhood rhyme stuck in your head."

Teddy stopped, the clicking of her heels falling short as she turned to look back at him. *I never said it was a rhyme.*

Stop it, another voice seemed to chime in, dismayed. *You're hurting. You've lost your parents. Elsie's missing. You are drowning, and you're grasping at straws.*

The Thread gave him a nudge. *So grasp, then. She's a healer, too. There's that.*

That, there was, indeed.

And there was no rule that said healing couldn't be the story he spun inside his head.

Spin it, then.

There was no denying the name. No denying those loose, coppery curls, cut to her collarbone, the deep blue eyes that went from ice to ocean without warning, the magic she didn't seem to like to practice.

"Your parents," he said softly. "You always call them Nerene and Roger, never 'Mom and Dad.' Why?"

Her eyes narrowed. "That's how they were introduced to me. It sort of stuck, I guess."

"How—"

"Teddy." She took a step forward, shaking her head. "Don't."

"I—I'm just trying to get to know you better—"

"And I'm telling you to stop."

His eyes were stinging as he looked away, nodding. "Yeah. No, of course, I'm—I'm sorry, I didn't mean to pry."

427

"Let's go," Risa said softly, gesturing to the edge of the compound after a moment. "Sam'll be waiting."

His feet were numb, finding the smooth paved walkway.

Don't pry.

She was sweet, like chocolate and wine, falling into step beside him, her shoulder brushing against his as they walked.

They're not her parents by blood. So, there's that, too.

She was right, you should stop—

Risa kicked a piece of ice with the toe of her shoe, sending it skittering along the path before them. "We need to be very clear. It doesn't matter what I call them, because Nerene and Roger? They're my parents."

"I didn't mean to say they weren't," Teddy muttered, giving her a side-long glance.

"I love them deeply."

He pursed his lips. "I loved mine, too."

Quiet fell between them, a renewed gust of wind making the basin roar, and her eyes flicked to his. "Loved," she echoed.

"You're a hypocrite, Theresa Barrett. You're happy to keep your secrets, but you can't help sticking your nose into everyone else's business."

The remark made her smile. "At last," she sighed, relieved. "Someone who understands me."

"They're dead," he said hollowly.

Her smile faltered, and she stopped, coming to a halt on the compound path. "What?"

"I loved them, past tense, because they're dead."

Such strange words, so heavy on his tongue, and yet they flew into the air like they'd been waiting there for years.

Had he wished them dead?

428

Was that what it meant?

That was impossible, though, because if he'd wished them dead, there wouldn't be this grief, rearing its head, conjuring ghosts on sidewalks and straws for the drowning and stories for the desperate.

"When," she breathed, brows knitted, tone flat.

"Few weeks ago. They..." He shook his head, trailing off, his eyes burning with tears as they found hers.

But she said nothing. She only turned on her heel, making for the gate.

"That's it? I—I tell you they're dead, and...and nothing?" He had to jog a few steps to catch up to her, anger sparking in his chest.

"Condolences," she clipped, voice cold, and with a word, she'd curdled the moon like milk.

SAM

"Destructive and powerful, thus fire is a double-edged sword."

-from 'The Advice of The Long-Dead' and Other Essays

The days were accumulating, gathering with ominous strength into something that was starting to look suspiciously like a week. And as is the consequence of such phenomena, Sam had found patterns emerging from the chaos of Elsie's arrest, patterns that he did not care for one bit.

It was this wretched routine of grieving, interspersed with anger and regret and the bitter taste of failed hope.

Grimacing, Sam let his fingers trail along the bloodied hole through the side of the jeweled bodice.

Desi had been cut out of it, the remnants left limply on the back of a chair in one of the more lavish guest rooms of the manor.

Like it mattered if she had a sitting area and a fainting couch when she'd been skewered by the chandelier.

Desi lay resting in the feather bed, tended to by a very grim-looking Isa, who'd been quick to shoo away the physicians doting over how many gold coins it'd take to find some gin and a saw for the hack-job amputation they'd been planning.

The captain, nor the diligent work of Risa and Teddy, hadn't saved the arm. But at least this way, it'd been taken with a little bit of dignity. Rather than a physician and a hack-saw and wagers on the outcome, it'd been done cleanly, with sutures and tonics and poultices and in the privacy of the manor room.

Desi's face had gone from porcelain doll to bruised apple—though with time, that, too, would heal.

"Sam."

It took him a minute to recognize who'd spoken, because that wasn't the girlish lilt he knew from their hours before the mirror.

The voice was quiet. Solemn.

He found her hand atop the covers as he sank down beside her, and it was an effort, summoning any semblance of a warm smile to give her. "Hey."

"Sam." There were tears in her eyes as they flitted to the bandaged stump of a shoulder.

"I know," he whispered, smile faltering.

"I just wanted to dance." Her curls were straggled across the pillowcase, frizzed and messy, her lips split and raw as she breathed the words.

He gave her fingers a squeeze. "You will again."

She shook her head, shoulders starting to quake with tears.

"I promise you will. Seamsters have a sense for these things," he nodded. His eyes flicked to Isa. "Can she stand?"

The captain paused in the midst of preparing a bit of salve. Then, with a sigh, Isa nodded, a hint of a smile behind those dark eyes.

Pulling back the blankets, Sam threaded an arm around her, helping her to sitting. "Alright, on three. One, two..."

She was on her feet—albeit leaning heavily against him—and gently, he slid his arm around her waist, cupping her hand in his.

"Look," he said softly, finding her eyes with a renewed smile. "You're doing it already. On your feet and waltzing. An historic recovery."

She wouldn't be on her feet right now if it hadn't been for Teddy and Risa.

Hell. She wouldn't even be breathing.

"It's backwards," Desi muttered tearfully.

He gave a quick glance to her left hand, sitting in his right. She wasn't wrong. "Maybe. But you've always done things differently, Desi." Carefully, he began to sway back and forth, drawing her in close. It was a far cry from anything she'd been taught. But it was dancing, nonetheless.

"At least they'll be talking about my introduction for years," she said at last, a little vivacity returning to her voice, and pulling back, there was something that might've been tiny smile on her bruised face.

Sam gave a quiet laugh. "That's the spirit. Just think, Des. You'll be the one that put Sam Alderton's introduction to shame."

"Alright," Isa warned, something playful in their voice, nevertheless. "That's enough of that nonsense. I don't permit my patients to go dancing off without a little rest first."

Helping her back into bed, Sam left her knocking back tonic after tonic from Isa's steady hand.

Strength was an odd thing, Sam thought, letting the door shut behind him. The cool air felt fresh in his lungs, better than the sick room, perfumed with ointments and tonics and bandages and heat.

For some, strength was not falling. It was refusing to let the knees buckle, to collide painfully with the ground.

Not for Sam.

Sam had been forced down too many times to believe that. He'd felt splintering wood beneath his hands as he braced himself. Waiting.

He occasionally told himself strength was knowing how to get back up—how often he believed it, he didn't really know. To rise, only to be knocked down again. It was something he had known well.

No, strength wasn't really something a person could have. To possess was to lose.

Strength was a found thing, small, like a hidden half-copper, brown and worn, hidden in between the paving stones of the crumbling road. Pummeled again and again, never relenting.

It wasn't forged in the furnaces of pain, amid the fires of *I'm doing this because I love you* and *Perhaps if you hadn't* and *It didn't really hurt, now, did it.* The heart that emerged was not of tempered steel. It was ash.

There was no glory in surviving. No victory in bearing those kinds of scars. No triumph.

He could remember when his ashen heart had started beating again, and a faint smile danced on his lips at the recollection.

It probably should've been Teddy that had kicked his heart into action again. That was how the stories went, wasn't it? He was supposed to fall in love, find his humanity in the arms of a lover.

But ashen hearts didn't work like that.

People often believed that ashen hearts couldn't remember how to love. That wasn't true, though. Those hearts loved with ferocity beyond comprehension.

What they couldn't remember, though, was that they were not some broken, twisted thing to be discarded like refuse. That their worth was not defined by the pain they'd endured. That just because their hearts were nothing more than smoking embers, that did not mean they couldn't be loved all the same.

"Sam." Clark's voice drifted lazily down the corridor behind him, and Sam paused, fingers brushed against the railing. "I was dearly hoping to catch you, love. Young Advocate Barrett, it seems, has taken to avoiding my messages, and so I ask: what news is there of our little heiress?"

A faint smile was tugging on Sam's lips. "Her name is Elsie," he said softly, "and her news is none of your gods-damned business."

ELSIE

Eyes were such strange things.

Their colors made no sense. Greens and blues and blacks and browns and misty, bloody reds, it was...nonsensical.

Like great globs of jelly, waiting for a pair of thumbs to squish them out, out, out—

"He says you're a descendant of Cora," Augustus said quietly, leaning against the wall across from her.

His visits were real.

She knew, because when the others came, they said things the real thems never would have.

Augustus was precisely as she remembered.

"She is Death," he said.

"*I* am Death."

His eyes were two disks, glowing in the dark. "Probably. You are strong. But it is unlikely you'll survive."

Maybe she would find her parents in the Beyond.

It was difficult, believing she'd been left for her own protection. Nobody left anybody with the Mirabeaus because they wanted them kept safe. Nobody left anybody with the Mirabeaus, if they were anybody at all.

Factionists—what a funny word, *fact-shun-ist*...

Clark was lying, lying, lying, and about what, she didn't know, because Augustus was not a *fact-shun-ist* with his drivel of religious zealously and the decided not-deadness of her, because wasn't that what the *action-fists* wanted, was her dead, dead, dead.

"I have no magic," she mumbled, tugging at the hem of her cotton shift.

Like the refrain would save her.

She didn't need magic when he had his faith.

"It is deep in your blood," he murmured unblinking. "You could not coax it out unaided."

"Unaided, like you're helping me," she spat, pushing herself to standing against the frozen stone wall. Her fingers traced the spaces between that had sucked away the slants, her hoarse voice scraping against the stone. "You're nothing more than a gods-damned page ripper."

AUGUSTUS

"There's nothing quite like a dysfunctional family dinner
to send one spiraling unstoppably downward."

~Mariann Bell

Augustus could feel eyes on him as he sank down at the rounded table.

"What happened to you," Cam frowned, glancing past her husband, the illustrious Senator Cormalum, to study Augustus. Her blonde hair was pulled back in a severe knot, her brow almost permanently creased in disapproval.

"Nothing."

You're a gods-damned page-ripper.

I am exacting the justice of the gods, I think they will forgive the breach of protocol, Augustus had snapped back. *And such shall be brought forth that the wicked will reap their sins with the scythe of their own making—*

Page-ripper!

"Well, that 'nothing' made your eyes all red," Cam snickered, her taunt drawing Augustus from the stinging recollection. Her gaze flickered to Fletcher, who'd conspicuously moved his seat as far away from Augustus as possible—not that it did much good. Dradan dining was, by design, intimate. "Baby brother's looking glum, too—why the dour mood?"

"Prison'll do that," Augustus shrugged. "He's pissy that he was fucking a traitor."

G𝖱ᴀɴᴛᴇᴅ ᴛᴇᴍᴘᴏ𝖱ᴀ𝖱ʏ 𝖱ᴇᴘ𝖱ɪᴇᴠᴇ ᴀᴛ ᴛʜᴇ ʙᴇʜᴇꜱᴛ ᴏꜰ Hᴇ𝖱 Mᴀᴊᴇꜱᴛʏ and on and on and on, and all it meant was that their mother was well enough to sit at the table but had refused to do so if one was absent, and he supposed it didn't matter, in the end, because Fletcher'd be back in his cell in two hours' time, anyway.

Fletcher was on his feet, fists clenched. "She is not a traitor!"

"Funny, I always thought betraying the realm counted as treason—"

"Why?" Alva glared at him across the table, a small ripple of power flying out. A warning. "Why do you have to be this way? He loves her, you don't have to be an ass about it. Just because you..." She trailed off, a look of dismay coming across her face as her eyes met his once more. "Isa *ended* it with you?"

"Get out of my head," Augustus growled, anger rising again.

"No, don't." Cam was leaning forward, amused, arms braced on the table. "Go on, Alva. Little brother likes his secrets—"

Fletcher raised an eyebrow, impressed. "Well, remind me to tell Isa that's a job well done—"

"That isn't funny," Alva snapped back. "He's hurt! I don't care what an ass he might be—"

Augustus's head was beginning to throb with violent irritation. It had been this way since they'd been born. At each other's throats. Competing in a game where Cam had been born the winner.

The soft click of a door opening met their ears, and the arguing ceased at once, voices silenced.

Bowyer had appeared, graying blonde hair swept back, the vee of his pale green tunic laced with thin, silver chords, matching silver buttons

438

falling at his wrists. Belted at the waist and falling loosely down to his knees, covering the dark trousers, it was the traditional attire of the Drada—he'd even gone so far as to shed his silver stole, though nothing would part him from the circlet atop his head.

And then there was her.

The reason they'd come.

A small woman beside him, her hand draped delicately over his arm, curls tumbling down only to be caught in a shimmering silver hair net, lest they run wild. Her gown was simple—the attire of one who was ill.

The faint scraping of chairs filled the reverent silence as everyone rose.

"Mm, I see they have decided to pretend they were not bickering like the children they are," Lilleana murmured, assuming her seat beside Bowyer. Her eyes flickered around the table, meeting each of them— save Cormalum, her only son-in-law for the time being—in turn. "They would do well to remember a mother's ears hear all."

Augustus fell down in his chair, letting out a quiet breath of relief.

Lilleana took a moment to settle herself, clear eyes finding Alva once more. "I want to start the meal," she continued on, reaching for her wine goblet, "by raising our glasses to my sweet daughter, who tonight, will be raised from mere novice to rank of mystic, in the tradition of our foremothers. To Alva."

The refrain echoed about the room, more somber than joyous, and Augustus heard the unmistakable sound of Cam's teeth being ground together in frustration. Alva was not the only daughter. Alva was not even the most important daughter.

But little Alva was a Listener, so fuck the rest of them, because she was the only one with their mother's gift.

At least this time, their mother's doting would pay off. Alva was dangerous—and too bright for her own good. It was only a matter of time before she put the pieces together. The mind couldn't be read like the pages of a book, but Alva didn't need the whole story. Just the right lines, and she'd know.

No, her talents would be better used praying with the mystics, listening to the harmonies of the gods spinning quietly in the heavens above. Perhaps the cool calm of the enclave would balance the fiery temper inside that girl. If she didn't listen to reason, maybe she'd be listening to the gods, instead.

~ • ~

Dinner lasted too long.

Augustus had more or less taken to counting the time with glasses of wine, each one tasting sweeter than the last. The morsels had long since worn out their welcome by the time the platters were collected, and with clenched fists, he departed without a word.

Drunk and frustrated, Augustus's feet carried him from the dining hall into the streets of Caelaymnis, towards the barracks. Their military—almost as pitiful as dinner had been. A tradition more than necessity, for show rather than substance.

Didn't matter. He ran the whole damn show. General Praequintelya, that was him.

And this fucking drama with Fletcher's little traitor.

Gods-damned page-ripper.

He was doing his duty to the city and the gods alike. Just like it was said, they'd scrub the corruption from the earth, let the corrupt suckle from the teat of...of...

He couldn't remember, just then.

The point stood, though.

He was standing before the familiar door. A small apartment in a row of other small apartments.

"Oh, gods." Isa was standing there, arms crossed, looking furious. Eyes like stars shown back, though. Beautiful. The warrior's physique was ill-hidden beneath the simple trousers and close-fit tunic, each curve, each muscle drawing the eye in.

Had he knocked on Isa's door? He must've.

"You're an idiot," Isa was saying, "You've lost yourself completely—"

"Stop it," Augustus snapped. Or, he meant to snap it. What came out was a bit of a slurred mess, sloppy and juvenile.

"If you're here to beg, you've come to the wrong place. Go home. You can manage on your own, as you and I both know."

"You—you—" But the words seemed to linger just out of grasp.

Each moment seemed clear, calm—but stringing them together to form some sort of sensical something or other...

That was it. He remembered why he was here.

"You had no right," Augustus blurted, smacking Isa's hand away where it'd lingered on his jaw. "E'ryone was asking questions, an' you think you have this—this—this moral high groun' but you don't, Isa! You don't!"

"Now, wait—"

"No! You wait! I am trying, Isa, trying to uphold everything tha—that this city was built on, because what else do I'ave? Tell me, what else, because Cam—Cam is the heir, and her 'usband's just trying to keep up with'er drama, an—an—an Fletcher's this stupid little justice boy with his nobility, and Alva, Listening, an' what does that leave, huh? I've got this," he stumbled, fingers finding the general's insignia on the coat of his uniform, and somehow, there was the sound of tearing fabric, the insignia in his hand, because he had to get it off, had to...

"This! Nobody else is even trying to protect our home, Isa! Nobody understands—they don't see! A—a Drada family died, didja know that?

441

Because a human settlement west foun'out what he was, and they—they killed him, an' his family, an—an' they had this little boy, too, jus' passin' through, but no, not enough—oh, think you can trust 'em, but you can't..."

Isa's brow was furrowed, lips pursed. "Augustus." A gentle thumb brushed something wet from his cheek—crying?

"I am doing the right thing," Augustus was insisting, chest tight as Isa ushered him inside. "I am—it's the right thing, I know it is..."

Protect his home. Blood magics were dangerous. Always had been. Always would be. Didn't matter whether it was six-hundred years ago when they'd string up anyone with a drop of magic, or whether it'd been last week, when Augustus himself had to unbury the corpses of his people to send them away with fire once more.

A child, ripped from the loving arms of his mother, executed mercilessly for magic he could no more control than any of them could master the changing of the seasons.

And Augustus was the monster for trying to protect his city.

Just another gods-damned page-ripper.

442

TEDDY

"I did not know one could have so much strength, until I met my youngest sister. Of course, I also didn't realize something so small could scream so loud—so, in this, I suppose, I am doubly gifted."

~Theodore Alderton

Hands braced on the bathing room sink, Teddy exhaled a long, ragged breath. His eyes burned with swallowed tears.

I will not fall. I will not fall. I will not fall.

One day at a time. That was what Risa said.

And for twenty-six mornings, he'd tried to take it one day at a time.

Twenty-six mornings, and Elsie was still gone.

The problem was, nobody seemed inclined to say where, precisely, she was. Nobody cared to hear petitions, nobody cared to shoulder the cause, nobody cared, period. She was a traitor, they said. They'd conduct their interrogations, as the law permitted, without the Hidden City's interference. The City had already freed the Commissioner.

Caelaymnis wasn't keen on watching another human walk free, too.

Adrian was fighting, Risa was fighting, hell, even Clark was fighting in his own twisted way, because Risa said she heard through the grapevine that he'd threatened his contact who imported the contraband supplies, promising pain unending if they didn't give up the information, which they hadn't, but it was a sort of nice gesture, all the same, he supposed.

"Hey." Warm hands were on Teddy's waist, and Sam slid behind him, pausing long enough to brush a kiss on his cheek before moving him gently aside. "You okay?"

Teddy nodded, folding his arms across his body as he watched Sam start the tap, a rush of hot water gushing forth.

Sam's cinnamon eyes caught his own in the mirror, giving him a skeptical look. "We don't have to do this, you know. Celebrate today. I'm sure she'd understand." His hands moved deftly, brushing the white shaving lather up his cheeks, down the stubbled neck.

Teddy sighed, sinking down on the edge of the bathtub.

"Not shaving today?"

He shook his head.

"Going rugged, I see." Sam was trying. At least there was that.

Instinctively, Teddy ran a hand along his jaw, feeling sandpaper beneath his hand. He kind of liked it. Today felt rough. So did he.

And maybe that was alright.

~•~

"I always loved the snow." Risa was leaning on the kitchen counter of Sam's apartment, staring out the window with a spark of excitement in her eyes.

"Yeah?" Teddy glanced up from the pie crust he was rolling out. The day had rolled in with a flurry of snow that had left all of Taylor Town coated in a thick, white blanket—though this hadn't prevented Risa from joining them all the same, as promised.

She nodded, finger lazily tracing the whorls of frost on the window. "It reminds me of being a kid. When did snow stop being so magical and start being such a drag? One day, you're staring at the snowflakes, wondering how the gods could think up so many different designs, the next, you're bitching about wet boots as you slog your way to the office—"

"Might want to go easy on the eggnog, there," Sam snickered quietly, passing through to refill his cup.

"Hey," Teddy warned, playfully swatting away Risa's finger dipping into the warm filling of the pie, "none 'til it's baked."

Risa scooped up a glob of sugar anyhow, a playful gleam in her eyes as she sampled the filling.

And for just a moment, he was back. Something about the mischievous smile on her lips, the way her hair looked kind of reddish in the morning light...

It stung. Like seeing through a window into a life that couldn't ever be.

Gesturing her out of the way, he laid the pie crust atop the pastry, brushing the flour from his fingertips. If Elsie had been here, she'd have helped with this, too, the way she had since she'd been little. He'd sit her right there on the counter, her feet swinging down, her little fingers wandering into the filling with almost as much presumptuousness as Risa's.

Soon. She would be back soon, they'd put this behind them, and she'd be right there, baking with him again.

The lies we tell ourselves.

"So, Leaving Day," Risa prompted. "Rather an ill-boding name, I think."

"Take it up with El," Sam shrugged.

Teddy nodded his agreement, retrieving his own glass of nog from the counter. "She never much cared for calling it something it wasn't. It was a nice spin, though, I always thought. This idea that...well, that her and I finding each other wasn't a fateful tragedy, but something sort of life-saving."

Elsie's birthday, they'd decided, was probably sometime in the fall. They didn't know.

So, instead, they—Elsie and Teddy, and eventually Sam, too—they celebrated the day she'd been left.

An attempt to take bitter abandonment and turn it into something sweet.

Teddy's eyes flicked to Risa. Since her bitter words at the compound, he'd decided to make an effort to shoot her as many significant looks as he could muster.

Perhaps he wouldn't be prying into her personal life any time soon. But that wouldn't stop him from letting her know what he knew—which at the moment, was nothing, but she didn't need to know that, and *oh, gods, she's not the only one that needs to ease up on the egg nog.*

"I, um...you know, I think I'll grab my sketch pad," Sam said slowly, glancing between them. "I find myself, uh, struck by the beauty outside, and I really—really should get the idea down..." Trailing off, he met Teddy's gaze for a moment. Then, with a quiet shrug, lips pursed, he left.

Leaning against the counter across from Teddy, Risa was watching him, eyes lost deep in thought.

What do you need.

"Can—can we talk about what happened in Caelaymnis?" Teddy said softly, steeling himself.

"No."

He blew out a breath, running a hand through his hair. "Alright, alright..." His eyes flicked about the kitchen. "I think I understand."

446

What do you need.

Worrying his cuticles, he moved to join her against the counter, their arms brushing. "I need you to know that you remind me of my sister."

"Criminal record aside, I'm flattered."

"Not El," he edged, glancing over. "My other sister. Tess. She'd be about your age, by now. And when we were leaving the compound—well, that rhyme, it reminded me of her, too, and we started talking about your parents...I let myself get carried away. You asked about my parents, and this—this thought just sort of popped into my head. What if I was the one that had to tell her they'd died? What if, through some stroke of luck, she'd made it out of this hell-hole of a town, only to come back, thinking her parents were still alive? It..." He sighed. "To be honest, it felt like I wouldn't be alone in the grief. El wasn't their kid. She was going through something different, something I couldn't understand."

"But if I were her, you'd have someone who got it," Risa mulled, nodding. "I get that."

"Exactly," he went on, finding her deep blue eyes drifting somewhere between ocean and ice. "I'd be able to say that it's alright to be conflicted—I mean, especially after what...happened to her. I'd say that I'm conflicted. That it—it has put her in my mind, more than she was already there, and that I miss her, now more than ever. And if you were her, I...kept thinking how lovely it would be, and I'd tell you how proud I was of you, making such a grand life for yourself."

Risa's eyes were swimming. "If I were her," she whispered, "that would be exactly what I wanted to hear."

"But you're not," he breathed.

"But I'm not."

447

ELSIE

"It is a singular tragedy, to wish action, when none is possible."

~from 'The Advice of The Long-Dead' and Other Essays

Against the cold stone wall, head in her hands, Elsie watched the flickering lights from beyond spill onto the barghest pacing before her.

There was a laugh, a pernicious little laugh, down the hall, and she was trying to tell if it was real or not.

Real, she decided.

The barghest halted its pacing, ears prickling.

"Bad dog!" Chim's admonishing voice echoed through the dungeon, and the little demon girl was shaking her finger at the beast, plumes of charcoal making the light hazy from where she'd popped into the cell. "You're a bad dog, you are being very scary! You are *not* going to get a treat for this!"

Elsie's hands fell as she rose, hope piquing. "Chim?"

Chim gave the barghest a scowl that sent it whimpering into the corner. "Naughty boy."

"Chim—"

The kobalde turned, hands on her hips. "I have been looking for you *everywhere!*" Her red hood was pulled back, inky eyes furious. "You've won this round of hide-and-seek. But it's my turn next, and I'm gonna hide so good, you'll see—"

Elsie let out a breath, deflating as she slumped against the wall in relief. "Chim, you have to get me out of here—"

"Well, what do you think I've been trying to do, silly?"

"Let's go—"

But Chim put up a finger, halting Elsie's words in their tracks. "Not. Yet."

Desperation was rising, fogging her clarity. "What do you mean, not yet—"

"I have a plan." Chim linked her fingers behind her back and began to pace, the air of a girl with an agenda. "I could get you out now. Or, I could get you out a little later, and we could also get that mean boy who put you here. I know *you* don't play games—"

"Get him." Vitriol overrode fatigue, and Elsie's fingers gripped the stones behind her. "Get. Him. I will play this game, I will wait, but you get him, Chim. Get them *all.*"

A fanged, devious smile spread across her face, and she rubbed her hands together greedily, cackling, and in a plume of smoke, she was gone.

Elsie sank down to sitting once more on the cold floor.

Gods bless the demon girls and the way they toppled empires.

AUGUSTUS

"I think there's a verse that goes 'free are the imprisoned and jailed are the jailers' or something, and honestly, it's such bullshit. Ask Elsie if she felt free in that cell—and if you don't walk out with a knife between your ribs, I'll eat my words."

~Captain Isa Mirestva

The sound of boots against stone filled the stairwell as Augustus spiraled towards the cells below, Isa following not far behind.

The weeks had been kind.

There was no better way to find the forgiveness of the *ro* than with a good bit of begging, it seemed.

Not that it was forgiveness, per say, that tempered Isa's reluctant break from the silent wall between them. But with vows to uphold all that was holy, vows that Elsie was given all the accommodations warranted her status, Isa had uneasily welcomed him back into their bed.

"And you still think Alva will go, even in spite of all that's happened," Isa was saying in an undertone. "You think she will forsake involvement in these affairs for the isolation that comes with her new mantle?"

"Oh, she will go. Perhaps not quietly, and not before trying to worm her way out of the obligation, but in the end, she will go," Augustus shrugged. She'd pull out all the stops, too, with her soft pink gown, the ice roses in her hair, ribbons, frills—as if any of that meant she couldn't raze the city in the blink of an eye. "Refusal would be tantamount to disavowing the faith. And how could she break with the wishes of an ailing mother?"

"And it doesn't strike you as contradictory," Isa countered, "that she's being forced to take the hood? Isn't that a bit at odds with the teachings?"

"This, coming from someone who's only seen the temple from a barroom window."

"You worship your gods, I worship mine. What are we doing here, anyway?"

Augustus glanced over his shoulder, glaring incredulously. "I was about to begin an interrogation. I don't know what you're doing here, except following me around, pestering me about Alva."

He didn't, in truth, know why he'd allowed Isa to venture into the cells below his sister's house.

Loneliness, perhaps.

Self-destructive, chaotic loneliness.

"You're a prick, you know that," Isa prodded, tossing an insolent gesture in for good measure.

Lips tugging upwards, Augustus grinned. "Yeah," he snickered, unlocking the iron door to the basement, "I know."

The corridor was cold, the lucents throwing dim light up and down the hall. It was quiet here, the unnatural silence seeming to slip into the crevasses of the between.

A Drada's life was full of noise. Heartbeats keeping time, the rush of air giving life to those around, the sweet whine of fabric-on-fabric, the intoxicating hum of skin-on-skin, a cry, whether loosed in agony or pleasure only the gods could tell...

In an instant, he'd turned on his heel, had, in a single, smooth motion, pinned Isa against the wall, heart pounding. Sounds to fill the silent corridor.

His breath was on Isa's neck as he inhaled deeply. Desire, laced with sweat.

Augustus took the moment. Isa—well, the gods had broken the mold when they'd created someone so beautiful. Dark eyes shining with the challenge, long hair pulled back into the knot of a warrior *ro*, Isa was pure grace.

It was a dance. Augustus could feel himself growing hard in anticipation as he ground Isa into the wall. Isa's sharp teeth found his ear, grazed it with such tenderness that Augustus couldn't stop the moan that escaped from his lips.

The sound of submission.

Isa moved, and their places had been reversed, a deep thud still echoing from where Augustus's back had been slammed into the cold stone. This was letting go. This was peace.

"Please," he murmured, eyes closing. Isa's fingers trailed the waistband of Augustus's uniform, the gray fabric now tight across the front.

"Beg me for it." A whispered command.

His heart was racing, breath quick. "Isa, please."

Isa's lips were soft, sweet against his own. "More."

"Please," he whimpered, needing Isa's hands to find their mark, "please..."

Amused laughter filled the corridor as the captain withdrew. "Mm, if only they could see the great General Praequintelya now," Isa snickered, taking a step back. "Begging like a pauper."

Face heating, Augustus opened his eyes, a smile nevertheless tugging

452

at his lips. "You're a piece of shit, you know that?"

"Yeah," Isa grinned, "I know." Arms folded coyly, there was mischief glinting in the captain's eyes. "What can I say? The training hall is one thing. This, though? One of us has to have some standards."

Augustus sighed, dropping his head. "Alright," he muttered, pushing himself off the wall, "let's go." Resigned, he made for the cell at the end of the hall.

"Try not to look too sad, lover. What was it you told me? Oh," Isa laughed, the sound like bells, "that's right—learn from your failures? Maybe you'll learn to beg a little harder next..." Their voice trailed off.

The lock had clicked open, the door had been pulled back.

"Oh, gods..." Any look of delight had faded from Isa's face, their eyes fixed on the open cell door with horror.

"Isa!" The traitor was trying to clamor to standing, her bloodshot eyes fixed on the silhouette of the captain in the doorway.

Isa whirled on Augustus, fury unlike anything he'd seen before burning in those onyx eyes.

And in that moment, he could almost feel it.

The shattering. The breaking, the irreparable, unsalvageable, undeniable breaking of the bond between them.

"El," Isa was whispering, a shimmering lucent in hand casting the cell in pale light as they knelt beside her, surveying the damage.

Loyalty before amity.

Nothing more. Nothing less.

"Please," the traitor was crying, "please help me..."

Isa was soothing her, holding her close in their arms, making promises they'd never be able to keep.

Loyalty before amity.

Isa was going to help her, he realized.

Isa, who even now, was crooning tales of her escape into her ear, and the hateful malice had been unmistakable in their eyes, flicking to Augustus.

The door flew shut with a reverberating clank, muffled shouts of protestation and sparks of futile magic fading as Augustus turned for the stairs.

It had been a mistake, returning to the room of Captain Mirestva that night. It had been a mistake, assuming Isa understood him. Understood who Augustus Praequintelya truly was. Understood the words he lived by.

Loyalty before amity.

They would say many things about Augustus Praequintelya.

He would not allow disloyalty to be among the slander.

They'd say many things about him.

How he delved into the darkest magics to save his city.

How he imprisoned his own lover for the sake of the realm.

How he was loyal. Loyal to the end.

CHIM

*"They paint the puppet masters as these old men,
dangling strings on a stage. I much prefer the idea we're
all simply the toys of a mischievous little girl, looking for
a bit of fun."*

~Elizabeth Clement Faulise

It had been Chaos that laid the path.

Such an entangled nest had been impossible to resist.

Mortals were such strange creatures, with their neat little rows in their neat little tapestries, a place for everything, and everything in its place, and that was how they'd fall.

Chim had placed a note, expertly forged, on a desk, because mortals loved finding letters. Elsie taught her that.

This was more hide-and-seek, so that the mean boy would find his lover, and mean boys were *so* predictable.

Mother Chaos whispered the rules into her ear, sent a song to the Listeners this very night, and so it made no matter. Mother Chaos saw the tapestry woven, saw the threads to be tugged at, and Chim *trusted* Mother Chaos, as all the kobalde did.

Trusted and served.

With such chaos, came power. The others would converge, soon.

There was one last piece to set into place first, though.

One little bargain of her own.

A prize, for winning this round.

She'd first traded a dockman for a bag of candy. A fair price, by any standard. Teddy didn't strictly know about the dockman, per say, not that knowing made it any less fair.

Now, she'd trade his sister for a hearth.

It'd been ages since she'd had a hearth. A home, really.

And tricksters were supposed to find their hearths, that was more or less the rule, but the last time she'd had a hearth, it hadn't really gone well, because an ax-man had to cut her out of the beast, but she'd had her revenge, in the end, and anyway, she was sort of wary of hearths.

A lot of kobalde went south with a bad hearth.

There'd been the pair of them who'd followed the candied crumbs right to the slaughter. Then there'd been the hearth-in-the-sky, and she didn't really fancy bone-bread.

But, then again, their hearth wasn't frosted and in the sky, and anyway, it was ordinary enough to probably be fine.

Their hearth had potential for chaos, it was true—potential a good kobalde would extort, because an ordinary hearth didn't have to be a *boring* hearth.

Time was of the essence, though.

And the chaos would not claim itself.

THE ENDINGS

What is there left to say.

She wished to write the endings.

And if it takes until my dying breath, I will fight for the endings she wanted to write.

~SAM ALDERTON,

EXCERPT FROM A LETTER DATED DECEMBER 30TH

RISA

"The one beckoned his brother to the field, a scythe
behind his back, for blood would stain the ground before
the morning was done."

~ 'Cautionary Tales for the Still Yet Living,' An
Anthology

A person is granted one—perhaps two—moments of pure clarity in the course of their life. Moments where the world comes into alignment, and nearly incomprehensible order arises from the mass of chaos of daily machinations.

And with the demon's words echoing in her ears, Risa had found such a moment. The kobalde had come, with terror and truth, whispering her secrets, spinning her chaos.

I would like to play a game, the kobalde had smiled.

She could see the vista, in all its terrible beauty, laid out for her taking.

Snow had been drifting down in fat, lazy flakes all day, and she wondered, now, if she peered out the window, if she might see how each would be woven into the blanketed town.

The girl's fanged grin was not half as unnerving as her unendingly pitted eyes.

Where the hell did you crawl from, you little demon child?

Night of the Leaving Day had fallen, and up came the kobalde, looking for a hearth.

Such things were legends of the Wild.

What hides Death inside the tomb, far from where the flowers bloom?

Is it Merchant, armed with Life, full of greed and hate and strife?

Is it King, sore and old, he whose kingdom will be sold?

Down the path and down the bend, where you'll find the River's End,

Bended knee with eyes unclear, mayhaps she be beneath the Weir.

"Risa." Teddy's hand was on her shoulder, brows knitted.

The kobalde was watching them with wide eyes, her words only moments passed, and yet, it felt like a lifetime.

Like worlds had passed Risa by as the seconds ticked on.

"I have to go," she breathed, breaking away.

"If this is true, we should be there," Sam countered darkly, already pulling a coat on. "You don't honestly expect us to sit here and—"

"Risa," Teddy echoed, and his eyes found hers, deep pools of blue. Imploring.

"It was Augustus." Her words were whispers. "He was the one. He's part of the ring. That's why he didn't want Fletcher investigating it. And I'll bet anything that the moment he realized Clark was a suspect, he arranged the deal with the medical supplies. He knew he couldn't take her with any other Drada around, and..."

And it was going to take a hell of a lot more than an epiphany to break her out.

"We have to go," Risa murmured, fishing deep within her pocket for the disc. "Now."

TEDDY

*"Twenty years an advocate, and there is one thing I have
learned to be an unequivocal truth: legality
is...overrated."*

~Adrian Lynch

Shaking, Teddy gave another unceremonious knock against the barrack door, earning a glare from a passing Drada, who'd winced at the reverberations.

Elsie. They were going to get Elsie back.

He knew the path to Isa's room like the winding game trails behind the farm, paths he'd trodden many times between visits to Fletcher's cell when he couldn't quite figure out what it was he needed.

Now, though, there was no question.

If Elsie was being held beneath one of the Praequintelya private residences, as Risa seemed to believe, they would need everyone.

His fist met the door again, agitation rising in the silence.

Where are you?

"Teddy?"

He started, turning to see a cloaked figure gliding down the corridor.

"Alva?"

She tipped her hood back, frowning. "What're you doing on the compound?"

"It's...I'm trying to find Isa, but..."

"Something is wrong," she breathed, eyes distant.

And he felt it, then.

A little ripple in the Thread.

Someone, traversing the wire, and it gave Teddy a little nudge, like it had in the meadow, when they'd watched the girl burn and he'd heard the ghostly song inside his mind sung from another world.

Shouldn't she be sequestered

Shouldn't she be with the mystics

Something uneasy was curling in his chest as he found her glowing eyes.

She should not be here.

Her frown told him she'd heard every doubt.

"Chaos called me forth," she breathed.

"Where is Isa," Teddy asked, voice thin.

She merely shook her head, grief in her eyes that could've only come from realization. "We need Fletcher," Alva whispered, turning. "Come."

~•~

The limestone steps flew by with ease as he followed her snapping cloak down the stairs to the juniper guard. A concussive flash with the snap of her wrist, and he'd collapsed, nothing more than a sort of piney mass against the wall.

Teddy could feel power rippling off of her now, the Thread trembling in tandem with her fury.

Whatever she was, whatever she could do...

464

It was not like the rest. And that scared him.

"Fletcher!" Her voice snapped down the corridor, and he was watching the grating with unease as they came across his cell.

"Elsie—"

"They found her," Teddy breathed, eyes stinging.

Fletcher's eyes asked one question, and one alone. *Alive?*

"Step back," Alva warned, shooing her brother to the furthest corner.

She closed her eyes, hands before her.

Then, slowly, she began to claw the air apart.

Except it wasn't the air.

Something was shimmering between the grating, and the silver was giving way. Her jaw was clenched in concentration, her chest starting to heave, little jewels of sweat beading at her hairline as she wrought the impossible bars apart. *No—*

The Thread was thrashing in his chest, caught in the battle between disappearing with the grate and flying towards the girl. Breath catching, he thrust a hand out against the wall, begging his knees not to buckle as the Thread gnawed through him, drawn away from the dormancy the prison was supposed to offer, snapping back in reflex to whatever craft Alva worked.

When she dropped her hands, panting, it was like someone had dampered the inferno, the only thing left smoke-filled lungs and stinging eyes.

Grating torn back, the silver bars had been twisted into unnatural knots, catching and snagging at Fletcher as he crawled through the hole.

Whatever she had done, it did not surprise him. Whatever she was, he knew.

Fletcher met his sister with a tight hug, half-holding her up as she almost collapsed. Words didn't come, though, his eyes flicking to Teddy, Alva in his arms.

FLETCHER

"Right or wrong, they will stand beside you, and this—
this is love."

-from 'The Advice of The Long-Dead' and Other Essays

Darkness had swallowed the City of Lights.

But this, the gods had foreseen, and as such, had given the Drada eyes that pierced the inky black.

Fletcher's knuckles rapped on a door in a seedy back alley of Caelaymnis, a pair of voices inside hushing.

A thoroughly disheveled looking Rodion answered, messy mop of black curls pulled back.

"They found her," Fletcher breathed. "Rodion, they found her, and I need your help."

To his credit, Rodion merely gave a curt nod. "Anything."

"You might be censured—"

"—don't care—"

"—arrested, maybe—"

"Fletcher." Rodion had snapped his name through the night, forcing his attention back. "I am with you, whatever it is."

"This isn't just another mission. If—if this goes poorly," Fletcher pressed, heart pounding, "they will take our heads for being traitors." The word hung heavy in the air, poison.

Loyalty before amity, the barracks seemed to call back across the city.

Rodion studied him for a long moment. Then, with a shrug, a grin began tugging at his lips. "I've had worse."

Relief washed through Fletcher, and he felt his breathing slow a bit as some of the sound came back into the world. The shuffle of his own hands against each other, moving to spite his nerves. The wind making the mountains sing in the distance, a chilling tune sent drifting over Caelaymnis, the unworldly voice seeming to send a name whispering through him.

Elsie.

Elsie.

Elsie.

"Isa—they're not here, are they?"

Rodion shook his head, brow furrowing. "Haven't seen them since this morning. They're not at the barracks?"

Panic was starting to rise in Fletcher's gut again as he followed Rodion inside. "No. Teddy and I both looked—"

"Did you check your brother's room?" Rodion asked, pulling on a tunic.

"Yes." He growled out the word, resentful, half-pleased he hadn't had to drag his friend from that traitor's bed, half-anxious at thoughts he didn't care to voice. His eyes flicked to Rodion, half-hopping as he tugged on the first pair of shoes he could find. "Augustus has Elsie. He's been lying about knowing where she is. He's running a ring, he..." Fletcher trailed off, words lost.

Mia turned the corner, buttoning her trousers. Swearing, her fingers cracked against the metal gromets of her pants, blood flying electric. "Shit. Isa's good folk, you don't think—"

"That *ro's* never had a problem speaking their mind," Rodion growled, turning for the door. "If Augustus thought they were a liability..."

Fletcher shook his head, following Mia into the street beyond. "I don't—Augustus..." He left the thought unfinished.

And Augustus loved them.

Deeply.

Reverentially.

That man, he had to remind himself, was dead.

Had died almost a year ago, in the highlands, at the knifepoint of a power-poacher.

And Isa could kick his ass any day, that much was clear. He'd watched his brother and the *ro* spar. It was the only time Augustus ever hit the mat in defeat.

I am so sorry, Elsie.

I am so sorry that I brought this world to your doorstep.

I am sorry that I was not the man you thought I was.

I am sorry about this nightmare.

Because, in the end, she'd been right.

That's what this was.

Just another nightmare.

SAM

"There is no worse feeling than that of inaction."

~Sam Alderton

Sam sat still in the armchair of the sitting room, waiting.

Tick.

It was a barren house, cold and empty.

Tick.

He'd lit the fires, though, and rustled up a few candles shoved in the back of a cupboard.

Tick.

And now, he waited.

Tick.

The idea that Clark had simply been a convenient soul upon which to place Augustus's blame...it made his skin crawl with mistrust.

Tick.

It felt accidental.

Tick.

Left too much unanswered.

Tick.

Elsie would kick down his door, demanding answers, though, as soon as she was back.

Tick.

As soon as she could restart her ashen heart.

Tick.

Tick.

Tick.

It had been this, or taking to the streets with Teddy.

His husband, though, was a man of movement, and Sam always felt in this, they were well paired.

One to move. One to stay

One to act, and one to think.

Two parts, moving in perfect time to one another, independent and reliant.

Chim was dozing on the hearth rug, curled like a cat before the fire.

I claim your hearth, she'd whispered, taking each of their hands.

Something had snapped through them, standing there, tying them, that, even Sam could feel.

Tick.

What game is this.

Why.

Fingers pressed to his temple, Sam tried not to watch the fire-shadows dancing for the demon-girl.

Tick.

Why had she talked about the Merchant armed with Life?

Tick.

And what was that, about hiding Death beneath the Weir.

Tick.

About the kingdom to be sold.

Tick.

About the River's End.

Tick.

Tick.

Tick.

ELSIE

*"They say death is the final act in the theater of life. To
the audience, staring at the curtain, perhaps this is true.
But, I ask, what of the actors behind the stage? What
becomes of them, after the house is emptied?"*
-from 'The Advice of The Long-Dead' and Other Essays

I think they're pulling me out of the slants

At least, that's what the whispers are trying to say.

*I heard someone tell me that, once, and I wondered what hellish dissociation
could be so strong you yourself have been ripped from the world.*

I know you I know you I know you

Elsie waded through the muddy memories of the before, through
the wash of slants and not slants and thoughts that seemed to belong to
another, another, another world, but each moment was a little clearer,
each blink of her burning eyes clearing away some of the reddish haze
burning down from the corridor sconces.

The cell door wasn't closing.

Isa. A rescue, as Chim had promised.

Their soft voice was on the air with words curling distant and pure,
singing to the sound of drums.

A sweet mezzo.

Her eyes were stinging, fixed on the door that served as a crushed velvet curtain to this beautiful twist like a knife between Augustus's ribs.

It wouldn't be long, now. Soon, she would be free.

Soon, she would have her revenge.

Heat was burning through her stiff fingers, something hot wrapping between them, around them—Isa, she realized had taken her hand.

A hush fell across this glamorous box, gilded in stone and sweat and blood and tears.

Best seat in the house to watch them fall.

Black eyes were glistening, beautiful and broken as the *ro* gave her hand a squeeze, gave a smile that was nothing but grief and mourning.

One deft movement, and a fur-lined cloak kissed her cheeks.

The music had faded, now, nothing but a lie, a treacherous, gorgeous *lie*, and still, the heartbroken clapped, for at last, the tragedy had ended.

The curtain had fallen.

Over. It was finally over.

FLETCHER

"She was vying for the throne. He was vying for a victory. It is terrifying, to imagine what the desperate would do, when cornered in their cages."

~Adrian Lynch

"We used to be close," Fletcher breathed, glaring at the monstrosity Cam called home. A lavish house on the banks of the river Weir. A wedding gift. A taunt, really. She didn't need it. The palace had been hers at birth. Had. Past-tense.

Because now, Cam's life was over.

It was hard to be sad about the sentence they'd pass. His grief about what his sister had been to him was soured by the knife she'd plunged into his back.

This would all be over soon.

Elsie.

He was going to see Elsie again.

He hadn't bothered to don the gray overcoat and trousers of his uniform—nor had anyone else, he noted. There was no time for such trivial formalities, and so he would find her, in the rough linens of his prison ware.

Adrian and Risa were already waiting.

The sound of bone on wood rapped through the long night. The sound of salvation. Of the passing of judgement. Of Elsie, in his arms again.

"What—"

"Cam Praequintelya," Rodion said, voice clear, crisp, "by the order of Commander Praequintelya, you are under arrest. The charges against you are as follows—"

She was struggling, magic flaring in her palms, the sound of boots on marble rushing forward, shouts, alarms being raised—

"What is the meaning of this?" Cormalum was running down the stairs, glaring, dark eyes flitting at the chaos. "Unhand her—"

"The charges," Rodion barked out, snapping the shackles shut before letting Cam fall to the floor, "are as follows. Blood Magic, Treason—"

Cam hissed, her lucent flying harmlessly into the wall of the shield that ensconced her, shrieking at her guards to attack, to fight, to do anything, something, to free her. But they did not look to her for a command.

They were eyeing Cormalum with hesitation.

"Cam," Cormalum breathed, brow knitting as he dropped to his knees, putting a soft hand against the shield that separated them. "Is this true?"

She was crying, now, chest heaving violently. "That girl defiled our laws," she choked, straining against the shackles. There was the scent of panic in the air, the primal terror of an animal cornered. "She violated them! You know this—"

"Senator." Risa's voice was low, hardly a whisper. And yet, it sliced through the noise, deadening the din in the foyer. "We have received intelligence that Ms. Mirabeau is being detained on these premises."

"There is a misunderstanding," he fumbled, rising clumsily to his

476

feet, dark hair askew. "I—that is impossible, why—why would we detain her..."

"Can our records show we have your full cooperation?"

"Yes, but—"

The soft padding of boots up the stairs interrupted him. Mia reached the landing, shaking her head. "Sir. I found something."

FLETCHER

"Someone said I rescued her, once. But I didn't. And she wouldn't have needed rescuing, anyway, if it hadn't been for the actions of a coward who thought she was his for the taking. She is no less strong, though, because she was the victim of his selfishness. She is no less brave, because this time, she couldn't break the walls down by herself. And she is no less human, for what was running through her veins. Remember that, when you think of her."

~Fletcher Praequintelya

Fletcher's heart was racing with anger and anticipation as he pulled open the iron door.

A dungeon.

She had turned their home into a prison.

Before them, a dark staircase spiraled downward, unfolding into blackness.

Instinct told him to flee.

To leave this place, to never look back, to let whatever vile, rotting magic that was brewing beneath them fade into forgotten memory, never to be stirred.

The dripping of water filled the passageway below, his breath frosting the air.

Cells lined the walls.

And not a soul could be heard.

The quiet sent his heart beating violently against his ribcage in angry protest, like it could beat hard enough for the two of them.

No. No, no, no, she had to be here, that was what Chim had said—

The cell door clanked open with a high-pitched squeal, the hinges groaning in anguish. The grinding of metal-on-metal was interrupted, though, with a rumbling growl that filled the corridor.

Snapping and hissing, an enormous barghest bolted forward, teeth bared, spines poised for attack.

Without thought, Fletcher's hands were up, a shield shimmering between the beast and the Drada. It must've sensed the fear in the air— fear for Elsie, fear for their safety, hell, even fear for his sister upstairs— as it hurled itself against the barrier.

"You know what to do," Fletcher muttered, glancing at Mia. "And do it quickly."

The shield—and his nerves—were beginning to fray.

A nauseatingly familiar electric crackle filled the air, and the whines of hunger had turned into howls of pain as the beast shuddered to the stone with starts and jolts.

And amid the screaming of the barghest, the shuffle from upstairs that was drifting down as an argument broke out beyond the stairs, he could hear it.

Da-dum. Da-dum. Da-dum.

Fletcher's shield fell and he was running past the beast that had come lunging down the corridor from that cell, holding onto that sound, that weak sound, faint in the din.

Da-dum. Da-dum. Da-dum.

479

His magic recoiled at the darkness, as his eyes searched through the black of the cell—

She was not alone.

Held close in Isa's arms, the captain's fingertips were outstretched, a faint shimmer of a shield around them both.

"Just me," Fletcher pressed, hands held up in surrender.

"Mirestva," Mia snapped, "what in the name of the gods—"

Isa let the shield fall, and Fletcher was on his knees beside her. "Elsie," he breathed, putting a hand on her shoulder, feeling hot tears on his face. She didn't stir. "Elsie?"

Da-dum.

So slow.

Da-dum.

Too slow, he realized.

Da-dum.

"Elsie, please!" He was begging now, his arms around her, holding her, trying to warm her—cold, she was too cold—

Da-dum.

Was he imagining it? His own heart was racing in his ears, the rush of blood almost deafening, mocking him—

Mia was beckoning the captain out of the cell, back from where they still knelt beside Elsie, making room for Risa.

The body in his arms was shivering—or maybe he was shaking, it was hard to tell—

"Honey, it's time to wake up now," Risa was urging, "Elsie, come on, sweetie, open those eyes..."

Her eyelids gave a shudder, and Fletcher was crying, silently thanking the gods above—

But where the emeralds should have sat on a field of white, there was only blood.

The whites of her eyes were shot with magic.

Damp—no. No, no, no—

Her body was damp, dripping, red—it coated his hands, his chest, his lips that had brushed against her forehead—

A deep cough wracked her body, making her seize and shake.

But his murmured words, choked out in a mixture of relief and panic, did nothing. There was no recognition in her eyes as they met his. She did not know him.

"No..." A look of terror was spreading across her face. She tried to pull away, to fight, and her ragged breathing became faster. "Please," she started to cry, red lines painting her hollow face, "no, not you again, please, leave me be! Let me die!"

Her voice cut through him. Cut through the corridor beyond, the house, the city—it had all gone quiet.

"Hey." Risa's voice was low. Calming, instructing, like a mother's call, and Elsie's eyes flew to hers. "Hey, it's alright. We're here to help."

"No," Elsie breathed, chest rattling faintly, "I don't want to see them anymore, tell him to leave—"

"I know," she soothed. Her hand was running easy strokes across Elsie's hair. "I know, honey." There was a vial in the other hand, uncorked quietly. "I promise that you don't have to see them, okay?"

"Really?"

Her breaking voice against the bleeding lips broke his heart.

"Really," Risa nodded, slowly moving the vial up, up, up, "but I need you to do something for me, okay?"

Elsie was crying again, body shaking. "Anything. Please, anything—"

"Drink this." And with that, Risa tipped the contents past her lips.

"Please." It was a mumbled plea now, her eyelids sinking again. "Please, you...you have to tell him..."

"I will," Risa breathed, holding her hand.

481

"No, you don't—you have to tell him you came? Because Teddy—Teddy has t-t-to..."

Her eyes were closed now, and Fletcher needed them open, needed her back, she needed to come back—

"Please...tell...you have to..."

Her body went limp in Fletcher's arms.

With a deep inhale, Risa rose, her movements quick, deliberate, now. "Can you carry her?"

Fletcher nodded, drawing her tight as he came to standing.

Light. She was too light. His arms should be straining from the weight, and yet...

As they emerged into the light of the corridor, a somber crowd greeted them. The body of the barghest had been moved, was sitting limply against the wall. Isa was watching them, arms folded tightly, dark eyes glistening. Mia's hand was on the captain's shoulder, a fist pressed to her lips as she shook her head.

Cormalum was standing, fists clenched at his side, face red with rage. "Take her away," he growled, pale eyes flashing, and Fletcher's fingers held tight. No. He couldn't be talking about Elsie—

"Get upstairs," Cormalum snapped, turning to one of the household guards, "and get that bitch out of my sight! I will see her tried, I will not rest until her head rolls, I will make her pay—"

"Fletcher." Risa's hand was on his arm, bringing him back. "Let them deal with Cam. Let's go."

FLETCHER

"We find comfort in our loved ones. Right or wrong, it is
an undeniable truth of our existence. And it guides us on,
and on, and on."

~Sam Alderton

Slouched in an armchair by a small fire downstairs, Fletcher sat in the
living room of his house in Caelaymnis, staring at the flames.

7,894.

7,895.

He had spent the last two hours counting her heartbeats.

Making sure that they pulsed on amid the terror that had yet to
dissipate from his heart.

Cam was being held in the palace cells. Her house was being
searched, and Cormalum was on the warpath. A messenger had been
sent to the house with the news nearly an hour ago. It had been a small
comfort.

But it was not nearly enough.

Soft steps coming down the stairs drew his attention, and Isa
appeared around the corner.

"How is she?" Fletcher asked, straightening.

"Resting," Isa sighed. "She's asleep. Risa gave her another sedative, and Teddy's sitting with her." And Alva had returned to their crumbling family, and Sam was making use of the kitchen, anxiously cooking to pass the time, and it still was not an answer.

Swallowing, Fletcher tilted his head back, fighting another wave of tears. "Thanks for staying."

"Of course." A pause. "Sir?"

Fletcher glanced over.

"I deeply regret that my involvement with the general—"

"Don't. Please. My brother's a piece of shit that can rot in the underworld. You don't need to pay for his sins."

Isa had stayed to care for Elsie. That was payment enough. It was the act of a kind heart that deserved better than whatever lousy, half-hearted affection Augustus had no doubt offered.

"I tried to take her," Isa said softly.

"What?"

"I tried to evanesce us both out. The cell wasn't barred in, of course, like the compound prison. Couldn't be, I guess, if it's a ring." Isa pursed their lips, raising an eyebrow. No. No, of course, they were right. The cells were barred in to quash magic, and therefore escape. But any such bars would render the efforts of a production ring weak, if not altogether inert. "But it was like she was—was stuck, or something."

"And you stayed," Fletcher edged, his head back against the cushioned chair.

"She is my friend. She asked me not to leave. She did not want to be alone. And so I stayed. Loyalty before amity, sir." Their dark eyes flicked to the kobalde on the rug. "And Elsie told me *she* said she'd go get help, anyway, so long as we got her a bag of sweets."

484

SAM

"Do no harm—to others, to yourself. That is the tenant
we live by. In this, we heal."

~Theodore Alderton.

The darkness felt unending.

But when dawn at last broke through the window, pale light crawling across the carpet, there was the unmistakable residue of an ashen heart that had lasted the night.

Sam had quietly taken his place beside Elsie. Had carefully taken her hand in his, had brushed his lips across the back of her hand, and her fingers had given a reflexive squeeze, faint, but there nevertheless.

Fletcher was laying down beside her, his arms protectively around her. He did not sleep. Eyes looking dark in the low light, they would periodically flash from Elsie to everyone else, then back to his companion again.

Risa kept vigil in her chair. But her blue eyes had long since drifted away from Elsie. Had landed on Teddy, where he was staring at Elsie from where he sat, leaning against the bedpost at the foot of the bed. The conflict in his eyes was unmistakable. The Thread, lashing out, only to recoil violently into himself—he'd whispered as much, and Sam knew it wouldn't stop him from trying to mend his sister, all the same.

Whatever they'd done to her, it could not be fixed with the hand of a Healer.

Whatever magic flooded her veins, time was the only recourse for remedy.

Eyes flickering back to Elsie, Sam's heart gave a lurch.

He loved her with a ferocity he hadn't realized was possible. Had loved her from the start, from the moment they'd met. Loved her wit. Her humor. The way she saw wonder in the world. Loved the resilience of her ashen heart.

It was said that the gods wield not weapons but fountain pens.

There were words, once. Murmured to him from a story as old time itself, given to him by a mother who loved him fiercely.

Words to restart an ashen heart.

You are strong, fiery and unstoppable.

He could still smell her, his mother, the tang of flowers and yeast.

You are power, a force to be reckoned with.

Her hair, beaded with sweat and snow.

You are goodness, worthy and pure.

His eyes stung with tears as he gripped Elsie's hand, and he knew. Knew it more strongly than he'd known anything before. *You are light that cannot be extinguished.*

EPILOGUE

Forcing open her heavy eyelids, Elsie blinked back the darkness—the sun had set, though, night falling through tall windows of her bedroom in Fletcher's house. Curled up beneath a soft throw on the window seat, she'd dozed off watching the glittering snowflakes gathering on the sill.

The shards of the person she'd been still lay scattered on her cell floor. She was all edges now.

And they'd best watch out.

It had been four days, out of the cell.

She hadn't meant to doze off, sitting there. But bathed in the last vestiges of daylight, her thoughts slowing as the storm beyond picked up, she had felt deeply at ease.

Her fracturing had been methodical. Her reassembly was haphazard, at best.

She would've happily traded her shattered soul for a kinder life. She was not stronger for what they'd done. They had not tempered her like fine steel, refining her through pain. They had gutted her.

And never would she thank them for her breaking.

Never would it be said that who she was, she owed to the page-rippers.

The parchment wrinkled softly beneath her fingers as she unfolded it again.

MS. Elizabeth Faulise, it began. The name cadenced oddly on her tongue.

The rest was trivial. The epitome of banal.

I was greatly relieved to hear of your release.

May the gods grant you a quick recovery.

Should you require anything during your recuperation, my services are at yours and on and on it went.

He hadn't needed more. Her name was promise enough.

May justice be served.

In Acquisition, Distinction, Protection,

Yours sincerely, Commissioner Clark Carson.

Oh, yes.

MS. Elizabeth Faulise, it began.

The world was waiting for her.

PRONUNCIATION GUIDE

Drada	draw-duh
Caelaymnis	sell-aim-niss
Vora	vor-uh
dhacrym	dah-krim
barghest	barg-hest
kobalde	ko-bal-duh
Insidiae	in-sid-ee-ay
Apoticaeum defuespes	apaw-tiss-ay-ee-um dif-way-space
Amdormvitae	am-dorm-vee-tay
Isa Mirestva	eye-za meer-est-vaw
Praequintelya	pray-quinn-tell-ee-a
Mia Siddeus	mee-a sid-ay-oos
Rodion Kastarae	road-ee-un kass-stare-ay

DECLARATION OF THE GUILD OF MERCHANTS

And heretofore we the Merchants, the Traders, the Barterers and the Bargainers, the Craftsmen, the Artisans, for the sake of our souls and the souls of all, enact our own governance, establishing and recognizing we ourselves as autonomous.

As such, we set forth these obligations, for the benefit of all, written henceforth to protect the endeavor of Acquisition, the honor of Distinction, and the duty of Protection, of which all in governance must swear to undertake.

By communal vote, one Commissioner Merchant shall supervise proceedings, in that they shall protect Acquisition through action as primary negotiator in matters concerning most or all districts herein, and guard Distinction through the levying of Protection, both in gold and armaments. The Commissioner Merchant presiding over this Guild remains the deciding vote within disputes, undertakes their co-conspirators as parties for which the Commissioner Merchant retains responsibility, and bear reasonable and just consequence over all within the territory. Let it be known I take this duty upon myself, that I, from this day forward, will guard these Districts beneath my wing for the sake of all, and should any seek to harm our people, our homes, our land, and our souls, they shall answer to me, for I be the Master of this Guild.

Signed,

Salem P. Aerdela

Acknowledgements

One would be hard-pressed to find another soul as kind or as loving as the one I have the privilege to call spouse. Unequivocally the Fletcher to my Elsie, the Sam to my Teddy, I could not have completed this project without the unending support of my husband. Our first years of marriage have been shaped by our Saturday mornings spent in the kitchen—he is cooking, and I read him the latest scenes—and our walks through the gardens, where we'd find a bench by the fountains to sit and review the manuscript, and truly, I can think of no better way to begin a marriage. My words cannot express my gratitude for the time, the kindness, and the love he has poured into this project. It is him, above all others, that helped me find a better ending to my story.

On this second edition (and third!), too, we've spent many hours talking about narratives and stories and sinking into a world of magic together, and I am humbled and feeling very loved, to have someone to devote so much time.

It is with the utmost gratitude that I would like to thank Lauren for her contributions to this project. A wickedly smart woman, she is quick to offer her unconditional support to the latest path her friend has decided to travel. She has, time and again, disproved the phrase *loyalty before amity*, because to her, they are one in the same. Thank you.

I cannot talk about devoted time without thanking Emily for the hours and hours they put in to illustrating the second edition of this book.

An enormous thank you to Jasmine for listening to me talk at length about this book as well.

My brother has always been an unwavering source of confusion to me, being both absolutely dear to my heart and completely aggravating, which, I think, are the best two things a person can be in this world, anyway. In an adjacent town or thousands of miles away, he can be counted on for a sarcastic remark and a fierce, almost violent kind of support that is, frankly, concerningly.

Thank you to Jen, for taking me into her program despite my eccentric resume. Frustrated with the job market, I rashly listed *author* under my list of qualifications when inquiring for work—thank you for taking me seriously, when I couldn't do that myself.

Of course, thank you to my supportive colleague, both creative colleagues and those who see me by day at the office, thank you to my friends and my community—really, thank you to anyone who nodded very politely whilst I once more talked about writing. Your sacrifice is greatly appreciated.

Much gratitude to all my very patient friends whose excitement for this project means the world to me. I hope that I can give all of you back the support and love you gave to me, and that we can continue to lift each other up.

I would also like to thank my dad, who imbued within me as a child the love of magic and fantasy. Each night, he would read to me, and together we got lost with elves and hobbits. As I drink my instant coffee and watch the maple seeds fall while writing these thanks, I am grateful that he gave me a love of adventure, the ability to see I can leave the world better than I found it, and the knowledge that if I believe in myself, I can make magic, too.

I would be amiss, too, if I did not thank a group of people I have spent a long time getting acquainted with, and who have helped me thrive more than they could ever possibly know. They have taken on a life of their own far beyond what I could have ever imagined, and for that, I will be eternally grateful. Elsie, who taught me to stop waiting for life to happen. Through her, I saw a fierceness to the world, an unwillingness to accept what we have been given. Her capacity for both love and anger are inspiring, and often, not mutually exclusive. Fletcher, who showed me what it was to see ocean waves when everyone else was looking at the fields of grass. His difference, his persistence in the face of the impossible, and his kind heart inspire me to love that much deeper. Teddy, who healed his author as much as his friends. He has a knack for unraveling personal complexities with astounding clarity, I think, and never were my own knots easier to unwind than when writing about him. Sam, who proved to me time and again that we do not become our hurts, and that the sins we commit are not who we are. His vivacity and unapologetic zest for life are beyond admirable, and exemplify a self-love to strive for. Risa, who made me feel less alone as she ventured far from home to make a life for herself. Isa, who proved to be the answer to so many of my own questions. Augustus, whose conflict is in the hearts of so many who are hurting. Chim, who showed me it was possible to keep childhood wonder, even as one accumulates years. To them all, who were unquestionably the victims of their author's imagination.

I love this book. I love what it has given me. I started writing this in the fall of 2017, shortly after getting married. My husband and I took a long weekend in the Poconos—he was there for a gig, and I was in the midst of the first draft of what would eventually become *Death and the Merchant,* and what a hellishly messy first draft it was.

I am so grateful to have had the chance to make it what it is now—

it's been a chance to work with and learn from some amazingly creative people, and I'm so excited to see what the next chapters have in store.

As I wrap this part up, with all this thanks and gratitude and such, I weigh whether my parting quip belongs. I am distinctly struck by remarks encouraging me to be less bitter and less petty, which I think is a funny thing to remark on when someone says they don't credit their accomplishments to walking a hard road. I eschew the idea that suffering makes art better.

That leaves me with this to say:

Cruelty does not serve us, our art, or this world, and to pretend as if we owe it a debt in exchange for honest art is to do ourselves and those around us a disservice.

Never will it be said that we thanked the page-rippers.

—C. H. Williams

About the Author

C.H. WILLIAMS is a fantasy author living in the Mid-Atlantic with his husband, a very spunky dog, and two troublesome cats. When not causing trouble or spending time doing foundry work with his husband, he can be found walking in the woods and listening to music. Before delving into the realms of magic, he worked as a classical musician, actively performing and conducting research about musicians' relationship to gender. He has since pivoted to legal work during the day and writing dark, contemplative fantasy at night.

www.ingramcontent.com/pod-product-compliance
Lightning Source LLC
Chambersburg PA
CBHW020621020726
47494CB00016B/1429